Betty Walker lives in Cornwall with her large family, where she enjoys gardening and coastal walks. She loves discovering curious historical facts, and devotes much time to investigating her family tree. She also writes bestselling contemporary thrillers as Jane Holland.

Wartime with the
Cornish
Girls

BETTY WALKER

avon.

Published by AVON
A division of HarperCollins*Publishers* Ltd
1 London Bridge Street
London SE1 9GF

www.harpercollins.co.uk

A Paperback Original 2021

First published in Great Britain by HarperCollins*Publishers* 2021

ISBN: 978-0-00-840028-6

Typeset in Minion Pro by Palimpsest Book Production Limited,
Falkirk, Stirlingshire

Printed and bound in UK by CPI Group (UK) Ltd, Croydon CR0 4YY

MIX
Paper from
responsible sources

FSC™ C007454

This book is produced from independently certified FSC™ paper
to ensure responsible forest management.

For more information visit: www.harpercollins.co.uk/green

In memory of my amazing mother, Sheila Ann Mary Holland, aka the novelist Charlotte Lamb, whose vivid anecdotes from a wartime childhood helped inspire this novel. Thank you, Mum!

CHAPTER ONE

Dagenham, East London, April 1941

Violet had known since leaving the café that she was being followed. She kept glancing over her shoulder, but in the thickening dusk she couldn't pinpoint her pursuer. The streets were dark, all lights out as usual, and whoever was on her trail was keeping furtively to the shadows. Not for the first time, she wished she'd accepted Fred's kindly offer to walk her home, since it was Mum's half-day at the café and she'd left work at lunch-time. But Violet hadn't wanted to lead Fred on; he was a real gent and very attentive, but not her type, and it would be wrong to pretend an interest just to avoid trouble.

Besides, it was high time she gave these nasty lads a piece of her mind. Following her about, whispering behind her back, pointing in the street . . .

Nobody should have to put up with this nonsense.

People had even started avoiding their little café, through no fault of her mum's. A widow now, Mum needed every penny she could get from her cakes and sandwiches, especially when rationing had made life so difficult.

Violet waited until she was nearly at the door to Number 27, then whirled, hands on hips, and glared into the shadows. She was tall for a woman, with a trim figure, and knew her height could sometimes be intimidating, so deliberately drew herself up and pushed her shoulders back.

'Right, who's there?' she demanded, putting on the no-nonsense voice she used with Betsy's two daughters, though they honestly didn't need to be kept in line. Poor girls, they'd just lost their mum and could hardly lift their heads for weeping. And she'd lost a much-loved sister. 'Come out and show yourself!'

To her surprise, it wasn't one of the unruly youths from the neighbouring streets, come to taunt her again, but Fred who stepped out of the shadows.

'Fred?' She couldn't hide the astonishment in her voice. 'What are you doing, for goodness' sake?' She shook her head, her heartbeat slowing as she realised it had been no foe, but a friend following her. 'Bloody hell, you gave me such a start!'

'I'm s-sorry, Miss Hopkins,' Fred stammered, removing his cap and turning it nervously between his hands. 'I didn't mean to frighten yer.'

'I told you, I don't need anyone to see me home from work.'

'But after last time—'

'I can handle meself just fine,' Violet said stoutly, though in truth she had been deeply upset by her last encounter with their less pleasant neighbours, a small group of troublemakers who called themselves the Dagenham Daggers. 'You'd best head off home now. I'm nearly at my front door, anyway.'

'If you're sure . . .'

In the far distance, there was the ominous drone of aircraft engines. They both glanced up at the darkening sky, knowing what that meant. Some poor soul was going to get it tonight, and you just had to hope it wasn't you. A shudder of fear ran through her.

'Of course I'm sure,' she said briskly. 'You shouldn't be out this late, Fred. There'll be another air raid tonight, like as not.'

'Goodnight, then.' Fred turned away, shoulders slumped.

But before he had taken more than three steps, a jagged stone came flying out of nowhere and hit Violet on the ankle.

'Bleedin' hell!' she cried out, hobbling towards her front door as she fumbled in her purse for her latchkey.

Fred turned at once, staring at the shadowy street corner opposite. 'Who's out there? Who did that?' His voice was suddenly strong and angry, and Violet could not help feeling grateful that he was still there. 'You cowards! Throwing stones at a woman?'

'She deserves it – she's one of *them*,' came the hoarse reply, and now she could see a grimy face in the shadows. Two or three grimy faces, she realised. Boys, not much older than her late sister's girls. Bareheaded street lads in filthy clothes. 'Gotta kick her out the street, see? Or she'll have the lot of us.'

'One of who? What are you talking about?'

The face came into sharper focus, a narrow chin with an even narrower body below it, but wiry, like a whippet's.

Patrick Dullaghan, self-appointed leader of the Dagenham Daggers.

'One of the Hun,' he said darkly, and stooped to pick up another stone from the street, weighing it in his hand. Two of the houses further down the street had taken a hit a few weeks before, and the road was still littered with debris. 'Hey, Fred, ain't you heard what folk are saying about Violet

Hopkins? Her brother-in-law's one of the enemy. A bleedin' German.'

'What rubbish!' Fred clapped his hands loudly, walking towards the lads. 'Don't talk such rot.' He was speaking loudly enough to make Violet nervous. She peered up and down the dark street for any sign of the air-raid wardens who often patrolled the streets, but there was nobody about. 'Off you go home, the lot of you. Before I report you to the police for assaulting a lady.'

The boys behind Patrick Dullaghan melted back into the shadows at that threat, but their leader hesitated. He threw the stone in a half-hearted fashion, missing her completely, before disappearing down the road while Fred glowered after him.

Shakily, Violet turned and struggled to fit her latchkey into the lock, groping about in the dark. Night had fallen while they were dealing with those nasty bullies. In the distance, she could once again hear the drone of engines high over London, but wasn't sure if they were enemy planes or their own boys.

'Ta, Fred.'

'Goodnight, Miss.'

Violet nodded and slipped inside, closing the door on him. But not before she'd seen the look on his face and known he'd been hoping for more than a 'Thank you'.

And something else, perhaps. The hint of suspicion.

Fred must have heard the rumours, though he had never mentioned them. But it looked as if he too was wondering . . .

In times like these, it only took a few whispers and most people would instantly assume guilt. No need for evidence, or a judge and jury. Not when the enemy was killing people in their beds every night.

She removed her coat and hung it up in the dark hallway,

closing her eyes briefly as she remembered the vicious look on Patrick Dullaghan's face, the sting of his words.

Gotta kick her out the street.

And what for?

Because her brother-in-law, a man who had bravely enlisted on the English side within days of the outbreak of war, was half-German.

He was also missing in action, presumed dead.

Not that any of that had stopped the whispers flying around Dagenham. Oh no, it had made him seem even more guilty. Not honourably dead. But *missing*.

Hurriedly checking her reflection in the hall mirror, Violet found she looked awfully pale, while her shoulder-length fair hair, swept off her face for work and set in a soft roll, seemed a little untidy. She patted her hair back into place and pinched her cheeks to bring the colour back.

'Violet? That you?'

She pushed into the sitting room to find her mother in the armchair, a woollen blanket over her knees, knitting patiently as she listened to the wireless.

'Who else would it be, Mum?' Violet whisked the tea cosy off the china pot on the table. The teapot was cool. 'Shall I make some fresh, or top it up?'

'Top it up, Vi, love.' Sheila clacked her knitting needles, her attention still half on the wireless, where a man with a plummy accent was droning on about the war effort. 'We're nearly out of tea leaves.' Then she stopped and frowned. 'You're late back. Any trouble at the caff?'

'No, all locked up for the night.'

'Were you dawdling again?'

'I had to do a stock-take. Time got away from me.'

'That's all very well, but what have I told you about being out so late?'

5

'Sorry, Mum.' Heading for the kitchen, Violet wobbled on her heels and winced at the ache in her ankle. 'Ouch.'

Her mother looked down and gasped. 'What's that? Vi, you're bleeding!'

Shocked, Violet glanced down too. Sure enough, the stone had hit her hard enough to break the skin. Luckily, she had not been wearing nylons – too expensive for work! But the small trickle of blood had been enough to alarm her mother.

'Oh, it was only them blasted Dagenham Daggers.'

'Language, Vi!'

'Sorry, Mum, but really . . . They're little better than thugs. Patrick Dullaghan threw a stone at me. I think they were lying in wait for me to come home from work.'

'Those horrible beasts. They ought to be dragged off to prison!' Her mother shook her head in angry disapproval. 'But in heaven's name, why throw stones at you?'

Violet hesitated, then said simply, 'Because of Ernst.'

Her mother's eyes stretched wide. 'They can't still think that my own son-in-law would be a . . . ?' She stopped short of using the word 'spy', but a familiar horror was in her voice. 'Mrs Chilcott told me what people were saying. But I thought that had all blown over. How can they make such mischief? Ernst is missing in action, for goodness' sake. And his girls have just lost their mother. It's too awful. My poor Betsy.' Tears sprang readily to her eyes at the name of her late daughter, who had left the shelter at the end of the street to return to her house for something – nobody quite knew what – and was found later in the rubble of her bombed-out house. 'Have they no sense of shame?'

Violet tried to imagine Patrick Dullaghan feeling shame, and failed.

'I don't think so, Mum.'

She sat to slip off her heels and rub her sore ankle. No

lasting harm had been done, she was sure. But what about next time? And that wasn't the only thing that worried her about tonight's attack. Her nieces, young as they were, had started to get a few hard stares from those street boys too. Lily had even reported someone shouting, 'Bloody Hun!' after her a few days ago. Next time, Patrick Dullaghan and his cronies might be throwing stones at the girls too.

Or worse.

'Perhaps we could talk again about Lily and Alice going down to Cornwall,' she said persuasively. 'You know your sister Margaret would take the girls if you asked.'

'Of course she would. And she'd put them to work too, on that blooming farm of hers. Anything for unpaid labour! My pretty little granddaughters herding cows in Cornwall? I won't allow it.' Sheila shook her head. 'I left the countryside behind when I moved up here, and trust me, it's no life for anyone. Fresh air isn't everything, you know.'

'Lily's a strong girl and so is Alice. And so am I, if push comes to shove.' Violet shrugged. 'If we have to go out herding a few cows in return for bed and board, so what?'

'No, I'm not listening.' Sheila clapped her hands over her ears.

'Mum!'

'Well, you know I couldn't bear for them to be so far away from their family.' Her mum dropped both hands into her lap again. She looked away, her lower lip trembling. 'They're still grieving, poor chickens. They need their gran.'

Thinking hard, Violet tried an argument she suspected might have a stronger effect on her stubborn mother. 'But the bombing's been so bad lately, surely it's time to—'

'We're safe enough in the Anderson shelter.'

Violet bit back her instinctive retort. Those Anderson shelters weren't worth tuppence in the event of a direct hit.

Besides, some of the bigger shelters had been hit in recent weeks, and dozens killed. And what about when they were taken unawares and had no time to reach safety?

Young Alice was a clever girl with only a few weeks left at school; with brains like hers, she had so much potential. And although Lily was seventeen now, she was still as sweet as she was innocent, spending her time helping out at the local hospital while she waited for an official war posting at eighteen. She often said she'd be happy to do her share in a northern factory, if that's what the Home Office chose for her, but would much prefer to work as a nurse.

Violet dreaded those lovely girls suffering the same fate as their mother had, blown apart and buried under rubble. The only thing for it was to take them both into the country, far from the bombs, and hope the war ended before Lily was old enough to be posted to a job away from her family. But their doting grandmother would take some persuading to part with her darlings.

'Well, let's not argue about it tonight. I brought some leftover liver and bacon back from the café. I'll freshen up the pot and put it on to reheat.' Violet got up and bent to kiss her mother's cheek. 'Please don't fret about those boys. They're bound to be shipped out to the country soon. If their parents can ever catch the little beggars, that is.'

She pinned a bright smile on her face for her mother's sake as she carried the teapot out to the tiny back kitchen, but inside she was furious.

Furious for Ernst, who was *not* a German spy, whatever ignorant fools like Patrick Dullaghan might say.

And furious for her mum, who had been doing her best to keep the old café going since Dad's death, and deserved better than whispers of 'Traitor!' behind her back.

Mum and Dad had warned Betsy what people might say

when she first announced that she was marrying Ernst Fisher, with his English father and German mother. The Great War had not long been over when they tied the knot, and people had tutted. But everyone had wanted to rebuild their lives, not dwell on the past. Or so Mum was always saying. So Betsy had married Ernst, both of them fresh out of school, and any bad feeling about his German heritage had been pushed out of sight. Until war broke out with Germany again.

Betsy had begged Ernst not to join up, terrified of losing him. But he had been adamant. 'I speak the language; I could be useful,' he told them all at a family meal, having packed in his job as factory foreman to join up. 'Besides, you think I want to see the look in people's eyes when I walk past? My surname may be English, but my Christian name is Ernst, and they all know it, even if you lot call me Ernest in public.'

'Only to help you fit in,' Betsy had said, clinging to him tearfully.

'I'll fit in better by fighting alongside these men,' Ernst had insisted, putting her aside and smiling bravely at Lily and Alice. 'I'll miss you all. But I'll write as often as I can. This will be for the best, you'll see.'

Ernst had left a few days later, and never come back.

He had been reported missing in action a week before Betsy was killed, and so there had been no chance to tell him of his wife's death.

Lily, and her sister, Alice, a precocious just-turned sixteen, had both been bullied horribly over their father's German connections. But the teasing had stopped after their mother died, presumably out of a sense of compassion.

And that should have been an end to it.

But it seemed Patrick Dullaghan and his blasted Dagenham Daggers were now turning their spite towards Violet instead.

How long would it be before the little brutes returned to taunting the so-called spy's daughters?

'I have to get those girls out of here,' Violet muttered, filling the teakettle and putting it on the gas ring to boil. 'But how?'

CHAPTER TWO

The Upside-Down Club, Central London, May 1941

'He's out there again tonight!'

Eva twitched back the curtain and gasped, her heart thumping.

Sure enough, the dark-haired RAF pilot with the Hollywood good looks was seated at one of the front tables, surrounded by his usual gang of uniformed friends, all chatting noisily over the band's playing. She had tumbled head-over-heels in love with him two weeks ago, when he first turned up and sat smiling directly at her throughout their number. To her delight, he had returned with his companions a few nights later, and this was now his fourth time at the club.

'Perhaps tonight's the night,' Karen said, and nudged her with a grin. 'Look, now he's going over to Walter. I wonder what he wants.'

Eva stared, her hand clutching the edge of the curtain. The good-looking young pilot had indeed wandered over to the manager of the Upside-Down Club, and was now talking in Walter's ear. It was all very mysterious.

Suddenly, Walter looked over to the backstage area, his eyes sharp and watchful.

'Oops!'

Hurriedly, Eva let the curtain fall back into place. They weren't supposed to peek out at the audience between acts; it was a serious offence and could lead to the docking of pay. Not that Walter was that strict. His bark was worse than his bite, as Karen regularly remarked. Sometimes he reminded her of her kindly Uncle Teddy, who had been charged with her care since her father left London.

Poor Uncle Teddy, she thought with sudden remorse. She had grown bored of working in a typing pool at his stuffy offices and had given him the slip one day, escaping to find work as a dancer. That had been about six weeks ago. She had left a note, telling him not to worry, she could take care of herself, and would be back in a few months. But no doubt Uncle Teddy would have fretted anyway. But really, he ought to have let her get a more exciting job. Didn't he know there was a war on and girls like her were determined to take advantage of the new freedom this brought?

Shirley, the backstage manager, was calling the girls together, clapping her hands. 'Five minutes to curtain up!' she kept saying as she checked everyone's hair and costumes.

A moment later, Walter appeared backstage, a folded piece of paper in his hand. 'Eva,' he said in his gravelly voice, roughened by years of cigar-smoking. 'There's a note for you. From some Yank out the front. Though I shouldn't really give it to you.' He shook his head at her. 'You know I don't like you girls getting too friendly with the clientele.'

Eva looked at him pleadingly. 'Please, Walter? Just this once?'

He handed it over but watched in disapproval as she opened it with shaking hands. 'What am I going to do with you? Shirley, can't you keep these girls in line?'

Shirley turned, hands on hips, her heavily made-up face crinkled in lines of disgust. 'I've told them, no boyfriends, or they're out. But I can't watch them every bleeding minute of the day, can I?'

Head bent, Eva read the note with mounting excitement.

Dear Miss Ryder,

Forgive my impudence in writing this note, but I have admired you from a distance for too long, and one of the staff was so kind as to furnish me with your name. May I beg you to join me in a glass of champagne after your act?

Your smitten admirer, Lt. Max Carmichael

'What does it say?' Karen tugged at her sleeve, her voice a high-pitched squeak. 'Tell me, tell me!' Wordlessly, Eva passed her friend the note, then laughed at Karen's wide-eyed expression of awe. 'Oh, doesn't he write lovely? *Furnish me with your name* . . . And a glass of champagne? With a pilot? My word, Eva, you lucky thing! You *always* get the good ones.'

Shirley grabbed the note and crumpled it up. 'That's enough of that nonsense,' she hissed. 'The curtain's about to go up. Into position, girls, quickly now!'

Everyone jostled into line behind the thick red curtain, seven girls in tight-fitting white uniforms and pillbox caps, listening for their cue as the band began to play their opening number. Eva was at the centre, as the tallest of the troupe, and arguably the most attractive, if you ignored the too-generous mouth and the upward tilt of her nose. But attractiveness, as she knew only too well, was not what ultimately mattered. Not with men. A pretty face was how you caught them. But not how you held on to them.

The good ones . . .

Eva said nothing, but she was thinking back over her past boyfriends with a flicker of chagrin. None of them had been 'good'. Or at least, not to her.

In fact, the men she seemed to attract usually turned out to be out-and-out bounders. They were only ever after one thing. And when she turned them down flat, they simply disappeared, running off to the next potential conquest. Leaving her broken-hearted and alone, wondering what she'd done wrong.

Though she was rarely broken-hearted for long, it was true. Her nature was too bold and resilient for feelings of angst to last much longer than a few dismal months. Sometimes only a few weeks, depending on how much the man in question had turned her head. Then she would be back on form, smiling and batting her eyelids, and hoping for the best from whichever young soldier had caught her eye this time.

Maybe she was a bit flirty at times. But, at only nineteen, she didn't feel she needed to worry too much about that. It wasn't time for her to settle down yet. And everyone said you had to kiss a lot of frogs to find your prince. Eva was intent on kissing as many potential princes as possible before the marriage trap closed about her. Though kissing was as far as it ever went, because she knew better than to encourage wandering hands.

The curtain rose, and they danced out together, arm in arm, singing and kicking their legs as high as their tight skirts would allow. Eva avoided looking at the front table where the RAF pilots were sitting, focusing instead on getting through the complex routine without any mishaps. But towards the end, she risked a quick glance in their direction.

Gosh, he was rather dishy!

Backstage again, Eva checked her reflection in the big

bulb-lit mirror that all the performers shared, elbowing each other for more space. Her face was glowing and needed a quick dab of powder before she was satisfied.

The band was playing a slower number now, as the evening drew towards its official close. She checked the clock on the wall. It was nearly half past eleven. The club was only supposed to stay open until midnight, but few people regarded the rules these days. So long as there were no lights showing, nobody seemed to care. Some nights Walter kept the place rocking until the early hours.

Suddenly nervous, she caught Karen's eye in the mirror and guessed what her curious expression meant. 'Five minutes,' she told her friend, 'that's all. He's probably just the same as the rest.'

'Aren't they all?'

'But he is offering champagne . . .'

'Yes, fair play to him.' Karen grinned. 'And he has the bluest eyes, don't you think?'

'I'm sure I didn't notice his eyes.'

'Of course not.'

'Though I do love blue eyes.'

'Me too,' Karen said dreamily.

'Especially when they belong to a gorgeous pilot.'

They both giggled, much to the annoyance of Shirley, who had appeared in the doorway tight-lipped and with folded arms.

'That's quite enough noise in here,' she grumbled. 'Settle down, would you? The punters will be able to hear you.'

Karen made a face at Eva, but said nothing.

Eva deliberately snatched up a scarlet lipstick and leant forward, artfully applying it to her lips while the other girls stripped off their costumes around her. Shirley's eyes widened.

'Walter shouldn't allow it.' She tutted loudly. 'You younger girls are under our care in this establishment.'

Her patronising tone made Eva's blood boil.

'I'm not under anybody's care,' she declared, and thrust the lipstick into her handbag before waltzing past the older woman with a defiant look. 'I'm nineteen, not nine, thank you very much.'

'Well, I never!' Shirley shook her head, lips pursed. 'You'd better watch out, young lady, with that attitude. Walter will give you the sack if you bring this club into disrepute.'

'Oh no, he won't,' Eva retorted.

'Is that right?'

'I'm his favourite. Walter would never sack *me*.'

A gasp from Shirley and a stunned silence followed that bold statement. But at least Shirley didn't bother to dispute it. Everyone knew Walter had a soft spot for Eva, and always gave her more leeway than the other girls.

Eva walked off without looking back, hands on hips, walking daintily on her high heels. She wasn't a big-headed girl, and she knew her luck was bound to run out one day. Luck had a nasty habit of doing that at the worst moments, she found. But for now, she intended to make the most of her natural advantages. Whatever the likes of Shirley might think of her.

The handsome young RAF pilots all stood up as a group, hastily scraping back their chairs and smiling as she approached the table. A little breathless, amazed at her own daring, Eva slid into the seat one of the pilots had pulled out for her.

'Thank you.'

'I'm so glad you could join us, Miss Ryder.' To her delight, she realised that Walter was right: the flight lieutenant was not English, but American! He had a marvellous twang to his accent, soothing as honey and like something out of the pictures. 'I'm Max,' he added, his eyes smiling, 'and yes, I'm from across the pond. But don't worry, I'm the only one. These other chaps are British.' He then introduced her to his friends, starting with the young man next to him, who winked. 'This is Mike, and that there is Eddie. The one with the stupid grin is Tommy, and the handsome devil on your other side is Mac. He's Scottish, you know?'

'Pleased to meet you all,' she said politely, looking round at them all. 'But do call me Eva. Miss Ryder sounds so stuffy.'

The flight lieutenant sat down, and all the other airmen copied him. 'A gal after my own heart, eh?' He held out a tanned hand and she shook it, thrilling at the way his lean fingers curled about hers. 'It's a real pleasure to meet you too, Eva. I've got to say, I couldn't take my eyes off you up there on the stage.' He shook his head, still clasping her hand. 'The routine was swell, and you're a real knockout.'

The other pilots agreed, grinning and banging the table enthusiastically.

Eva smiled too, a little breathless. 'Thank you.'

Max released her hand at last, looking round for a waiter. 'We were just about to order some more drinks. Would you care for a glass of champagne, Eva?'

'I thought you'd never ask.'

He laughed and waved a hand at a passing waiter, who happened to be Bertram, an old sweetie and one of Eva's favourites at the club. He threaded his way towards them with a harassed expression, balancing a tray of empties on one hand.

'Sir?'

'We'd like a bottle of champagne.'

'Which kind, sir?'

Max stared at him, taken aback. 'There are different kinds of champagne?'

'Yes, sir.'

'I see.' Max hesitated, glancing awkwardly at Eva, who carefully said nothing but examined her nails for chips in the varnish. There were always a few at the end of a long night at the club. 'Well, bring us whichever champagne is the most popular. And six glasses.'

'Very good, sir.'

Bertram hurried away with a grunt. He was a kindly man in his sixties, always dapper in his waiter whites, but over-worked by Walter.

As the band launched into one of the latest swing tunes, Max pulled his chair closer to Eva's and began to tell her about himself. He described his parents' bean farm out in Missouri, his little sister Pam and how she made sure to write to him every week he was away from home. Eva listened, charmed by his warmth and the expressive glint in his eyes. He wasn't just good-looking, she thought. He was friendly and down-to-earth, too. And there weren't many men like that about, she thought, instinctively drawn to him.

'How come you're in the RAF, then?' she asked at last, curious. 'I mean, you're an American. Why fight for our country?'

'I flew crop planes back home, so I decided to volunteer.' His face sobered. 'My grandfather was born an Englishman, from Surrey, and I could see how unhappy he was about these damn fascists. He wants America to join the war, crush them for good. But while I couldn't do anything about our foreign policy, I was able to cross the border into Canada and volunteer my services as a pilot. They sent me over to England for training with the RAF, so here I am!'

'How brave you are. I wish I could do something more useful.'

'Oh, I'm no braver than anybody else.' He winked at her.

'You keep us entertained; I fly a plane.' When she looked at him closely, wondering whether Max thought less of her for being a dancer, he said more seriously, 'We all do our bit in our own way.'

Eva smiled. 'I hadn't thought of it like that. But yes, I suppose you're right.'

'And it's fun, in a mad kinda way. I wouldn't miss this for the world. Even the damn air raids.' Max met her eyes. 'Being so close to death . . . It makes you feel more alive, don't you think?'

She nodded, captivated by his charm. 'Yes, absolutely.'

While they talked, the other pilots smoked and chatted among themselves, only casting the occasional sideways glance at her tight-fitting stage costume. She didn't mind the attention though. Most men stared and didn't care a jot if she saw them. It was nice not to be leered at for a change.

The champagne arrived, and everyone had a little in their glass. Eva knocked hers back without hesitation, and saw Max's surprised look. Probably not the ladylike thing to do, she thought with sudden chagrin.

Since her mother's death, she'd been brought up by her father, who was a military officer and often absent or too preoccupied to notice her. Eva loved him dearly, but instilling proper manners in his rebellious daughter had not been high on Daddy's list of parental duties. And once war had been declared, and her father had been packed off to the back of beyond, somewhere down in Cornwall, she'd barely seen him.

Suddenly, the eerie, all-too-familiar whine of the air-raid siren rose above the swing music. The band stopped playing at once and began to pack away their instruments, and the singer slipped away backstage for her coat.

Once, the band might have carried on playing through the air raid, like the band on the *Titanic* was reputed to have done when the iceberg famously struck. But there'd been a near-miss the other week, completely demolishing a building a few doors away, and since then Walter had made the decision to call it a night whenever the sirens went off.

Eva jumped up too, straightening her skirt. 'I'm sorry,' she told the soldiers with genuine reluctance, for she did not often have a chance to talk to such interesting people, 'but we have to head to the shelter now. It's only a few hundred yards down the street. Will you come?'

She managed a smile, but could have screamed with frustration. They had been getting along so nicely. As far as she was concerned, the timing couldn't have been worse. Drat those German bombers!

Flight Lieutenant Carmichael seemed to share her disappointment. But he was preoccupied, glancing doubtfully at his friends. 'We should probably report back to base. It's quite a drive away.' He got up too, swiftly followed by the others. Around them, everybody was knocking back their drinks and filing towards the front entrance. 'But I can walk you to the shelter first.'

'Thank you.'

Outside on the dark London street, people were quickly making their way towards the shelter, some in dressing gowns and slippers, summoned from their beds by the siren. Above them, the night sky was lit up with criss-crossed searchlights and the frequent flash and crack of anti-aircraft guns.

Rather cheekily, Max took her hand as they hurried down the street together. Eva was surprised but decided not to pull away, even though it was a bit of a liberty for a man she had only just met. He had such an irresistible smile, after all.

But before they could reach the underground station where she had spent so many nights before, Eva heard the terrible whistle of a bomb descending.

'Bomb incoming!' someone shouted. 'Run for the shelter!'

The whistle grew louder and louder as it hurtled towards the earth, almost directly overhead.

People started to scream and run all around her.

'Quick!' Max pushed her through the churning crowd towards the mouth of the underground station entrance, only a few feet ahead but packed with people. 'You get to safety, honey.'

Eva protested and tried to turn around, but stumbled on her heels, pushed along by the crowd of hysterical club-goers on every side. She could hardly breathe, she was pressed in so tight. They were nearly there, nearly at the shelter.

Suddenly, she felt herself lifted off her feet as though flying . . .

Then everything went black.

CHAPTER THREE

Near Porthcurno, South Cornwall, June 1941

Hazel caught a glimpse of her curvy reflection in the small mirror over the mantel, and hurriedly pulled her long dark hair forward to hide the livid scar above her eye. The ugly bruise on her cheek had long since vanished, but the scar remained, an unsightly reminder of her husband's famously short temper. No amount of face powder could entirely conceal it, though she had applied plenty this morning. But if she set her curls more loosely than usual, and left off her headscarf, it might do to draw the eye away.

She had been thankful when Bertie had left, nearly two months ago now, heading back to his regiment after a mercifully short leave of absence, during which time he had mostly been drunk, though not too drunk to insist on his conjugal rights. She still didn't know where he was stationed, as he hadn't been allowed to say where the regiment would be sent next, except to hint that it might be overseas.

Her husband would be back again one day though, unless the enemy finally did for Bertie Baxter. It was wrong even to think it, but some nights Hazel wondered what it would be like to get that telegram and know herself to be a free woman.

Pushing aside such unloving and downright wicked thoughts, Hazel carried the meagre breakfast of one fried egg on buttered toast across to the kitchen table, and put it down with a smile in front of her son.

'There you go, Charlie,' she said, doing her best to sound cheerful, though such a small breakfast was hardly enough to keep a strapping young lad going until lunchtime. 'Get that down you. Then it's off to school, you hear me?'

Charlie made a face. 'I don't want to go to school.'

She sighed, sitting down opposite him and pouring herself a cup of weak tea. She wasn't hungry this morning, which was a blessing, as there were no more eggs anyway. But if their best layer, Henny Penny, could be persuaded to do her duty for King and Country, that would only be a temporary problem.

Thank goodness for having their own hens! There were folk in the big cities who hadn't seen a real egg in months . . .

'Come on, love, we've talked about this.'

Charlie stuck out his chin, only fifteen years old but already every bit as stubborn as his dad. 'I want a proper job, Mum. All them sums and writing tests. What's the point of them?'

'So that you can do better than your dad,' she replied sharply, then regretted it when she saw unhappiness cloud his eyes. She bit her lip, then leant forward and squeezed his hand. 'Everyone has to go to school, love. Not much longer, eh? Then we can talk about jobs. Maybe the war will be over soon, and your dad can help you find work.'

'As a brickie?' Contempt thickened his voice. 'No thanks.'

Bertie had been a brickie and a labourer before the war.

'It's a living,' she told him defensively.

'You call this living? There's got to be something better than this.' Charlie shovelled some of his egg into his mouth, then glanced about the small kitchen with its faded cabinets and dusty plasterwork, shaking his head. 'If you ask me, that's why Dad signed up so quickly. To get away from . . . all this.'

She flushed, knowing he had been about to say 'get away from *you*,' and had changed his mind to spare her feelings.

Only a few days ago, during a blazing row about their lack of money, Charlie had demanded to know why she had married his dad in the first place.

'It's not like you were in love with him,' her son had said bitingly.

Hazel had wanted to deny that, but couldn't.

She and Bertie had married for the oldest of reasons, and the worst too, she often felt.

Bertie Baxter had been a handsome brute as a lad of seventeen, and boldly charming where other boys – like George Cotterill, with whom she'd been good friends since they first started at the village school together – had been shy and tongue-tied. He had turned her head with his unflagging interest, even though her father, then a teacher at the local school, had declared Bertie 'beneath' her and forbidden their friendship.

Only just sixteen herself, Hazel had made a mistake in walking out with Bertie, and an even stupider mistake when she gave in to Bertie's endless wheedling to let him have his way with her.

Her parents had been appalled when she admitted to being several months gone, earning her the strap from her usually mild father.

Bertie had finally agreed to marry her, under pressure from his stern grandfather, who had once been a village smith and was still the size of a barn door. For a while, Hazel had been happy, with a new babe in her arms and a good-looking, hard-working husband to care for. But within a few years her husband had turned sour, perhaps resentful that his easy, carefree days were over, and that was when the drinking had started, and with it the debts they could ill afford to repay.

There had been other women too, of course.

But Hazel, listening to her mother's advice, had decided to turn a blind eye to these strayings. 'You're his wife – he'll always come back in the end,' her mum had told her. 'Least said, soonest mended.'

For once, though, Mum had not been right.

Things between her and Bertie had gone from bad to worse, and a few years back, he had moved from yelling at her in one of his drunken rows to slapping her. The first time it had happened, she had retreated in tearful silence, and Bertie had been shocked and apologetic the next day, promising it would never happen again. But, of course, it had. Often enough for his violent outbursts to have become almost normal.

'Come on, I'll walk with you to the crossroads,' she told her son as he pushed his empty plate away, then unfastened her pinny and hung it up behind the kitchen door. 'Put your shoes and coat on. Hurry now, or you'll be late for the bus.'

Hazel took her bicycle from the shed, and wheeled it to the garden gate.

Together, they set off at a walk from the row of cottages for the crossroads, where they usually parted – her son heading for the bus stop a mile further on, and Hazel cycling the rest of the way to work.

Except that today would be different.

She had been offered work at Porthcurno's Eastern House, where telegraph cables came ashore from America and around the globe, and where something connected with the war effort had been going on for months. It was all supposed to be hush-hush, but everybody in Porthcurno had known something unusual was happening as soon as strangers turned up and began digging into the cliff.

In this tiny Cornish fishing port, nobody could keep a secret for long. Or so it had seemed to Hazel before the outbreak of war in 1939.

Since the war though, something had changed in the very air of the place. For a start, the old communications station had been reorganised early on, with trucks of military personnel arriving in droves, along with fresh-faced trainees from the country's top universities. Sentry posts and barbed wire fences had gone up first, meaning access to most beaches and cliff paths was impossible, and Ministry of Defence signs had appeared throughout the valley, mysteriously announcing, 'Strictly No Entry By Order'. All winter, explosives had been laid and tunnels dug into the cliff to house the new equipment and personnel, because it was considered safer underground from an aerial attack. 'A shortcut to the pub' had been the official reason given for the sudden excavations, as though the locals would swallow such a tall tale!

But nobody said a word.

Whatever was happening at the old communications station, it was clearly connected to the war, and that meant top secret and not to be discussed.

Still, the idea that this sleepy little village was now a key bombing target for their enemies kept Hazel nervous in her bed at night. And she was not alone in her fears. These days, people went to work with grim faces, and came home tight-lipped.

To an outsider, Porthcurno might seem idyllic. But London – and indeed the whole of Britain – relied on this remote spot on the Cornish coast for the most vital weapon of all in this very modern war.

'Information,' she whispered under her breath.

'Sorry?' Charlie looked at her quizzically. They had reached the crossroads, where he knelt to retie one of his trailing shoelaces. 'What did you say, Mum?'

She managed a breezy smile. 'Nothing, love.' She kissed her son on the cheek, and nudged him away down the lane towards town. 'I'll see you tonight.'

'Have a good day!' he called back over his shoulder.

Hazel nodded, raising a hand. Only when he had turned away did she allow her smile to falter and slip. She waited until her son was out of sight before getting on her bicycle and cycling slowly towards Porthcurno.

She had not yet discussed her new job with Charlie. The truth was, she was afraid. Afraid of messing up, making a fool of herself, and possibly damaging the war effort. And she was afraid it would be beyond her skills. She had taken on occasional secretarial work for a local attorney once Charlie was old enough to go to school, until Mr Beddowes had retired. But nothing skilled.

Since then, she had done odd jobs here and there, whatever she could get, to make a little extra money towards the house-keeping. Bertie was notoriously mean with his wages, preferring to spend them in the pub or on a card game than hand them over to her. Now that he was away fighting, there were too many nights when the cupboard was bare, and she and Charlie had to dine on bread and cheese, if they had it.

Then last week, after she'd put a note in the local Post Office asking for work, George Cotterill had come to the house after dark, looking like an undertaker in his dark suit and hat, and offered her a job.

'It's at the communications station,' he'd said, rather unnecessarily, for George more or less ran the place. 'Eastern House. We're short-handed at the moment, and could do with someone like you.'

Hazel had been amazed. 'Like *me*?'

Whatever could he mean?

'Someone discreet,' George had said softly. 'Someone who can keep a secret.'

Hazel had blushed, for she knew what he was referring to.

One time, when they were both teenagers, she and George Cotterill had exchanged an ill-judged kiss after a local wedding. Ill-judged, because he'd been dating her older sister at the time, not because Hazel hadn't liked him. She had always liked George. But then she and Bertie had started seeing each other, and after that it was too late to go back. Not even when her sister had moved away for work, never to return to Porthcurno.

One kiss, that was all.

But ever since that night, Hazel had averted her gaze whenever she passed George in the street, and had never spoken a word to anyone about that strange, exhilarating moment.

She had accepted the job, no questions asked. They needed the extra money.

But she was worried.

Unlike her, George Cotterill had never married, and she had often lain awake at night wondering how different her life might have been if only . . .

If only.

Two of the stupidest, most wasteful words in the English language.

'If ifs and ands were pots and pans,' her gran used to say, quoting an old saying she loved, 'there'd be no work for tinkers' hands.'

She clearly remembered swimming in the River Camel with George and some other kids during the school holidays when they were all about ten years old. George had seemed so clever, telling her how river currents and estuaries worked, while the other boys skimmed stones or splashed about in the shallows, making the girls shriek in horrified delight and run back to the bank.

She had even had a little crush on George around that time, she recalled with a blush. But it had never seemed like the right moment to say anything.

All the same, she hadn't waited for George to be free when they were teenagers. She had married Bertie instead, and given birth to dear Charlie, the most precious person in the world to her. And she was still married to Bertie, for better or worse.

Those were the only things that mattered now.

She freewheeled for a while, bees buzzing about her in the sunshine. Then she began to climb a steep hill, pedalling hard until she had to get off and walk. In a few minutes, she was within sight of the guardhouse beside the new fence of barbed wire that encircled the valley, keeping locals out.

'Good morning, Miss.'

She showed her ID card, feeling a little awkward under the curious gaze of the guard, but was allowed through after answering a few questions.

She walked on through the heavily fortified grounds and began the climb up to Eastern House. Once beautifully white, the familiar façade was now camouflaged, draped with green and brown netting to blend into its background. She barely recognised it. And it was so busy. There were soldiers everywhere, more than she had ever seen in one place in her life, smoking in the sunlight, marching to and fro, or shouting coarsely to one another as they unloaded equipment from covered trucks.

Several men paused to stare at her as she passed. One even pushed back his cap and wolf-whistled, giving a loud guffaw when she turned to glare at him. Blessed with a curvaceous figure, she often garnered male attention. But fear of antagonising Bertie had made her wary of even looking sideways at a man, and though her husband was away, she still found it uncomfortable to deal with.

Eventually, she came to the entrance to the new communications station, hidden safe underground behind Eastern House, where the enemy's bombs could not reach it.

As the hill steepened for the last few hundred yards, Hazel wheeled her bike more slowly, studying the gated fence of barbed wire curiously. She had never been inside Eastern House before or its newly fortified compound.

There was a soldier lolling on the gate, rifle slung over his shoulder, not much older than her Charlie. He straightened, watching as she approached.

Hazel's nerves worsened.

She didn't know the soldier and he didn't look very friendly. Yet why should he?

Ahead of her, the Atlantic glittered in a long blue swathe stretching as far as the eye could see. Birds sang in the hedgerows, and in the fields butterflies danced among the bright gorse bushes. It seemed impossible in this remote spot, only a short distance from Land's End, that a careless word could cost the lives of thousands. But she knew it to be true. For if Porthcurno Station was compromised, the information channelled through it every day would be too. Messages between Britain and its allies, for example.

A droning noise made her stop dead.

Both she and the guard looked up at the same time, squinting into the sunshine. A small plane was high overhead, light glinting off metallic wings. As it turned, banking further west, she saw the familiar red, white and blue round insignia of the RAF.

One of ours, she thought, with a quick stab of relief.

'You can't come in here,' the guard said lazily as she reached the gate, eyeing her legs with vague interest. He had a Welsh accent. 'So off you pop, before you land yourself in hot water.'

Hazel didn't like the way he was looking at her. 'I was told to report here this morning,' she said firmly, secretly wishing she could just turn around and cycle home. But they needed the money. And she certainly wasn't going to leave before she had seen George Cotterill. Otherwise he would think she had bottled it.

'Oh aye?' He lit a cigarette, his manner unhurried. 'What's your business, then? Come to mop out the ablutions, is it?'

'I'm to report directly to Mr Cotterill.' Hazel spoke with the no-nonsense tone she used with Charlie when he was being difficult, and saw from the way the soldier's eyes widened that it was having an effect. Either that, or George's name had been enough to put the fear of God in him. 'So you'd better let me in straightaway. Or I promise it'll be you in hot water, not me.'

The young man took a quick puff of his cigarette, studying her more closely, then nodded and unlocked the gate. 'In that case . . .' He gave her an unexpected wink as she walked past him, still pushing her bicycle. 'Mr Cotterill, eh? Should have said so at the beginning. George has got taste, I'll give him that.'

'I beg your pardon?'

But he had already turned away, saluting the men who were emerging from the station entrance. Two were soldiers of senior rank, from the pips on their shoulders, and the third was George Cotterill himself.

George was talking, but stopped when he saw her. 'Mrs Baxter,' he said at once, and came forward to greet her. They shook hands awkwardly over the bicycle. 'I'm so glad you're here.' He hesitated. 'Look, I'm a little busy right now. But if you leave your bicycle here and head that way, someone will show you to my office. Then we can discuss your duties.'

'Whatever you say,' she replied shyly.

George left her and escorted the two soldiers through the gate, where they headed towards a parked vehicle, all talking in low voices.

Catching the young soldier's eye, Hazel stiffened at his insolent smile and turned away. She propped her bicycle against the wall and headed in the direction George had indicated.

She only had to wait about ten minutes in his private office, standing in front of George's desk because nobody had told her to sit, before the door opened and he came in, smiling, seeming to fill the space with his tall frame.

'Hazel,' he said, then corrected himself with a wry smile, 'I mean, Mrs Baxter . . . I'm very pleased you chose to take the job.'

'Well, it's good money,' she said bluntly.

She saw an odd flicker in his eyes, and knew her too-quick response had offended him. But that had to be the way of it. Best George understood from the start that she was not here for him. That what had happened between them as kids was ancient history, and this now . . . This was purely business.

She was a married woman, after all.

'Of course,' he said, as though she had spoken those last words aloud. 'Your husband came home in the spring, didn't he?'

'Just for a few days, on official leave.' She felt awkward, unwilling to discuss Bertie with him. It felt too much like disloyalty. 'He's gone back now,' she said starkly, and some devil prompted her to add, 'to do his duty.'

'Quite right too.' George sat down behind his desk and

gestured her to sit too. 'If it were up to me, I'd gladly join a regiment and do my bit too. But I suffer from a mild hearing problem, called tinnitus, so they turned me away at the recruiting office. Perforated my eardrum as a boy, you see, and my hearing never really recovered.' He shuffled some papers on his desk, clearly embarrassed by having to reveal this failing. 'Luckily, I'm good at paperwork. Organising things. This is the kind of war work I can do.'

Hazel could see that she had nettled him. And she felt guilty. She hadn't known about his hearing problem.

'It all counts,' she said firmly.

'You'll be given a uniform. White blouse, buff skirt and matching jacket. It will be your responsibility to keep them in good condition, and make any necessary repairs. You can see Mr Frobisher about that tomorrow; he has the keys to the staff wardrobe.' He handed across a few sheets of paper. 'Could you read and sign these? Then pass them back to me. I can't proceed until that's done.'

'Sorry?' She glanced down at the sheets, confused. 'Wh-what are these?'

'You've heard of the Official Secrets Act, I suppose?' When she nodded, George passed her a pen and then sat back in his chair, watching her. 'That's what you need to sign if you want to work here. You have to swear never to reveal anything you see, hear, or do at Porthcurno Station, for the rest of your life.' He paused, holding her startled gaze. 'Not even to your husband.'

33

CHAPTER FOUR

The train gave a tremendous jolt and braked, finally coming to a halt. The unexpected stop threw her forwards, almost off the shiny old fabric of her seat, and Violet's eyes flew open in surprise. She grabbed at the heavy bag on her lap before it could fall, and checked its contents for the umpteenth time since leaving home: purse, ration books, identity papers, a creased old photo of Mum and Dad on their wedding day, and all her other knick-knacks. Nothing seemed to be missing.

She peered at the photo before putting it carefully away, no longer able to see her mum's face properly. It was nearly dusk outside and the carriage was gloomy.

'What the bloomin' hell was that?' she demanded.

Opposite, Lily turned to stare out of the window at the passing countryside. 'I dunno, Aunty Vi. Maybe we hit a cow.'

Her eldest niece was flushed and wide-eyed, as she had been ever since they left Paddington, her face glowing with excitement. Lily had never been out of London in her life. Her long fair hair was braided in pigtails and tied with red ribbons, topped with a tartan beret that had belonged to her late mother.

Alice, looking up from her book at last, gave a snort of disbelief.

'What was that noise for?' Lily turned to her little sister with an impatient expression. 'Honestly, cows are *everywhere* down here. Sheep too, fields and fields of them. I must have seen more than a hundred sheep since we left London.' She paused, raising an eyebrow. 'Perhaps if you took your nose out of that book, you'd see a few animals too.'

'I'm not interested in cows and sheep,' Alice said disdainfully, finally releasing the end of her own fair pigtail, which she'd been sucking for miles. 'The only animals that interest me are the ones that live wild on the savannah. Like rhinos and springboks.' She held up her book, an adventure story set in Africa. 'Now *those* are worth seeing.'

Lily shook her head in disbelief, but didn't bother to argue. She was too used to her younger sister's strange reading habits.

Curious herself, Violet got up and tried to peer out towards the front of the train. If they had hit something, they might be stranded here all night, she worried. But they couldn't have hit a cow, because a moment later, with a few jerks and noisy creaks, the train started to move again. They all peered out of the carriage, and saw a level crossing in the twilight, with a car pulling away, its headlight beams picking out hedgerows and the white roll of steam across the fields.

They were sharing the carriage with several other people, including an important-looking man in a suit and bowler hat, squeezed up beside Alice with obvious distaste. When the man checked his watch, as he had been doing most of the way, Violet asked quickly, ''Scuse me, what's the time?'

He hesitated, then said reluctantly in a posh accent, 'Nearly half past ten.' Then added, 'We're running late. Should have been in Penzance an hour ago.'

She thanked the man politely, but could see from his

contemptuous shrug that he didn't think much of her and the two girls.

Yawning, she stretched out as best she could in the cramped space, and rubbed her tired eyes. It had been such a long, dreary journey. She'd been trying to catch some much-needed sleep before their arrival in Cornwall, and had only just managed to doze off when the train driver had braked so suddenly. Now she felt worse than ever.

Less than ten minutes later, the train slowed again for a station, and the faint sound of a whistle was heard above the noise of the engine.

Everyone piled out of the train, grumbling at its late arrival. The three of them were a little slower than most, weighed down with so much luggage. Violet slipped her bag strap about her wrist, then glanced up and down the platform; but there were no porters in sight.

'Come on, girls,' she said, trying to sound cheerful. 'Grab your bags and let's see if we can find your Great-Aunt Margaret.'

The three of them struggled down the platform with their heavy bags. Violet was also lugging a second suitcase containing shoes and coats for the winter, just in case their stay in Cornwall turned out to be a lengthy one. She'd told her mother they would probably be back before winter set in. But she had been saying for months that the war must surely be over soon, and the longer it went on, the more hollow those words sounded . . .

Most people had left by the time they reached the station entrance and peered out into the dark and lonely evening. There were no cars waiting, only cars pulling away. There was not even a bus, as it was so late.

Violet again felt a stirring of alarm. What if her aunt had forgotten to pick them up?

Lily looked nervous too. 'Where's Great-Aunt Margaret?'

'How am I supposed to know?' Violet snapped, and saw Lily's face fall. Hurriedly, she added, 'She's probably just late, love. I sent that letter nearly two weeks ago. I know there's a war on, but she'll have got it by now.'

'Maybe she's changed her mind,' Alice said gloomily, sitting down on her bag.

'I hope not.' Lily's voice was faint. 'We've got nowhere else to stay.'

'Oh, don't fret,' Alice told her sister. There was the ghost of a smile on her lips as she rummaged in her pocket, eventually pulling out a dusty-looking ginger biscuit. She took a bite and seemed satisfied. 'It's nearly summer. The weather's perfect for sleeping out-of-doors, especially here in southernmost Cornwall. All we need to be comfortable is a sturdy hedge and a couple of blankets.'

'I'm not sleeping under a hedge!' Lily exclaimed, and burst into tears. 'Aunty Vi, you're not going to make us sleep under a hedge, are you?'

'Don't be daft. Your sister's only pulling your leg.'

'I am not,' Alice protested through a mouthful of crumbly biscuit. She held up the adventure novel she had been reading on the train. 'It's not a big deal. Big game hunters sleep outside all the time.'

'This isn't Africa and we're not big game hunters,' Lily pointed out.

Alice shrugged and said nothing in reply. Instead, she put away the book and finished her mouthful of biscuit before getting up and peering out into the dusk again.

With a sense of relief, Violet heard the roar of an engine in the quiet evening. Was it a car coming towards the station?

Seconds later, she pointed up the road. 'Look, girls, I can see headlights. Maybe that's your great-aunt now.'

Sure enough, a vehicle pulled up beside the station entrance a moment later, and someone leant out of the driver's side. Only it was not a car, but an open-backed truck, and not Aunty Margaret, but a man Violet had never seen before in her life.

The driver looked to be in his sixties, with a heavy beard flecked with grey, and sharp, narrowed eyes under bushy eyebrows. He looked Violet up and down in a way she found uncomfortable, then gestured to the back of the truck.

'I'm Stan Chellew. You must be Violet and the girls.' His thick Cornish accent growled out of the dark at them. 'Hop in quick, then. We're not supposed to be out on the roads this late. Not after dark.'

Dimly, she recalled that her aunt had remarried after her uncle's death five years ago. They had been invited to the wedding, but Dad had been too ill to travel and Mum had not wanted to leave him alone. Violet and Betsy could have taken the girls down on their own, of course, but the train fare all the way to Cornwall had been so steep, it had not seemed worth it just for a weekend. So they had declined and posted off a wedding present of some lace instead. Enough to make a nice tablecloth and some napkins besides. Not the finest, but all they could afford.

'You're me Uncle Stanley?'

'That's right. Your aunt sent me to pick you up but I had some jobs to do first.' He banged the side of the truck, his face impatient. 'Come on, tick tock. Violet, you sit up front with me. The girls can ride in the back with the bags. Just unhook the back flap and climb up.'

Violet helped the girls load the bags while Stan sat unmoving at the wheel, the engine running noisily, then she checked they both got aboard safely.

'Aunty Vi, this truck smells 'orrible,' Lily whispered.

'Hush,' she whispered back urgently, unwilling to offend their benefactors. 'Find somewhere clean to sit and hang on, there's a good girl.'

Alice had already found a corner to anchor herself in, but Lily was peering about in obvious distress.

'I don't think there is anywhere clean to sit,' Lily was saying, a hint of tears still in her voice. 'There's . . . muck . . . everywhere.'

Unfortunately, it seemed that Stanley had good hearing for a man in his sixties. 'It's been used for carting sheep, is all. Sit on your luggage if you're that bothered by the shit.' Again, he banged his fist on the door panel. 'That's it, let's go. I'm missing my bed for this nonsense.'

Hurriedly, Violet gave Lily a reassuring smile, then closed up the rusty back flap of the truck and checked it was secure. She climbed into the passenger seat beside Stanley and closed the door, though it did not seem to hang right on its hinges.

Violet clutched her bag tightly in her lap. It was dark and stuffy in the cab interior. Stanley himself was huge, taking up most of the space, and stank of whisky and tobacco besides.

She caught the gleam of his eyes as he studied her, and quickly turned her head, looking ahead at the road and refusing to show any nerves.

'It was very kind of you to come out and collect us,' she said, recalling her manners rather late. Not that her uncle cared much about manners, she thought; he had none himself, that was bleedin' obvious. 'We've very grateful.'

'Huh' was his only reply, then he revved his engine and pulled violently away, the truck shuddering as he engaged gear.

Violet braced herself against the dashboard with a quick hand, hoping to goodness that the rickety passenger door, which was rattling and banging with every jolt, would not suddenly open and throw her out onto the road.

Uncle Stanley drove fast, tearing along narrow lanes and through gloomy crossroads without braking and seemingly with little regard for the possibility that he might meet another vehicle. But she supposed it was unlikely anyone else would be out after dark on these roads, and if they were, there would be the warning of headlights. All the same, she could not help wondering what might happen if any livestock had got loose, or if someone was on foot, heaven help them . . .

The girls gave a series of squeaks and squeals as they were thrown about in the open back, and Violet bit her lip, glancing at Stanley in amazement that he did not slow down. She hoped her nieces would not be hurt or, worse, tossed out onto the road at this mad pace.

But after a few miles, their cries died down to only the occasional moan, presumably as both girls accustomed themselves to their predicament.

'How is Aunty Margaret?' she asked at last, loudly enough to be heard over the roar of the truck engine. 'Well, I hope?'

'A touch of rheumatism,' he shouted back, and again she caught the gleam of his eyes looking her over. 'She could do with a hand about the house.'

'Well, I'm happy to help.'

'And on the farm too,' he added gruffly as though she had not spoken, and changed gear again as the truck began to labour up another steep hill. Cornwall seemed to be mostly hills, she thought grimly, used to the relative flatness of the East End. They would soon develop new muscles just walking about the place. 'Everyone works here in the summer. Yon two girls can pull their weight too.' He paused. 'They look strong young things with a bit of meat on them. Just right for land work.'

Violet said nothing, glad he could not see her expression in the dark. But she'd begun to wonder if she had done the right thing by dragging the girls down to Cornwall. They might all be safer here from bombs than they were in London. But she had a feeling Uncle Stanley was not to be trusted with her two young nieces.

Aunt Margaret was waiting up for them at the farmhouse, standing in the doorway with a lamp. Stanley finally helped with the bags, only to dump them in the hall for them to carry upstairs later. But Margaret was welcoming at least. She had even warmed a chicken and vegetable pie for them to eat, despite the late hour. After all the hugging and crying, the three of them sat down to eat, ravenous after the long journey.

'How's Sheila?' her aunt asked, watching them eat. 'I've not seen your mum in years. Is she still running the café?'

Violet caught her up with all the family news, only briefly touching on the girls' father, still missing in action, before talking about her work in the café for a while.

'And you've brought your ration books?' Aunt Margaret asked as they washed up their plates afterwards. 'Because I'll be needing them if I'm to feed three extra mouths. You'd better let me have them tomorrow morning.'

Violet felt uneasy about parting with the ration books. What if they needed to go back to London later? Without those books, she and the girls would be in deep trouble. But what choice did she have? And she was sure her aunt could be trusted.

'Of course, Aunty Margaret.'

After dinner, Uncle Stanley had disappeared, so they had to drag their heavy cases upstairs to the back bedroom on their own, thumping noisily up the stairs.

It was too late to unpack, and Violet was far too exhausted to hunt for everyone's night clothes, so all three of them simply kicked off their shoes and dived into the large double bed, still fully clothed, and drew the cool eiderdown up to their chins.

The room was chilly, to say the least.

'Move over, Alice,' Lily groaned from the middle, 'you're taking up all the room.'

'I'm taking up just as much room as I need.'

'Then you need to stop eating so many biscuits, you great lump.'

'I don't think that's going to be a problem here, do you? That pie was gorgeous, but did you notice the cupboards were bare?' Alice paused significantly. 'I checked. Not a biscuit barrel in sight.'

'Button it, girls,' Violet hissed at them, only too aware of how quiet the house was and how easily their voices might carry. The last thing she wanted was to get thrown out almost as soon as they'd arrived. 'There's a war on, and I'm sure your great-aunt does her best with rationing. Anyway, she'll have our ration books next time she goes shopping.' She was horribly uncomfortable, perched on the lumpy edge nearest the door. 'Alice, pet, are you sure you can't squeeze up a little?'

There was a faint rustling of the eiderdown as Alice moved up about half an inch, protesting, 'Fine, but that's as far as I can go, honest. If I fall out of bed in the night . . .'

'Then I'll chuck a pillow down after you,' her sister told her, remorseless, 'and we'll all have more room to breathe.'

CHAPTER FIVE

'But what exactly happens at Eastern House?' Charlie asked again, persistent in his curiosity.

'I can't say,' Hazel said, tight-lipped.

'What do you mean, you *can't say*?' Charlie stared at her, nonplussed. 'I thought you were offered a cleaning job, Mum? How can a cleaning job be a secret?'

'If I could tell you, it wouldn't be much of a secret, would it?' Flustered by her son's endless questions, Hazel continued pushing her bike along the lane in stubborn silence. But it was clear from his glare that he was never going to give up asking. 'Look, I'm not supposed to tell you anything about what goes on up there. I know you're my son, but them's the rules. "Not your husband or even young Charlie," that's what I was told.'

'But everyone knows about the works up at Eastern House.'

'Yes, but knowing and talking are two separate things, aren't they?'

'I can hardly talk about what goes on up there,' her son pointed out crossly, 'since you won't tell me anything about the place except that it's top secret.'

Hazel wished she could be more open with him. But George Cotterill had been so stern. Besides, the realisation that she – Hazel Baxter of Number 3, Sea View Cottages Terrace – had signed the Official Secrets Act was enough to make her quake in her boots. She could be arrested just for saying the wrong thing to the wrong person. And that included Charlie.

The locals knew something was going on up at Eastern House. They'd seen and heard the works for themselves over the winter, all the noisy blasting and digging into the cliffs.

What they didn't know was why it was necessary.

Yes, everyone knew that telegraph cables came ashore at Porthcurno, because they'd been there since the Victorians laid the first transatlantic cables. What they didn't know was that the Home Office had established one of their main listening stations behind Eastern House, all safely hidden underground, with messages vital to the war effort passing through there every day between Britain and its Allies.

And she wasn't going to blab any of that to her son.

'Sorry, Charlie. Just keep in mind what the posters say,' she reminded him gently. 'Mum's the word. There's a war on!'

They stopped at the crossroads, and she kissed him goodbye, seeing the frustration in his face. 'Maybe one day I'll be able to tell you about it. But not now. Now off you go to school.'

He hesitated. 'I wish I didn't have to go.'

'Oh, for God's sake, not this again. You have to finish your schooling before you get a job. Qualifications, that's what you need. And that's final.'

'But that's so unfair!'

'Life is unfair, love. But if you put your head down and

work hard, and always do what you're told, you should end up with a steady job . . . and never have to worry about money like your dad and me.'

He made a face. 'You only have to worry because Dad can't stay off the sauce,' he said flippantly.

'Charlie!'

The boy clammed up then, and headed off down the road towards town without another word.

Fretting about the time, Hazel watched her son until he was out of sight, then got on her bike and pedalled as quickly as possible towards her new job. It wouldn't do to be late. Not on her first day.

Soon she reached the menacing barbed wire fence that separated the St Levan valley from the rest of the coastline, and flashed her ID at the guard with more confidence than the day before. Once through the checkpoint, she got off her bike, wheeling it slowly past the guardhouse, and walked the rest of the way uphill to the looming edifice of the communications station. It was steep but she was used to the hilly lanes around Porthcurno, so was barely out of puff by the time she reached the top.

Close up, Eastern House was a large white rectangular building with huge windows and an imposing façade that looked over the valley. But she supposed it must be hard for an enemy bomber to spot from above, and that was what counted. From any distance, it would be hard to distinguish the camouflage-draped building from the surrounding rocky cliff and shrubs. Especially at night.

'A cleaning job' was how she had described her role here to Charlie.

But she had kept quiet about the dangers involved, not wanting to worry the boy. Because it would be dangerous, wouldn't it? She was working at a top-secret site that would be high on the enemy's list of bombing targets if they ever found out about it.

All the more reason not to talk about what the government was really doing at Eastern House, she thought grimly.

Once through the gate, she leant her bicycle against the wall, straightened her crumpled skirt, and headed for the back door.

The guard gave her a sharp look. 'New staff?'

'That's right.'

He turned, holding the heavy door open for her. 'There you go, Miss.'

'Mrs,' she corrected him.

He grinned. 'Right you are, Missus.'

She hesitated in the doorway, feeling a little overawed by the large building and the uniformed soldiers wherever she turned. The war had always felt so far away in this remote spot, right in the heart of the Cornish countryside. But now, seeing barbed wire everywhere and having to sign the Official Secrets Act just to take this job . . .

It brought the war in Europe much closer to home.

'I was told to report to Mr Frobisher,' she said, suppressing a shiver. 'You wouldn't happen to know where I can find him?'

'Beats me, Missus. Try the mess.'

'Sorry?'

The soldier grinned again, and pointed down the narrow corridor that lay ahead. 'That way, all right? Follow the smell of bacon and sausage.'

Hazel thanked him, and hurried down the corridor. The place did indeed smell of fried food, making her suddenly quite ravenous. They must feed their soldiers and trainees well here, she thought enviously, remembering the doorstep slice of toast with a scraping of butter and marmalade she had managed to grab before heading out this morning.

At the end of the corridor was an empty room set with several benches and tables. The benches had been pushed back, and the tables were piled with dirty plates and cups. It looked as though a small army had just left the room.

Halting on the threshold, she caught her reflection in an adjacent windowpane and nearly shrieked at the unruly mess that was her hair. Embarrassed, Hazel tutted loudly and smoothed her hair back down until it lay flat again. The wind must have caught it while she was cycling here.

'Mrs Baxter?' An elderly man with a stoop had appeared out of a small side room. This had to be Mr Frobisher, she decided. He had silver hair and a pronounced chin, and deep-set glaring eyes. He did not sound very friendly. Quite the opposite, in fact. 'About time too. I've been waiting for you.'

'I'm sorry.' Hazel lurched forward and shook hands with him, which left him looking even more horrified. Perhaps she wasn't supposed to have done that. 'George . . . That is, Mr Cotterill didn't say what time I was to be here. Just morning.'

'You've missed breakfast.'

'Oh, I already ate at home.'

His glare became more pronounced. 'I didn't mean *your* breakfast, Mrs Baxter. I was talking about the personnel's meal. I was expecting an assistant to help with cooking and laying out. But you never arrived.'

'I'm so sorry,' she said again, mortified now.

'Never mind, you're here now. You can help clear the tables first. Then I'll show you your other duties.'

'Yes, sir.'

'Uniform first.' Frobisher gestured to her to follow him to the staff wardrobe. There, he handed over a buff skirt and jacket, roughly her size, and a grim-looking white blouse so large it would probably swamp her. 'You can change in the staff lavatory. You'll find that outside the back door.' He pointed her in that direction, adding, 'You'll need to wear an apron over your uniform for some jobs. They're kept in the second pantry. And put your hair up tomorrow.'

'Yes, Mr Frobisher.'

He shook his head. 'I told Mr Cotterill I didn't want a woman. Always fussing with their hair, I said, instead of doing their job. But he didn't pay any attention. And look at all the make-up you're wearing!'

She said nothing, but glared at him over her armful of clothes.

'I'd better show you around first.' They entered the small, high-ceilinged kitchen, the air moist and rich with cooking smells, all the windows steamed up. 'I suppose I ought to be grateful you're a Mrs, not a Miss.' He looked round at her with narrowed eyes. 'You *are* married, I hope? Not widowed? Because I won't stand for any nonsense.'

By which he must mean flirting with the soldiers, she guessed, still blushing from the comment about her made-up face. He wasn't to know she'd put on more powder than usual today to conceal the fading marks above her eye. She didn't want people knowing that Bertie knocked her about and pitying her. That was her business, nobody else's.

'I'm married. My husband's gone to war.'

She didn't know why she had added that. It was surely more information than this grim-faced antique needed to hear. But Frobisher merely shrugged and handed her a stiff white apron from the pantry.

'Very well,' he said. 'Once you've changed into your uniform, take a tray and load it with plates and cutlery from the mess hall. Bring them back to the kitchen. Once all the tables have been cleared, wipe them down with soda and hot water.

Cleaning cloths are by the sink. Then wash all the dirties, dry and put them away in the second pantry, and re-lay the mess hall for luncheon at noon. Eight men to a table.' He paused, peering at her with rheumy eyes. 'Is that clear?'

'Yes, Mr Frobisher.'

'I'll be preparing luncheon in here. Once the tables are laid, you can come and help me. Learn where everything is kept. And no helping yourself to any food. Domestic staff only eat after personnel have left the hall. Not before.'

'Yes, sir.'

'Well, don't just stand there,' he snapped. 'Look lively! Whole bloody country's gone to the dogs since this war began.' He shook his head, looking her up and down with obvious distaste. 'Did you bring a headscarf?'

She bit her lip. 'No, sir.'

'Good God.' Frobisher waved her away impatiently. 'I want your hair properly covered tomorrow. With a net or a scarf. Is that understood?'

Hazel nodded and scurried away with a mumbled apology, red-cheeked and feeling like an idiot schoolgirl after that telling-off.

And she hadn't even started work yet!

She got changed in the unpleasant-smelling outside lav, tucking in the over-large shirt as best she could, and then headed back into the kitchen to grab a clearing tray.

Mr Frobisher paid her no attention, intent on unwrapping some smelly cheese.

Armed with a large metal tray, she looked about the untidy mess hall with a sigh. It would take ages to clear this lot up single-handed and then lay the tables all over again. But she had no intention of complaining about her lot. It was good honest work and she was pleased to have it.

Charlie desperately needed new shoes, and her wages

would pay for them – and far more, if she could make it stretch.

After taking off her buff jacket, Hazel rolled up her shirt sleeves and set to work, clearing the dirties, scraping plates and gathering soiled cutlery. Not that there was much food left on the plates. These lads had an appetite; that was clear.

George had told her at the interview that the main building, owned by the London-based Cable and Wireless company but commandeered by the government for the war effort, was for recruits to their training schedule, but since the outbreak of war, extra recruits had been allocated to Porthcurno. The young men were learning to receive, decode and pass on messages around the globe, many of them vital to defeating Britain's enemies. George had not elaborated, and he hadn't needed to. By working here, even as only a domestic, she would be contributing to the war effort, and that was good enough for her.

After washing and drying all the dirty plates and cutlery, and putting everything away – not a simple task, since she hadn't a clue where anything was stored and she didn't dare disturb Mr Frobisher to ask – she laid the table for luncheon as instructed.

All that work finished at last, she stretched out her aching back with a groan, and then hurried back into the kitchen for her next orders.

'Mr Frobisher?'

She had last seen Mr Frobisher in his apron, bent over the main preparation table in the kitchen, grating several vast hunks of strong-smelling local cheese.

Now he was nowhere in sight.

Hazel hesitated, uncertain what to do. Not wishing to stand about idly, she decided to spend a few minutes exploring. What harm could it do?

Following the corridor further on, she found a side door standing ajar, and peered out. To her disappointment, there was nothing outside but a cramped, dusty yard, set immediately below the looming bluff of the cliffs.

The house had been built up against the rock, she realised, stepping outside to cool her flushed cheeks. There was barely enough room to swing a cat; she counted nine steps from the door to the cliff wall. But a sea breeze was whistling through the yard, warm and salty, and sunshine picked out delicate ferns and gorse bushes clinging to the rock face higher up.

Hazel felt her heartbeat slow. She stood there for a rapturous moment, eyes closed, her face lifted into the brilliant light, listening to the mournful cries of seagulls.

It was so wonderfully peaceful, she thought, when Bertie was away at his soldiering. Whenever he was back home, angrily drinking and shouting, and sometimes hitting her and Charlie, it felt as though her soul were being ripped apart. Only his absence could begin to heal the wounds he inflicted, inside and out. Which was a wicked, disloyal thought indeed. But one she could not seem to shake these days.

'Hello,' a familiar voice said.

Startled, she spun round, blinking and confused.

George Cotterill was watching her from the doorway. He looked so distinguished in his dark suit, yet somehow down-to-earth too, his tie slightly askew, his black leather shoes dusty. Out here in the light, she could see the fine silver strands threading the dark hair at his temple. It gave him such a distinctive air she was struck dumb and could only stare, irresistibly drawn.

If only she could find this man as attractive as a fence post, and twice as dull. Then she would not be suffering these wicked thoughts. She was a married woman, for goodness' sake, and had a child besides. But her heart had other ideas.

'Cat got your tongue?' George asked her, almost mischievously. 'Sorry, did I make you jump?'

'Can I help you, Mr Cotterill?'

That wiped the smile off his face. He had been leaning against the doorframe, but straightened up now, clearing his throat. 'I just wondered how your first day was going.'

'Perfectly well, thank you.'

'I dropped into the kitchen. But there was nobody around except Frobisher.' He hesitated. 'I think he's been looking for you, actually. Better make your way back before the old boy blows a gasket.'

'He's a character.'

'Made an impression on you, has he?'

'I'll say.' Hazel smiled. 'He wanted to know if I was really married, or if the "Mrs" was just to keep men at a distance.'

George looked at her, suddenly intent, and she lowered her gaze. For a moment, there was silence in the backyard, broken only by the gulls crying out overhead as they circled on the warm air. Her heart was beating unnaturally fast, she realised with a guilty start. What on earth was wrong with her?

'Well,' she added quickly, 'I'd best get back to the kitchen, like you said. It wouldn't do for Mr Frobisher to find me standing about gossiping.'

George moved aside to let her pass, but put a hand out, catching her forearm before she could escape. His fingers were warm on her bare skin.

'Wait,' he said softly. 'Really, how is it going? Frobisher's bark is worse than his bite – don't mind him.' He paused. 'You'll let me know if you run into any trouble, won't you?'

'Trouble?' Hazel met his eyes, bewildered. 'What kind of trouble?'

'With the men.'

'Sorry?'

'This place is crawling with soldiers.' His mouth quirked in a humourless smile. 'Don't tell me you hadn't noticed.'

'I'm sure I can cope. And wearing this outfit,' she said, glancing down disparagingly at the grim buff skirt and voluminous shirt, which desperately needed to be taken in, 'I doubt many will be looking my way.'

George Cotterill looked her up and down too, his eyes narrowing, and for a moment she felt quite awkward under his gaze.

Then he nodded and released her.

'Well, I hope you settle in all right,' he said, and hurried away.

Back in the kitchen, Hazel endured Mr Frobisher's ill-tempered reprimand without a word in response. She very much hoped George was right and the old man's bark was worse than his bite, because his bark was bad enough.

But later, stirring a vast tureen of thick vegetable soup that smelt delicious, she could feel a slight burning tingle on her arm. She knew what it was, too. The place where George's hand had touched her bare skin.

Guilt surged through her again, and she bent to focus her attention on her task, stirring so hard the greenish soup began to whizz round and Mr Frobisher gave her another scolding. Her marriage might have become a sham, but she and Bertie were still legally man and wife. And no amount of wishful thinking could change that hard truth.

CHAPTER SIX

When Eva finally woke up after the air raid, she could smell starch and strong disinfectant, and could barely move her legs. Panic flooded her. What on earth? Her blurred vision slowly cleared to reveal whitewashed walls and another identical bed opposite, only its unfortunate occupant was swathed in bandages like an Egyptian mummy. Another woman in a bed further down was sitting up, reading a magazine.

So she was not dead, as she had half-expected when the bomb fell, but lying in a hospital bed. Groggily, Eva stirred under the tightly tucked-in sheets and blankets. Her mouth was dry, her head throbbing, and she hoped grimly that she too was not swathed in bandages.

What had happened after the explosion?

She had a vague memory of coming to for a few seconds, first under a heap of bricks, her face covered with dust and the night sky above riddled with searchlights. Then again at first light when they found her under the rubble. She recalled two men in ambulance armbands bending over her. She had managed to tell them her name, but passed out with the pain when the bricks were finally lifted away.

I must have cut my head open, she thought, recalling the taste of blood in her mouth.

But what about the rest of her?

Glancing down, she was relieved to see both her hands lying on top of the white blanket, nastily cut and bruised, and smeared with some kind of greasy ointment, but uncovered. Presumably then, they were still working.

Tentatively, Eva wiggled her toes. It hurt, especially in the tight confines of the bedding, but the white blanket twitched at the base of the bed.

Both legs still intact.

Her relief was so immense, she gave a little sob.

'Ah, thank God, you're awake at last!' Surprised, she turned her head on the pillows to see Uncle Edward at her bedside, lowering the newspaper he had been reading. He looked very smart as always, wearing a dapper, double-breasted suit, though his usually cheerful face was wreathed in concern for her. 'You've been asleep for two whole days, my dear. We thought we were going to lose you.'

'Uncle T-Teddy? What are you doing here?'

'Picking up the pieces after my errant niece had a wall collapse on her, of course.'

'*A wall*?'

'A bloody great building, to be brutally frank. But don't worry about that now. You don't recall what happened?'

'There was an air raid. We were running for the shelter at the end of the road. A bomb fell right beside us.' Everything was aching now, and a pain shot through her right hip as she moved. 'I guess we didn't all make it.'

'That's about the size of it. You're lucky to be alive, if you ask me.'

'Oh!' Her cheeks had blenched and she felt faint. She'd suddenly remembered Max and the other dashing pilots from the club. All those people too, on their way to the shelter. And her friends in the club: Karen, Walter, even grumpy Shirley . . .

She was alive. But what had happened to them?

'Was anyone k-killed in the blast?'

'Seven dead at least, others seriously injured. They're still digging through the rubble, in case there are other bodies.' He saw her horrified expression, and paused. 'You look like you've seen a ghost. Friends of yours, were they?'

'I can't stay here. I must get up, I need to find someone . . .' She tried to swing her legs out of bed, but her body was wobbly and the room began to spin. 'Oh, my head!'

'Don't try to get up, silly girl.' Her uncle gestured her to lie down again. 'That's the ticket. Now, who do you need to find?'

'There was an RAF pilot called Max,' she said, blinking away tears, 'and . . . and all my friends from the club. Dancers, you know?'

'I've no idea about them, I'm afraid.' Edward shook his head at her. 'Eva, you make me despair. You run off, leaving only the barest of notes, and drop me right in it with your father. For weeks, I've had people on the lookout for you. When I finally get a report, it's because you're in a hospital bed.' His tone became stern. 'What on earth were you doing at that dive of a night club, besides getting yourself blown up?'

She turned her head away, nettled by his disapproving tone, and looked longingly at the covered jug of water on the cabinet next to her bed.

Edward correctly interpreted her gaze, and poured her a glass of water. 'There you go, my dear,' he said more gently, helping her to sit up again. 'Just a few sips, mind. No gulping it down. You've had a bit of a shock, that's all.'

'Th-thank you,' she whispered.

He waited while she drank, then took away the glass.

'Come on then, missy,' her uncle said, and wagged a finger at her. 'Let's hear the whole sorry tale.' He adjusted her pillows, and sat back down. 'What's your excuse this time for nearly getting yourself killed? You've done nothing but get into scrapes since your mother died. Now this . . .'

She flinched at the mention of her mother, who had died of tuberculosis when Eva was only fifteen.

'You can't blame this on me,' she exclaimed, stung by the accusation. 'It was an enemy bomber. I didn't stand in the road and wave my arms about, begging to be hit.'

'You might as well have done, wandering the streets of London at that time of night. My God, have you never heard of curfew? That bomb missed you by a few feet, Eva. You were damn lucky not to be crushed to death, or lose a limb, instead of just getting knocked out for a couple of days with a bloody bad headache. Though the doctor says you should take it easy for a while. Concussion, and all that.'

'But I need to find out what happened to Max and the others.'

She was getting agitated again.

'You're not going anywhere for a few days at least,' her uncle said firmly, and stood up to call a nurse. 'In fact, you might as well know, I've been in touch with your father, and he's come up with a plan to keep you out of trouble for a while.' She groaned in despair, but he paid no attention. 'Look, Gerald may be on the other side of the country but he deserves to know his daughter is safe. He asked me to watch out for you, and I haven't exactly done a bang-up job of that, have I? Every time I take my eye off you for five minutes, you give me the slip and end up somewhere completely unsuitable.' He paused. 'So, your father and I have decided on a change of tactic.'

She stared at him, already feeling mulish. 'Whatever it is, you and Daddy can forget it. I'm a grown woman now, Uncle Teddy. I don't belong to anyone but myself.'

'Now listen, kitten,' he said, and patted her hand. 'Your dad's not been himself these past few years. Not since your mother passed, in fact. And you know what it would do to him to lose you too. So, why not just play along for a bit? Until this blasted war is over and life can go back to normal.'

Eva looked at the ceiling and rolled her eyes, waiting to hear whatever the men in her family had decided was best for her – while determined to do the exact opposite.

Her uncle started to ramble on about some top-secret facility in Cornwall where her father was now based, part of a new communications task force, and that they'd jointly decided she should head down there too, rather than stay in London at the mercy of the menacing German Luftwaffe. It was all she could do not to swear and toss a pillow at her uncle's head, though in truth she was feeling a bit too weak even for pillow-throwing.

When would her family realise she wasn't a child anymore and didn't need them telling her how to live her life, however well meant their interference was?

She wasn't really listening to Uncle Edward anymore. What had he said? *Seven dead at least, others seriously injured.* All she could see was the face of that brave pilot, careless of his own safety, pushing her out of the bomb blast . . .

CHAPTER SEVEN

More accustomed to the noisy streets of London's East End, with its powerful smells and constant bustle, Violet was entranced by the peace and sheer beauty of the Cornish countryside. The farmhouse was close enough to the coast for them to see the Atlantic, a deep blue glittering all the way to the horizon.

She had visited Southend as a child on a family holiday, so it was not her first glimpse of the sea. But Lily and Alice had never been to the coast, let alone seen an ocean. Both girls had got up on their first morning in Cornwall and stared out of the bedroom window, speechless with astonishment and delight.

'Goodness,' Lily had murmured, her eyes wide. 'All that water . . .'

'Can we go to the shore? Can we learn to swim?' Alice had been incandescent with excitement. 'Can we take rods and nets, and catch fish?'

Violet had laughed, pleased to see the girls happy for once. 'One thing at a time. First, we need to unpack our bags, and find out if your great-aunt has any jobs for us. Remember, she and Stanley only agreed to take us in if we'd help out around the farm. But I'm sure there'll be time to go to the beach one day.'

'And swim?'

'Well . . .' Violet had bit her lip, suddenly unsure. 'I can't teach you, Alice. I don't know how to swim myself. But maybe you could paddle.'

Alice had looked disappointed.

Their first week at the farm had flown by. And not for a good reason. It turned out that Margaret had plenty of jobs lined up for Violet and the girls, and it would have been awkward to refuse. So each day was filled with relentless, back-breaking activity: mucking out pens and stables; carrying water in heavy pails and mopping stone floors; feeding chickens – the only job all of them loved – and helping out with the daily milking of Stanley's dairy herd, which included walking alongside the cows as they trudged the half-mile between their field and the milking shed. The fields were muddy, despite the dry weather, and Lily was scared of the cows. There had been a lad who'd helped out before, but Stanley had resented the cost of his weekly pay packet, and they – as Margaret had pointed out with relish – only needed the cost of bed and board.

Violet seemed to have been lumbered with most of the indoors work, which meant she rarely got to wander outside in the glorious, bee-rich fields and meadows. The girls, on the other hand, got more fresh air and hard work than ever before, falling exhausted into bed every evening, footsore and pink-cheeked.

Seeing their situation without rose-tinted spectacles, Violet guessed their extended family had only taken them in as refugees in order to use them as unpaid servants. It was a punishing regime. She watched the girls struggle to stay cheerful and uncomplaining, and wondered if she had made the wrong choice, bringing them to Cornwall.

But the alternatives were unthinkable.

Violet herself was used to hard work and long hours from helping her mother out in the café, and she was determined to keep on Aunt Margaret's good side by not complaining. Assuming she had a good side, that was.

If her aunt and uncle threw them out, they'd all be in serious trouble, stranded without money or any way of returning to London.

She was still suspicious of her uncle, however. She feared Stanley might be the kind of unscrupulous man who would make a pass at her or even young Lily, despite being their relative, even if not by blood. Not that he had made a move on her, or said anything tasteless. It was more instinct at first, just the sidelong way he looked at the girls at meal times, his eyes narrowed as he chewed his meat.

Violet might not be very experienced with men, but she could tell a lecherous man when she saw one. Still, she consoled herself that while the two girls were out all day, working around the large farm, they should be safe enough from interference.

Unfortunately, her aunt and uncle soon realised that Alice was the smartest of them all, and a bit of a whizz with numbers, as the winner of her year's coveted Maths Prize. She was summoned into the barely used dining room after their evening meal one night, and told she could leave the farmwork for a while and help out with the accounts instead.

'Me?' Alice looked surprised. 'But I'm only just sixteen.'

'You mind your manners, girl, and pay proper heed to your great-uncle,' Margaret said sharply. 'Or it'll be the worse for you.'

Violet stiffened, exchanging an outraged look with Lily.

But she said nothing. She felt sure her aunt was all mouth; she couldn't be suggesting she'd seriously punish Alice for disobedience.

'All right,' Alice sighed. 'What exactly is the problem?'

'The problem is, I can't make head nor tail of them figures for the bank,' Uncle Stanley whined, shoving a dirty old ledger under the girl's nose. 'You done well at school. You have a look through that damn book, and tell me where I been going wrong. It shouldn't take more than a few days.'

'A few *days*?' Lily echoed, sounding shocked.

'It's a big book,' he pointed out.

Alice opened the ledger dubiously. 'Very well. I'll try.'

'Excuse me? You'll do more than try, young lady!' Margaret surprised Violet by suddenly turning sour. 'Here we are, feeding you greedy lot, and keeping all three of you under our roof for no payment in return but your help about the place, and you give me that mealy-mouthed look when we ask for a little extra help.' She mimicked Alice's voice, only in a more ungrateful tone. '*I'll try.*' Then shook her head. 'It's downright unchristian.'

Alice stared up at her, clearly astonished and unsure what to say.

Angry and upset for her niece, and sensing possible danger ahead, Violet put what she hoped was a reassuring hand on Alice's shoulder, and felt her thin body quiver.

'You don't have to do this if you don't want to, Alice,' she said firmly.

'You mind your own business!' Margaret snapped.

Violet stiffened, trying not to snap back at her aunt. Without warning, Margaret had suddenly become as unpleasant as Uncle Stanley.

Before they left London, Mum had warned her to beware Margaret's manipulative nature. But Violet had not completely believed it until this moment. After all, her aunt had been nice as pie at the beginning. Had it all been an act, intended to make them feel safe and settled at the farm, so they wouldn't leave when the real demands started?

'This *is* my business,' Violet told her aunt, chin up. 'Alice is still a minor, and she's under my charge, not yours.' Margaret's eyes widened at this mutiny, and she opened her mouth to respond. But Violet pressed on regardless, trying to find a compromise. 'Young people her age need to be outside in the fresh air. Not cooped up in a stuffy room, looking at figures all day. She can keep working on the farm, like we agreed when we arranged to come here.'

'That was before I knew she could add up,' Stanley growled.

Violet forced herself to smile at him in a placatory manner. It would do none of them any good to scream at the man, much as she longed to.

'Perhaps Alice could set aside some time every evening after dinner. Then we could sit with her, and help her together.'

But Stanley screwed up his face in stubborn lines. 'They need this book at the bank by Friday afternoon, or else I won't get my loan for breeding costs. And if I don't increase the herd, the farm could go under.'

It was Tuesday evening.

'A loan?' Alice, who had been running a finger down the uneven columns of figures in the ledger, looked up sharply.

'Um, I see your problem, Uncle Stanley,' Violet continued warily, 'but Alice is a bit young to help you apply for a bank loan.'

She strongly suspected he wanted Alice to make his accounting look better than it was, maybe even falsify some figures, so the bank would look more favourably on his loan application. Which would be illegal, of course. She couldn't allow him to coerce her innocent niece into something like that.

'Perhaps . . .' Violet herself knew very little about maths and accounting. But what else could she do? 'Perhaps I could help you instead.'

Stanley studied her suspiciously. 'You know about accounting and so on?'

'I've helped Mum out at the café with her books from time to time.' She crossed her fingers behind her back. It wasn't quite a lie, more of a massaging of the truth. Her 'help' with the accounts had mostly been moral support and lots of piping hot tea. But he wasn't to know that. 'I'm sure it can't be much different.'

Stanley said nothing.

'Very well.' Margaret also looked unconvinced, but she nodded. Maybe she too did not quite trust her husband to be on his own with the girl. 'That's settled then. You can look at the farm books in the mornings, and Alice can check your working in the evenings.' She clapped her hands. 'Upstairs with you now, Alice. It's past your bedtime!'

Violet sat down with the farm ledger the next day, and struggled to understand the figures. The book was a mess, numbers crossed out and columns added up incorrectly. But it was clear to her that any substantial loan was unlikely to be repaid in a hurry, going on the prices paid for beef in the previous few years. With the war on, everything had become very stretched, and although the farm had received a subsidy from the government at one point, it had not been spent very wisely.

On the same grounds though, she doubted the bank would refuse a small loan for breeding costs. People needed meat more than ever now, and increasing the size of the dairy herd would help with that.

That evening, Uncle Stanley came into the kitchen while Violet was making dumplings for a stew, and put a hand on her bottom. Casually, as though it meant nothing.

Violet jumped away at once, wiping floury hands on her pinny.

''Ere, what you doing?' she demanded, copying the strident tones of Thelma, the cleaning woman at her mother's café. Thelma's shrieks always worked on the hard-faced working men in the East End, so she felt fairly certain they would work on a Cornish farmer. 'You keep your hands to yourself!'

Stanley shrugged, unconcerned by her fierce reaction. He merely helped himself to a piece of chopped carrot and wandered out of the kitchen without another word.

Violet stared after him in despair. It had only been a gut feeling before. But now she knew for sure that she couldn't trust Uncle Stanley alone with her sister's girls. Not if he could behave like that and show no shame whatsoever when called to account for it. The man was a predator.

But how could she keep Lily and Alice safe without causing her aunt offence?

CHAPTER EIGHT

Hazel did not know when she had last felt so bone-weary.

Two of the soldiers guarding Eastern House had fallen sick – something they ate, a fellow soldier had suggested – and had vomited in the entrance hall, an hour apart. Just as she had finished mopping up the first lot, feeling pretty sick herself at the stink, the other soldier on guard had thrown up too, all over her neat, shining floor.

It had been enough to make her weep.

But she had smiled cheerfully as the soldier was helped away. 'Not to fret,' she'd told the young man, who was apologising profusely, 'I'll soon get this cleaned up.' And she had hurried away to fetch a fresh bucket of steaming hot water and disinfectant.

Before the end of her shift, three more soldiers had fallen sick. But luckily they had made it to the lavatory in time, and she had not been needed for mopping duties.

Mr Frobisher angrily dismissed rumours that something he served had caused the sudden epidemic of sickness. 'My kitchen is perfectly clean, and all my meals are made with good healthy food. I'll take issue with any man who says otherwise.'

In the afternoon, George came and had a stern look around the kitchen, pantry and store cupboards, which were all spotless as always. He talked at length to Mr Frobisher, and they both decided it must be a tummy bug, and not the food, that was to blame.

Hazel scrubbed her hands well after each clean-up, and again before going home, and hoped that would be enough. She was a little disappointed that her work at Eastern House was not more exciting, as she had hoped it would be when George first approached her about a job. But it was better than not working at all, like many of the other wives and mothers she knew, and at least there was some satisfaction in helping the war effort at one of the most important secret facilities in the country.

It was raining when she cycled home, head down against a stiff wind, and she was drenched by the time she reached the little row of cottages, most of them already with lit windows. The sky was gloomy with heavy rainclouds, and her own cottage was dark, no lights on inside.

'Charlie? I'm home, love,' she called through the curtain that hung between the kitchen and the sitting room to keep out the draughts.

There was no answer.

She went upstairs, but his bedroom was empty.

'Charlie?'

She stood on the silent landing and wondered where on earth he could be. School had finished long ago, and the bus would have dropped him off at least an hour before.

Perhaps he had chosen to go home with a friend tonight. He did that sometimes, to play a board game or kick a ball. Though in this rain?

Before she could start to fret over his absence, Hazel changed into dry clothes and dried off her hair briskly with a towel. She hung her damp uniform over the rack beside the Rayburn, where it would dry overnight. She had chosen to keep the Rayburn running on a low heat through the summer, as their other stove ring ran on gas, whereas it cost little to top up the Rayburn with sticks and dead branches gleaned from the fields and hedgerows. Then she set about putting away yesterday's cleaned dishes and making a cauliflower cheese for dinner, her hands working on automatic.

But while she worked, there was a little worry nagging at the back of her mind.

Where was Charlie?

She kept checking the front gate and the road. But Charlie did not arrive home. By the time the dinner was almost ready, the worry had turned to fear.

At last, as she considered whether to eat alone or keep the dish warming on top of the Rayburn, the front gate creaked, and a moment later Charlie appeared in the doorway.

She had not meant to scold him, but couldn't help it.

'Where on earth have you been?' she demanded, her relief turning at once to anger. 'Have you seen the time? I've been out of my mind with worry.'

'Sorry, Mum,' he said sullenly.

He dragged off his wet coat and cap while she fussed about him.

'Look at you, boy. You're soaked to the bone!'

'I'm fine,' he insisted, but there was a red spot burning in each cheek and she thought there was a wild look in his eyes. 'Leave me alone, would you? And don't call me boy. I'm not a kid anymore.'

'Why are you behaving like a child, then? Coming home so late . . .'

'Dad does it often enough,' he countered.

She felt her stomach lurch at the surly tone in his voice.

Charlie had always been such a good lad. But the way he was looking at her left her sick with anxiety. She had seen that contemptuous look on Bertie's face too often.

Charlie wasn't turning into his father, was he?

'Now, listen here,' she began, her voice rising with fear, but he shook his head and pushed her away.

'No, you listen.' He swallowed hard, then blurted out, 'I'm a man, you hear me? Not a boy anymore. And I've had a letter from Dad.' He dragged a sodden-looking envelope out of his pocket and flapped it at her. 'He says I should . . .'

When he hesitated, she shook her head in despair. 'Oh, what now?'

Charlie's face hardened at her tone. 'Dad says that I'm old enough to join up. Or as good as. And that I should, too.'

Hazel couldn't believe what she was hearing. 'Please tell me you're joking.'

'He says I can go out there and join him, and all the other men in the regiment.' When she tried to snatch the envelope from him, Charlie whisked it away and thrust it back into his pocket. 'No, Mum. Not this time.' He stood a little straighter, facing her. 'This is my decision, and you're not going to change my mind.'

'Now, Charlie . . .'

'No.' He glared at her. 'Dad's head of this family, not you. And this is men's business, none of yours.'

'Pardon?'

'You heard me.' He looked her up and down scathingly. Another unpleasant trick he had learned from his no-good father. 'What does a woman know about fighting a war? It's death and glory, Dad says. Not cooking and cleaning.'

It was on the tip of her tongue to lash out at him, to explain how women were fighting the same war as the men, only here, on the home front: going without, making do on very

69

little, raising kids alone, working in munitions factories and carrying out other traditionally male jobs, all without complaining and for the good of Britain.

Exactly as she was doing in Porthcurno, in fact!

But Hazel bit back her retort, struggling to hold on to her temper. Charlie had that stubborn look she knew only too well, his chin jutting, his cheeks flushed with defiance. Getting angry would not help her, only push him further away.

Bloody Bertie!

Didn't her husband understand their boy could be killed if he joined up? She suspected he was only encouraging their son so he could get back at her, aware that she had previously vetoed the suggestion of Charlie signing up as soon as he was old enough. Or perhaps Bertie wanted someone there to skivvy for him, to get him extra tea and tobacco rations, and get involved in his idiotic moneymaking schemes. It would be typical of Bertie to pull such a selfish, self-serving stunt, a man who had never truly cared about anyone except himself.

But saying so would not be helpful.

Charlie knew his father's faults but had never seemed to care about them. Or not when it suited him to turn a blind eye instead.

Hazel took a deep breath. 'Be sensible, dear Charlie.' She tried reasoning with him instead of arguing. 'You can't join up to fight. You're too young.'

'Dad says they won't care about my age at the recruiting office. He says they're desperate for more men.'

More volunteers for death, she corrected him miserably but silently. God, she hoped he was wrong. Because if not, those recruiters deserved to be horsewhipped, sending mere boys away to war. But she kept a sympathetic smile pinned to her face.

'The law's still the law. And you're not sixteen yet. They'll ask for identity papers, and turn you away when they see your age.' She crossed her fingers behind her back, hoping she was right.

His lip trembled, and then his face fell. 'You think so?'

'I know so.'

'But I should try, at least.'

'You don't look old enough, darling. Best to wait until you're older.' She bit her lip, seeing that she nearly had him, and added lightly, 'It would be embarrassing to be turned down, wouldn't it? In front of all the other recruits . . .'

That did it.

'I suppose it would, yes.'

'And you wouldn't be sent out to join your dad, anyway. New recruits to the Cornish regiments don't fight straight-away. They have to be trained first. It can take months. And I don't know where your dad's regiment is stationed at the moment. He wasn't allowed to tell us where he was going, remember? But you heard him hint it might be overseas.' She paused. 'So the war may likely be over before you see your dad again.'

'I hadn't thought of that.'

'Well, never mind, eh? Fighting isn't the only way you can help the country. You just concentrate on your schoolwork and everything will work out – you'll see.'

Her son pulled out a chair and sank down at the kitchen table as though his legs would no longer carry his weight. He stared at the wall opposite where a photograph of a much younger Bertie hung, smiling broadly and moustachioed.

'All the same, it's not impossible. I could change the date on my identity papers.' There was a sullen look on his face. 'Some of the lads at school say they don't look that closely when you enlist.'

'Don't you dare, Charlie Baxter!'

71

'But, Mum—'

'How about some supper, love?' She put a hand on his shoulder, and felt him tremble. 'Just this once, I'll let you eat before changing out of your wet clothes. It's so late, you must be starving. And no more talk of breaking the law, you hear me?' Briskly, she carried the still-hot dish to the table, and removed the lid. A rich and tangy smell filled the kitchen. 'It's your favourite, cauliflower cheese.'

He smiled, but only faintly. 'Thanks, Mum.'

She undid her apron and sat down too, beginning to spoon the steaming cheesy mix onto his plate for him, as he hadn't moved.

'So, what else did your dad say in this letter?' she asked, her heart beating fast, but trying not to show her concern.

Charlie blinked and stuttered through a few things from his dad's letter, even laughing while recounting some knock-about anecdote from the trenches. But later, there was a faraway look in his eyes as he scooped up his supper, and she knew the idea of joining up had not left him. Though her son was unlikely to mention those secret yearnings again. Not now he knew how much she disapproved.

Death and glory.

Oh God, she thought wretchedly, *why did I have to marry such a fool?*

But she feared Bertie could be right about the local recruiters. Everyone on the coast was so sure Germany was about to invade, some of them might turn a blind eye to a boy's age in their desperation to get more men trained and ready to fight.

She pushed the cheesy cauliflower about her plate, her movements listless, feeling a little queasy. She had successfully stalled him for now. But that truce wouldn't last long. Not if she knew his stubborn nature.

How on earth could she distract her son from enlisting?

'You not hungry tonight, Mum?' Charlie asked as he finished his plateful, glancing curiously across the table.

'Oh.' She realised she had barely eaten anything. 'No, I suppose I'm not. Feeling a bit off-colour, that's all. Some of the soldiers were sick today. Perhaps I've caught something.'

'Can I have the leftovers?'

She had been keeping the rest to go with tomorrow's dinner. But she smiled, and pushed the dish of cauliflower cheese towards him.

'You go ahead, love. Fill your boots.'

CHAPTER NINE

Eva was pleased to be met off the London train by a friendly young corporal in a tight-fitting uniform, who opened the door to his car and urged her to 'Hop in, Miss.' He had a strong northern accent that was quite hard to understand at first, but apparently the train had pulled in late to the station and he was now running nearly an hour behind schedule. 'Don't want to miss your dinner, do you?'

By which she guessed it was him who didn't want to miss his dinner.

'Something tasty tonight, is it?'

'Dunno about the main course, Miss,' he said, jumping in behind the wheel and starting the engine with a loud judder. 'But it's Spotted Dick for afters, and that's my favourite.'

'Oh, mine too,' she said cheerfully, though it wasn't. But she knew better than to make a chap feel as though they had nothing in common. 'I hope it comes with custard.'

The corporal pulled away from the station with barely a glance behind, clearly in a hurry. 'There'd be a riot if it didn't, Miss.'

Eva clutched her handbag on her lap, and stared out of

the window at the summer evening. The town was still quite busy, as it was a Friday evening, and the first pub they passed was doing a roaring trade, people drinking outside in the sunshine. She got the feeling they did not suffer much from bombing raids down here, and felt a stab of envy at such a carefree existence. Still, it must be dull to only have a pub for amusement, or the occasional parish hall gathering on holidays.

As the car made its noisy way through narrow streets, she caught a glimpse of the sea in the near distance, sparkling blue over the crest of a hill, and a wild green coast, its high cliffs dashed by white-capped waves.

'Oh, how beautiful,' she gasped, leaning forward to see more, but the low, white-washed cottages closed in, preventing her from catching the view again.

'First time down here in Cornwall, Miss?'

'That's right.'

He risked a quick glance at her, his grin a bit cheeky. 'City girl, are you?'

'I might be.'

'Most of the lads down here are townies, me included. So we don't judge.'

'I'm glad to hear it, Corporal.'

'Call me Geoff,' he said with a wink, and stuck out a hand. 'Short for Geoffrey.' She shook it, a little alarmed as the car veered about the road, but to her relief he hurriedly returned to steering. 'How did you get them scars, Miss, if you don't mind me asking?'

She stiffened, and put a hand to her hurt cheek. The ridges still felt rough under her fingertips from where she had been hit by flying stone.

'A bomb fell near where I was standing.'

'That's bad luck.'

'The others I was with that night would say I was the lucky one,' she said sharply, not keen to talk about her near-death experience. 'If they'd survived, that is.'

She had tried to find out more information about those who'd been around her when the bomb fell, but in the chaos, it seemed survivors had been taken to different places. And nobody she'd spoken to had known where she could find the names of the dead. She had gone back to the tiny house she'd been sharing with several other dancers, to collect her belongings, but nobody had been home.

She would have persisted, but Uncle Teddy had taken her straight back to his flat after that, not even allowing her to visit the club and ask there. He hadn't trusted her not to give him the slip again, he'd said bluntly, though with a twinkle in his eye.

'Come on, Miss, what's *your* name? I've told you mine,' Geoff said, undeterred by her mealy-mouthed answers. 'Or is your name top secret?'

'I'm Eva.' She hesitated. 'Eva Ryder.'

'*Ryder.*' Geoff slowed, looking round at her with wide eyes, then continued, 'As in, Colonel Ryder, our commanding officer? Wait, are you his daughter? The one who's always getting in such trouble?'

'Guilty as charged.'

'Flippin' 'eck,' he said in a blank tone, and pushed back his cap to rub a sunburned forehead. 'Is that why you're here? Was the colonel worried for you in London, with all the bombs falling?'

'Something like that.' She crossed her legs, and saw his sideways glance, followed by an appreciative look in his dark eyes. 'Are there many soldiers stationed at Porthcurno?'

'Hundreds.'

That surprised her. 'Why so many?'

'I take it you don't know anything about Porthcurno?'

'I thought it was just some obscure coastal outlook.' When he laughed, she realised she was missing something important. 'Why all the troops then?'

'Oh no.' He shook his head, changing down through the gears as the winding country road grew steep. 'If you don't know, Miss Ryder, I'm not going to be the poor sap who spills the beans and earns himself a court martial. You'd best ask your pop, not me.'

'My *what*?'

'Your poppa. Your daddy.'

She smiled at his northern accent. *Hundreds* of troops, though? What on earth was this place? Porthcurno had been kept top secret, indeed. She had never even heard of it. Though that was presumably the point. Loose lips sink ships, she reminded herself.

Being banished to stay with her father in the back of beyond would not be too much of a drag if there was a large populace of soldiers on hand. Maybe a summer romance wouldn't be out of the question in Cornwall.

She thought yearningly of the brave American pilot who had saved her life that night by pushing her towards the shelter. She could barely remember what had happened in that split second, except that the world had turned black. But she could still recall his handsome face, smooth accent, and impressive rank. Flight Lieutenant Max Carmichael.

Such a gentleman!

'Here we are,' Geoff said, as the car suddenly began to descend a narrow, rattling track with trees on either side. 'Porthcurno.'

She looked up, blinking, and was dazzled by the sun on the wide blue waters ahead. The cliff was jagged with outcrops of rock, much of it hidden behind trees and what she realised as they came closer was camouflage netting. On the hillside running down to the beach was a vast, white, stately Georgian house, much of its roof and walls covered with yet more camouflage netting.

'What's that?' she asked, pointing at the house, surrounded by clusters of buildings.

'That's Eastern House.' Geoff slowed for a checkpoint of barbed wire across the road, manned by guards with rifles slung over their shoulders. 'Porthcurno Headquarters, some call it.' He glanced at her. 'You like the look of the place?'

She caught a glimpse of whitish sands at the end of a narrow V-shaped valley, and smiled. 'Oh, very much.'

Two minutes later, as the vehicle crawled up the steep slope towards Eastern House, she saw a door open at the top, and a familiar figure emerge.

'Daddy!' she cried, a sudden delight sweeping over her, and as soon as Geoff drew up, she had the door open and was out, running across to the colonel, who caught her up in a fierce embrace.

'Welcome to Porthcurno!' her father boomed, swinging her off her feet, then spoiled the welcoming effect by squinting down at her in the sunshine. 'I just hope you're going to behave yourself, missy.'

CHAPTER TEN

Violet was feeling cornered, and it wasn't a comfortable sensation. Though not by the leering Stanley, for once, but her aunt instead. While they were peeling potatoes in the kitchen together one night, Aunt Margaret had asked at length about London and her sister's health, and now seemed baffled that Violet was still unmarried.

'But why ever not?' she kept asking, frowning. 'You're not that bad-looking a girl. Is there something wrong with you?'

Violet tried not to glare at her. 'Of course there's nothing wrong with me, aunt. It's just the way things are.'

'I suppose you turn them off.'

'Sorry?'

'Being so gobby and independent. Men don't like that.'

Violet felt her cheeks redden and struggled against a bitter tide of outrage rising in her chest. She felt strongly her status as an unmarried woman, due to no fault of her own but to the shocking loss of her fiancé to a sudden bout of influenza, and to have salt rubbed in that wound was unnecessarily painful. She had long since accepted that she would never again love someone as deeply as she'd loved Leonard.

Her aunt had never been a very sympathetic woman, to put it mildly. But as Margaret had grown older, she seemed to have become nastier than ever. Small wonder her mother had refused to abandon London and her beloved café, and travel down to Cornwall with them. No doubt Mum felt that even the risk of nightly bombing raids in Dagenham was preferable to sharing a home with her unpleasant sister!

Violet said nothing, though. What was the point?

But her aunt wasn't finished. 'Your sister managed to catch herself a husband, God rest her soul. She was a good girl, and pretty too. Such a tragedy, that bomb. I cried when I heard. But then there was all that fishy business with her husband.' She shook her head in disapproval. 'That's what happens when you marry a Hun. I sent your sister a letter, warned her not to do it. But some people won't be told.'

Violet restrained herself from saying something rude in response. She was usually the type to speak first and apologise afterwards. But she had to think of the girls now. Lily and Alice were depending on her to keep them safe and with a roof over their heads.

Aunt Margaret paused, thinking. 'Hold on, you were engaged once too, weren't you? I remember your mother sent a letter about him years ago, though she's never mentioned him since. Some young man you met at a dance. Whatever happened to him?'

'He died.'

'Oh.' Her aunt blinked. 'What of?'

'I don't want to discuss it, if you don't mind. He died, that's all.' She felt the old agony rise inside her and pushed it away with a supreme effort, saying grimly instead, 'But I don't do a lot of dancing these days.'

Her aunt stiffened. 'You know, your cheeky East End ways aren't needed down here. We don't talk to each other like that here in Cornwall.'

'Who's being cheeky?'

But her aunt merely huffed away in a mood, muttering something under her breath about ungrateful relatives and how they ought to be put out on the street.

Violet wanted to break down and weep. Or shout after her aunt angrily. Probably both at the same time, giving how up-and-down her moods were at the moment. But she did neither, because she wasn't free to express her pain and distress at being reminded of Leonard's death. Not here in her aunt's home. Instead, she merely gritted her teeth, put her head down, and continued to peel potatoes for supper.

Some young man you met at a dance.

That dance seemed so long ago now. In fact, she realised, it was five years since she'd lost her handsome, laughing Leonard – and not in heroic action abroad, but to something as commonplace as the flu. Though she was confident he would have enlisted if he had lived to see the war.

At the time, Betsy had insisted she would get over it eventually. 'Grief doesn't last forever,' her older sister had assured her.

Yet five years later, Violet was still grieving, waking with a heavy heart most days. Or was it sadness over Betsy's own death she was feeling? Perhaps she'd seen too many deaths and too much unhappiness lately, and it had become muddled in her heart.

All she knew was that she would never fall in love again. This was her life now, a lonely spinster looking after her sister's children, and it would never get any better.

And here she was, unable to tell a soul how she felt.

Inside, she was desperate, wishing there was something,

anything, she and the two girls could do to escape this wretched place . . .

She did eventually manage to escape a few days later, but only for a short period, to take her nieces on the bus to the nearby town of Penzance. Aunt Margaret and Uncle Stanley did not try to stop them, though they grumbled horribly about having to do all the chores themselves. But Violet made a point of saying she was writing to her mother about their time in Cornwall, and waving the letter in the air several times as she talked. Her aunt peered at it without saying much, then shrugged and left them to it. Obviously she was happy treating them like unpaid servants when nobody knew about it, but she didn't fancy her sister knowing what she was up to.

It was only a 'very occasional' bus service to Penzance, she had been warned by a smiling lady at the bus stop, and not terribly reliable. Having been told the last bus would trundle through the town at about six o'clock, she decided they would return to the main Penzance stop by half past five at the latest, which should be plenty of time.

In Penzance, they were surprised to see so many buildings in ruins.

'Don't tell me the bloody Jerries have been at it down here too,' Alice sighed, peering over a wall at what was left of an old warehouse. 'Is nothing sacred?'

'Language,' Violet warned her niece automatically, though she too felt dismayed to see so much evidence of bombing on the quiet Cornish coast. 'It does look like it though. I suppose no towns are safe these days.'

They spent a few pennies in the tiny row of shops along the High Street, where Violet sighed over fabric rolls in the dressmaker's window, wondering if she could afford a yard or two to make new summer dresses for the girls, though her dressmaking skills were not as good as Betsy's had been. Later, they helped themselves rather extravagantly to three ices, which they devoured on a bench on the seafront, staring out at the shining blue waters.

'What's that?' Lily asked in an awed tone, pointing at the strange craggy landmass out in the bay, covered mostly in trees, with a turreted castle-like structure on top.

'That's St Michael's Mount,' Violet said, looking over. 'They're selling postcards of it in the High Street – didn't you see them?' When her niece shook her head, she continued, drawing on old stories her mother had told her and Betsy when they were kids, 'I think it used to be part of the mainland. Only the sea rose in a terrible storm one night and it was drowned.'

'Some Cornish people say it's the last remnant of a magical land,' Alice said knowledgably, 'that was swallowed by the sea centuries ago, because of a spell put on it by a wicked fairy.'

'Oh!' Lily stared at her for a moment, then blinked. 'That can't be true!'

'Of course it isn't true, you goose,' Alice told her older sister in scathing tones. 'I didn't say it was true, only that's what some people believe. Some very *silly* people, if you ask me.'

Violet grinned to herself.

'You do say some blooming odd things,' Lily accused her sister.

'Language,' Violet murmured.

'Sorry, Aunty Vi. But she can be so aggravating sometimes.' Lily paused, peering at the shimmering horizon, one forearm raised to shield her face from the bright sunlight. 'What's on the other side of this sea?'

83

'America, if you go the same way as that ship and turn right towards the Atlantic,' Alice replied at once, nodding towards the misty outline of a large ship far out to sea. 'Or down towards France, Spain, and North Africa that way,' she added, pointing vaguely in the other direction, past the mysterious crag of St Michael's Mount.

Violet slipped off her shoes and wiggled her hot, aching toes in the sunshine, hoping nobody would mind. 'I wish we could see it without all the barbed wire and stone blocks.' Much of the beach had been fortified, and in the distance she could see pillboxes along the coast and even on St Michael's Mount, spoiling the natural look of the place. Such a shame, she thought sadly. But she supposed it was better than leaving Cornwall wide open to an invasion force. 'The water does look nice and cool, though.'

Alice looked at her hopefully. 'Ooh, can I walk down to the water? I could take my shoes and socks off, and have a paddle.'

'Not right here,' Violet said, studying the heavily fortified beach, dotted with warning signs not to go into the water. She put her shoes back on. 'There's probably mines and all sorts here. Let's walk along a bit, see if we can find somewhere quieter.'

They walked along the seafront until they'd left most of the houses behind, stopping at a narrow strip where a mucky-looking stream ran down towards the water below the looming cliffs.

'This don't look too bad,' she said, not seeing any wardens in sight, 'but mind you watch your step. And if any soldiers come along, get back up the beach smartish. You hear?'

Alice stared at her. 'We can't go down there on our own.'

Violet peered dubiously at the beach. It looked to be mostly rock and shingle. But it was also hot and she was tempted.

It had been such a long time since she'd had a nice paddle, and that had only been on the foreshore of the Thames.

'I'm not sure . . .'

'Well, we are.' Lily dragged Violet down the shingle. 'You're coming too, Aunty Vi. And no arguments.'

Laughing at their fierce expressions, Violet allowed the two girls to haul her across the narrow, rocky strip of beach to the water's edge, where pretty scallops of white waves were rippling in. There, the three of them pulled off their shoes and bared their feet for paddling.

The water was freezing at first, and they giggled and half-screamed, running back and forth in the shallows with their dresses held up to prevent the hems getting wet, though they still got splashed. Violet stared out at the misty horizon and wondered what lands really did lie that way.

'That looks refreshing,' a man's voice said from close behind her.

Embarrassed, Violet spun round, and found a sun-browned, dark-haired man watching her from only a few feet away. He smiled at her confusion, and touched his cap.

'Sorry if I startled you,' he said, his voice deep, his accent dreamily Cornish. He had such large, dark, liquid eyes with long lashes, it was hard not to stare into them. Especially given that he was five foot five or maybe six, and she was tall for a woman, so they were almost eye-to-eye with each other. 'I didn't mean no harm. I was only admiring you three young ladies having such a good time in the sea. Almost as though there wasn't a war on.'

Three young ladies . . .

She was hardly *young*, Violet thought, hot-cheeked and thrown by the unexpected compliment, though she was clearly younger than him. She reckoned him to be about thirty, perhaps, while she was only twenty-seven. But she had been brought up in the East End, and knew that men had to be treated carefully. Even the friendly ones could mean trouble.

'Is it off bounds, this part of the beach? We didn't see any warning signs down this end.' She glanced around, half-expecting to see other angry strangers condemning them for trespass. But the man was alone, leaning on a walking stick. 'Sorry if we disturbed your walk.'

'No need to apologise, Miss. I wasn't so much walking as taking my time with a slow stroll along the seafront. Until I saw you three, that is, and decided to come down and see what was going on.' The dark-haired man paused, looking past her at the other two, who had come mincing out of the shallows with raised skirts to stare at him. 'Besides, it seems to me that people don't have a good time often enough these days. What with this war on, and all.'

'That's true,' she agreed warily.

'Would you like to paddle too?' Alice asked the man with her usual boldness. 'You can join us if you like. It's wonderful and cooling, just right for hot feet.'

'Alice!' she hissed.

'What?' Alice blinked at her, surprised, then glanced at the man. 'You're not offended, are you?'

'Not a whit, Miss,' he said politely, but to Violet's shock and dismay, he tapped his left leg with his walking stick, and it clanged like metal! 'But I've only the one leg these days, and I wouldn't want to unnerve you with such a sorry sight.'

Violet did not know where to look. 'I'm so sorry,' she blurted out. 'I'm sure my niece didn't mean to upset you.'

His smile was slow but sad. 'I'm not upset. It is what it is.'

'But I'm sorry too. That's my younger sister, Alice. She's got a right mouth on her; she's always making people feel uncomfortable.' Lily came inching up the beach towards him, twisting the damp hem of her dress between her hands. 'I hope you don't mind me asking, but how . . . how did you lose your leg?'

'Lily!'

But the man did not seem offended by that question either. 'I was in the navy when war was declared, and proud to serve my country. Only our ship got hit in the night by one of them sneaky German U-boats, and down it went to the bottom like a stone. Only a few dozen of us survived, and I lost my leg.' He shrugged. 'Lucky to be alive, the doctors said.'

'But you don't think so?' Lily asked, her eyes wide.

'Not much for a one-legged man to do when there's a war on,' he said, without sounding even slightly sorry for himself. 'I do my bit. Volunteering for this and that, and some training for the Home Guard. But I'd be no good if the Germans landed, would I?'

'You look pretty strong to me,' Alice said helpfully.

He smiled again, though this time the smile did not quite reach those large, dark eyes. 'My mother's happy that I came home from the war, even if not in one piece.' He nodded up the beach to where a middle-aged woman in a wide-brimmed hat sat watching them from a bench. 'So I try not to complain.'

'What about your wife?' Violet asked impulsively, and saw from the quick narrowing of his eyes that this time he *was* offended.

She was so embarrassed, she could have thrown herself in the sea there and then.

'I'm not married,' he said quietly. 'That is, I was engaged when I went away to war. But not when I came back.' Again, he tapped his metal leg. 'If you see what I mean.'

'You mean, your fiancée wouldn't have you once you'd lost your leg?' Alice's voice was high with outrage. 'But that's bloody awful.'

'Language, Alice,' Violet muttered, but nobody paid her any attention.

'Can't say as I blame her,' the man replied with a shrug.

'You *should* blame her, trust me,' Alice retorted, earning herself a stern look from Violet, who was trying to think of a way to drag the girls away without making it obvious they were fleeing the beach.

There was something about this noble, suffering man that stirred her so much, Violet felt quite uneasy in his presence, fearing he must be able to see her feelings in her face. He was nothing like Leonard, for instance, who had laughed and joked constantly. Perhaps almost too much, she now wondered. It had been hard to talk to her fiancé about anything serious, and certainly he had never made her fear he could read her thoughts.

But poor Leonard had only been in his early twenties when he died; this man was older, and had seen far more of the world.

'Yes, sounds like you was well shot of that one,' Lily said naively, in agreement with her sister for once.

'Girls, we ought to go,' Violet said, having thought of a polite enough excuse. 'We don't want to miss the bus.' She made for the dry spot higher up the beach where they had left their belongings.

After a short hesitation, the girls followed her up the beach, both grumbling under their breaths but not daring to openly defy her. Not in front of a stranger, anyway.

To her dismay, the man was still behind them.

She pulled on her shoes in a hurry, not even bothering to dry her feet properly with her handkerchief.

'Bus?' He stood a few feet away, studying her partly bare legs with obvious interest. Something in his own face made her sure he'd spotted her high colour and drawn his own conclusions. She lowered her eyes, quickly jumping up again and pulling her dress down to cover her legs. 'Whereabouts are you staying? Evacuated from London, were you?'

'How do you know that?' Lily asked, staring at him astounded.

'Those aren't Cornish accents,' he pointed out gently, then grinned when she bit her lip, his whole face changing. 'You're not living here in Penzance, I take it?'

'We're staying with our aunt and uncle on a farm near Porthcurno,' Alice said before Violet could stop her.

'And how d'you like that?'

Alice pinched her nose contemptuously. 'Whole place stinks of cow poo.'

He laughed. 'That's the country for you.'

Lily made a face, clearly wanting to join in with the conversation. 'And they work us like slaves, all day long! This is the first time we've managed to escape.'

'Work you like slaves?' he repeated, his smile fading. 'That doesn't sound too good. Safer than London though, I guess.'

Violet met his eyes shyly, as that last comment had been directed at her. 'We're glad to be out of the city,' she agreed, 'but it's harder work than what my sister's girls are used to. Still, I suppose they'll soon build up their muscles. We all have to pull our weight in this war, don't we?' Lily had finally got her shoes back on, so Violet picked up her bag and shot him a quick smile. 'Well, we'd best be getting back to the workhouse. It was nice to meet you.'

'You too.' He stepped back, taking off his cap as though in respect. 'The name's Joe, by the way. Joe Postbridge.'

'I'm Violet Hopkins.' She introduced the girls too, as it

would have been rude not to. And she even shook his hand when he offered it.

He had a firm grip, but not a threatening one. It was the hand of an outdoors man, she thought, very aware of how his fingers curled about hers momentarily before he released her. Strong fingers, sun-browned and calloused.

And a warm smile to go with the handshake.

His mother drifted towards them, her face in shadow under the wide brim of her hat. 'Hello,' she said in a deep Cornish accent, when Joe had introduced them. 'How do you do? I'm Edna.' She seemed like a nice woman, her smile especially warm towards the girls when she heard they had lost their mother. 'Oh, you poor dears.' Perhaps seeing how uncomfortable they were with her quick sympathy, she changed the topic. 'But what lovely fair hair you both have. And such charming manners. Are you enjoying Cornwall?'

As the girls replied to her questions, Violet realised with a start that Joe Postbridge was watching her, not listening to his mother.

Suddenly, she felt embarrassed and overheated, tucking her hair behind her ears and not knowing where to look. She was behaving like a schoolgirl!

As soon as it felt polite to do so, Violet said a hurried goodbye and shepherded her nieces up to the main road without looking back, damp feet squelching in her shoes, her heart beating uncomfortably fast.

'Aunty Vi, your face is awful red,' Alice said as they waited for the bus back to Porthcurno, gazing at her innocently. 'You must 'ave caught the sun.'

'I daresay,' she said, and set her lips tight.

It would not do to think about a man this way. Not even for a moment. Not even in the privacy of her own head. She was here in Cornwall to ensure her nieces' safety, not go all gooey-brained and dewy-eyed over the first interesting man she had met in years.

When the war was over, she would be taking the girls straight back to London, hopefully to be reunited with their missing father. There could be no future in a relationship with a Cornishman.

And she knew it.

CHAPTER ELEVEN

Hazel wiped her face with a damp cloth, and closed her eyes until the next wave of sickness had passed her by. She stayed where she was, leaning over the kitchen sink for a few minutes, letting her wobbly legs rest. Then she heard Charlie's feet on the stairs and straightened, hurriedly running the tap on full to clean out the sink and clear the air of that sickroom smell.

By the time Charlie came bursting into the kitchen, she was almost herself again, turning to smile at him as though nothing was wrong.

But her son was not a fool. He stopped on the threshold, staring at her. 'What's the matter, Mum?'

'Nothing.'

'Smells like you've been sick.' He nodded at the cloth still crumpled in her hand. 'You not feeling well? Did you catch that illness from the soldiers?'

'I must have.' She threw the cloth in the wash basket, and rinsed her hands. 'But it's not so bad. Just a bit of dizziness.'

'You should stay home. Don't go to work today.'

She gave a croaky laugh. 'We need the money, Charlie.

You know that. And I'm perfectly fine. I didn't sleep well, that's all.'

His stare was frustrated. 'Well, I can't make you stay home. But I bet if Dad was here, he'd be able to stop you.'

She didn't like where this was going. More and more these days, her son was beginning to sound scarily like his dad, thinking he could force her into things and that, as a male, he had a God-given right to do so.

'Charlie, look . . .'

'Sorry, Mum, I'm already late.' He grabbed an apple from the fruit bowl on the table, dragged his satchel over his shoulder, and headed out of the door. 'See you later!'

The silence in the house felt heavy and overwhelming once the door had slammed shut behind Charlie. If only she could find a way to get through that defensive armour of his.

But at the same time, Hazel felt a tremendous sense of relief that she was finally alone. It had been so hard to keep the distress and fear out of her face. She couldn't let him see what was happening deep down, that this queasy feeling, the wobbliness, the light-headed sensations she had felt on rising for the past few days were not down to any sickness she might have caught at Eastern House.

No, this was far worse than any tummy bug.

Hazel had sat down last night and checked through her diary, looking back at discreet red crosses beside certain dates for the past few months, and then done the necessary calculations on paper . . . and discovered the awful truth.

She was pregnant.

There was no other possible explanation. She had missed her usually regular-as-clockwork time of the month a couple of weeks back, and thought perhaps it was the worry and stress she was feeling over Charlie that had caused her to skip a period. But then her breasts had begun to tingle in an oddly familiar way, feeling fuller than normal, and queasiness had become a problem. Still she had thought nothing of it. Her bosom was often fuller just before her monthlies, and more sensitive than usual, and the sick feeling over the past few days she had put down to this bug going round among the soldiers.

But put together with her absent monthly bleed, and this new uncomfortable feeling of always being on edge, the symptoms could only add up to one thing.

But a baby . . . ?

Carrying Charlie had been hard work. She was not cut out for pregnancy, the doctor had told her. How could she cope with another one, so much older this time around, and struggling on her own without a husband to lean on for help? Especially once she grew too obviously pregnant to hold down her job.

She could hide her pregnancy for a few more months, of course – and she must, to keep the household going. The meagre weekly allowance she received as a corporal's wife, even with a few shillings extra for a child, was not sufficient for their needs.

But pregnant women were not supposed to go out to work, not even with a war on. George was not blind, and neither were the rest of the staff and soldiers at the listening post. Someone at Eastern House would notice her expanding girth eventually, and then she would lose her position, and with it, their only steady income apart from what she received as an army wife.

It had been so long since she had slept regularly with Bertie, it had not occurred to her that such a thing could happen. She and Bertie had made love – if it could be called that – when he was last home on leave. But it had been a hurried, fumbling event, and she had not even considered the possibility that it could have consequences. Which seemed like the stupidest possible thing now, given the evidence before her.

What on earth was she going to do?

Very late for work by the time she'd pulled herself together, Hazel had to cycle hard through the lanes, puffing up and down the slopes between their row of cottages and Eastern House, barely looking where she was going. It was a damp morning, rain spitting into her face and dripping off her hat brim, a white, clammy mist hanging gloomily over the sea. Her mind was focused completely on the shock she was suffering, this upsetting realisation that a tiny life was growing inside her for the second time – and was not entirely wanted. It was that terrible awareness – that she did not wish to carry Bertie's child, even though he was her husband – that was causing her the most pain.

She bicycled with more than usual difficulty up the grim incline of Tinker's Hill, and then whizzed down the other side at speed, grabbing on to her rain-sodden hat as the air snatched at it.

A loud hooting brought her back to reality.

Something large and frighteningly solid loomed out of the mist ahead. It was a van, taking up nearly the entire lane, and to her horror it wasn't showing any signs of slowing or moving aside.

Hazel jammed her handlebars sideways in a desperate attempt to avoid a head-on collision.

The butcher's delivery van roared past, young Donald at the wheel, apparently oblivious to the fact that he had nearly run her off the road.

Suddenly, the front wheel of her bike struck a large stone

jutting out of the grassy hedgerow, and she came to an abrupt halt. The bike wobbled and toppled over.

She fell with it, crying out in alarm.

For a moment, she lay there on the road, too winded to move. Then the cold of the rain-wet ground began to creep into her bones and she moaned, disentangling herself with an effort from the spinning front wheel.

'Bloody 'ell,' came a cry from across the road, in the direction of Chellew Farm. 'I saw the whole thing through the kitchen window. That idiot nearly mowed you down.' A woman with smooth fair hair, the light shining through it like a halo, crouched down and stopped the front wheel from spinning, then bent to give her a sympathetic look. 'You all right? Any broken bones? Cracked ribs? Or a cracked head, maybe?'

'I . . . I don't think so,' Hazel muttered, though she couldn't help wincing at the pain in her knee. 'Thanks, but I have to get back on the bike. I'm late for work.'

The woman studied it dubiously. 'You sure about that? Front wheel looks awful bent.'

'Then I'll push it.'

'In your state?' The woman folded her arms, clearly disapproving. She looked to be a few years younger than Hazel. 'Look at you, your knee's bleeding. And you could have been killed. Them at work can wait another few minutes, surely?'

'Sorry.' Hazel shook her head, stumbling back to her feet with the woman's aid. 'I . . . I can't risk being given my notice.'

'I know that feeling. Here, careful there . . .' The woman supported her as she staggered sideways. 'Look, why not let me patch your knee up, at least? There's dirt in that cut. And you don't half look pale.'

Hazel had dragged the old bicycle upright and was staring in consternation at the front wheel. It hadn't buckled, thank

God, but there was a distinct bend to the frame. The woman was right, she couldn't possibly cycle on it. Charlie could probably straighten it out for her tonight with a hammer. But she would have to push the bloody thing all the way to Eastern House, and then home again this evening, unless she could wangle a lift from someone.

And the rain was coming down harder now, dripping off the end of her nose.

She felt thoroughly miserable.

'My hat,' she whispered, and bent to retrieve it.

Her flimsy Macintosh parted, and that was when she saw her knee, muddied and blooming with scarlet just above the hem of her work skirt, the buff fabric bloody too – where it was not stuck to her skin.

The world spun with another wave of sickness, and she nearly fell again, barely regaining her balance as she tried to straighten, hat in hand.

'That's it, you're coming into the house with me,' the woman said, almost crossly, and slipped an arm under her shoulder, supporting her back to Chellew Farm. 'I'm Violet Hopkins, by the way.'

CHAPTER TWELVE

Eva woke up on her second day at Porthcurno almost too stiff to get out of bed. But she could hear a bell ringing below, and knew it meant breakfast was ready. If she missed it, she had been told, there would be nothing more to eat until lunchtime. And she was famished, probably thanks to the fresh country air.

She groaned as she stumbled out of bed, then dragged down the blackout curtain and made a disappointed face at the rain misting up her window, the sea beyond Eastern House a vague whitish-grey today, seagulls circling and crying mournfully over its expanse as though in complaint at the rain.

Where had all the gorgeous sunshine gone? It was like being inside a cloud.

This sudden shift in weather suited her mood though, she had to admit. Every damn muscle in her body ached, and that included her heart.

She had dreamt about poor Flight Lieutenant Carmichael again during the night, and now she could not seem to shake those dark images. They had been walking together down an unlit London street, holding hands and laughing, when suddenly his hand had slipped from hers. She had turned in surprise, but found the handsome pilot was no longer there. And where he had been standing was a deep, smoking hole in the road.

She had screamed in horror, staring down into the blackened crater, which seemed to go on forever into the bowels of the earth, but nobody heard. Or at least nobody came to help her. Then a bright flash lit up the whole sky, and when she looked up, a terrible force swept her off her feet and carried her away into burning darkness . . .

If only she knew what had happened to her saviour.

It had been lovely to see her father again when she arrived at Porthcurno – she could not deny it. They had been apart too long, mainly because of the war, but also because of a basic clash in their outlooks on life. Her father was a sweetie. But since her mother's death, he had developed a tendency to disapprove of Eva's modern lifestyle, always trying to cramp her style by imposing Victorian rules she was frankly disinclined to follow.

It came of being a colonel, she supposed. All those soldiers at his beck and call. But she wasn't one of his men, she was his daughter, and that meant she sometimes needed her freedom. Because staying with him invariably involved early nights and bracing walks in the country, such as the one he had inflicted on her yesterday afternoon.

But Daddy was trying his best to get closer to her again – she had to admit. Yesterday, he had stridden across the Cornish cliffs in the sunshine, while she struggled to keep up with him. He had not seemed to notice that the wind was whisking her hair every which way, or that her flimsy shoes were not designed for long country walks, nor her body used to miles of tramping up and down steep slopes.

'Look at that,' he had boomed in his commanding officer's voice, pointing his walking stick at armed military outposts, or grim little pillboxes dug into the cliffsides, or yards of barbed wire bristling across sandy beaches far below, sounding every bit as proud as though he had improved the Cornish countryside with such horrid accoutrements. 'This whole coast is heavily fortified. No chance of the enemy getting even one hairy toe on shore without losing said toe.' He had nodded with obvious satisfaction. 'Jolly good, don't you think?'

'Absolutely lovely,' Eva kept repeating in a dreary tone, wishing she was back in London, where bombs might be falling, but at least there was fun to be had every night, even in the blackout.

'What's up, Miss Moppet? Why the long face?' he demanded at one point, no doubt catching the ennui in her voice at last. 'Don't you like the fresh air?'

'This air isn't fresh,' she replied at once, sniffing in the country smells with vague disgust, having twice almost trodden in some brownish substance he had described as 'cow dung'. 'It's positively reeking. And my feet hurt.'

'Your feet? But you've hardly walked five miles.'

She was aghast. 'Five miles?'

'No need to get upset. We'll soon get you fit out here, my dear. Another month here, your leg muscles will be strong as iron, mark my words.' He swung his arm wide, indicating the glittering sea and rugged Cornish coast. 'Now come on, isn't this a pretty sight?'

She had to admit, it was very pretty. But it wasn't London.

'I'm a city girl. I prefer streets and buildings.'

'But surely this is more satisfying, my dear? Earth and sea and sky. All this greenery everywhere. Human beings were made for exactly this kind of terrain. Not for blasted city streets. You should use your legs for walking long distances.'

'My legs were made for dancing, not walking,' she told him tartly. 'And ladies aren't supposed to have leg muscles like iron. Trust me, Daddy.'

'Well, maybe not. But you'll soon come around. Anyway, your uncle told me on the telephone that you'd had a bit of a rough time in London. We can't be having any more wild behaviour – do you hear? No more dancing the night away with all sorts, and nearly getting your head blown off in the process!'

Eva rolled her eyes, staring at a herd of lumbering cows in the distance. She could see two girls in drab coats trudging along through a field with them, presumably taking them to or from the milking shed. Land Girls, from their uniforms. She'd heard that the Women's Land Army had been re-formed, and women from cities and towns were now being encouraged to work on farms instead of in factories.

What an awful life!

But some women liked that kind of thing. Fresh air and early rising, and all that. Not her! Thank goodness it wasn't compulsory. Though if the war went on much longer, she imagined it soon would be.

Her father glanced at her averted profile, and relented. 'Now, Eva, don't look so glum. It's not the big city, but it's a marvellous part of the world.'

'It's not my cup of tea, Daddy. When can I go back to London?'

'Never,' he said shortly, 'if I have my way.'

Eva glared at him, too furious to trust herself to speak. She was no longer a child. What right did he have to keep her here?

'Look, you're not confined to quarters,' he continued, frowning down at her, 'but I'd rather you didn't leave the camp for the time being. Not until I'm sure you're capable of behaving in a rational manner.' He shot her a meaningful look. 'Anyway, I need to find you work here if you're to avoid being drafted God knows where. You don't want to end up making bombs in some factory up north, do you?'

She folded her arms, reluctantly aware that he was right. 'No.'

'Then be a good girl and do as you're told.' With a quick smile, he added, 'Besides, we have plenty of dashing officers here in Porthcurno to squire you about the place when I'm busy. So you won't be lonely. I'll introduce you to a few of the chaps at dinner tonight. How's that?'

Dashing officers . . .

She knew the type he meant. Clean-cut, fresh-faced boys straight out of Oxbridge, the kind he wouldn't mind seeing her settling down with as soon as possible, or else confirmed bachelors with silver streaks in their hair, older straitlaced men who were unlikely to tempt her into any misbehaviour.

Nobody even remotely like her fallen flight lieutenant, in other words.

But she would play his game for now, Eva decided.

The alternative would mean trying to find her own way back to London when she was flat broke. Plus, the room she had rented there would probably have been given to someone else by now, and it was not easy to find new lodgings in a city where half the houses had been reduced to rubble and the other half might follow at any moment.

And she definitely wanted to avoid being made to work in a factory.

'Sounds absolutely lovely,' she repeated, following him back along the cliff path to Eastern House, and childishly putting her tongue out at his back.

There were no bars at her window or barbed wire outside her door. But it seemed she was to be a prisoner here at

Porthcurno, all the same. As much a prisoner as those unfortunate country girls she'd seen with the cows, in fact.

Well, her father had told her often enough that it was every prisoner's duty to try and escape. So, he could hardly blame her if she slipped the leash once or twice. And her first act of rebellion was already taking shape in her head. Cornwall or not, there had to be *somewhere* in these godforsaken parts where people danced and had a good time.

And if there wasn't, she would jolly well invent one.

CHAPTER THIRTEEN

Violet helped the woman hobble across the muddy yard and into the farm kitchen, ignoring all her protests that she didn't need her cuts cleaned and that she was going to be late for work. 'Better safe than sorry,' she told her firmly, and sat her down in the rickety chair at the head of the table. 'What did you say your name was? Hazel?' She hunted on the dresser for the tin where her aunt kept bandages, pins, and an assortment of medicinal creams in case of accidents about the farm. 'I'll soon get that knee cleaned and patched up, and then you can be on your way. Where do you work?'

Hazel hesitated, looking furtive. 'Erm, just down the road a bit,' she said reluctantly, removing her wet coat so that Violet could hang it to dry by the range. Underneath the coat, she had a curvy figure, the kind Violet had always rather envied, and was wearing what looked like a domestic uniform. 'Another couple of miles.'

Violet had not been that way since arriving at the farm, so wasn't sure where Hazel meant. She had only taken the bus into Penzance, which they'd caught by following one of the narrow lanes in the other direction.

'Well, you won't get anywhere fast pushing that bike,' Violet said, wondering why she was being so secretive about where she was going. 'Maybe my uncle can give you a lift. He's probably about the farm somewhere.'

'That's very kind, but I'd rather not bother him.' Hazel bit her lip, examining her cut knee. 'Ouch, this is worse than I thought.'

Violet filled a bowl with hot water from the kettle that stood permanently heating on the range, then took a clean cloth from the drawer. She sat down next to Hazel and gave her a soothing smile. She knew what it was like to be hurt and sitting in a stranger's house; there had been several close calls during the bombing in London, when she and the girls had fled after nearby houses had been demolished. Though this was hardly on the same scale, the woman did seem rather shaken, and definitely worried about her job.

'This work of yours, what is it you do?'

Again, that tiny hesitation. 'Cleaning and cooking, mostly. I . . . I'm not supposed to talk about it. Sorry.'

Violet was intrigued now. 'War work, is it? Well, bless me. I didn't know there was much of that going on down here.' Then she considered the troop trucks she had seen driving past, and the occasional heavily guarded convoy. She'd assumed they were heading to some kind of training area further up the coast; it had never occurred to her that tiny Porthcurno itself might be concealing a military base. 'Sounds very hush-hush.'

'That's r-right, it is.'

The woman sucked in a breath as Violet dabbed at her bloodied knee with the damp cloth. 'Sorry,' she said quickly.

'No, it's fine. Best to get it clean.'

'That's the spirit.'

Violet kept wiping the wound as gently as she could until

all the mud and grit had gone, then she bathed it with clean water, dried the whole knee, applied one of her aunt's medicinal creams, and tied a bandage around it.

'I won't tie it too tight or you won't be able to bend your knee at all,' she said, and went to wash her hands at the sink. 'Feel better?'

'Much, thank you.' To her surprise, Hazel was already halfway across the kitchen, heading for the range to collect her coat. She dragged it on and hobbled to the door, peering out into the rainy yard. 'The rain seems to be slowing. I'd best be on my way.'

'What difference can five minutes make? Let me try and find my uncle. He's got a truck, he could put your bike in the back.'

'No, honestly . . .'

Her aunt bustled into the kitchen at that moment, arms full of washing, and stopped dead at the sight of a strange woman in her kitchen. Only apparently the woman was not as strange to her as she was to Violet, because her face darkened and her lips pursed up in instant dislike, and she gave a fierce squawk-like cry.

'Hazel Baxter! What are you doing here?'

Frozen in the doorway, Hazel looked back at her with a hunted expression. 'H-Hello, Mrs Chellew. Sorry to disturb you. I was just leaving.'

'So I should think,' Aunt Margaret said sternly.

'Thank you again,' Hazel said awkwardly to Violet, and then ran out across the yard, pressing her wet hat back on.

Aunt Margaret shook her head, then turned her attention to Violet, an angry light in her eyes. 'And what,' she asked in glacial tones, 'was that Awful Woman doing in my home?'

'Awful Woman?' Violet stared at her aunt in surprise. 'She had a nasty accident on the road, and I offered to help, that's all. Some fool in a van nearly hit her bicycle, and she came a right cropper, bloody knee and all.'

'Very Christian of you, I'm sure. Only next time, leave the woman to fend for herself. Hazel Baxter is not welcome in this house. Her or her family.'

Violet stood by the open door, watching Hazel outside in the rain as she picked up her battered bicycle and began pushing it along the road in a slow, jerky fashion. She had seemed a polite enough woman, if a little nervous, and clearly very countrified, her hair cut in a dowdy style and not wearing any make-up. Though here in Cornwall it hardly seemed worthwhile bothering with lipstick. Not when cows were the only ones to see it most days.

'Why ever not?'

'Because of the Awful Man she married. Bertie Baxter.' Aunt Margaret deposited her armful of washing in the wicker basket by the door, ready for the next sunny day, her voice full of loathing. 'The man's a drunkard and a liar and a thief.' To this list of serious defects, she added more darkly, 'And an adulterer.'

'Sounds like his poor bloody wife needs our pity, not our contempt.'

'What did you say?' her aunt demanded, staring.

'You heard me.'

'How dare you use such language under my roof?' Margaret exploded, and pointed a bony finger at her. 'Why, you're lucky I don't toss you and your lazy nieces out on your ears, talking to me like that.'

Violet folded her arms, her temper rising sharply. 'Like what, exactly?'

'Like the East End guttersnipe you are.'

Well, what a bloody cheek, she thought angrily. It was all she could do not to throw something at the unpleasant woman. But Margaret was still her aunt, and it was true she did not want to risk the girls' safety by saying something she would regret.

Instead, she snatched up an old sheet from the washing basket and ran out into the rain, covering her head to avoid getting drenched.

The road outside was empty. But Hazel had not gone far. She was about five hundred yards down the road, a misty figure under the drizzle, limping as she pushed her bicycle.

''Ere, hang on a minute,' she called after Hazel, splashing through puddles as she hurried after her. 'Do you need a hand?'

Hazel looked round in surprise, stopping. 'No, thank you.' She glanced back at the farmhouse, half-hidden behind high banks of grassy hedgerows. 'I'm sorry if I got you in trouble. Are you one of those Land Girls? Do you work for Mrs Chellew?'

'God, no, nothing like that. She's my aunt, the old dragon. She and Uncle Stanley have been putting us up at the farm while the Germans are bombing London. But they're driving me mad.'

'You're from London?'

She grinned at the woman's wide-eyed stare. 'What, don't you know what an East Ender sounds like?'

'I knew you weren't a local. But I've only heard London accents at the pictures in Penzance, and I wasn't sure . . .'

'Well, pay no attention to what Aunt Margaret says. I was happy to help. And your old man sounds like a right sod.'

Hazel looked flustered. 'Oh, did she . . . I mean . . . How embarrassing.'

'Oh, don't worry about that spiteful cow.' Violet realised the rain had almost stopped, and rolled up the sheet that had been covering her head. 'Look, yours is the first friendly face

I've seen since we arrived. Maybe we could meet for a cuppa sometime. Not at the farm though,' she added quickly, seeing Hazel's horrified expression. 'At yours, if you like. Maybe when your husband's not at home.'

'Bertie's a soldier. He's away fighting.'

'Nothing to stop us, then. I miss having a good gossip over a cup of tea. And I'd do anything to escape the farm for a few hours.'

'Did you bring family with you from London?'

'My sister's two girls are with me.' She paused. 'Betsy died in the bombing.'

'I'm so sorry.'

Violet nodded her thanks, and squeezed her new friend's arm. There was a sudden lump in her throat. 'There's a war on, these things happen,' she said gruffly, and changed the subject before she could embarrass herself by crying. 'Look, let me know where you live, and I'll pop round for tea one afternoon. If you ever get a day off, that is.'

Hazel explained where she lived, and Violet nodded, having a vague idea where she meant.

'They work us pretty hard, but I'm usually free on Thursday afternoons,' Hazel said, then added hesitantly, 'You know, they might be looking for new domestic staff where I work. One of the women just left because she was expecting, and another is moving to Exeter at the end of the month.'

Violet stared. 'You're saying there's a job going at this place?'

'Maybe, I'm not sure.'

Her heart swelling with excitement, Violet did not know what to say. But her mind could not help skipping ahead to a new future. She had been so miserable since leaving London, she felt almost sick with it. This could be her chance to escape the farm. But what about Lily and Alice? She couldn't just abandon them.

109

Hazel shot her a harried smile. 'I've got to go, but I could ask someone on your behalf if there's work available. It's all top secret though. They don't just take anyone.'

'Understood.'

'We can talk more on Thursday.'

'Can't wait,' Violet said, and let her go. 'Take care of that knee, love.'

Walking back to the farm, she could not get rid of the notion that a job at this top-secret place could save her from working on the farm. Perhaps save all three of them if there was more than one job available. With at least two wages coming in, they might be able to find a room to share nearby, or even two rooms. Then they could escape the farm altogether.

Her aunt was waiting in the kitchen to give her a stern tongue-lashing. Her uncle appeared too and gave her a dressing-down for having spoken rudely to her aunt.

But nothing either of them said could dampen Violet's spirits. She went off whistling under her breath, and it was hard not to let her rebellious thoughts show on her face as she finished her chores that evening. She was bursting to tell Lily and Alice of her encounter with Hazel, and the possibility that there might be a job going elsewhere. But she didn't want to raise the girls' hopes only to dash them.

After all, what if she applied for work, but was turned down on account of her missing brother-in-law being a suspected spy?

That would be too awful.

It was a thought that kept her awake most of that night, suddenly unsure what to do. Perhaps it would be safer to stay at the farm and put up with her aunt's mean behaviour and her uncle's occasional leering. Better the devil you know, she thought unhappily.

Her brother-in-law was not a spy, she felt sure of it. But

she doubted anyone would bother to ask her opinion. They would be more likely to suspect her too. They were at war with Germany, and anyone who fell under suspicion of working against Britain was considered guilty from the off, and that included their families.

Down here in Cornwall, that dangerous business with Ernst had seemed so far away, like another world they had left far behind. But she knew these family secrets had a way of coming out eventually, however well hidden.

CHAPTER FOURTEEN

Eva was running, newspaper held over her head against the pelting rain, when she bumped into a woman pushing a bicycle up the slope to Eastern House, and nearly sent her flying. 'Oops, sorry!' She grabbed at the handlebars, righted the bike, and threw an apologetic smile at the woman, who had stumbled sideways with a startled cry. 'Gosh, you're drenched. Come on, I'll help!'

Wheeling the bike together, they ran the last few yards to the covered area near the side entrance to Eastern House, where a couple of soldiers were standing about, smirking as they dragged on their roll-ups just out of the rain. Beyond them were rolls of barbed wire and a gatehouse, guarding the entrance to a tunnel that ran under the cliff.

Eva's father had pointed out the doorway on his brief tour of the campus, and told her the area was strictly forbidden, which had of course made her instantly curious to know what they were hiding inside there.

'Need a hand, ladies?' one of them called out cheekily, giving Eva a knowing wink. 'I've got two here I could lend you.'

The soldier got a fierce glare from Eva for his trouble.

'Watch out, mate, that's the colonel's daughter,' his friend muttered, and the men fell silent, shuffling their feet.

The woman was looking uncomfortable, and not because of the soldier's suggestion. Eva studied her quickly, her eye falling on a rip across the hemline of her skirt, barely concealed by the sodden, clinging raincoat. There was a bloodied bandage under there, wrapped about her knee.

No wonder she had been pushing the bicycle instead of riding it. And now that she had a chance to examine it, Eva could see that the front wheel was in a bad way too. She doubted it was even roadworthy.

'That knee looks bad,' she said briskly. 'Taken a tumble on the road? I can have a look if you like. I've got some training.'

Her father had insisted she took a course in basic nursing at finishing school, and though she had not yet needed it except for the occasional cut and graze, it always made her feel more confident when people were hurt.

The woman did not look very grateful for the offer though.

'I'm not supposed to use this entrance,' she said breathlessly, removing her soggy-looking hat and wiping damp hair out of her face. Her accent was thoroughly Cornish, rich as a cream tea. 'And I have to put this old thing away in the bike shed, or I'll be in hot water for sure.' She looked Eva up and down, and then added awkwardly, 'Thank you ever so, but my knee's just fine. And I . . . I'm terribly late as it is.'

'You can blame me. Tell them it was the colonel's daughter's fault.' Eva stuck out a hand. 'That's me, by the way. Eva's my name.'

'Hazel Baxter.'

They shook hands.

'Where's this bike shed, then?' Eva gave her a friendly smile. 'I only arrived two days ago, I'm still learning my way around. Dad gave me the guided tour but only the official stuff. Which didn't include bike sheds or which door I'm supposed to use.'

'It's round here,' Hazel said, wheeling her bicycle along the back wall of Eastern House to a narrow lean-to.

Rain poured off the roof and splattered on the ground as Hazel pushed her bike inside, then hurriedly led Eva further along to a door that opened onto an echoing corridor. They banged inside the house and slammed the door against the downpour, both stopping just inside to wipe their wet shoes on the coarse matting that passed for a door mat.

'Look,' Eva said, stamping her feet, 'you're a local girl, you must know the answer to my question.'

'Wh-what question?'

'Is there any dancing to be had round here? A pub with an upper room, maybe? Or a night club?'

'Dancing?' Hazel looked at her blankly, sodden hat still clutched in her hand. 'I . . . I don't think so.'

'What? You're saying you Cornish lot never get your glad rags on and dance the night away?'

'At a wedding party, maybe. Or a Church Friendly.'

'What's that?'

'Sometimes the local church will run a dance to get the community together, maybe to raise some funds for repairs too. We're quite isolated out here, and the bus doesn't usually run late enough for a dance in Penzance. Though on a Friday, you can catch the bus back after the pictures. Well, you could, until the Germans started bombing them. I don't think the picture house is open anymore.'

'A Church Friendly sounds promising.'

'Except now there's a war on, they've stopped the Friendlies too. Because we can't go out after dark. Not unless it's an emergency. Lights aren't allowed.'

'You don't need lights if you're walking.'

'True,' Hazel said dubiously.

'Is there a church nearby?'

'In the valley. It's not too far, I suppose.' Hazel made a face. 'Not sure what the vicar would say to a dance though. He's a bit of a . . . well, a curmudgeon, my dad used to call him. And he might object if it risks his church getting blown up!'

'There can't be much bombing round Porthcurno, surely?'

'Not too much, no. But they reckon the Germans know about the listening post now. Only they don't know where exactly.'

'Hence all the camouflaging on the buildings and cliffs.'

'That's right.' Hazel nodded sombrely. 'Probably not a good idea to hold a dance, not with all the bombing in Penzance lately. Don't you think?'

'It should be fine, so long as we keep the blackout curtains up.' But Eva found herself instinctively fingering the scar along her jawline.

'What happened to you there?' Hazel's curious gaze lingered on the faded cuts and bruises that still showed under Eva's face powder, then she blushed. 'Sorry . . . None of my business.'

'Oh, it's no secret. I nearly got myself blown up in London.'

'Blown up?' Hazel looked shocked.

'Yes, bit of rotten luck. But not as rotten as some. I lost friends that night.'

'How dreadful.'

They were still standing just inside the back entrance, dripping all over the floor. What would have been the servants' entrance a few decades back, Eva guessed, before the Great War. Everyone was more equal now, and quite right too. She set the wet newspaper she'd been using as an umbrella

115

on the floor to dry, and straightened, realising too late that they were being watched.

There was a group of clean-cut young men in dark suits huddled in conversation in the corridor. Some of them, she noticed, were rather dishy. Though a bit youthful for her tastes.

'Hey, who are those boys?' Eva whispered to Hazel, nudging her with a sharp elbow. 'Nice suits.'

Hazel peered round at their audience, and her eyes widened. 'Trainees,' she whispered back.

'What kind of trainees?'

'Right clever ones. They work in the underground rooms. Listening to all them secret messages that come in along the undersea cables, I daresay.'

'How exciting.'

But Hazel clapped a hand over her own mouth, clearly aghast. 'Oh Lord, I shouldn't have said that. Me and my runaway tongue. You know what they're always saying, careless talk costs lives.'

'I won't tell anyone,' Eva said soothingly.

'Yes, but I had to sign the Official Secrets Act on my first day. I . . . I could probably be imprisoned just for telling you that.' Hazel turned pale. 'Or shot, maybe. Do they shoot people for talking out of turn?' She bit her lip. 'I've got a son. Charlie. He's only fifteen. He needs his mother.'

'And he's not going to lose you over a few words spoken out of turn.' Eva used her most reassuring voice, leading her further along the corridor. But Hazel did not seem reassured, tears welling in her eyes. 'Listen, I don't think anyone's going to shoot you. Or clap you in irons either, so please don't look so pasty-faced. There are no Germans here.'

'Is that you, Eva?'

'Oh, blimey.'

116

She turned guiltily, recognising the deep, booming voice that had echoed down the corridor. Until he found her something more useful to do, her father had told her strictly not to loiter about the main house, but to spend most of her time in her quarters, reading improving books or sketching in the small hardback book he had provided for her artistic endeavours. Almost as though, as she had said at the time, she was back in finishing school.

But who could stick to such a monastic routine? Certainly not her . . .

'I'd better go,' she told Hazel hurriedly, adding, 'But let's get together later and talk about organising a local dance. It'll be a blast, I promise.'

She strode past the gaggle of young men, who were now standing straighter and carefully averting their eyes, and navigated her way past the guards to stop at the bottom of the stairs.

'Yes, Daddy?'

'Ah, Eva, good.' Her father gazed down at her from the floor above, a pipe in his hand, a cloud of thick smoke about his head. To her relief, he was smiling. Not on the warpath as she'd feared, then. 'I thought I could hear your dulcet tones. If you've done with your chit-chat, come up here a minute, would you? I need to talk to you.'

She ran lightly up the stairs, and hugged him. 'Good morning, Daddy.' She coughed as his pipe smoke wafted about her. 'Goodness, that reeks!'

'I'll open a window. Your mother could never stand the smell of my pipe either.' He patted her cheek affectionately. 'Come into my office, my dear.'

His 'office' was a converted sitting room with high ceilings, its faded grandeur quite appealing after the stark décor of her bedroom in the officers' quarters. There was a tarnished gilt mirror over the mantel, a vast potted plant that gave the room the air of a jungle, and several sofas and armchairs dotted about. The floor-length curtains were only partially open, so the room was both dimly lit and steamy as hell, not least because the old-fashioned ceiling fan was stationary.

She did not sit down but explored the room restlessly, only stopping to study a row of framed photographs on the wall, all very stiff and starchy-looking men with grey hair and bushy beards, presumably previous occupants of the house.

There was a large metal radiator near her foot. She could hear a faint tapping from the metal, as though it was cooling. Why would they be running the heating in summer? The weather was damp, for sure. But it was not cold.

Her father opened one of the windows a few inches, barely enough to let the smoke escape, and then sat down behind a large mahogany desk near the fireplace.

'Now,' he said briskly, not wasting any further time on pleasantries, 'you can't spend your time here wandering about like a schoolgirl, with nothing to do but chat to my staff and generally get underfoot.'

'Now, that's not fair.' Eva put a hand on the radiator. It was cold. But she could still hear a repetitive tapping from the metal. 'I've only just arrived.'

'Nonetheless, my dear, I do feel I should put you to work in some capacity. I apologise, I know your sainted mother would turn in her grave if she could hear those words, but . . . There is a war on, after all, and unmarried young ladies are expected to pull their weight.' He tapped his smouldering pipe out into a huge glass ashtray. 'Only problem is, I haven't the faintest idea what you can do.'

'Well, I can't cook for toffee. So the kitchens are right out.'

'You've some nursing skills.'

'True, but no empathy.'

'I've never met a nurse with empathy yet.'

'I can't stand the sight of blood,' she lied, not wanting to spend the rest of the war cooped up at a nurse's station, bandaging the wounded or cleaning out bedpans. 'And as for diseases . . . No, thank you.'

He frowned, looking at her suspiciously. 'Cleaning, then.'

'Daddy!'

'Well, for goodness' sake . . .' He shook his head, sounding exasperated. 'What did that finishing school teach you, apart from how to avoid hard work?'

'I can speak several languages, including German,' Eva pointed out meekly.

'We all speak English here.'

'Not in your intercepted messages from the enemy.'

The room went quiet.

'That's men's work,' her father said in the end, and shook his head. 'And there's a lot more to that job than *eins, zwei, drei*.'

'You mean, like cracking codes?'

'Exactly.'

'Spelling out a message in Morse code?'

'Ah now, there you've got me. It's a damn shame, but these boys, they haven't learned Morse code, and we don't have the personnel on hand to teach them. People stopped using it, you see. Now it's come back because of the war, and it's a full-time job manning the machines and writing down the messages that come through.'

'Dah-dah dah-dah-dah di-dah-dit di-di-dit dit,' she said dreamily.

'I beg your pardon?'

'Dah-di-dah-dit dah-dah-dah dah-di-dit dit.'

'Eva?'

'M.O.R.S.E,' she said, spelling out the letters she had just

119

heard being tapped out through the metal radiator beside her. 'C.O.D.E.' She turned to her father, grinning. 'Sounds like somebody's using your heating system to teach Morse code!'

Her father stared at her blankly. 'Good God.' Then he slammed a hand down on his desk, so hard that his pipe jumped out of the ashtray. 'What a fool I am. I taught you Morse when you were a little girl. You used to send me messages through the wall with it at home.' He laughed heartily. 'SOS, and so on. And *where's me dinner*?'

'I haven't forgotten.'

'Well, there's a turn-up.' He got up and strode across the room. Flinging the door open, he bellowed down the landing, 'Templeton? In here a minute!'

A moment later, a man strolled through the door who had Eva's instant attention. Somewhere around thirty, by her guess, he was tall and athletic-looking. Attractive, too. Clean-shaven but with dark sideburns that lent his face a hard-edged air, and cheekbones that would not have looked out of place on the cover of a fashion magazine. Despite her father's urgent summons, he showed no sign of hurrying, but walked with his hands stuck in his trouser pockets, his shirt slightly dishevelled under his tweed jacket. He was more Oxford don than daring flyboy, it had to be admitted. But she liked intelligent men.

'Colonel Ryder?' he said coolly.

'Templeton, this is my daughter, Eva. Come down from London to stay with me.' Her father looked on with satisfaction as they shook hands. 'Eva, this is Professor Templeton. He used to teach mathematics at Cambridge but I'm glad to say he's been seconded to our unit for the duration of the war. Excellent fellow, very good with the men.'

So, she hadn't been too far off with her assessment of him,

Eva thought, and covertly looked the professor up and down. In a just world, he would be far too sexy for a dusty old Cambridge don, of course. But there was no arguing with those leather patches on his elbows. Or the tortoiseshell spectacles he wore with debonair aplomb.

Teaching mathematics at university and now seconded to a listening post? She suspected he must be a code specialist, but said nothing. That kind of information was definitely need-to-know-only, and she'd promised her father she would try to be more discreet at Porthcurno.

'My daughter heard your message through the radiator,' the colonel said proudly.

'My message?' Professor Templeton repeated, turning to look at her in surprise.

'Morse code,' her father explained, and tapped the start of the message out again on his desk. '*Dah-dah dah-dah-dah,* and all that. Taught her myself when she was a child. What do you say to that, Templeton?'

The professor, who had been looking Eva up and down in his turn, raised one eyebrow in admiration.

'I say it sounds marvellous, Colonel. I was using the radiator to demonstrate Morse code to some new trainees.' He smiled at her. 'But it seems you don't need lessons, Miss Ryder.'

'I could probably do with a quick brush-up on basics,' she admitted.

'How astonishing.'

'Because I'm a woman?' she asked, a little tartly.

'Because so few people know the code these days, actually,' he told her, and again she read amusement in the lift of one eyebrow. 'I'm not that much of a dinosaur.'

Her father cleared his throat, glancing from one to the other. 'I thought she could help out around here, Templeton. An extra pair of hands. Or ears, in this case. What do you think? Could you put her to use in the training school? I'll be frank, you'd be doing me a favour.'

'It would be my pleasure, sir,' Templeton said, and clasped his hands behind his back, a faint smile on his face as he gazed directly back at her.

'Will you be free later to show her around?'

Templeton turned to look at him. 'The underground area too, sir?'

'Good God, man, she can hardly help you out if she can't accompany you into the tunnels.' Her father took a manila folder out of his desk drawer. 'You'll have to sign these papers, Eva.' He removed several sheets and passed them across the desk to her. 'Official Secrets Act. Not allowed to work here without that.'

'Of course.'

Her father nodded at the professor. 'That will be all, Templeton. I'll send my daughter through to the training room when she's done here.'

'Very good, sir.'

Once the professor had wandered out again, closing the door behind him, Eva took an ink pen from the desk and sat down to read through the Official Secrets Act she had to sign. Though it was hard to concentrate. Her heart was beating fast and she felt light-headed, her cheeks suddenly warm. The professor was nothing compared to Max, of course. But she couldn't help being drawn to his warm smile, and there was no harm in looking.

She only hoped her father wouldn't notice her response to meeting Templeton. He had an annoying way of interfering in her affairs.

'Excellent, excellent.' Her father gave her a brusque, approving nod. 'Well, that's taken a weight off my mind. It seems you do have a useful skill, after all.'

'Yes,' she said, and signed her name with a bold flourish. So she was to be permitted entrance to the underground rooms, along with those young men in suits. Not to mention the dashing Professor Templeton in his tortoiseshell spectacles. This was better than lounging about in her room all day with some improving tome. She only hoped her rusty Morse code would be up to the job. 'Rather exciting, isn't it?'

'That's one way of looking at it.' He frowned, flicking open a dossier on his desk and picking up his pipe again. 'No funny business though. Understood?'

'Funny business?'

'No getting giddy over all these trainee chaps.'

'Oh, Daddy!' Eva handed him back the signed documents, shaking her head in mock hurt. 'I do wish you would learn to trust me.'

'Hmm' was his dry reply.

CHAPTER FIFTEEN

Violet stretched up to unlock the feed store, and groaned at the pain in her back and thighs. She'd told her aunt on arriving that she wasn't afraid of hard work. But the sheer number of jobs that needed to be done about the farm, and the long hours they involved, had changed her mind.

Her heart had begun to sink whenever her uncle sent her on an errand, as more recently these had included chopping logs, digging holes for fence poles and then sinking them – one of the most physically exhausting tasks she had ever been given – and she had even been sent clambering up onto the old stable roof to check its state of repair. Now every muscle in her body was aching, and she never wanted to see another hammer or axe again. Except she would, and possibly even later that day.

This morning's task was pleasant enough, though. Feeding the chickens, scattering seed and grains across the dirty backyard where they pecked merrily at her feet, clucking and hopping about.

'Isn't that Lily's job?' she'd asked her aunt on being instructed to add chicken feeding to her list for today.

'She's helping your uncle in the barn this morning.'

Violet had looked round at her, surprised. 'In the barn? Why's that, then?'

'Never you mind,' her aunt had snapped, tea towel in hand as she dried the breakfast dishes Alice had just finished washing. 'Moving hay bales, I daresay. Just get on, would you? Standing about gossiping and poking your nose in where it isn't wanted . . . This isn't a holiday camp, you know.'

Cleaning out the sink, Alice had rolled her eyes at this aggressive response, and then shot Violet a warning look when she opened her mouth to reply.

They had all agreed not to antagonise Aunt Margaret this week, not after the huge fracas caused by Violet allowing That Woman to enter her kitchen.

Remembering her promise, Violet didn't press the point, but nodded and went about her chores without further questions.

'Yes, Aunt.'

Apparently, Hazel Baxter was despised by Aunty Margaret and Uncle Stanley for having 'a drunkard and a liar' as a husband, an unpleasant man who'd once had the temerity to speak rudely to Margaret at a local fete, and had ever since been considered their enemy. The husband had left Cornwall now for the front, but the feud still continued in his absence, with Hazel one of a long list of locals thoroughly loathed by the ageing couple.

'There you go, chickens,' she said, nudging one persistent little pecker away with her foot. 'Yes, cluck, cluck, cluck. That's enough for now.'

That poor woman, she thought, putting the chicken feed back in the wooden store near the barn. Her husband's bad behaviour was hardly *her* fault. But Aunt Margaret had refused to listen to reason, as usual, describing her scathingly as 'no better than she ought to be,' whatever that was supposed to mean.

Hazel had seemed a perfectly nice woman, Violet thought, if a little frazzled and uncommunicative. Though that was understandable, given her accident, the heavy rain and her lateness for work, any one of which would be enough to upset anyone. Besides which, she had helpfully suggested there might be an opening available at the Porthcurno listening post, if any of them wanted alternative employment.

But how could any of them leave?

Violet imagined her aunt's fury if she chose to work elsewhere than at the farm, and knew it to be impossible. She could fantasise about giving up her chores on the farm. But that was all it would ever be. A silly daydream. Her aunt and uncle would turn them all out on the street if she dared take a job at what Uncle Stanley had called 'the listening post' the other night, not realising she could hear their whispered conversation, and she had the girls' welfare to consider. She might just be able to support herself, but Alice and Lily too?

She was about to return to her chores in the house when a muffled cry made her turn in sudden consternation.

What on earth . . . ?

'Hello?' she called out, looking about the farmyard and adjacent buildings. 'Is . . . Is someone hurt?'

But now there was only silence, apart from the busy clucking of chickens.

Had she imagined it?

Almost ready to give up, she heard the cry again, a kind of stifled, wordless scream. This time she was sure it had come from inside the barn.

Running towards the closed double doors, Violet dragged them open, staring inside. She couldn't see anything but stacked bales of hay at one end, the sunny air spinning with dust motes and pieces of hay.

'Lily? Is that you? What's wrong?' She stumbled inside, peering desperately about. 'Please answer me, sweetheart.'

There was a strange scuffling sound, then one of the stacked hay bales tumbled to the floor, revealing a red-faced Lily kneeling up in the straw, her dress half off one shoulder, her long fair hair dishevelled.

Violet stopped dead, shocked. 'Lily?'

'Oh, Aunty Violet . . .' Lily's voice broke, her eyes full of tears. 'Please don't be cross . . . It wasn't my fault. I . . . I tried to stop him.'

'Stop who?'

Then another hay bale fell away, and there was Uncle Stanley, also red-faced and puffing, hurriedly snapping his braces back into place.

Violet felt sick. 'Uncle Stanley? Wh-what have you done?' Though she did not need him to answer that; it was obvious what had been going on. Horribly obvious. She could barely speak, suddenly light-headed and breathless with disgust. 'And to Lily . . . She's only a child, for God's sake!'

'Get out of my barn,' he thundered at Violet. 'Nosy bloody crow! What business is this of yours, eh? She bain't no child, she be a grown woman, near enough.'

'I'm so s-sorry, Aunty Violet. I didn't know what he were up to till it were too late.' Lily wept, head down, hair hiding her face. The girl was clearly ashamed, as though she were to blame for this. Which she absolutely wasn't. 'I told him no. Only he wouldn't stop . . .'

Violet felt genuine rage, then, and understood how it would be possible to kill someone out of pure fury.

But she could not kill him. That would not help the girls.

'Come with me, love.' Ignoring her uncle's blustering

protests, she took Lily by the arm and helped her out of the barn, discreetly tidying her clothes and hair. To her relief, he did not follow but stood watching them in silence. 'That's it. Of course it's not your fault. It's your uncle's fault.'

But Lily merely shook and continued to weep, incoherent now.

Carefully, Violet avoided the kitchen, leading her niece through the side door and into the quiet back room where she did the accounts. 'Here, sit down.' She arranged a blanket over Lily's knees, and gave her cold arms a rub. 'I'll make you a hot sweet cup of tea, dearie. That will help with the shock.' She gritted her teeth at the lost look on Lily's face. 'That vile perverted man. He should hang for this. His own bloody niece!'

'He never . . . He didn't . . . I mean . . .'

Violet peered into Lily's tear-streaked face, and then took a deep breath, secretly relieved. 'He didn't manage to do it?' she whispered in the girl's ear. 'Is that what you're trying to say?'

Swallowing hard, Lily nodded.

'Well, thank God for that.' Violet took a handkerchief from her pocket and dried her niece's face as best she could. 'Not that he doesn't still deserve to hang. Or lose his man parts.' She smiled at Lily's strangled sob of laughter. 'But that's a mercy, at least.'

She was furious. But it would not help them if she attacked her uncle and got arrested for assault – or worse. And the last thing her niece needed was a policeman asking her horrible, embarrassing questions and making her feel even worse than she probably did right now.

But the man did need to be confronted for his crime.

Confronted and shamed.

'I'll fetch you a cuppa, love. You stay here and don't fret too much.' Violet straightened. 'Aunty Vi's going to fix this.'

She found Alice coming downstairs, and after a brief explanation that skirted the worst facts, sent her in to look after Lily.

Uncle Stanley had returned from the barn and was speaking to his wife in the kitchen. Loudly and bitterly. Some ludicrous tale of how Lily had 'come onto' him and then claimed he had tried to touch her. None of which was true, he was explaining.

Fuelled by outrage, Violet paused on the threshold to the kitchen, rolled up her sleeves, and then marched in with her head held high.

'Your husband just tried to rape Lily,' she announced to her aunt in a voice that shook with emotion. 'Don't listen to his barefaced lies. You and I both know what he is. So no more of this nonsense. The only reason he didn't succeed is because Lily put up a fight, good sensible girl that she is.' She met her aunt's shocked stare with folded arms and a piercing glare of her own. 'Now, what are you going to do about it?'

Stanley hunched his shoulders and looked away, dark red staining his cheeks.

To her surprise though, Aunt Margaret did not even blink. 'I'm going to do what I should have done days ago, and throw all three of you out on your ears.'

'Excuse me?'

'You heard me.' Margaret stood in front of her husband, as though protecting him. 'You, and that tramp Lily, and her nasty little sister, can all find somewhere else to live. Think you can come down here with your filthy London ways and seduce my husband . . . Oh yes, I've seen the way you look at him. You and those dirty girls. And Lily . . . She's a tart, let's face it. Making out she's shy, like butter wouldn't melt . . . But all the time, waiting to sink her claws into my man.' Her aunt pursed her lips, a cruel smile on her thin lips. 'I'm doing you a favour. Plenty of trade in Penzance. I daresay you three could make a small fortune on your backs there.'

'How dare you!'

'Go on, upstairs and pack.' Her aunt pointed to the door. 'And no stealing anything. Or I'll have the police on you, you hear me?'

'Call the bloody police,' Violet said, hot-cheeked and shaking, unable to hide her anger now. 'I think they'll be interested in what I've got to say.'

'Constable Black, you mean? He plays cards with Stanley at the Cross Four Ways pub.' Her aunt gave a short laugh. 'Go ahead and tell him whatever you like. It's a young girl's word against Stanley Chellew's. And I doubt the constable will believe an East End tart like her over a proper Cornishman.'

Violet was furious; she wanted to slap her aunt. But it was clear that Margaret was serious. She would cheerfully dub the whole family liars rather than see her husband get into trouble with the law. And given that they were outsiders to this small, close-knit community, the chances of the local police believing Lily's word over Uncle Stanley's were remote. Instead, Lily would almost certainly find herself branded a liar – and promiscuous, too. Awful though the alternatives were, she couldn't put poor Lily through such a terrible ordeal.

'And what do you think Mum will have to say when she hears about this?' she asked, her voice dangerously quiet.

Margaret hesitated. 'I don't care what my sister says.' But she looked a little afraid at last. 'Besides, London's a long way off. What happens down here is none of her business.' With bared teeth, she added defiantly, 'And this is my house, young lady. You three are not welcome anymore. So you'd better pack up your things and get off our property.'

'Who's going to do all your chores?'

'Three mouths less to feed sounds like a good deal to me,' Margaret said shrilly. 'Besides, we can get half a dozen girls like you off the Land Army, and do far better for it from the government. I've been telling Stanley for weeks to join the scheme. Now he'll have no choice.' She snatched up a potato off the table to throw at her. It missed and rolled harmlessly away, but Violet could see Margaret glancing about for something else to throw. Something bigger and more painful, no doubt. 'Go on, get lost!'

Violet turned on her heel and left the kitchen. She collected a shocked Lily and Alice from the back room, and took them upstairs to pack their things. They had not brought much to Cornwall with them, so it didn't take long. There were a few odd items still lying about the house, but as she told the girls, there was no time to look for them.

They were being evicted, and that was an end to it.

'Are we really, truly, leaving the farm, Aunty Vi?' Alice whispered as they crept down the stairs, bags in hand.

'Yes,' she said shortly, trying to hold herself together until they were out of the house, at least. 'Grab your coats and hats off the hall stand, and let's go.'

She listened at the kitchen door, but there was no sound from inside.

'I'm so sorry, Alice. I'm so sorry, Aunty Violet.' Lily was dragging her coat on, red-eyed and subdued now that her crying fit was over. 'Th-this is all m-my fault.'

'Don't let me hear you say that again,' Violet told her bluntly. 'You understand? This is not your fault. It's Stanley's fault. And I'm going to make him pay for what he's done to you, mark my words.'

But Lily looked away, blinking miserably.

Gathering all her strength, Violet pushed open the kitchen door and stared across the room at her aunt, who was standing by the table with folded arms and pursed lips.

There was no sign of Uncle Stanley.

'I'll be needing our ration books back,' Violet told her bluntly.

Her aunt shuddered, then pointed to the Welsh dresser. 'Behind the best teapot. And mind you only take your own. I won't stand for no thieving.'

Violet repressed a desire to shout a very rude word at her.

Extracting their ration books, she stomped out of the kitchen without a word of goodbye to Margaret.

'Come on, girls,' she said cheerily, like they were going to the park, not leaving the only roof they had over their heads. 'Let's get out of here.'

They slipped out through the front door, laden down with bags and cases, and trudged across the cobbled farmyard to the road. It was a good day to be thrown out, Violet thought with a touch of irony, the ground reasonably dry and the sun shining brilliantly over the sea. A downpour would have added considerably to their woes.

All the same, she stood motionless on the road for a moment, peering up and down with absolutely no idea which way to turn.

Left or right?

'Which way, Aunty Violet?' Alice asked, shifting her heaviest bag to the other hand. 'Where are we headed?'

I don't know, Violet thought wretchedly, her heart pounding. But she could not let her uncertainty show. Not to these two helpless girls who were both looking to her for guidance.

Turning right would lead them to the listening post at Porthcurno, a half hour's walk if they didn't dawdle. There might be work there, Hazel had said. Maybe work for all three of them.

On the other hand, a left turn would take them to the bus stop and the resort town of Penzance. Except she barely had enough money for the bus fare, and what would they do once they were there? Where would they spend the night? She had a sudden terrible vision of them all sleeping under a hedge, or on a town bench under newspaper, and begging for food tomorrow, while she racked her brains for how best to raise three train fares back to Dagenham and her mother.

Except the enemy were bombing both Penzance and London. It was no safer anywhere else than here. And something might yet turn up for them.

Violet forced a brave smile to her lips. No point crying over spilt milk, she told herself. 'Right,' she told them firmly. 'We're going to Porthcurno.'

CHAPTER SIXTEEN

'Hazel?'

Startled by the echo of George's deep voice right behind her, Hazel jumped round, dripping mop in hand, and stared at him wide-eyed.

She had been tasked with mopping floors once she'd finished clearing the tables after lunch, and still had several rooms and corridors to go. The soldiers in particular tended to traipse in and out of the house with mud on their boots, and without a thorough cleaning once a day, the place soon looked like a mess. It wasn't her usual job, of course. But it gave her a chance to escape the steamy heat of the kitchen, where Mr Frobisher was preparing several large summer fruit puddings for tonight's meal.

'You gave me a fright!'

'Sorry,' George said awkwardly, and stood looking at her, jingling some loose change in his trouser pocket. 'I seem to be making a habit of that.'

'Maybe if you stopped creeping up on people . . .'

'Not sure I do much creeping,' he said, glancing ironically

at his large feet. 'Maybe you were mopping so loudly, you didn't hear me.'

'Maybe.' She gripped the mop handle tightly, trying not to appear too friendly. 'Can I help you, Mr Cotterill?'

He cleared his throat. 'I wondered if you . . . erm . . .'

'Yes?'

'More of a request, really, but I wondered if you . . .' George frowned, cutting himself off. 'Hang on, what have you done there?' He gestured to her knee, and she blushed under his scrutiny, horribly embarrassed. 'That looks painful.'

'I took a tumble, that's all.'

'How did it happen?'

'A van driver nearly ran me off the road yesterday morning, driving like a maniac. In the rain too. I came off my bike.' Hazel made a face, tugging at the hem of her skirt to cover the cuts and bruises. 'It's nothing, really.' She managed a half-smile. 'The bike looks worse.'

'Do you know who the driver was? Not one of ours, I hope? Or I'll have someone's guts for garters, knocking you off your bicycle like that.'

'It wasn't an army van. Please don't make a fuss.'

'But you could have been killed.'

'Only I wasn't.' She stuck her mop back in her steaming bucket of hot water, and sloshed it about a bit, staring at the soapy water instead of at him. Her tummy was turning somersaults at the look in his eyes and she dreaded him knowing how she felt. 'It was just an accident. Sorry, I've a mountain of work to do. This is usually Amelia's job. But she's still off sick, and there are so many rooms to clean . . .'

'I'll sort out a cleaning detail to help you. Three men be enough?'

'Soldiers? Cleaning?'

'Why not?' He grinned, instantly looking younger without that worried frown. 'It's part of the job. Plenty of young men out there with little to do but hang about in the sun, smoking and pretending to be on guard duty. They might as well give you a hand.'

'I couldn't! I wouldn't know what to say to them.'

'Mop here, mop there?'

Hazel laughed reluctantly. 'What was it you wanted to speak to me about, anyway? Since this water's going cold now, might as well be a reason for it.'

'Yes, sorry, I . . . erm . . .' His eyes met hers at last, and she felt a jolt at the intensity of that stare. 'I wondered if you might be free to go out for a drink one night. At the pub.'

She stared, not sure she had heard him correctly. 'A d-drink? With you?'

'That's the general idea, yes. To catch up properly, you know. Have a good chin wag about old times.'

'Oh, Mr Cotterill, I really can't—'

'George, please.'

'I'm sorry, but I couldn't possibly go for a drink with you.'

'Why not?'

Hazel avoided his gaze, horribly uncomfortable at the confused note in his voice. If he knew about the baby she was carrying, she thought miserably, he would not be so interested. Well, he would know soon enough. And then she would lose her position, like as not.

'I didn't take this job on to . . . to be able to see you again, George. I took it on to earn some housekeeping money. For Charlie, you know.' Her cheeks felt flushed. 'I know you want to be friends. But I'm a married woman.'

'Can't a married woman have friends?'

She gave him a direct look, then. 'Not men friends, no.'

Not men friends like *you*, she was thinking. Not men friends she fancied.

'That brute doesn't deserve you,' he said grimly.

His straight talking shocked her.

'Maybe not, but that brute is still my husband.' She slopped the mop back onto the floor, and began cleaning again, swishing the water about furiously. 'Better move now, Mr Cotterill, before your feet get soaked. Thanks for the offer of some help, but I prefer to manage on my own.'

'So I see,' George said, and strode away without another word.

Later, Mr Frobisher came to find her, a sour expression on his face. 'I need you in the kitchen again. To prep for tonight's dinner service and . . . and to clean up.' With lips pursed as tight as if he were sucking a lemon, the cook gave a bitter little shake of his head. 'One of my puddings exploded. It's made a right bloody mess. Strawberry mush all over the floor, like half a battalion died there.'

Hazel bit her lip rather than laugh. 'Oh dear.'

'Come on.' He nodded to her bucket of dirty water. 'And make sure you empty that before someone trips over it.'

She had almost finished the mopping anyway, so nodded and followed him wearily to the kitchen, mop in one hand, heavy bucket in the other.

'Excuse me, Miss? Are you Hazel?'

She turned in surprise, and found a heavy-set, grey-haired soldier peering down the corridor after her. The man looked almost anxious, his brows drawn together in a frown, and her first horrified thought was that Charlie had been hurt.

'Yes, I'm Hazel.' She licked dry lips, her heart thudding. 'Why . . . Why do you want to know?'

'There's someone asking for you. Down at the checkpoint.'

With a small cry, she dumped her bucket in the middle of the corridor, ignoring Mr Frobisher's remonstrations, and ran past the soldier to the side door.

But when she hurried down to the checkpoint in hot sunshine, she found not Charlie, nor some teacher from the school come to give her dire news, but three bedraggled-looking young women waiting at the guardhouse, appearing wretched and tired, and laden down with bags and suitcases.

Well, one woman about her own age, and two girls, she corrected herself, staring at the three of them in blank astonishment.

'Ah, there you are,' said the soldier on the gate, a little gruffly. 'This woman won't go away. She claims to know you. But she hasn't got a pass. Only her identity papers.'

'Thanks,' Hazel said dubiously. She turned to the woman, her tone cautious. 'It's Violet, isn't it? From Chellew Farm.' She gave them a half-smile, not wanting to seem rude but not sure what this was about. 'What are you doing up here? And why did you ask to see me? I was in the middle of work, I could get in trouble for coming out . . .'

She stopped, seeing tears well up in Violet's eyes, and noticing the miserable expressions on the faces of the two girls beside her. Her nieces, as she recalled.

'What's the matter? Has something happened at the farm?'

'Mrs Chellew, my aunt, has thrown us out. We've nowhere to stay.' Violet paused, a red spot of embarrassment burning in each cheek at having to admit her misfortune in front of the soldiers, then added in a wavering voice, 'And no money for food, or the fare back to London.'

'Oh dear!'

'You said there might be work going here.' Violet glanced at the soldiers behind the roll of barbed wire, guarding the tunnel into the cliff, then studied the dripping mop that Hazel belatedly realised she was still clutching. 'We're honest and hardworking, and we'll do anything, me and the girls. Mop floors, clean tables, cook food. Whatever's needed.'

Hazel did not know what to say.

'Please,' one of the girls said plaintively. The youngest one, she guessed. 'We can't go back to the farm. My uncle attacked Lily, and then my aunt threw us out. Like it was our fault!'

'Oh my goodness!'

'Hush,' Lily told her sister with undisguised horror. 'Keep your mouth shut, would you? There are people listening!'

'Yes, no need to wash our dirty linen in public, Alice,' Violet said quickly, though she also gave the girl a hug as though to show there were no hard feelings. Over the girl's head, she threw Hazel a desperate look. 'If you could help us, love, even if it's just to find a bed for tonight, I'd be so grateful. I'm at my wits' end. I don't know what to do. I'd manage on my own, I'm sure . . . But I've got these girls to think of.'

'Of course.'

'I'm sorry for calling you out of work. I hope you won't get into trouble for it. But you're the only other person I know in the whole of Cornwall.'

'It's all right, I'll cope.'

Hazel could imagine how it would feel to be stranded in some strange part of the country, with no money or anywhere to stay, and with Charlie to look after. But that didn't help her know what was for the best. After all, she was just one of the domestic staff. And with everything so top secret around here, she guessed it wouldn't be easy for three strangers to walk up and demand a job. Not at Porthcurno.

'Thing is, it's not up to me. Or I'd say yes right away. You'll need to speak to Mr Cotterill. He does all the hiring of staff.'

'Mr Cotterill,' Violet repeated, handing her coat and bags

to the two girls, and then tidying her hair with obvious determination. 'And how do I find him?'

'He's right here,' a voice said behind Hazel.

It was George, coming down the slope to the gatehouse with a cool expression. He did not look at Hazel, as though still offended by her rejection of his help and determined not to make eye contact. He nodded to the guard instead, and then took a moment to study the three visitors.

'Good morning,' he said to Violet in a civil enough tone, his gaze skimming the younger two. 'I'm Cotterill. What seems to be the trouble?'

'No trouble at all, sir,' Violet said quickly, her London accent even more out of place in the warm Cornish sunshine than when Hazel spoke to her in the farmhouse kitchen. 'I'm just after a job. Three jobs, in fact. For myself and my nieces.' She gave him a broad smile, showing neat white teeth. 'We're hard grafters and won't make no trouble.'

'I'm sure you're all excellent workers,' George told her. 'But I'm not sure we have any domestic positions free at the moment.'

Hazel looked at him in surprise but said nothing. She had only just complained to him about the sheer amount of work being heaped on her shoulders, with several domestic staff off sick, and some kind of tummy bug raging in the camp . . . And here he was, turning away three able workers?

'Could you make sure, then?' Violet asked, and one of the listening soldiers chortled at her cheekiness. She gave the man a fulminating glance, then turned back to George, wringing her hands. 'Sorry to be so forward, Mr Cotterill. But there ain't no point beating about the bush. If you turn us away, odds are good we'll be sleeping under one tonight.'

George frowned. 'Under what?'

'A bush.'

The soldier lounging by the guardhouse laughed again. This time it was George who shot him a stern look, and the young man straightened to attention, his grin fading.

'What on earth are you talking about?' George seemed impatient to be back at his post. 'Why would you want to sleep under a bush tonight?' He scanned their faces. 'Are you evacuees? Didn't you have a home appointed to you?'

'We come down together of our own choice. Nobody took us in official-like. The girls are just out of school, and I'm looking after them, see?'

Violet explained her situation briefly, though Hazel could tell from her hesitations and uneasy smiles at her nieces that she was leaving plenty out. Certainly, she failed to mention the attack on Lily. Her story was that she had fallen out with her aunt and uncle at the farm, and all three of them had been thrown out after a 'family row'. Now they were homeless and penniless, and would be grateful for any employment that would enable them to buy their fare back to London.

George's eyebrows had risen during her account. It was clear he too had spotted her omissions, though was too polite to suggest Violet was lying. But at this last admission, he seemed almost shocked.

'You intend to return to London? During these bombing raids?'

'I don't have no choice, sir. If I can't feed these girls and keep a roof over our heads, I'll have to take 'em back.'

George sighed. 'I don't know . . .' he began dubiously, but Hazel interrupted him, rather more boldly than she had intended.

'I'll vouch for her,' Hazel told him. 'Her name's Violet Hopkins and she was very kind to me when I fell off my bicycle.'

He turned his head, considering her. 'I beg your pardon?'

'Violet took me into the farm kitchen and saw to the cuts on my knee.' Hazel saw his gaze flash down to her legs, and felt a little wobble inside. Which was wrong of her. Truly wrong. She had determined to keep George Cotterill at arm's length, and instead all she could think about was getting closer to the man. She continued more firmly, 'Also, she looks strong and capable, and I could definitely do with another pair of hands about the place.'

'I see.'

'Several pairs of hands, in fact.'

'Hmm.' He stuck his hands in his trouser pockets, and turned back to Violet, giving the woman a long searching look. 'We're very careful who works at Eastern House. You have up-to-date identity papers with you?'

'Oh yes, sir.'

'And these young ladies?'

Violet introduced her nieces as Lily, the eldest, and Alice, the one who had spoken out of turn earlier. 'They're both good girls, and willing to work hard. We've all been pulling our weight on the farm, so we're used to early starts and long hours.'

'Very well,' he said slowly. 'I'll need to check your credentials first, though. And check your story with your aunt and uncle. I know Mr and Mrs Chellew, so that won't take long. But it could take a day or so to verify your identities, I'm afraid. You'll need to give me your details, then come back later.'

'But we've nowhere to stay. I thought if we could start work today, we might get a small advance on our wages, just a few bob for a shared room nearby.'

'I doubt there are any rooms currently available in Porthcurno. This whole area is under military control, and we've billeted most of our personnel hereabouts. But I can give you a letter for the evacuees officer in Penzance. He should be able to find you temporary accommodation in one of the outlying villages, where there's less chance of bombing.'

'I'd rather not live that far away, thanks,' Violet said frankly. 'We can't afford the bus fare to and from Penzance every day.'

'I'm sorry,' he said awkwardly. 'I know it's not ideal. But it's the best I can suggest until all the formalities have been completed.' George managed an apologetic smile. 'Better than sleeping under a bush, surely?'

Looking downcast, Lily picked up her bag and hoisted it onto one shoulder, wincing as she did so. 'If we have to walk all the way to bloody Penzance, we'd better start soon,' she told Violet in a low voice. 'Unless His Nibs is planning to lend us the bus fare.'

Hazel couldn't bear the unhappy looks on the two girls' faces. She tried to imagine how she would cope if it was her and Charlie in the same position, and felt awful.

'You can stay with me,' she said impulsively. 'At my cottage.'

Everyone stared round at her in astonishment. Especially George, whose frown told her instantly that he thought it was a bad idea.

These three were complete strangers to them, it was true.

But there was a war on, as everyone kept reminding her. And in wartime, you had to make sacrifices. And help others worse off than yourself.

'It's a small house – we don't have much room,' she admitted. 'But my Charlie would give up his room for you and your two girls, I'm sure, and sleep downstairs on the sofa. Bit of a squeeze, but better than hiking all the way to Penzance and ending up miles away.'

'You mean that?' Violet asked.

'Now, why wouldn't I?' Hazel drew a breath, ignoring George's hard stare. 'If you can wait about here another couple of hours, you can all walk home with me. My bicycle's off the road, you see. But it's not too far.'

Over the barrier, Violet gave her a brilliant smile. 'Oh, bless you, bless you,' she said breathlessly. 'We've our own ration books with us. So no need to worry about extra food.' She hugged her nieces hard, who both squealed and giggled. 'You hear that, girls? We've got a home to go to tonight.'

As they walked back up to Eastern House from the checkpoint, George touched Hazel's arm. 'That was a very kind gesture,' he said quietly. 'Especially given your situation.'

Hazel found it hard to breathe. What on earth did he mean by that?

'What situation?'

'There's not really room for so many people in the cottage, is there?'

She almost sagged in relief. For one terrible moment, her heart thudding violently, she had feared George knew about her pregnancy. Which was impossible. She had only just discovered it herself.

'It'll be fun,' she said defiantly. 'We'll all bunk up together.'

'I'll contact the evacuee officer anyway, make sure you get proper remuneration for your generosity. And don't forget to use those ration books she offered you. With three more people in the house, you'll need all the help you can get.'

'Thank you.'

His eyes met hers. 'You're sure about this, Hazel? Three strangers . . .'

'She was desperate. And those poor girls. Did you see their faces?'

'I did.' George was frowning though, as though something else was fretting him. 'You're a good woman. I only hope you won't regret it.'

'I won't,' Hazel said, with more confidence than she felt. Then added, with a touch of desperation, worried that he could see how much she liked him and eager to put him off the scent, 'And the three of them will be company for me and Charlie, won't they? What with Bertie off with his regiment . . .'

George looked away and did not reply.

CHAPTER SEVENTEEN

Professor Templeton gestured for Eva to follow him out of Eastern House. 'Now, would you like to see where you'll be working?'

'I certainly would,' Eva said promptly.

'It's all underground, I'm afraid.'

'I don't mind that.'

Eva felt excited, the skin tingling on the back of her neck, and not just because this handsome man was standing so close. This was the kind of war work she relished!

They were permitted through the barbed wire barrier, showing the guards their special passes, and they walked out of brilliant sunshine into a shady tunnel entrance. Templeton had already explained that the tunnel led deep underground, to rooms so shrouded in mystery that even the guards on the barrier were not sure what lay within.

A short walk further on, there was a second entrance, covered by a vast studded metal door with another guard posted in front of it. It was a blast door, she was told, meant to protect those inside in the event of a bombing raid.

'What I'm about to show you,' Professor Templeton

announced, halting outside the closed metal door, 'is strictly classified information. Everything within these fortified underground chambers has been declared top secret, by order of the government. Not to be disclosed to anyone outside a need-to-know-only basis, in other words. I cannot stress enough how important this is. You have now signed the Official Secrets Act and are therefore bound by its strictures. Failure to follow these instructions as I have explained them to you could mean imprisonment or even death . . .' He stopped, regarding her gravely. 'Are you even listening to me?'

Eva looked up with a guilty start. Realising he was merely repeating the dire warnings her father had already drummed into her, she'd become bored and started studying her finger-nails instead, one of which was looking distinctly ragged. She could hardly tap out good code with a wonky fingernail, after all. But she realised he might not understand such niceties, so thrust her hands hurriedly behind her back.

'Of course,' she said coolly. 'You were threatening me with imprisonment or even death if I blab about what I've seen. Is that about right?'

'That's it precisely.' He nodded to the uniformed guard waiting a few feet away at the metal door. 'Sergeant?'

'Right you are, Professor.' The soldier touched his cap badge in a kind of quasi-salute, then operated the heavy door, which rolled open with a slow, majestic motion, making a grating sound. Once it was fully open, he nodded them inside. 'Watch your step now, Miss. Wouldn't want you to fall over in those heels.'

She flashed the sergeant a sharp look, aware of amusement in his face. 'I shall be careful, Sergeant. Thank you so much for your concern.'

The space beyond the metal door was dimly lit and claus-trophobic, its ceiling slightly rounded, strongly reminiscent of the underground tunnels in London, except without the rushing air from the passage of trains.

As the metal door closed behind them, Eva felt a little apprehensive, as though she was entering a wormhole headed for the centre of the Earth. But she refused to be cowed. She followed the professor down the corridor without hesitation, studying everything closely as she passed, information boards covered in sheets and posters, and flickering lights set into the wall. The tunnel twisted and narrowed, soon opening into a large, airless room filled with desks and rows of cabinet-like machines, glass doors revealing strange coiled instruments inside, many of them whirring and clicking. Other machines were spewing forth ticker tape at a phenomenal rate, seemingly disregarded by those working nearby.

After the relative peace of the Cornish countryside, the noise underground was quite incredible, echoing off the tiled walls and ceiling. Eva had to resist an urge to clap both hands over her ears. She might have been inattentive and answered a bit flippantly when Templeton delivered his stern warnings, but in truth, she didn't want them to think her unfit to be down here, doing a man's job.

But that was not what caught her attention. The room housed about twelve personnel, at a guess. Some of them were the very young trainees she had seen hanging about Eastern House, others were silver-haired men in suit trousers and clipped-up shirt sleeves, bustling to and fro between the desks.

Two or three looked round as they entered, and at least one young man gave a silent whistle and nudged his friend, who also stared in her direction.

Obviously, they did not see women down here very often.

'Gentlemen,' Professor Templeton announced loudly, straining to be heard above the clack and whirr of machinery, 'this is our newest recruit to the training programme, Miss Eva Ryder. Yes, Ryder. She's the colonel's daughter and has been granted clearance to work on certain instruments.' He cleared his throat as everyone stopped work, turning to stare. 'I trust you will extend her every courtesy.'

'Hello,' Eva said breezily, raising a hand.

Nobody answered.

After a brief silence, all but one went back to what they had been doing before. One of the older men came over and shook her hand, introducing himself as Willie Topping, and offering to help Templeton show her round the place.

'I can manage, thanks,' Professor Templeton told him, and Willie did not comment, but headed back to his seat with a shrug and continued with his work.

Oh well, not a very friendly lot, then. But she was used to getting the cold shoulder. In the club, some of the other girls had looked on her with dislike, saying she'd been born with a 'silver spoon' in her mouth. But she had never let their distrust stop her doing what she wanted and enjoying herself whenever possible.

Certain instruments?

'What do all these machines do?' she asked Professor Templeton in a whisper, burnt up with sudden curiosity.

'You don't need to know. You won't be expected to take on a full role here. Just send and receive Morse code messages in that room there.' He pointed down a corridor.

'But can the enemy intercept any of these messages?'

'Not the ones that come through our underwater cables. Those are impossible to intercept, always have been. They'd have to have a spy in the room for that.'

She shuddered. 'What a horrible thought.'

'That's why we're so careful to hand-pick everyone who comes through those blast doors and into the listening post.'

She stared about herself, entranced. 'There are so many machines down here. And they're so noisy! Goodness, what does this one do?' They were passing a large metal machine, whose cogs seemed to be rotating wildly. Beside it, another machine had some kind of spinning disc. 'Or that one? Am I allowed to know?'

'I suppose it won't do any harm. You are the colonel's daughter, after all.' He gave her a wry smile. 'That's an Interpolator. The other one is a Synchroniser. It regulates the pulse rate of messages coming through the Interpolator. And that odd-looking box on the end, with all the wires and cables sticking out, is an aerial patch panel. For hooking the listening machines up to an aerial, so they can send and receive messages. Then there are the wavemeters . . .' He laughed at her bewildered expression. 'Never mind. You'll get the hang of this place eventually.'

Turning on her heel, she caught sight of a large black box covered in dials and switches, with headphones attached, and suddenly knew she'd seen something like it once before, with her father back in London.

'I know this machine. It's a receiver, isn't it?'

'Well done, yes. That's an AR88 Receiver. Standard listening equipment. You'll probably get a chance to use one later on,' he said, then added carefully, 'assuming you show any aptitude for the job, that is.'

Patronising beast, Eva thought crossly, shooting the professor an irritated glance, but did not comment. Instead, she stopped in front of one of the larger metal cabinets, captivated by its rows of shiny spinning coils.

'This one looks fearfully complicated,' she said. 'Like it could make you a cup of tea while you're waiting for a message to come through.'

'That one's out of bounds. Best steer clear, Miss Ryder.'

Templeton led her past the rows of desks and machines into the side corridor he'd pointed out before. Tables had been arranged neatly along the wall, stacked with boxes, paper files and other oddments, and the way through was narrow. 'The training room is this way. You'll spend your first few weeks down here, learning the ropes and committing various codes to memory. Unless we need you on the Morse code interceptor.'

'Sounds like fun,' she said, perfectly serious.

He crooked an eyebrow at her. 'Trust me, not everyone would call learning strings of codes fun. It can be intricate, back-breaking work, and requires a lot of brain power. But at least you've got a head start, already knowing Morse.'

Eva crossed her fingers behind her back, hoping her Morse would pass muster and wasn't too embarrassingly rusty. 'Dot dot dot,' she muttered, 'dash dash dash, et cetera.'

'That's the stuff. I'm sure you won't have any problems.'

Eva hoped he was right.

She was keen to appear confident and capable in front of Professor Templeton. A modern woman, ready to cope with anything the war might throw at her. But the truth was, she did feel nervous. Some of these machines looked rather tricky, and though she knew they wouldn't expect a mere trainee to operate them, it did make her wonder how easy she would find this job, working down here in the underground tunnels.

He had made it clear she might occasionally be asked to work night shifts as well as during the day. But what if she got tired and slipped up?

It would be too awful if she made a stupid error with some vitally important message. An error that could cost brave men and women their lives. That was her real fear.

At the other end of the corridor, Templeton pointed to a large crate of rubber gas masks. 'In case of a gas attack,' was all he said.

She nodded silently, aware that she might be putting herself in danger by working down here. But no more than being in London at the height of the bombing raids, and she had somehow survived that, she reminded herself, walking with a brisker step. A gas attack might sound scary, but it was no worse than having a house fall on your head.

He opened a door into a smaller room and flicked on the light. 'This is us, Miss Ryder,' he said, gesturing to one of a number of desks set with chairs, like a classroom. 'Please, take a seat.'

She sat down with a smile, crossing her legs and smoothing her skirt over her knee. 'Call me Eva.'

'Probably best if I don't, Miss Ryder.' But Professor Templeton sat down at the next desk, pulling his chair closer. He indicated the blackboard on the wall ahead. Several words had been chalked out in a list at the top of the board, and below them was a series of short sentences. 'Using just your fingertips, could you spell out those words at the top in Morse code?'

'Oh, is this a test?'

'I just need to assess your capabilities, that's all. No need to be worried.' He nodded to the blackboard. 'Try tapping out the first one. Sword.'

She was mesmerised by those dark eyes. 'Sword . . .'

'In your own time.'

She blinked, feeling like she was under a spell, then nodded and tapped out the five letter codes for 'Sword', the first word on the list.

'Excellent.' There was a faint surprise in his voice, as though he had not entirely believed her father when he claimed she knew Morse code. 'Now the next one.'

The next word on the list was 'Cabbage'.

'Very good,' he said when she tapped it out correctly. 'Keep going. Work your way down the list. I'll tell you when to stop.'

Tap tap tappity-tap. Tappity-tap tap tap.

His gaze had become admiring by the time she reached the end of the list. 'No mistakes at all. That's truly impressive. I thought we might be here for hours, but at this rate . . .' He sat back, watching her. 'Now for the short sentences. Let's see how you are with a complete message.'

She studied the list of full sentences on the board, and felt her heart sink. 'You want me to tap all *that* out?'

'If you would, please.'

'Very well.' Eva tapped out laboriously, 'How much is that doggy in the window?' and then sat back in triumph. 'There you go.'

He studied the code, and then shook his head. 'Nearly right.'

She was dismayed. 'I made a mistake?'

'Only a small one. You gave a long dash there instead of a short one.'

'Oh, for goodness' sake!'

'Miss Ryder, please take this seriously. Any mistake, however tiny, could cost lives. Sometimes hundreds of lives.'

Eva stared at him, feeling cold. That was precisely what she was afraid of.

'Hundreds?'

'Hard to imagine, isn't it? That you and I, sitting underground here in Cornwall, could influence the course of a battle raging on the continent, or even further afield?' He spoke softly, but she heard the stress in his voice. 'These cables stretch globally, remember. Sometimes we're responding to messages from thousands of miles away. But a single mistake in either deciphering code or sending replies could be fatal, and that's why it's our solemn duty to get it right.'

'Yes, of course,' she said faintly.

'Try another sentence on the list and see if you can get it right this time,' he said gently. 'You weren't far off with that first one.'

This time, she tapped out the sentence more carefully, furrowing her brow in fierce concentration, and to her relief he gave her a quick smile at the end, nodding.

'That's perfect.'

'Thank you.'

'But a little too slow.'

'Oh.' She felt as though the wind had gone out of her at this criticism. 'I was trying so hard to get it right, I . . . I couldn't go any faster.'

'You'll get faster as you get more used to it.'

'I'm not sure I'll ever get used to the idea of so much responsibility.' She read the next test sentence on the list, and shook her head, perplexed. 'And some of these messages are just bizarre. I mean, what are four-and-twenty blackbirds, and why does someone need to bake them in a pie? That's from a nursery rhyme, isn't it?'

'I know some of the sentences must seem odd to you. But the majority of our messages are delivered in a recognised code form, and those receiving them at the other end will usually have a code book to hand that they can check.'

'That's fascinating.'

'In this job, you'll have to get used to some unlikely wording. Indeed, you may not know what the message you're sending means, it could be so top secret. But that needn't concern you. Our chief task at Porthcurno is to decipher incoming messages, deliver them to headquarters, and pass on any replies that come back down the line.'

'Headquarters?'

'Electra House, in London,' he explained. 'The operators

154

there have to answer to the secret service in their turn. But the important thing is to follow orders to the letter. Literally, in this case.' He folded his arms and nodded to the blackboard. 'Better keep going, Miss Ryder. Try the next one. And this time, concentrate on increasing your speed. See how much faster you can go.'

The next hour was spent enjoyably tapping out messages in Morse code, as fast as she could, then listening to Professor Templeton as he tapped out words and phrases for her to decipher. Overall, she thought he seemed pleased with her progress, and certainly she was making far fewer mistakes at the end than when she had started. But he made no attempt to flirt with her, or respond to her smiles.

It was really quite disheartening.

As he had said, the work was deadly serious, and it was clear duty came first for Templeton, even if that meant ignoring the woman sitting next to him.

But Eva refused to give up hope.

Besides, apart from her secret fears, she was having a fantastic time. She pored over training manuals under his expert guidance and refreshed her understanding of codes and ciphers. Mathematics and logic had always been her favourite subjects at school, but her teachers had barely touched on such delights, the curriculum placing more emphasis on those skills that would make her a good wife and mother, with less time spent on academic topics.

'Talking of new things,' she said, as Professor Templeton was packing away the message charts he'd produced from a wall cupboard for her to study, 'did you know this is my first time in Cornwall?'

'Mine too,' he said, closing the cupboard.

'So we're both strangers in a strange land.' She hesitated. 'I haven't even seen the beach here yet,' she said, though she'd caught a glimpse of it from the cliffs, while out on a walk with her father. 'Porthcurno Beach is supposed to be famous, isn't it? Popular with Victorian tourists, I believe.'

'I wouldn't know. I'm from Surrey myself.' But he turned, smiling at her, suddenly more relaxed than she had seen him before. 'That was good work today, Miss Ryder. I have some reports to do this afternoon. But we'll take up your training again tomorrow.'

Oh, for goodness' sake! Her attempt to lure him down to the beach had flown over his head, it seemed. But Eva was not to be so easily deterred. More training meant more time alone with him. More opportunities to get to know him, and perhaps work out how to attract his attention.

'I can't wait,' she said, returning his smile warmly.

'You can join the other trainees in our next session,' he said, dashing her hopes of another intimate hour or two in his company. 'No reason why not. Some of the lads are more advanced than you at signals training. But you're clearly a very bright young woman, and with a little extra study you should soon catch up.'

'Extra study,' she repeated in a hollow voice, following him back into the corridor.

'Don't worry, you won't be at a disadvantage with the men.'

'Won't I? When they've already been here for weeks, training with you?'

'That's a fair point.' He hesitated, running a hand through his springing hair. 'I could help with that, I suppose. Talk you through some of the more advanced techniques before you meet the other trainees. We could schedule an hour after dinner tomorrow night.' He cleared his throat, suddenly awkward. 'For, erm, study purposes.'

'I study best in the open air,' she said, lying blithely. She rather liked the thought of spending a warm summer's day outside with this man. 'It's this dratted heat. It stops me being able to concentrate.'

'I see.'

'Maybe we could take a little walk down to the beach?'

Professor Templeton gave her a searching look, then said, to her surprise, 'Yes, why not? Though I'll need to clear it first.'

'With my father?' Her voice was a squeak of disbelief.

'Good God, no.' He gave a short laugh. 'I meant, with the officer on duty tomorrow night. The beach itself has been mined in places and is guarded against enemy attack. But we might be able to approach it, at least.' His gaze met hers, and she felt suddenly breathless. 'Assuming you aren't worried by a little danger, Miss Ryder?'

CHAPTER EIGHTEEN

Violet could hear birdsong nearby. She rolled over with a groan, heavy-eyed and confused. What was going on? It was already daylight and her aunt had not yet come up the stairs, banging a saucepan with a ladle and demanding they get up to start work. Then she realised she could not hear the distant lowing of cows, and when a vehicle rattled loudly past her window, she sat up with a start, abruptly remembering that they had left that awful farm and moved in with Hazel Baxter and her boy three days ago.

It had been the height of luxury to spend three whole days in Hazel's lovely old cottage, sitting out in the sunny back garden and sometimes helping with the housework in return for their bed and board. She didn't know when she and the girls had last enjoyed a proper holiday. But after labouring for weeks on the farm, rubbing shoulders with her short-tempered aunt and uncle, this short break had left all three of them rested and restored.

Best of all, Hazel had told them the good news over dinner last night . . . Their identity papers had passed muster and they could finally start work at Eastern House.

'Morning, Aunty Vi,' two cheery voices chirped, and she turned her head, blinking away sleep.

Alice was sitting on the edge of the bed she was sharing with Lily, her older sister carefully plaiting her hair. Both girls stared at Violet's head.

'Bird's nest hair?'

Always the diplomat, Lily bit her lip. 'Not too bad. Though it could probably do with a comb-through.'

Hurriedly, Violet licked her fingers and smoothed her disobedient hair down into some semblance of order.

'You've been asleep ages,' Alice complained, though she did not seem too upset. 'I've been downstairs already but nobody's about yet. So I came back to bed.'

'And woke me up,' Lily said plaintively.

Violet swung her legs out of bed, feeling more rested than she could remember for ages. 'I slept so well. What time is it?'

Lily nodded to the small mantel clock Hazel had given them when they moved in, after setting up a spare trestle bed next to the bed Charlie had given up, decked out with sheets and blankets and makeshift pillows. They were all sharing the son's bedroom, while Charlie very kindly had moved downstairs to sleep on the sofa. It was obvious that Hazel doted on him, and why not? He seemed like a nice boy, polite and helpful, though he became a little shy and tongue-tied around the girls.

'Nearly half past seven,' Lily said with a grin, her face lit up with pleasure. 'Imagine that, Aunty Vi. I like staying here with Hazel. She cooks nice grub, and we don't have to get up with the bleedin' lark!'

'Language, Lily,' Violet warned her with a click of her tongue, but without much heat. The girl was getting a bit old to be told off for colourful language, and it wasn't like Violet

159

herself never used the odd swear word. 'All the same, let's not be late for work on our first day. Better get washed and dressed.'

Lily made a face. 'If I can get to the wash bowl over Alice's mess.'

'My books are not mess!' Alice complained.

'Well, do your best,' Violet told them, yawning as she stretched out her arms, 'and Alice, do pack your books away for now, there's a love. You can't read them all at once.'

Yes, it was a bit of a squeeze, Violet thought, glancing about the cramped cottage bedroom with a feeling of resignation. And the work at Eastern House wouldn't pay very well, according to what Hazel had told them. Though that was assuming they could even get work there for more than a few days while other members of staff were off sick. But it would be a thousand times better than slaving unpaid for Aunty Margaret and Uncle Stanley. With all the horrors that had involved, she reminded herself, including poor Lily's assault in the barn.

And the girls seemed much happier here.

Violet only hoped her usual bad luck wouldn't strike again, like it always seemed to, and spoil things for the three of them.

Downstairs, Violet popped to the outside lavatory, which to everyone's relief did not involve picking their way through a nettle patch, as it had done at the farm. Returning to the kitchen, she found Hazel at the stove, an apron wrapped about her waist and a pan sizzling cheerfully on the flame.

She was uncomfortable to see her cooking, given how much hospitality they had already enjoyed from the woman.

'That's not for us, is it?' she asked, peering over Hazel's

shoulder at the sausages spitting in the pan. 'I thought we agreed we'd each cook our own food. You've done enough, putting us up like this, and your poor boy having to sleep on the sofa. It wouldn't be fair on you to do all the cooking too. Though I must say,' she added with a grin, her tummy rumbling, 'those sausages smell tasty.'

'Oh, I don't mind. Besides, it's cheaper to cook all the food at once.' Hazel looked pale, but she flashed her a brief smile. 'Oh, before I forget, these are the last of the sausages until I go shopping with the new ration books.'

'Thanks for the reminder, love. I'll bring them down to you.'

'Thanks.'

Violet paused in the doorway. 'He's a fair geezer, that Cotterill bloke. Thought he was going to turn us away. But you sweet-talked him nicely.'

'Me?' Hazel shook her head, and pushed the spitting sausages about the pan with a long-handled fork. 'I didn't do a thing.'

'If you say so.' Frowning, Violet studied her new friend's averted face. 'You all right, Hazel? You look a bit peaky.'

'I . . . erm . . .' Hazel grimaced. 'It's just the smell of these sausages, first thing in the morning. I can't stand . . .'

She clapped a hand over her mouth and rushed out of the back door into the garden. Seconds later, Violet could hear the sound of retching from outside. She could also hear sofa springs from the sitting room next door, and then the shuffle of heavy footsteps. The lad, no doubt, getting up for his breakfast.

Hurrying to the back door, she closed it and returned to the stove just in time for Charlie to pop his head into the kitchen. The young lad had not dressed yet, still in striped pyjamas and a pair of battered-looking slippers.

'Hello, Miss Hopkins,' he said, yawning sleepily behind his hand.

'Call me Violet. Or Vi, if you like.'

He grinned. 'I was looking for Mum. Do you know where she is?'

Violet turned a sausage over before it burnt, careful not to let the spitting fat scald her.

'Popped out to the loo,' she said casually.

Definitely a nice lad, she thought, watching as he shrugged and helped himself to a cup of water. She had been impressed by his helpfulness when they all trailed in after Hazel that first evening. Young Charlie had set to work willingly enough, soon shifting his things downstairs to the sofa and fetching up the trestle bed from the shed. But she'd also noticed he was a bit sniffy with his mum at times, and guessed there must be some ongoing quarrel there. Charlie was in his mid-teens though, so that was no surprise. At his age in the East End, he'd probably belong to a gang, and be out fighting or worse most nights. Here in Cornwall, she could tell he was chafing at the bit and desperate to be free of his mother's apron strings.

At dinner last night, she had spotted him eyeing Lily sideways at the table, who had returned a few shy smiles. Violet had been unsure at first, and then made up her mind not to worry about it. A little country romance might suit the girl, make her less homesick. But only so long as it didn't turn serious. Lily was still recovering from that ordeal with her uncle, damn his wandering hands, and the last thing the girl needed was to get her heart broken by a local boy.

Now, Charlie gave a grunt. 'Better get dressed then, I suppose.'

'That's the ticket,' Violet said breezily, and waved the long-handled fork in his direction. 'Breakfast is nearly ready, anyway.'

162

The boy nodded. 'And your girls? Are they awake too?' He glanced up at the ceiling as though expecting to see a head pop through the floorboards. 'Lily up yet?'

Violet smirked, recognising the hopeful note in his voice. 'Shouldn't you be getting ready for *school*?' she asked, emphasising the word 'school' to remind him he was younger than Lily.

Charlie blushed, and disappeared back into the sitting room.

Hmm, possibly a situation to watch.

Violet lifted the heavy pan of sausages off the heat and went outside.

She found Hazel in the act of leaving the red-brick outside lav, her face a ghastly white, a hand at her belly. It was obvious what had just happened.

'How far gone are you?' she asked bluntly.

Hazel did not bother to deny that she was pregnant. And why should she, as a married woman? She whispered, 'Not too far. Bertie came home on leave in the spring.' Some women would have been ecstatic at such news. But she was not smiling. 'I was so shocked when I realised what had happened. I mean, it's been years since I had Charlie. So I never thought . . .'

Violet saw the unhappy expression in her eyes, and guessed this surprise pregnancy was far from welcome. What she couldn't work out was why.

'What's the matter, love? Not keen on having another kiddy?'

Hazel hesitated, then shook her head.

'It shouldn't be too much hard work for you,' Violet said firmly, though she was still confused. She gave Hazel a quick hug. 'You can't be much past thirty.'

'It's not that.' Hazel bit her lip, and her eyes swam with tears. She lowered her voice even further, until Violet had to bend close to catch the words. 'Me and Bertie . . . It's not been right for a while. He drinks, you see.'

He drinks, you see.

Those four simple words hid years of pain, Violet thought, suddenly angry for her friend. Belatedly, she recalled what Aunt Margaret had said about Violet's husband – a drunkard and a liar. Spiteful as her aunt was, it seemed she had been right on this occasion. But the little 'un was in there now, and no amount of wishing would get it out. And maybe a new baby would bring Hazel some comfort during this awful war. Though it was clear she couldn't see the positive side of things just yet.

'Well, no use crying over spilt milk,' Violet said, as cheerfully as she could manage. Her tummy rumbled noisily and she grinned. 'My belly thinks my throat's been cut. And we must be running late. Best go back inside before the kids start helping themselves to everything in the cupboard.'

'Thank you,' Hazel said awkwardly, 'and I'm so sorry about this. I thought I was over the morning sickness. It was just the smell of frying . . . It set me off again.'

'Don't you fret. I'll serve breakfast.'

'Wait.' Hazel caught her arm as she turned away, her look fearful. 'Look, you won't say anything in front of the kids? Charlie doesn't know. And I'm not ready to tell the world yet. Just in case . . .' She sucked in her breath. 'That is, until I'm good and sure.'

She meant until she was sure she wasn't going to miscarry, Violet thought. Her sister had miscarried twice in the early weeks, so she knew all about the misery that could bring. Best to spare the boy that knowledge, no doubt.

'My lips are sealed,' Violet told her, and mimed buttoning her mouth. Then she added, as an afterthought, 'So, if you're not up to eating breakfast today, does that mean one of them sausages is going begging?'

CHAPTER NINETEEN

On arriving at Eastern House, Hazel took the two girls and Violet to see George Cotterill first, to make sure their paperwork had passed scrutiny and for them to sign the Official Secrets Act. Violet seemed to find the interview nerve-wracking, chewing on a nail until it was ragged. But George was happy enough with his new employees, shaking all their hands and welcoming them to Porthcurno with a friendly smile.

'How are you settling in at Mrs Baxter's cottage?' he asked Violet.

'Me and the girls are over the moon, sir. Such a lovely view from the windows, and all as snug as can be,' Violet said enthusiastically. 'I can't thank Hazel enough for putting us up.'

'She's a very generous lady,' he agreed, glancing at Hazel.

Hazel could not help beaming with pleasure. 'You should come round one evening,' she said impulsively. 'Have dinner with us.'

But his smile faded at her words. 'Sorry, I . . . I have to go' was all George said, before picking up a clipboard and hurrying out.

He barely looked at me, Hazel thought unhappily, watching him go. She had spoken above her station and been put in her place. George Cotterill was her employer at Eastern House and she had asked him to dinner as though they were equals. But he'd asked her out for drinks before, so why not? Still, the last thing she needed right now was George on her mind, along with Charlie wanting to enlist and the complication of her unwanted pregnancy . . .

'Mr Frobisher next,' she said with forced cheerfulness. 'To sort out uniforms for you all, and get your cleaning detail.'

Mr Frobisher had clearly been made aware of their arrival, as he was not surprised when they trooped into one of the pantries in search of him. He seemed deeply displeased by the idea of two young women on his domestic staff, looking Lily and Alice over with pursed lips and a disapproving glare. But he unlocked the staff wardrobe and waited for them to take turns changing in the cramped outside loo, the only ablutions the cleaning staff were allowed to use at Eastern House.

Soon all three of them were kitted out with uniforms like Hazel's own, a plain white blouse with buff skirt and jacket.

'Ugh, this feels like sackcloth,' Lily complained, plucking at the rough yellowish-brown fabric of her skirt. 'And it smells like it too. I'm wearing a potato sack.'

Mr Frobisher shot her a sour look, but clearly disdained speaking to a Young Person. 'Buckets' was all he said, and handed Hazel one, then passed the other to Violet in a forbidding manner. 'Make sure you add disinfectant as well as soap. One of the men was sick and it needs clearing up.' He made a face. 'It's this nasty thing that's going round. If I didn't know better, I'd swear the enemy was behind it.'

Hazel blenched, hating this kind of job. Especially when

she had only recently been unwell herself. And how embarrassing to have been caught by her house guest!

She avoided Violet's gaze.

But to her relief, the Londoner didn't even glance in her direction. Violet was a good sort, Hazel decided. A little rough round the edges, but with a friendly smile. Heart of gold, as her mother might have said.

'I don't mind a bit of mess, Mister,' Violet said cheerily.

Hazel part-filled her bucket from the steaming water-boiler, adding disinfectant as well as detergent, then Violet followed suit while Mr Frobisher, arms folded, watched intently.

'That's me done.' Violet swung her bucket so the hot soapy water spilt over the edge onto the tiled floor. 'Oops, sorry.'

'Be careful there,' Mr Frobisher growled, but Violet seemed unabashed by his tone.

'Sorry, Mister.' Violet winked at him. 'Now, don't you fret. I'll soon get the hang of it. I'm glad to have the work.'

'Hmm.'

'And no bombs falling. That's the best.'

'Yes, very well. Less talk now, more listening.' With a disapproving air, Mr Frobisher told Hazel, 'The, erm, mess to be cleaned up is in the listening room. You'll need to pass through the checkpoint, but just tell the guard that Mr Frobisher sent you, and why. They may ask to see your identity cards.'

'The listening room? You mean, in one of the underground rooms?'

Hazel was amazed. She had never been asked to clean up in any of the underground rooms before. The area was top secret and constantly guarded.

'They have their own cleaning staff, ordinarily. But the duty man's off sick himself. I was asked to provide suitable

cleaners from among the domestic staff to fill the gap.' Mr
Frobisher studied them both down the length of his lofty
nose. 'I would say your talents make you two an obvious
choice for this job.'

''Ere, you calling us scrubbers?' Violet demanded, her
colour suddenly high. 'Not very complimentary, are you?'

Hazel tensed, expecting Mr Frobisher to issue some stern
reprimand. But although his face stiffened, 'On your way'
was all he said in response to her outburst. Then he nodded
to Lily and Alice. 'You two girls, stop smirking and follow
me. I've plenty of kitchen work for you to do. You can start
by tidying up the store cupboard.'

'Bye, Aunty Vi,' the girls chorused as they were led away,
looking a little nervous.

Violet waved, then once they were out of sight she blew
out her cheeks with a look of exasperation. 'Bloody rude
man.'

Hazel was astonished by her courage. Especially given that
she was so new to this job, and to Cornwall. If Hazel were
to be shipped off to London and given a job in the city, she
would be speechless, or at least very shy. And she certainly
wouldn't have dared give her boss any cheek.

'I don't know how you got away with that,' she whispered
to Violet as they trudged away, buckets in hand. 'I thought
he was going to tear a strip off you.'

'Oh, I've met his sort before,' Violet confided, not bothering
to keep her voice low. 'Loud enough, but they're all bluster.
They only bully you until you stand up to them. That surprises
'em, see? So they scurry off with their tails between their legs.
Like that one did.' She jerked a thumb over her shoulder
towards the kitchen door. 'Trick is, not to let the nasty
blighters get away with it. Soon as they start hectoring, you
come back fast. Shuts most of 'em up right away.'

Hazel did not know what to say. But she could not help laughing. And then could not seem to stop, snorting with giggles, her shoulders shaking.

'What now?' Violet asked, stopping to gaze at her. Her tone was a little aggrieved, as though she thought Hazel was making fun of her. Which she wasn't, of course. She thought Violet very brave and rather wonderful too. 'Did I say something funny?'

'No, sorry . . . It was just the thought of Mr Fr-Frobisher . . . scurrying . . . with his tail . . . between his legs,' Hazel somehow managed to reply between hiccupping laughs. 'Like a scared rabbit . . .'

Violet laughed too, then also could not seem to stop.

By the time they reached the barbed wire barrier in front of the tunnel that led to the underground listening post, both of them were shaking with laughter, their buckets swaying, steaming water sloshing onto the ground.

The two guards stared at them in blank astonishment. The older one pushed back his helmet to scratch his balding head.

'You two got a touch of the sun, or what? Only listening post personnel get to go inside.'

'Sorry.' Hazel sobered, and hurriedly passed across her identity card. 'Mr Frobisher sent us. We have to go into the listening post. Apparently someone was sick in there?'

He took her card and studied it, then took the one Violet was holding out. His brows rose. 'Essex?' he said with a long whistle. 'That's next to London, isn't it? You're a long way from home, ain't you?'

'I've heard that's going round. You're not Cornish either, are you?' Violet held out her hand and he returned her card, clearly taken aback by her pert reply. 'Ta, love.'

Hazel took back her card and tucked it back into the pocket

of her cleaning apron. 'Everything all right, then? Can we go in and clean up the mess?'

'I suppose so, if Mr Frobisher sent you. But don't take too long, or I might have to come in after you.' The guard gave her a wink, and nodded to his younger companion to move the barrier aside. 'Best watch your step, girls. It's bloody dark in there. Takes a minute or two for your eyes to adjust.'

Hazel peered over his uniformed shoulder at the narrow gaping tunnel he was guarding. The army had dug it deep into the rocky hillside, like the entrance to a mineshaft. They had tried to keep it quiet, but people in Porthcurno knew it was there, even if they didn't know what it was for. The official line had been a shortcut to the other side of the headland, where there was a pub, but nobody had believed that story.

She could understand why its true purpose had to be kept as quiet as possible though. If the enemy ever found out about the tunnels at Porthcurno, fire would rain from the skies every night until they were destroyed, the buildings flattened and everyone here killed. Including her, and possibly Charlie, if their little row of cottages caught a stray bomb. None of them would stand a chance.

And maybe the Germans already knew about Porthcurno, and were merely biding their time, trying to pinpoint its exact location before striking.

Suddenly all the laughter left her, and Hazel felt only apprehensive. She didn't like the idea of going underground. And not just because this might already be an enemy target, for all she knew. She'd never liked confined spaces, and the thought of going inside the cliff, with all that weight of earth piled on top of their heads . . .

The idea made her feel queasy again.

Violet seemed to catch her mood, her lips tightening. But

she gave Hazel a nudge with her elbow. 'Come on, then, love. That floor won't mop itself.'

Hazel nodded silently.

One after the other, heavy metal buckets sloshing with water, the two women walked out of bright sunshine and into the tunnels under the hillside at Porthcurno.

CHAPTER TWENTY

Eva did not know when she had ever been so frightened. Never in her life, she decided. She wasn't the type to frighten easily, as even her father would admit, and when that bomb fell, killing so many around her, there had been no time to feel fear. Now, though, there was time. Too much time, she realised, glancing up at the relentless ticking arm of the wall clock. What was she supposed to do? Who should she speak to first?

She gazed about the room, but everybody else had gone outside for their morning tea break. She would have joined them, having fallen in love with the tangy sea air and bright Cornish sunshine. But one of the noisy machines had started clacking and spitting out tape just as she was leaving. The young man who was usually on duty during tea breaks had gone pale earlier this morning, and abruptly thrown up, leaving Eva herself feeling a little sick too, just at the vile smell. The sergeant on duty outside had come in and helped him to his quarters, and nobody had been sent to replace him yet.

'Some tummy bug going round,' the sergeant had remarked

cheerfully, touching his cap as she stepped out of the way. 'Sorry about that, Miss.'

'Where's the duty orderly?' Templeton had asked the man irritably, making a face at the smell. 'That mess needs cleaning up.'

'Orderly's sick, sir.'

'For God's sake!'

'Don't you worry, sir. I'll get the cleaners sent in, have that gone in a jiffy.'

'See that you do, Sergeant.'

But the promised cleaners had not yet arrived, and the rank air in the underground tunnels had now grown almost unbearable. No wonder everyone had piled outside for a ciggy at break time, desperate for fresh air. Meanwhile, an important message had arrived, and Eva had been the only one there to intercept it.

Eva read the message again, still unsure what to do.

It was in code.

POLLY PUT THE KETTLE ON

The cryptic line was followed by a numerical sequence. Fear turned to sudden exhilaration as her brain began to work again. It was an identification number, which she was pretty certain must indicate a vessel in their fleet. There would be a code book somewhere, to check the number against. And though she had no idea what *POLLY PUT THE KETTLE ON* might mean, it had to be important, otherwise why send the message?

Closing her fist about the precious message tape, Eva dragged open the heavy listening room door, and then rushed down the dimly lit corridor to the outside world. But her passage was blocked by two figures ahead, silhouetted against the sunshine.

She blinked and stopped dead, startled by this unexpected sight.

As they came closer, Eva saw them more clearly. Two women in buff uniforms, each carrying a mop and a steaming bucket that stank of disinfectant.

'Oh, thank God!' she exclaimed, recognising one of the women as Hazel Baxter. She pivoted on her heel and pointed back down the corridor. 'The mess is down there. It smells appalling. Thank you so much, Hazel, and, erm . . .' She peered at the other woman, who seemed younger than Hazel, with a pretty, flushed face and shining eyes. She was also slightly taller than Eva, which was unusual enough to intrigue her. 'I'm sorry, we haven't met.'

'No, Miss.' The other woman gave her a sweet smile. 'I'm new here – it's my first day. I'm Hazel's friend.' She had a strong East End accent, like several of the club girls she'd known in London. 'My name's Vi.'

'Vi,' Eva repeated blankly.

'Violet, I mean,' she said, then added hurriedly, 'Violet Hopkins.'

Eva smiled in return, hearing the slight awkwardness in the woman's voice. She knew how it felt to be nervous and in a strange place.

'That's a Cockney accent.'

Violet laughed, apparently a little bolder now. 'That's right. I'm from Dagenham.'

'I love the East End!' Eva could not help gushing, suddenly nostalgic for the life she'd left behind in London. 'How long have you been down here?' Belatedly, she recalled the message still clutched in her hand. 'Oh, but look, I don't have time for a proper chat now. How about later? I get lunch at noon, maybe meet you out on the front lawn if you're free? I'd love to chat about London.'

Violet grinned. 'That would be smashing.'

'I'm Eva Ryder, by the way.'

'Pleased to meet you.' Violet tried to shake her hand while holding a bucket and a mop, but couldn't quite manage it.

'Lovely to meet you too, Violet. Sorry, got to dash!' Eva squeezed between the two women, shooting the Cornish-woman a quick, encouraging smile too. 'Good to see you again, Hazel.'

She noted that Hazel was looking pale and a little unwell, and hoped the dreaded tummy bug hadn't spread to her too. But she had not seemed particularly happy the other day either. Perhaps all she needed, like Eva herself, was a pick-me-up.

Hurrying away, she called cheerily back over her shoulder, 'You and I still need to organise that dance, remember?'

The noisy echo of her heels on the concrete floor drowned out Hazel's reply. Which was a pity. Eva couldn't wait to spin and twirl on the dance floor again, even if it was only in a tiny parish hall. But however desperate she was to organise a local dance, and hopefully cheer both herself and Hazel up in the process, there was no time now to waste on such idle chit-chat. Not when the message in her hand could be a matter of vital national importance.

As she burst out of the dark tunnel like an avenging angel, the corporal on guard duty in the sunshine jumped to attention, a lit cigarette in hand. No doubt, he had just settled down for a crafty smoke.

Swiftly moving the barbed wire barrier back for her to pass through, the soldier asked curiously, 'Everything all right, Miss?'

'I need to speak with Professor Templeton urgently,' she said crisply, using the authoritative voice her father used when speaking to his men. 'It's a matter of grave importance. Is he still having his tea break?'

'As far as I know, Miss.'

'Thank you.'

Sure enough, she found Templeton on the sunny front lawn, a cup of tea and plate of biscuits by his side, along with several of his young male trainees, all of them smoking. The trainees looked round at her with disapproval as she approached them, for not all of them had yet been allowed to man the machines underground, despite weeks of training, while she had been whisked in there double quick.

She could see the customary accusation in their eyes.

Favouritism!

She was the colonel's daughter, after all.

But although that could not be excluded as a possibility, Eva preferred to think of her promotion as a reward for natural aptitude. Besides which, most of these boys were too young even to shave. The older lads had mostly all gone off to war by now, so she supposed Templeton's pool of trainees must be increasingly restricted.

'Might I have a word, Professor?' She hesitated, not wanting to discuss potentially top-secret information in front of these boys. 'I've found something that might be of interest to you.'

'Spit it out, then,' he said.

Eva raised her brows in surprise, and saw him blink. Perhaps he was used to talking to his male trainees in that peremptory tone, but he would have to be a damn sight more polite if he wanted to keep in her good books.

Templeton stood up, knocked out his pipe in the ashtray, and gave her an uncertain smile. 'Perhaps if we walk towards the sea a little way?'

Eva nodded and followed him.

'What's all this about, then?' he asked as soon as they were far enough from the house that others couldn't overhear them. His brow furrowed as he studied her face. 'You look flushed. I hope you're not unwell.'

'Never better.' Eva held out the crumpled message, and he took it, frowning as he unfolded the narrow slip of tape. 'This just came through. Marked top secret.' She bit her lip at his grave expression. 'I hope I didn't break any rules by bringing it out of the room. Only there was nobody else there, you see. Tea break. I didn't know who to show it to. But it seemed important. So I thought . . .'

'No, you did the right thing.' Professor Templeton read the message again, and then looked up, meeting her eyes with a worried smile. 'Thank you, Miss Ryder.'

'Eva,' she reminded him.

'I'll deal with this.'

A little disappointed, though not showing it, she asked, 'Is it important?'

He hesitated, pushing the note into the top pocket of his jacket. 'I'm sorry, I can't give you any details.'

'I understand.'

'But, yes, it's incredibly important. This message will save lives.'

She exhaled, nodding. 'I'm so glad.'

'Jolly good show, Miss Ryder.' To her astonishment, he clapped her on the back as though she were one of his male trainees, so hard she rocked on her heels, blinking. 'If you'll excuse me, I need to get this information to the colonel straightaway.' Then he left her without so much as a backward glance. 'Mum's the word!'

He meant she shouldn't say a word, of course.

As if she would!

Eva gave a silent inward groan as she stood there alone, gazing down the narrow tree-thick valley towards Porthcurno beach. The sun sparkled on the sea, a slight breeze tipping each wave with charming white flecks. It was an idyllic scene.

There was something intriguing about the professor.

Something different and worth pursuing, she decided. She was not a shallow person, or at least, she hoped not. Deep inside, she was still aching for Max, the pilot who had so bravely put her life before his own.

She would never forget Max Carmichael.

Never.

But when bombs were falling and people everywhere were in danger of losing their lives, it was vital to stay alive and follow the promptings of the heart.

What else was there to live for in times of war?

Professor Templeton was going to be tough work though. She could see that now. She'd thought from his warm smiles earlier that he had finally seen her as a woman. But just now, when she gave him that message, she might as well have been a tree. Eva winced, sure she could still feel the imprint of his broad hand between her shoulder blades. He had practically walloped her! Hardly the kind of contact she had hoped for from the gorgeous professor.

She was going about this all wrong, she thought, suddenly inspired. What she needed was a chance to whisk those spectacles off his handsome face, and have him look at her more closely. Close enough to see she was a woman, and not one of his male protégés.

She walked back towards the house with renewed energy.

Templeton and the other trainees had vanished back inside, and the lawns were empty, tea break over. But Hazel appeared, peering out of the doorway to Eastern House, one arm crooked to shield her eyes against the bright sunshine.

'Miss?'

'Are you looking for me, Hazel?' she asked, surprised.

'Sorry,' Hazel said breathlessly, as though she'd been running, 'I didn't mean to interrupt your break. Only you went and forgot this.' She was holding up Eva's purse, which

179

she must have left on her desk in the listening room. 'Thought you might need it.'

'Thank you.' With a grateful smile, Eva went up the steps and retrieved the purse. 'That's very sweet of you, Hazel. But please, call me Eva.'

'Oh, I couldn't, Miss. You're the colonel's daughter.'

'Never mind that.' She drew Hazel to one side, her mind already working swiftly. 'Look, did you get a chance to find out if we could hire a local hall for that dance? I'm going crazy here. I need to do *something*.'

Hazel bit her lip, glancing over her shoulder into the house. 'I can't talk now, Miss . . . I mean, Eva. It's Violet's first day, and I've left her alone with all them machines.'

'Three minutes, that's all I need.' Eva gave her an encouraging smile, linking arms with the Cornishwoman. She didn't buy that shy, uncertain act. Not one little bit. Something about Hazel told her the woman had a core of steel. And what she needed right now was someone she could depend on to get things done. 'Come on, have you got any good news for me?'

CHAPTER TWENTY-ONE

Violet finished mopping up the mess on the concrete floor, head down, trying not to look at the fearfully complex click-clacking machines all about her. The noise they made left all her nerves jangling. She had never been good with tech-nology, and still hated the telephone. But Hazel had told her these telegram machines saved lives, carrying all them messages from across the Atlantic and right round the world, so she guessed they were worth protecting in these under-ground tunnels.

Of course, the smell of sick in an enclosed space had not helped Hazel's condition, and Violet, spotting her wan face, had found an excuse to send her friend out into the fresh air again. 'Oh look,' she'd said quickly, pointing, 'Eva's left her purse. You should take it to her before she misses it.'

Hazel had gratefully accepted the mission, but had not come back yet.

It made Violet a little nervous, being here on her own.

A top-secret underground room!

But she had to admit to being curious too, finally plucking up the courage to peer at a few of the machines nearby and read some of the important notices on the wall, though they meant nothing to her.

Young men started to come down the tunnel into the listening room, chatting and laughing with each other as they came back off their tea break. Some in shirt sleeves, others in flannel jackets, they looked posh, fresh-faced with floppy hair, and most were very young, less than twenty years old by her guess. A few glanced at her with little interest before heading for their stations further into the tunnels. The others paid her no mind at all, striding past as she shrank against the rough tunnel wall, dripping mop in hand.

It was like being blooming invisible.

Posh types were like that though, weren't they? A woman with a mop in her hand wasn't anyone important to them. She could be a German spy, and they wouldn't take no notice of her. Not even if she was creeping about, reading their top-secret bleeding messages.

'You there, what are you doing?'

Violet jumped guiltily, turning to see a soldier in his forties with one of those twirly handlebar moustaches, glaring at her like she really was a spy.

That would teach her to stand about daydreaming instead of doing her job!

'I was just cleaning the floor.' Violet turned red despite herself as heads turned all over the room, the young men staring round at her in silent accusation.

The soldier with the big moustache jerked his head back towards the entrance. 'Right, well, you appear to have finished now. So, on your way.'

'Yes, all right.' She gathered up both her own bucket and mop and those that Hazel had abandoned, and struggled away down the corridor, metal buckets clanking together, the two dripping mops leaving behind a trail of soapy water. 'Oops . . . Sorry.'

The soldier folded his arms and watched her go, clearly unimpressed.

At the barbed wire barrier, she met a flushed and harassed-looking Hazel.

'Here's your mop and bucket,' Violet told her breathlessly, handing them over once the grinning soldier had moved the barrier to let her pass. 'I wish you'd come back a bit sooner. Left me in the bleedin' lurch, it did.'

Hazel stared. 'What do you mean?'

'Some bloke threw me out. Seemed to think I was up to no good.'

'Oh no, and on your first day too! I'm sorry it took so long.' Hazel showed her round to the back of the house. There was a small yard back there, and a covered area with a drain where they could ditch the dirty water and prop the wet mops. 'I tried to get back as soon as I could. But Eva – Miss Ryder – she wouldn't let me go. She's got some mad scheme. I don't know what to do about it.'

Violet leant against the back wall in the sunlight and pulled a packet of fags from her apron pocket. 'Is it our break time yet?'

'Not even close.'

'I'm having a smoke anyway. Two minutes, all right?'

Hazel hesitated, then shrugged. 'I suppose so.' She glanced at the back door. 'Frobisher shouldn't see us back here, not at this time of day. He'll be too busy in the kitchen. First luncheon sitting's at noon, and he likes everything prepared and set out on the tables in good time.'

'Wonder how my nieces are getting on.' Violet made a face. 'Poor little mites. I wouldn't change places with them, not for the world. He looks a bit of an ogre, that one.'

'Oh, he's not so bad.' Hazel shook her head when Violet offered her a cigarette. 'No thanks, I don't smoke.'

'Suit yourself.' Violet took a long drag and blew a smoke ring, watching it dissolve as it drifted upwards in the sunny air. 'Keeps me going, a smoke between jobs. And stops me thinking about food.'

'Oh, food!' Hazel clutched her tummy. 'I'm so hungry these days.' Then her face fell, as if she had suddenly remembered about her pregnancy. 'When I can keep the stuff down, that is.'

Violet closed her eyes, letting the sun play against her lids. She could get used to this new life, outdoors so much, and this bright Cornish air, the smell of the sea . . .

Suddenly homesick, she wondered what everyone was doing back in Dagenham. How her mum was, and their neighbours, and the café. Every night at bedtime she prayed that the bombs would miss everyone she knew, and named them all, and even mentioned her mother's little café where she had worked for so long.

She wasn't a fool, though. She knew perfectly well that everyone in the East End must be praying the same thing, and not everyone got spared, did they?

Still, she always stuck her hands together and muttered the words all the same, because what was there to lose? Nothing, except a few minutes every night before her head hit the pillow. Maybe God was listening, maybe he wasn't. Maybe there was no God, as many had begun to mutter since the bombing started, because if there was a God, why would he let so many kids die, or leave them orphaned and alone? But it was worth the effort, praying.

She took another drag on her ciggy, pushing her fears away. But there was a sick feeling in the pit of her stomach. She hadn't heard from her mother since moving into Hazel's place, when she'd posted a quick note back home to let Mum know where she was. That didn't mean anything, though. Mum might have written back, but the letter could have been lost. Post Offices and depots were bombed too, weren't they?

Or more likely, her mother was busy and hadn't known how to reply to her letter.

Violet bit her lip. She hadn't gone into much detail about what had happened, not feeling it right to put such an embarrassing fact into a letter where anyone might read it. Especially when it was about her niece, who was still so young and innocent. It wouldn't be fair for Lily to be marked out in some way by what her uncle had tried to do. But that was what happened when scandalous stories like that did the rounds, wasn't it? The girl suffered while the man got away scot-free. It was the way of the world, and she knew it, but it still wasn't right.

'You all right?' Hazel asked, peering at her, which was when Violet belatedly realised she had been talking about the necessary evils of rationing, and how much she and Charlie missed some of the foods they couldn't get hold of anymore, not for love nor money. 'I don't think you've been listening to a word I've said.'

'Too much sun, that's all,' Violet replied shortly, then dropped her fag and ground it out under her heel. 'I'm not used to it.'

'I hope you're not going to get sick too. You look a bit peaky.'

'So do you, love.' Violet couldn't resist giving her friend a quick nudge. 'But that's not surprising, given your condition.'

'Shush!' Hazel looked about herself, horrified. 'Keep your voice down!'

'Oops, sorry.' Violet realised too late that several windows were open above them. She had forgotten that Hazel probably wouldn't want her pregnancy to be widely known. Once people knew, she would lose her job here, for starters, and then Violet might lose her own too, not to mention the girls. 'My effing mouth! It just slipped out.'

'Please be careful.'

'I will in future, cross my heart and hope to die.'

'Thanks, though I'd rather you didn't!' But Hazel was still frowning. 'Look, Violet, are you sure there's nothing bothering you? You really don't look too clever.'

Violet hesitated, about to tell her friend what was wrong, but then abruptly changed her mind. She wasn't ready to share her fears about her mum back in Dagenham. Hazel might mention it in front of Lily and Alice, and then they'd get upset for no good reason. Until she heard to the contrary, she had to assume everyone back home was safe and well. Just as they were, even if things hadn't quite worked out as planned.

'I'm just feeling a bit dicky, love. Best get back to work though.' She shot Hazel a falsely cheery smile, and winked. 'Come on, let's see what them girls are up to in the kitchen, shall we? Bet they've got that old bloke in a right stew by now.'

But as she hurried back into Eastern House, Violet stopped suddenly, her eyes widening in shock.

Right behind her, Hazel bumped into her back. 'Watch out!'

'S-sorry.' Violet put a hand to her heaving chest. 'Clumsy me, eh? Told you . . . It must be a t-touch of sunstroke.'

But it wasn't too much sun that had made her stop dead, and she knew it.

There was a dark-haired man standing a few feet away, deep in earnest conversation with George Cotterill, the kindly fellow who'd agreed to give her and the girls a job. Violet could only see him in profile, but she'd recognised him at once, and felt her heart rate suddenly accelerate.

It was Joe Postbridge, the man from the beach at Penzance.

CHAPTER TWENTY-TWO

Hazel moved past Violet, who was still rooted in the middle of the corridor, a flush in her usually pale cheeks. What on earth was wrong with the East End girl today? She had seemed lost in her memories outside, her mind elsewhere while Hazel was talking. Either that or she had been bored rigid by all her talk of cookery and ration books, and hadn't bothered responding. Now her eyes were wide and her mouth was partly open, and if Hazel hadn't known better, she would have said Violet was panting . . .

Then she saw George Cotterill up ahead, and the question died on her lips. If he'd been looking harassed earlier, he now looked positively furious.

Whatever could be wrong?

He was talking to a man she knew vaguely, Mr Postbridge's nephew. His name was Joe, and he'd just moved in to Swelle Farm, not far from Eastern House. Joe's uncle Harold, a widower, had passed away earlier that year, and Joe had inherited the farm from him. Which was quite a step up in the world for a lad who had lived most of his life in a tiny two-up, two-down, terraced house in Penzance with his mother, his father having died of pneumonia some years ago.

The young man was lucky to have such an inheritance, she thought, especially given the dreadful bombing of his ship, which had cost him a leg and sent him home early from the war. A man with only one leg would always struggle to find work, and Joe had been his uncle's favourite as a boy, a frequent visitor to Porthcurno over the years.

Now he was here, leaning on a stick and talking to George in his low, deep voice, and whatever he was saying appeared to have rattled George no end.

'Come on!' Hurriedly, she dragged a stiff-legged Violet by the arm past both men, giving George and his visitor a polite smile, and hoped he wouldn't notice they'd been slacking in their duties. 'Mr Cotterill. Mr Postbridge.'

George merely nodded at them both without speaking, his face preoccupied. But Hazel knew she was not imagining the quick glance that flashed between Violet and Joe.

In the kitchen, Mr Frobisher was out of sight in one of the side pantries. But he could be heard instructing the two girls in the correct stacking of dishes in the china cupboard, while they chorused, 'Yes, Mr Frobisher, sir,' in docile tones after every command.

Hazel put her hands on her hips, staring at Violet. 'What was all that about?'

'What do you mean?'

'For goodness' sake! I saw the way he looked at you.'

Violet's eyes were like saucers. 'Who?'

'Joe Postbridge.'

'You know him?'

'Of course I know him, I've lived here my whole life. I know everyone. Though Joe and his mother live in Penzance. Or rather they did, until quite recently.'

'You mean, Joe lives here in Porthcurno now?' Violet's voice was squeaky.

'He just inherited his late uncle's place, Swelle Farm, a mile or so up the road. He was really close to his uncle, especially after his dad died. I think they only moved in last week, because of the bombing raid in Penzance. I heard it was really bad.' Hazel looked at her friend, churning with curiosity now. 'Come on, spill the beans. How on earth do you know Joe?'

'Why do you think he knows me?'

'Because I saw his face. He was surprised to see you, I can tell you that. Surprised . . . and pleased too.'

Now Violet's cheeks were a deep rose-pink. 'Oh, really? You think so?'

'I'm waiting.'

Violet bit her lip, looked at the open door to the side pantry, then whispered in a low voice as though worried her nieces would overhear, 'All right, all right. I met him on the beach at Penzance a little while ago. Such a gent. And so good-looking.'

'And?'

'And nothing. We chatted for a bit, then I had to take the girls to catch the bus back to Porthcurno.' Violet shrugged. 'That's all.'

Hazel was disappointed. 'Nothing else?'

'Cross my heart.'

'The way Joe looked at you, I thought he must be on a promise, at least.'

'Oh, don't!' But Violet giggled, suddenly looking five years younger. She touched her hair, self-conscious. 'He did give us a good looking over though, didn't he?'

'I'll say.'

'And I did like him. Such a nice way of talking. And that Cornish accent. He must charm the birds out of the trees, that one. I could listen to him all day.'

Hazel wondered if that was why she had been so far away this morning, but merely said, 'You don't mind about his leg, then?' If Bertie came home from the war with an injury, she wouldn't think any the less of him. But they were married. 'I mean, Joe's a looker, for sure. Always has been. But it don't put you off none?'

'Why would it?' Violet's eyes were shining. 'He served his country, didn't he? As far as I'm concerned, the man's a bloody hero.'

'And you aren't worried by the other thing?'

'What other thing?'

'Well, his shortness.' Hazel hid a grin, baiting her friend a little. 'What is he, five foot five?' She looked Violet up and down. 'You're a little mismatched.'

Violet stared at her, then sucked in her breath when Hazel burst out laughing. 'You effing tease! You're bloomin' pulling my leg, ain't you?' She laughed too. 'As if it matters that I'm taller than him.'

'Sorry, I couldn't resist.'

'What on earth do you two squawking hens think you're doing?' Mr Frobisher had emerged from the side pantry with a gigantic tureen in his hands. He glared at them disapprovingly. 'You ought to be setting an example to the younger women. Not behaving like a pair of cackling fishwives on market day.'

Behind him, Alice and Lily peered at them, both girls bright-eyed and pink-cheeked, hands clapped over their mouths as though to stop themselves from laughing. They had seemed overawed on first meeting Frobisher this morning. But no doubt they'd heard plenty more choice comments like that from him, and were having trouble not openly sniggering at him now.

Violet went quite red herself, as though this insult were the last straw. Her voice shook as she stuttered, 'F-Fishwives? Why, you—!'

Hazel caught her arm, shaking her head in warning. 'Shush,' she mouthed.

He shouldn't have said that, it was true. But if Violet antagonised him, they might both find themselves out of work. And Hazel needed this job desperately.

She turned to Mr Frobisher, a quick apologetic smile on her face. 'Sorry, sir. We were just letting off steam. It's nasty work, cleaning up in them tunnels. And in this heat too. It won't happen again, I promise.'

'Hmm.' Mr Frobisher walked in a stately fashion to the table and deposited the tureen there, then whirled to fix them both with a beady-eyed look. 'Well . . .'

'What can we do to help with lunch?' Hazel asked.

'Wash your hands first. Thoroughly, mind, with hot water and soap.'

'Yes, Mr Frobisher.'

'Then you can finish laying the tables out in the mess. You'll see the girls have already cleared the breakfast things away, and scrubbed down the wood to my satisfaction.' He turned to Alice and Lily, whose giggling faces fell into docile lines at once. His eyes narrowed suspiciously, but all he said was 'Hurry about your chores, then. You know what to do.'

'Yes, Mr Frobisher,' the two girls chorused demurely, and scurried to their separate stations, Lily stirring today's soup, which smelt like pea and ham, and Alice peeling and coring apples for dessert.

Hazel and Violet took turns washing their hands with strong-smelling tar soap, then changed their damp aprons for clean ones, and carried the large cutlery and condiments baskets between them into the mess.

Slamming knives and forks down higgledy-piggledy on

the well-scrubbed tables, Violet muttered a few choice insults about Mr Frobisher that meant nothing to Hazel, thankfully. Probably some East End slang. But after a few minutes her friend seemed to calm down, going back and straightening the place settings.

'Do you really think he likes me, then?' Violet asked, stretching across to position salt and pepper shakers in the middle of one table. 'Joe Postbridge, I mean.'

'It looked to me like he did, yes.'

A slow smile crept across Violet's face, and again she looked years younger. 'Well, I like him as well. Mind you, we only got five minutes to speak on the beach. And I was too shy to say much. Proper tongue-tied, I was.'

'Sometimes words aren't what's important.'

'I wonder what he's doing here.'

Hazel thought about it, adjusting the knives and forks she'd just laid out. 'Probably something to do with his farm. With all the new soldiers arriving, I expect George is looking for fresh sites for them to set up camp.'

'Talk of the devil,' Violet muttered in warning.

With a start, Hazel realised that the door into the mess hall had just opened. She raised her head from her work only to find herself looking into George's serious eyes.

He crooked a finger at her.

'A minute, Hazel?'

She put down her cutlery basket, and followed him outside into the echoing corridor. Her heart was beating fast, and she had to focus on not seeming flustered. Had she done something wrong?

But what he said took her completely by surprise. 'I've found you a car,' he said, and jangled a set of car keys from his fingers. 'I need you here on time, and I know you don't have enough bicycles to go around.'

Hazel stared at him in astonishment. 'A c-car?'

'It's an old van, actually. It was round the back of the stores. Nobody seemed to be using it. I cleaned it out and got it running again.'

'Oh, George!'

'It was the least I could do, given your transport issues. Though don't tell any of the other domestic staff, or they'll all want a car.' It was a joke, but she could tell he was half-serious. 'You know what people are like. I don't want to be accused of favouritism.'

'I won't say a word.'

'You know how to drive, I suppose?'

'I've passed my test.'

'Excellent.' George glanced over his shoulder as though worried someone might be listening, but the corridor was empty. There were still about forty-five minutes until first sitting for luncheon. He lowered his voice, standing a little closer. 'Look, I'm going to run you ladies back to the house myself tonight, then walk home on foot. Just to reassure myself the car's in good working order.'

'There's no need,' she began, but George held up a hand. 'I insist.'

Hazel felt a glow inside at the warm look in his eyes, the protective tone in his voice. And then hated herself for feeling like that. What was wrong with her?

'Thank you,' she said softly, smiling.

He smiled too.

For a moment, there was an odd silence between them. His serious gaze met hers, and for once she did not look away.

'See you outside at the end of your shift, then,' George said, and strode away.

Hazel watched him go, and could not decide what to do,

twisting her fresh apron in her hands until it was horribly creased.

What she felt for George Cotterill was wrong, plain and simple. Yet she could not help liking him. Even loving him, perhaps, as she had loved him once before, though without really understanding the meaning of the word back then. She did not love Bertie anymore. That was becoming more obvious with every day that passed. She rarely even thought of him now, except with a sense of fear and loathing. But she was still his wife, and moreover, was carrying his child.

Some things mattered more than love, especially in times of war.

Like duty.

She would do her duty, of course, and steer clear of George Cotterill.

Yet somehow that promise rang hollow this time. She had smiled at him just now. And spoken softly. And George had smiled at her too. The way a man smiles at a woman when they have a secret understanding.

Something had shifted between them. Hazel wasn't sure exactly what or why. But she was in deep trouble, and she knew it.

CHAPTER TWENTY-THREE

Eva almost forgot to meet Hazel during the lunch break, but dashed out of the tunnel and over to the front lawn just in time to catch her getting up to leave. 'I'm so sorry,' she said breathlessly, 'I got caught up with work. You're not off, are you?'

Hazel was with the new woman, Violet, and two fresh-faced girls, who got up from the striped deckchairs they'd been occupying and studied her with undisguised interest. They were clearly both relatives of Violet, because all three shared the same pert, turned-up nose and thin, mobile lips. Not to mention the same sharp-eyed watchfulness.

The younger girl crammed a rough-cut sandwich triangle into her mouth, staring at Eva, but at least knew enough manners not to eat with her mouth open.

'Sorry, girls, have I spoiled your lunch break?' Eva pumped their hands heartily up and down in turn as Hazel introduced them. 'Hello, Lily. Hello, Alice.' She grinned at their startled looks; no doubt they weren't used to being greeted so enthusiastically. 'I'm Eva, and I need your help in organising a dance. You game for that?'

The older girl brightened at once, her sulky expression

turning to enthusiasm. She was astonishingly pretty, Eva decided, with lovely flaxen hair and huge eyes. 'Just try and stop me!' she exclaimed, her East End accent strangely at odds with her beauty. Then she faltered, looking sideways at the two older women. 'If Aunty Vi will let me, that is . . .'

'Oh yes, please, Aunty Vi,' the younger one agreed, swallowing the last of her sandwich before continuing with a disarming honesty, 'I mean, it's not bad being 'ere instead of at the farm. It beats pulling up taters all day long, that's for sure. But a dance would be . . . Well, better than taters, anyhow!'

Eva laughed at her pleading expression. So, these two charmingly outspoken girls were Violet's nieces. She wondered fleetingly where the mother was, but decided not to ask. They were from the East End, not from around here. And she had lost too many people in the nightly bombing in and around London not to realise that stupid questions like that, more often than not, led to horrific answers.

'Well, Aunty Vi?' Eva asked Violet instead, as brightly as she could. 'What do you say? In or out?'

Violet seemed to be in a daze, not quite listening. Instead, she was looking at Lily. 'I s'pose so. If you girls want to have a dance, then yes, why not? Though Hazel's the one who knows what's what.'

'Hazel?' Eva turned to her hopefully.

'Well, there is a church hall to the west of here, about a two-mile walk.' Hazel looked dubious. 'If we can get permission from the vicar, that is.'

'Sounds perfect,' Eva said, pleased by the idea of a venue so close to the camp. 'And perhaps you should leave the vicar to me.' She tapped a finger against her lips, thinking hard. 'Hmm. Does this vicar have a wife?'

Hazel nodded. 'Mrs Clewson.'

'Then I shall pay Mrs Clewson a visit. Though it might be a good idea if you were to come with me, Hazel.'

'Me?' Hazel's eyes widened.

'Of course. I'll need you to make the introductions.' She tipped her head to one side, regarding Hazel curiously. 'What's the matter? Is the vicar's wife a bit of a dragon?'

The girls giggled, but Hazel looked even more uncomfortable.

'No, it's not that. But Porthcurno . . . It's a small place and people gossip.'

'About you? Surely not.'

Hazel seemed embarrassed. 'My husband Bertie hasn't always behaved in a respectable fashion – let's put it like that. And we've never been big churchgoers. I'm not sure I'd be welcome at the vicarage.'

'Nonsense.' Eva gave her an encouraging smile. 'I need you there. You know the area, I don't. But if you need support, maybe Violet and the girls would like to come too?' She looked at them. 'How about it, girls? Do you fancy a walk to the vicarage one day soon, see if we can squeeze a biscuit or two out of the vicar's wife?'

'Yes, please,' Lily and Alice chorused, grinning with pleasure.

Violet darted a quick glance at Lily's shining face, and said to Hazel, 'That does sound like a nice day out. Maybe on our next afternoon off?' There was a pleading note to her voice. 'I'll come along to back you up.'

'Oh . . .' Hazel rolled her eyes. 'Very well, then.'

'Excellent, thank you.' Eva gave Hazel a hug, squeezing her tight. 'Then it's as good as done. Soon, we'll all be dancing our feet sore and having a whale of a time at the old church hall.'

'You don't know much about the Cornish if you think that,' Hazel said drily. 'We tend to do things *dreckly*.'

Eva frowned, not understanding. 'What does *dreckly* mean?'

'Only that we like to do things in our own good time.' Hazel straightened her white headscarf, which had become lopsided during Eva's hug. 'Or never.'

'Oh, nonsense! Tell you what, once we've decided on a date for the dance, I'll design a poster, and do a few copies. Maybe you girls could stick them up here and there. Church porch, bus stops, lamp-posts . . .' Eva came to a halt, looking round at their laughing faces. 'What? Have I said something funny?'

'Bus stops? Lamp-posts? This isn't a big town; this is the countryside,' Hazel explained gently. 'The bus stops where it always has, or where you ask it to. There isn't usually a bus stop. And we don't have many lamp-posts out here in the middle of nowhere.'

'So, how on earth do we tell people there's going to be a dance?'

Hazel grinned. 'Word of mouth, of course. People have a way of knowing what's going on round here, even without lamp-posts and bus stops.' She chewed thoughtfully on her lip. 'Though we could put a poster up in the mess, if Mr Cotterill or the colonel don't disapprove.'

'You can leave those two up to me,' Eva said confidently, and saw a flicker of what looked like disapproval in the other woman's face. Now whatever had she said wrong?

'What about the local paper?' Alice piped up.

'Oh, that's a jolly good idea,' Eva said warmly, smiling round at the younger girl. 'Maybe you could write a note for the Penzance newspaper, as soon as we know the date, and cycle over there with it.'

'I'd like that,' Alice said, her eyes glowing.

'Well . . .' Eva could hear the rumble of male voices as the code-breakers and trainees left the mess hall and made their way back towards the underground listening post. 'Time for me to dash, I'm afraid. Work calls! But let's talk again soon. Once you've squared things with the vicar, Hazel. Then we can all get our posh frocks sorted out and buff up our dancing shoes.'

There was a short silence.

Eva glanced back at Hazel, who was still looking a little miffed, though she couldn't imagine why. And now even Violet had an uncertain frown on her face, while Lily was gazing away into the distance, apparently in a world of her own. What a crew! Still, beggars couldn't be choosers, and this was what she had to work with. And to be fair, some of the dancers she'd known at the club in London, whom she'd tried to organise into asking the manager for better pay, had been even less promising material.

'Meanwhile, I'll get cracking on that poster, and Alice can start drafting something for the local rag. All we need now is a firm time and date for the dance.' Eva smiled at them winningly. 'How does that sound?'

'Excellent,' Alice declared, and sucked on the end of her braided hair, seemingly oblivious to any tension in the air. 'Truly excellent.'

The sun was still warm, though it was already evening. Eva had intended to take a wander outside in the leafy grounds of the officers' quarters where she had her room. But after a long shift, her feet were aching, so on getting back to her room, she'd kicked off her shoes and sat cross-legged on her bed, working on a design for the dance poster.

She'd only been there about fifteen minutes when a loud 'tick' at the window made her raise her head in surprise. Nothing else happened, so she continued her sketching. Seconds later, a louder 'tick' was followed by an ominous 'crack'.

Someone was throwing stones up at her window!

'Who on earth . . . ?'

Eva jumped off the bed, abandoning her poster design, and pushed up the sash window, sticking her head out to peer down into the bushes below.

Professor Templeton, in the act of throwing another pebble up at her bedroom window, lowered his arm sheepishly.

'Sorry,' he said, and dropped the stone back into the undergrowth. 'So you are in, after all. I was beginning to wonder.'

She was rather enchanted by this boyish tactic of gaining her attention, but surprised too. 'Haven't you heard of using the stairs?'

He stuck his hands in his pockets. 'Ah, well, yes. But I didn't fancy running into the colonel. I'm not sure if he'd approve of . . .' He stopped short, and then seemed to focus on the plain white blouse she had worn to work. 'Oh, have you forgotten about our walk to the beach? I've cleared it for this evening, just as you asked.'

'Of course not,' she said, smiling. 'But I thought we were going after dark. Which isn't for ages yet.'

'The moon's too full. Sergeant Cryer reminded me when I was asking about a moonlit walk. It's what they're calling a bomber's moon in London.'

She knew exactly what it meant when the moon was full in the capital: a rain of death and destruction. Yet somehow she had not expected the same horror to be enacted in the heart of the quiet Cornish countryside.

'Even down here?'

'Jerry's intent on blowing us all to kingdom come, I'm afraid, even down here. Besides, we're a target. The Germans know there's a listening post in Cornwall. We got a heads-up a few months back that they'd be sending bombers along the coast, looking for the place.'

'Oh, my God!'

'Don't worry. They haven't managed to pinpoint our position yet.'

Eva shivered, gazing out at the empty, still-blue skies above the shimmering sea. How foolish she'd been, to assume that by coming down here she was somehow escaping the war. All that death and mayhem in London . . .

'What a dreadful thought.'

'Sorry to burst your bubble,' Templeton said regretfully. 'You've been lucky, not having to go down into the bunker yet in the middle of the night. Someone should have told you to keep shoes and a dressing-gown by the door, just in case.'

'That bad?'

'Not recently. But we had a few close calls last month at the full moon, so everyone's on high alert at the moment. Sky-watching, you know?' He made a face. 'Anyway, thing is, the sergeant warned me off the beach tonight. We'd be too visible. Best I can offer is a gentle cliff walk before sunset. How does that sound?'

Eva nodded unhappily. She would have loved to wander across the pale sands of the beach with him in the moonlight. But now she knew about the bombers, she dismissed that as an impossible dream. The last thing she wanted was to bring that dark rain of devastation down on peaceful Porthcurno. Maybe one day when the war was finally over . . .

'Sounds delightful.'

Professor Templeton smiled with obvious relief, and bent to pick up a small wicker hamper at his feet. 'Borrowed this from old Frobisher in the kitchen. He's packed us a half bottle of wine and two glasses,' he explained, seeing her curious glance. 'And something to eat. Thought it might make up for not being allowed on the beach.'

'Oh, you darling!'

His mouth split in an appreciative grin. 'So you'll come down, then?'

'Give me a jiffy to change into something fresh, and I'll be with you,' she promised him, shutting the sash window without waiting for his reply.

Dragging the curtains across for privacy, she threw off her dull work clothes, gave herself a quick cold splash at the washstand, sprayed some perfume on her underthings, and combed out her hair.

A little over ten minutes later, Eva ran down to meet him in flats and a pretty summer frock. She would have preferred to wear heels. But all her heels were deeply impractical for a cliff walk, unless she wanted to end up plunging to her death.

Anyway, she suspected Professor Templeton wouldn't mind her wearing flats. Not when it made her a little shorter than usual. Men often found her height intimidating, she had discovered to her cost, and wearing heels tended to wound their fragile egos further. Perhaps he wasn't bothered, of course, being fairly tall himself. But she wasn't taking any chances. Not on a first date.

'You look . . . nice,' he said, studying her, then held out his arm.

She slipped her arm through his, and they started to walk towards the headland. It was a glorious evening, and the walk took them along a narrow woodland path under overhanging trees. It was really quite romantic, she thought, seeing the occasional white flash of bunny tails as rabbits scurried off through the undergrowth at their approach.

At the end of the wooded glade, they stopped at a lonely guard post to show the signed permission slip Templeton had wangled from Sergeant Cryer, and then took the upper path away from the sands, up into the sunlit evening.

'I'm sorry about the beach,' he said as they came out on

the cliff walk and paused to look down at the white sands and boulders of Porthcurno Beach.

It was just as well they hadn't gone onto the sands, she thought, gazing with dismay at the newly installed rolls of barbed wire strung along the top of the beach, and the vast anti-landing obstacles, scattered at intervals along the shore-line, intended to hinder a German invasion from the sea. Not exactly the romantic setting she had imagined. No wonder her father had steered her away from this spot during their walks.

'Pooh,' she said lightly, 'who cares about a moonlit beach? We'll have a gorgeous red sunset instead, and over the Cornish cliffs too. Not to mention wine.'

Templeton met her eyes, smiling. 'You're a good sport, Eva.' He hesitated, as though about to add something, then seemed to change his mind. 'Look, I'll get you back to your room before the moon rises, never fear.'

'Thank you,' she said, gazing out at the bright, sparkling tide as though that was all she cared about. 'Oh, isn't the view here marvellous? Shall we find somewhere to sit down and drink that wine?'

But secretly, Eva was hoping for just a little moonlight on their walk back, even if she had to delay things a trifle, in order to get the moonlit kiss she'd been dreaming of.

CHAPTER TWENTY-FOUR

Although their day shift had officially finished, George Cotterill had asked them to stay on for an extra hour to cover for the evening shift. One of the staff had gone down with the dreaded lurgy, Hazel was told, and she did not know how to say no to the request. So, even though the two girls were dragging themselves about wearily, flushed and droopy-eyed, she agreed they would stay on until the evening meal had been laid out and eaten, and all the tables cleared for the morning.

Once they had finally hung up their aprons and head-scarves, they traipsed down the steep slope to the guardhouse barrier to be let out.

That was where George had said he would meet them.

Hazel walked slowly, wheeling her bicycle, glad she would not have to ride it home. George had told her to bring it to the guardhouse, despite having a lift home, because apparently there would be 'plenty of room for a bicycle' in the back of the van.

How big was this van, anyway?

She still couldn't quite believe her luck, that George Cotterill had promised her a vehicle for getting to and from work, and had even said she could fill it up the first few times with army fuel at the depot. In this time of shortages and rationing, she couldn't imagine anything more generous.

But was it really *luck*?

She was uncomfortably aware that George had a soft spot for her. Had his feelings prompted this gesture?

She hated the idea that people might be gossiping about her behind her back, perhaps suggesting that she and George were carrying on together. Which they absolutely weren't, of course. But she could imagine what Bertie would make of such rumours, if they reached him at the front, courtesy of one of their interfering neighbours.

'Is that it? Is that going to be ours?' Alice exclaimed suddenly, pointing ahead.

Hazel stopped dead and could only stare, dumbfounded, at the large white van with a faded red cross on its side.

Surely not?

But yes, George was there, leaning against the bonnet with his arms folded and a smile on his face.

Violet too had come to a halt, right beside her. She exchanged glances with Hazel, then rubbed her tired eyes as though not sure she entirely trusted them. 'I don't believe it,' she said blankly. 'An ambulance? He's giving us a bleedin' ambulance?'

'And from the Great War, by the look of it,' Alice muttered, her eyebrows so high they almost disappeared into her fringe.

'I . . . I'm sure there's a good reason for that,' Hazel said, on the defensive at once. She didn't want George to think them ungrateful. 'And it's better than walking, isn't it?'

'Oh, a thousand times better, Aunty Hazel,' Alice agreed hurriedly, giving her arm a reassuring squeeze, then spoiled the effect by adding, 'so long as it doesn't break down.'

Aunty Hazel?

Hazel didn't know where to look. But she rather liked the affectionate way Alice had said that. Charlie had been so distracted and withdrawn for months now, she had forgotten how it felt when someone was nice . . .

'I love it,' Lily declared, having walked all the way round the ancient, battered vehicle. She ran a hand over the faded red cross on its side panel. 'It's romantic.'

George, who had been just about to hand the keys over to Hazel, paused, staring at the girl. 'Romantic?'

'Of course. Think of all the wounded soldiers it must have carried from the battlefield to the hospital, and all the nurses who tended them, in their smart white uniforms.'

Hazel bit her lip, struggling not to smile. Violet had told her that Lily had some vague aspirations of becoming a nurse, despite the fact that the girl apparently went queasy at the sight of blood.

'Or all the dead bodies it must have held,' Alice pointed out ghoulishly.

'D-dead bodies?' Lily repeated in a faint voice, and abruptly withdrew her hand from the red cross, folding her arms across her chest instead. 'Ugh, that's horrid, Alice. You've gone and ruined it for me now.' She took a step backwards, turning to Violet in pale-faced entreaty. 'I . . . I hope it's been cleaned out inside. I mean, proper cleaned out. With disinfectant and all. Because I don't think as how I can get inside, otherwise.'

Hazel smiled at last and met George's amused eyes, and looked swiftly away.

Oh goodness, she mustn't look at him like that!

'I doubt it carried many wounded soldiers, Lily,' George said, giving the girl an understanding smile as he took the bicycle from Hazel, wheeling it to the rear. 'Sorry to disappoint you, but this old ambulance hasn't been used abroad. It came to us from the cottage hospital at Penzance, one of their cast-offs. And yes,' he added, grinning at Lily's suspicious stare, 'it's been thoroughly cleaned out since then.'

Violet had opened the double doors at the back and was sniffing inside. 'Hmm,' was all she said, but ruffled Lily's hair when the girl started to protest. 'That's enough, scallywag. There's plenty of room in the back here, and it's better than Shanks's pony.'

George had been loading the bicycle into the back of the former ambulance, but his brows drew together at this curious slang. 'Shanks's what, sorry?'

'She means walking,' Alice explained simply.

'Ah, right.' George stowed the bike, then came back and opened the front passenger door, which creaked noisily. He gestured Hazel inside. 'It's probably over twenty years old, and not in the best condition, it's true. But it's safe enough, according to the army mechanic who checked it over, and it's yours if you want it.'

Hazel climbed inside gratefully, her feet aching after the long day, and glanced through the narrow partition into the back. 'Everyone all right back there?'

There were two padded benches, one to each side, where presumably they had laid the sicker patients for transport. The girls were already seated together on one side, looking cheerful enough about this new adventure, with Violet sitting opposite, gripping onto a hanging strap with a fearful expression.

'I'll say!' Alice exclaimed, grinning broadly.

Lily said nothing.

'Just don't turn us over,' Violet muttered. 'I'd rather walk if it means not dying.'

George laughed, and then closed the back doors on them.

He climbed into the front seat and started the engine. The battered vehicle vibrated beneath them, but otherwise seemed sound enough as he turned it in the dusty track beside the barrier and then coaxed it up the hill out of the valley. As they drove, he showed Hazel where the various controls were, and told her what to say when she took it for refuelling at the army depot.

'Here, listen to this,' George said as they reached the main road, leaning forward to push a button on the dashboard. A jangling siren rang out in the evening air, turning heads among a squad of soldiers marching past on their nightly patrol. One of the men saluted him, and George grinned, raising a hand in response.

Hazel clapped her hands over her ears.

'Sorry,' he said, and turned the siren off. 'I thought the girls might enjoy it.'

'That was amazing,' Alice shouted from the back.

'Bleedin' deafening, that's what it was,' Violet said unappreciatively, but Hazel could see she was smiling, and no longer clinging for dear life to the hanging strap.

'At least you won't have any trouble clearing sheep out of the road,' he said.

The others laughed, and even Hazel had to join in. 'Poor sheep,' she said, lowering her hands to her lap, 'they'd be terrified.'

He shot her a smiling look, then transferred his attention back to the road as they rounded a corner perilously close to the cliff edge.

'It's very good of you to let us have this,' she began carefully, but George shook his head, again refusing to allow her to thank him.

'We need you at Eastern House,' he said in a low voice, for her ears only. 'I'd put you up there in the staff quarters if I could, save you a trip every morning. But I know you'd rather be at home for Charlie.'

'That's right. Charlie needs me.'

'Let's hear no more about it, then. You needed transport.' He tapped the dashboard. 'This was the best I could do.'

'Well,' she said archly, 'there is a war on.'

He threw back his head and roared with laughter.

Hazel had never seen him so relaxed, and found it hard not to stare. It must be all this sunny weather, she decided, looking back at the road when he glanced in her direction. Even with the back-breaking work every day, somehow it still felt like a holiday. And she guessed that Violet and the girls must feel about the same, having escaped the horrors of the Blitz for the rural peace of Cornwall.

They passed the turn to Swelle Farm, and she thought suddenly of Violet. 'That's where Joe lives now,' Hazel called into the back, and the three of them scrabbled to see, though a house sign and a narrow winding lane with overhanging trees were their only reward. 'That was his uncle's farm, the one he's just inherited.'

'I bet it's right big and posh,' Lily breathed, in awe.

'I wonder how many sheep he's got,' Alice said, gazing at the long field running up to the woods that hid the farm-house.

Violet stared the longest, then sat back with a sigh once the house sign and field were both out of sight. 'It's so strange to think he lives so close to Eastern House. He didn't mention he was about to move here, that day we met him on the beach.'

'He's always been a very private person,' Hazel turned round to say. 'And I believe his mother wasn't too keen on leaving Penzance. That's what I've heard, anyway.'

'Listening to village gossip?' George shook his head, an

amused note in his voice. 'Whatever happened to "careless talk costs lives"?'

Hazel blushed, and faced front again. 'Gossip can be useful, sometimes.' She smiled. 'Anyway, I doubt Joe's mother would be of much interest to the enemy.'

Soon, the row of terraced cottages was ahead, and her own modest home. Hazel's smile faded as she thought about Charlie, how surly and defiant her son had been recently towards her. She was worried about him. The problem was, he was at that age where lads are trying hard to be men, so don't like to take a woman's advice, even their own mother's.

But perhaps if a man were to take him aside, find out what was troubling the boy, that might be just the ticket.

'Might I ask you a favour, George?' Hazel looked at him, twisted up inside with sudden, brutal anxiety. 'That is, I mean . . .'

She didn't want him to take this the wrong way.

'Anything,' he said quickly.

'It's my Charlie,' she blurted out before she could change her mind. 'I've been having trouble with him.'

'Too many women in the house for him, is that it?' George slowed, pulling up outside the row of cottages. He lowered his voice. 'Especially two girls about his own age. Perfectly understandable.' He called through to the back. 'We're here, ladies! You should be able to open the doors from the inside.'

With wild whoops, Alice and Lily threw open the double doors at the back, clambering out. The ancient ambulance rocked as they jumped down, followed in a more stately fashion by Violet, who kept muttering under her breath about preferring to walk. No doubt being trapped in the back of the lumbering old vehicle all the way home had left her feeling a bit queasy.

Hazel did not get out. She watched the other three make their way indoors, Lily retrieving the key from under the loose slab as she had been shown.

'No, that's not it,' Hazel said, remembering some of the scenes with her son, heated conversations that had left her upset and unsure what to do for the best. 'Charlie . . . He's been talking about joining up.'

'Wants to do his bit for King and country?' George gave her a sympathetic smile. 'Well, what lad doesn't? I wouldn't worry. He's still at school. Too young for the armed forces.'

'He's fifteen, and he says . . .' She bit her lip, tears pricking at her eyelids. 'Charlie says they turn a blind eye at the recruiting office. That he can change the birth date on his identity papers, and nobody will be any the wiser before it's too late and he's been shipped out.' She was finding it hard to keep her voice level, a wobble behind her words. 'It's because of his dad not being here. I mean, they don't get on that well. But a boy needs his father, doesn't he? And with Bertie at the front, I can't seem to make him see sense.'

'Hazel, please,' he said soothingly, 'don't get yourself in a state.'

Hazel.

He usually called her Mrs Baxter, as though he needed a constant reminder that she was a married woman.

She shivered, despite the heat in the enclosed space.

'But what am I going to do?'

'I'll have a word with the lad, all right? Put him straight on a few things.' He hesitated, looking at her uncertainly, then patted her hand with an awkward air. 'I hate to see you so upset.'

Hazel said nothing, head down, hunting through her pockets in vain for a handkerchief. Much to her embarrassment, she could feel a tear rolling down her cheek. She hadn't intended to cry in front of him. She never cried in front of Bertie or Charlie these days, however upset she was feeling inside. In these terrible times, she saw it as a wife and mother's job to be strong and unshakeable. But George's quiet sympathy had been the last straw.

'Here,' he said, producing a clean white hanky. He leant across and dabbed at her eyes, his touch soft as a butterfly's wings. 'You can't go inside like that.'

'Thank you.'

His face was so close, she was looking straight into his eyes. It was hard to ignore the attraction between them, sitting alone with him, only a few inches apart. He was so bloody kind – that was the problem. The complete opposite of Bertie. A man she could rely on, not someone who would let her down time and again.

Hazel gave a little gasp, struggling against the feelings coursing through her. His lashes flickered down to hide the tormented look in his eyes, as though he felt the same.

'Oh, Hazel,' he murmured.

She looked at his handsome face and stupidly did not move away, helpless to resist. Which was when the impossible happened, as she had known it must in the end.

George cupped her cheek with one hand and leant forward to kiss her, ever so slowly, watching her face, giving her plenty of time to wriggle away or call a halt.

Only she did not take the chance to escape.

His lips were gentle but insistent.

Guilt swamped her.

This was so wrong, she thought wildly. It was only a kiss, perhaps, but it must count as adultery, and she had made an oath to God in church, never to betray her husband.

Still, she did not push George away, even raising her head and kissing him back for a brief moment of madness. Bertie had betrayed her often enough, after all. And it was so lovely to be held close and kissed at last, and not out of brute need but tenderness . . .

So what happened next was entirely her own fault, and nobody else's.

CHAPTER TWENTY-FIVE

Violet glanced out the front window at the pair still sitting in the ambulance out the front, and was shocked and amazed to see George Cotterill kissing Hazel.

'Bloody hell!' she muttered.

It was just as well the girls had both gone out the back with her washtub to get the dirty laundry washed before supper. But they'd be back soon enough once they'd wrung the wet clothes through the mangle.

Then she heard feet thudding on the stairs, and caught a glimpse of Charlie running past at top speed, his face bright red. The front door was wrenched open, then the boy tore across to the ambulance, shouting, 'Get your filthy hands off my mother!'

Violet bit her lip, not sure whether to follow him out or leave well alone.

Charlie must have been up in his bedroom when they came home, she realised, the small room overlooking the front, which they had invaded on their arrival. Getting fresh clothes, she imagined.

Poor boy – what a thing to see. His mum kissing another

man while his dad was away at the front. Though from what she'd heard about Hazel's husband, he wasn't exactly an ideal man. And George Cotterill seemed to be a good one, as men went. But she doubted the lad would see it like that. Your dad was your dad, whatever he might have done.

George Cotterill had stumbled out of the driver's seat and was facing off against the boy, who was almost as tall as him. He had his hands up and was clearly trying to defuse the situation, but Charlie was yelling insults at him.

'Whatever's going on?'

Lily was in the doorway, staring at her, a dripping blouse over her arm.

'Nothing to do with you, missy,' Violet told her hurriedly.

'But that's Charlie, isn't it? And in a right temper, by the sound of it.'

Sure enough, Charlie's voice could be heard outside the house, his rage and misery loud as a thunder crack.

'None of your business. You get on with wringing out them clothes, then hang them over the range to dry. And keep Alice with you too.' Violet bustled to the front door, hoping things wouldn't turn violent out there. 'I'll go see what's to be done.'

Some of the neighbours were looking over their gates, drawn out by the boy's yells. Hazel was out of the vehicle too, reaching for her son, a look of unhappy entreaty on her face.

'Come on, now,' Violet said firmly to Charlie. 'Let's take this inside, shall we? You've got an audience.'

'I don't bloody care who hears me. He was kissing my mum!'

'That's enough,' George Cotterill told the boy, a dark red in his cheeks. 'Think of your mother and keep your voice down.'

Not exactly very discreet, was he, kissing a married woman

right outside her own house? But she supposed they hadn't really been thinking things through at the time. She'd seen the two of them together earlier, the awkwardness of their stilted conversations, and guessed that had been their first kiss.

Violet grabbed Hazel by the arm and drew her back towards the house, ignoring her protests. 'Best leave them to it, love.' She glanced towards the nearest neighbours, an elderly man and woman who had come out of their front door to stare. 'No, don't look back at them. Head up, and smile. Like there's nothing wrong. That's the ticket.'

Inside the house, she left the front door slightly ajar and gave Hazel a hug. 'There, that's better,' she said in a low voice, not wanting the girls to hear. 'Now, don't you fret. It'll all turn out right.'

But Hazel was clasping her flushed cheeks in horror. 'I let him kiss me. And Charlie saw us. What was I thinking?'

'We all make mistakes. Your boy will understand.'

'No, he won't. And he'll tell his dad next time he writes. Oh God!' Hazel had gone pale as a pint of milk. 'Bertie will be so angry. He'll come straight home and murder George, I just know it.'

'I don't think they let soldiers come home to kill their wives' lovers.'

'It's not funny. You don't know my husband. Bertie's . . .'

'Not a nice fella?'

Hazel shook her head wordlessly, and then buried her face in her hands, shuddering violently. 'Oh God, oh God! Whatever am I going to do?'

'First things first.' Violet shoved Hazel none too gently towards the stairs. 'You want my advice, love? You go on upstairs. Wash your face, change out of your uniform, and try to calm down.'

'But Charlie—'

'Leave all that to me,' she told Hazel firmly. 'Trust me, I'll get your lad indoors without any more hullabaloo.'

Truth be told, Violet was worried sick. No point saying that out loud, of course. Not right now. But Violet had thought, when she and the girls found shelter with Hazel, that would be them snug and cosy until the end of the war. Now this trouble had come along, and she could see the husband back on leave next chance he got, kicking them all out. First thing an angry man does in that situation, she thought anxiously – blame the company his wife's been keeping.

As soon as Hazel had disappeared upstairs, she checked the girls were getting the table laid for supper, and then hurried out of the cottage.

Charlie was still yelling at George, who was trying to calm the boy down. 'It's not what it looks like,' he kept repeating raggedly, but she could see in his face that he was worried too. 'Just a misunderstanding, son.'

'I'm not your bloody son. And there's no misunderstanding. You were kissing my mum. I saw the two of you.' Charlie stopped dead and jerked his head round at the sound of someone approaching, and gave Violet a sullen look when he realised it wasn't his mother. He pointed unsteadily at her, 'And you can get lost too!'

'Hey, now, that's enough,' George told him, frowning. 'You keep a civil tongue in your head when you talk to a lady.'

'She's no lady! Her and them East End girls . . .'

Violet crossed her arms, struggling to keep a lid on her own temper. Cheeky little sod, she was thinking. What was he trying to say about her dear Alice and Lily? As if they weren't the hardest working and best-behaved girls in the world . . .

But all she said, a little tartly, was 'No need to be rude.'

'Probably best if you can go back inside,' George Cotterill said quietly, his gaze shifting to the watching neighbours.

'Probably best if you take yourself home,' she said in dry response, and saw his eyes widen. 'Look, I know you're my boss, and I'm sorry if I'm not tugging my forelock hard enough.' Now his eyes were like saucers, and fixed on her face. 'But this here's my home now too, and I'd just as soon take this business indoors, thank you. Not have it aired in the street where anyone can hear.'

'This isn't your business,' the boy began, but she ignored him.

'Off you go,' she told George, and shooed him away. He hesitated, then threw her the keys to the van, and started to trudge up the hill, presumably heading home.

Pocketing the keys, she whirled on the boy. 'Now you. Indoors, if you please.'

'Get lost!' he growled again, and stared after George, his face still darkly flushed, a martial light in his eyes.

'You listen here,' Violet said sharply, standing between him and his target, 'I don't much care what you think of me. But you've upset your mum, and for what? Some little peck on the cheek? Your dad's not here, true enough, and I suppose you think you should step up, be the man of the house in his absence. But all you've done here tonight is make a fool of yourself. In front of the neighbours, and my nieces too.' She tutted loudly. 'What must Alice and Lily think, seeing you like this, throwing your weight about in the street like a regular hooligan?'

Charlie glared at her, fuming silently, hands curled into fists at his sides.

'And speaking about them like that,' she added, lowering her voice in case her nieces were listening, 'with so little respect. Is that what those girls deserve?'

She must have hit a nerve there, because the light in his eyes died, and the boy hung his head at last, shuffling his feet.

'I didn't think so.' Violet stepped aside, pointing him towards the house. 'Now, get in there, and wash up before your supper. And no more of this nonsense!'

After he'd gone back inside, she stood there for a moment, looking back up the hilly road they'd taken from Porthcurno. The sun was setting, bathing their little patch of Cornwall with a soft golden light. She didn't think she'd ever seen anything so beautiful as this view, and couldn't quite take it in; it was so different from the dark, grim, smoky streets she'd been born and brought up in. The road back to Porthcurno bobbed up and down, rising and falling with the land. But several headlands away, she could see what looked like the slate roof of an enormous farmhouse, with a suggestion of whitewashed walls beneath it, all lit up for a moment by the last rays of the sun.

Was that Joe Postbridge's farm?

Oh, she'd so liked the look of him on the beach. It was stupid, perhaps, after only one chance meeting, but she'd spent a few restless hours most nights since then, dreaming about his warm, dark eyes. Not to mention that quick, dry smile, and the easy way he'd had with the girls. She'd taken an instant shine to him, all right.

Down on the beach at Penzance, Joe had seemed just like her. A little bit broken, a little bit defiant, but definitely an ordinary person from an ordinary family. Someone she might be able to trust, if fate was ever to throw them together again.

Yet far from being an 'ordinary' man, Joe Postbridge owned a whopping great house and a ton of land, and was probably fighting the ladies off with his stick.

Violet's shoulders slumped, and she turned away from that

gorgeous view. The argument between Charlie and George had left her nerves frayed. She couldn't help wondering what would happen if she and the girls ended up getting kicked out on the street again, how she would cope . . .

She made her way wearily back into the house and shut the door without looking back at that great big farmhouse on the hill. It was just another dirty trick fate had played on her. But she'd had her fair share of dirty tricks – like the one that had robbed her of a sister, and those girls of a mother – and she knew how to deal with them.

Chin up, eyes front, and keep buggering on, as Mr Churchill would say.

CHAPTER TWENTY-SIX

Eva inhaled the warm salt air and stared out across the bay at Porthcurno. The sun was slowly slipping below the horizon in the far west, casting a gorgeous reddish-orange patina across the land and sea.

'I could fall in love with Cornwall,' she declared.

'Only with Cornwall?' Professor Templeton asked, and she suddenly realised how close beside her he was.

Gosh, that was rather a daring question, she thought, and turned with a cautious smile. 'Hard to think about anything else, faced with this super view,' she said, and saw his lips twitch at her diplomacy.

The professor had been the epitome of charm during their clifftop picnic, topping up her glass with a very drinkable white Burgundy, plying her with Cornish cheese and biscuits, and never making a single move in her direction. Playing the gentleman, she had decided, only too happy to take things at a gentle pace. She had still not decided how she felt about him, after all. Sometimes physical attraction was not enough, and only led to trouble later on.

Now, though, the picnic was over, and he had just finished

222

packing everything away in the hamper. With the sun so low, it would soon be dusk. The perfect time for a seduction, if one were planned.

And here he was, close enough for her to touch, with his handsome cleft chin and the sun-tipped waves reflected in his glasses.

It was now or never.

Eva chewed delicately on her lip. Time for a little push, perhaps.

'Do you need to wear those all the time?' she asked, perhaps spoiling the moment, perhaps encouraging him to move closer, she wasn't sure.

'My glasses?' He shook his head. 'Not always, no.' He removed his spectacles, and slipped them into the top pocket of his jacket, which he had worn relentlessly throughout their long picnic, despite the summer warmth. 'Though if I get too close to the cliff edge, please let me know.'

She laughed.

Templeton looked her up and down, using his lack of glasses as an excuse to take a step nearer. Exactly as she had planned. 'I like the way you laugh. You laugh quite a lot, I've noticed.' At her raised eyebrows, his mouth quirked in a smile. 'That's not a criticism, but a compliment, trust me. I spend much of my time with very serious young men. It can get wearing.'

Eva was able to see his eyes properly for the first time, without the rather intimidating barrier of horn-rimmed glass between them. His eyes were blue as chinaware, tiny pale flecks flaring out from an intense pupil. There was an air of vulnerability about him, she decided, with his glasses off. Which was almost certainly why he wore them so constantly, despite not really needing to. He looked younger too, and his smile was disarming.

'All right, Miss Ryder, you've been giving me a pretty

thorough once-over,' he said, studying her in his turn. 'What's the verdict?'

'Oh, definitely guilty.'

He grinned. 'Damn.'

'And call me Eva,' she reminded him. 'Miss Ryder sounds so stuffy.'

'Sorry, I forgot.'

'Not terribly flattering.'

'Maybe not, but you are the colonel's daughter. I want to make sure I'm according you the proper amount of respect.'

She tried to suppress her snort of laughter, and failed. Which was very unladylike of her. 'Well, if we're talking about names, I can't go on calling you Professor Templeton like we're in a classroom. Not now you've been practically hand-feeding me cheese and biscuits for the past hour. It's far too lofty and distant.' She gave him a coaxing smile. 'What's your Christian name?'

'Reginald,' he said with obvious reluctance.

'Talk about lofty and distant.' She teased him with her eyes. 'May I call you Reg? At least when we're alone together.'

'To be honest, I can't stand Reg or, worse, Reggie. It makes me feel like I should be flogging second-hand cars for a living.' He hesitated again, studying her smiling face. 'My family and close friends call me Rex. Don't ask me why. I think it started when I was young, and sort of stuck.'

'Rex it is, then.'

'Not too lofty? It means "King" in Latin.'

'I rather like it.' There was a sudden stillness between them. Now or never, she thought again, and lunged impulsively upward on tiptoes to kiss him – just as he stooped, presumably to do the same. Their faces collided with a bruising shock, and they fell apart, her with a gurgling shriek, him looking distinctly flushed and uncomfortable.

'Oops,' she said, rubbing her forehead.

'Great minds . . .'

'Hit each other in the nose?'

'So it would, erm, seem.' Rex – was that honestly his family nickname? – cleared his throat, and then seized her with a manful fervour, one arm encircling her waist, the other stroking down the back of her summer frock. 'Miss Ryder . . . I mean, Eva.' He gave a hoarse laugh, as though mocking his own awkwardness. 'If you would do me a favour by standing still for a moment.'

She raised her face to his, waiting mutely, eyes closing instinctively as his dark head lowered to hers.

Now or never!

Finally, his lips met hers, firm and persuasive, and at once his strong arms tightened, pulling her close against his body.

Eva's eyes flew open, then shut tight again. She did not know what to do, her whole being having been thrown into turmoil by his kiss. She'd been kissed quite a few times before, and not only by one person, she had to admit. She considered herself something of a connoisseur when it came to kisses. But this was something new. Something beyond simple kissing. And though she was not altogether comfortable with it, it was certainly exciting.

After several minutes, Rex pulled back to gaze down at her flushed, upturned face. 'Eva?'

'Hush, please don't speak.' She kept her eyes closed, safe in the circle of his arms. 'I don't want this moment to end.'

'Everything has to end sometime.'

'Not this.'

'Open your eyes,' Rex insisted, 'and look at me.'

Eva squinted up at him. 'Must I?'

'Absolute necessity, I'm afraid. Come on, time's up.'

'One more kiss?'

He gave a laugh. 'Temptress!'

But he didn't refuse her request, one arm curling about her waist as he bent to kiss her again. This time, his kiss was deeper, more intimate. It left Eva decidedly hot and tingling, and in need of a cool flannel. Definitely not a sensation she had ever experienced before. Indeed, by the time he released her, she felt quite pink-cheeked and as though she were floating on air. Which wasn't a particularly clever thing to be doing at the edge of a cliff!

'I say.' He straightened, breathing rather heavily. 'You're one hell of a kisser, Eva Ryder.'

'You're not exactly a dullard in that department yourself, Professor Templeton.'

'Thank you, I'll take that as a compliment. I think we'd better get back though. Before we lose our heads and do something we might both regret.'

She blushed at the amorous look in his eyes. Though if Britain lost the war, God forbid, or Eastern House was bombed to smithereens, she might die without ever having known love. And she was damned if she'd let that happen.

'Who says I'd regret it?'

Rex's eyebrows rose steeply, but he didn't pursue that dangerous question, smoothing back his hair with a quick hand. 'Look, you're a marvellous girl, Eva, and I've enjoyed this evening tremendously, don't get me wrong. But your father's a colonel, and I may not be one of his men but I still have to answer to him.'

'You're not afraid of my father, are you?'

To her surprise, he didn't take offence, merely grinning. 'If your father misses you tonight, he'll have me strung up for this little jaunt, and no mistake.' He straightened her crumpled dress, his touch suddenly respectful. 'Best I whisk you back to your quarters before the moon rises and we make an easy target for Jerry.'

The sun had set while they were kissing and night was already falling, Eva realised, peering about herself in the soft twilight.

'I suppose that's sensible.' Eva gave him a quick smile, willing her heartbeat to return to normal. 'Maybe you could come in for a cup of tea when we get back?' When he said nothing, she felt awkward, adding with a laugh, '*Polly put the kettle on*, and all that. Did you ever get that sorted out?'

Rex remained silent, his face unreadable in the poor light.

'I'm sorry,' she said, flustered by her lack of discretion. Though it was only the two of them there, so what did it matter? 'Top secret, I suppose.'

He took a sudden step towards her, looming large in the dusk, and she reversed in trepidation, only to find herself stumbling over loose stones on the cliff's edge, her arms flailing as she began to topple backwards.

'Watch out!'

Rex caught her by the hand. She didn't dare look down, but heard the relentless rush and drag of the tide below, unseen in the thickening air, and was suddenly afraid.

For what felt like an eternity, though was probably only a few seconds, they stared at each other through the twilight, unmoving. Then they both heard the approaching drone of an aircraft engine, coming low and fast along the coast.

With a swift glance at the sky, Rex dragged her away from the cliff edge. 'That was a close shave,' he said, steering her back onto the rough grass where they had eaten their picnic.

She did not know what to say.

'Don't worry, it's one of ours,' he continued, misinterpreting her confused expression. He nodded after the camouflaged biplane that had already soared past them, probably heading for the nearest airfield. 'Been doing a quick recce of the Cornish coastline, I should imagine. Making sure our sea defences are up to scratch and no enemy planes are about. They fly the coast quite frequently these days.'

Eva stared at him, wondering if she'd imagined his hesitation a moment before, when her life hung in the balance.

'Well, that was a very enjoyable picnic.' Rex picked up the hamper and gave her a reassuring smile, as though nothing untoward had happened. 'Ready to go?'

CHAPTER TWENTY-SEVEN

Violet knew a moment's apprehension as the old ambulance rounded the corner, the girls in the back shrieking with laughter, and she saw the vicarage for the first time. It was a handsome building, bathed in the warm glow of late afternoon sun, with ivy on the red-brick walls and smooth green lawns to the front. Behind the house, she could see the church itself, squat and grey, but with a spire reaching above the trees, past rooks' nests cradled between spindly branches, into a still-blue sky.

'This is the vicarage,' Hazel said, not looking much happier than her, and slowed to a halt beside the other cars parked on the gravelled drive. 'And the hall we want to use is just beyond the churchyard, though you can't see it from here.' She parked next to a dark green army truck. 'Looks like Eva's here already. She must have got a lift from Eastern House.'

Violet got out, retying her headscarf under her chin. 'Good,' she said shortly. 'Maybe she's already done the asking, and we'll be able to leave double-quick. I've never been one for religious types.'

'Me neither,' Hazel agreed, checking her reflection in her

pocket compact. 'Bible-bashers leave me cold. But Eva's right. We can't do this without the vicar's say-so.'

'Don't see why Eva couldn't have come on her own,' Violet grumbled.

'Would you want to have tea with the vicar's wife on your own?'

There was a soldier leaning against the truck's bonnet, idly smoking a cigarette. He grinned at the girls as they tumbled out of the back doors.

'Hello,' he told Alice with a wink, and then straightened at the sight of Lily, who was rapidly growing up. 'Here to see the vicar too, eh?'

Lily smoothed down her fair hair, a little flushed. The two girls had been messing about in the back, but suddenly she was all cool dignity, ignoring the soldier's interested look as she stalked past him.

'We're having tea with Mrs Clewson,' Alice told him frankly. 'Maybe cake too, Aunty Vi says. I hope she's right. I like cake.'

'So do I,' the soldier replied, amused.

'Come along, girls,' Violet said, hurriedly leading them to the front door of the vicarage, not sure she liked the way he was studying Lily. 'Alice, for Gawd's sake, stop chatting to strangers like that. You never know who you're talking to.'

'He was just a soldier,' Lily pointed out on her younger sister's behalf, glancing back at him furtively. 'And he spoke to us first. Where's the harm in being polite?'

'Corporal,' Alice stated.

'Sorry?' Lily frowned at her.

'He's a corporal.' Alice tutted. 'You should look at their arm badges and give them the correct rank. I've been reading all about army ranks in that magazine Eva lent us.'

'That's Miss Ryder to you,' Violet told her.

'There she is!' Her face animated, Alice pointed through the front bay window of the vicarage. Inside, they could see Eva in a striking hat, sitting down to tea with a middle-aged lady. 'And they do have cake. Look, Eva's eating some.' The girl was breathless with excitement. 'I hope there's enough to go round.'

'Alice, for goodness' sake!' Lily nudged her. 'Behave, would you? You're not a little kid anymore.'

'But cake, Lily . . .' Alice groaned, staring through the window.

Violet exchanged a wry glance with Hazel. 'Anyone would think she was a starvin' orphan. But she ain't had cake in a good long while, that's all. Not since we left London, I don't think. Only the odd biscuit. And she is very partial to cake.'

'She's not the only one,' Hazel said.

Alice was already on the doorstep. 'Can I ring the bell, Aunty Vi?' she asked cheerfully, reaching up for the iron bell-pull.

But the door opened before the girl was able to pull on the bell, and Violet found herself facing a severe-looking man in black clerical dress with a white dog collar. *Oh blimey,* she thought, suddenly filled with trepidation and wishing herself anywhere but there.

'Good afternoon, Vicar,' Hazel said politely, 'I believe we're expected.'

'Of course.' The vicar smiled too, looking a little less severe. 'How do you do, Mrs Baxter? And how is your son?'

'We're both very well, thank you.'

'I'm glad to hear it. And these other ladies are friends of yours, I presume.' The vicar turned to study Violet, who put her chin up and stared back at him, determined not to be intimidated by a man of the cloth. 'I don't believe we've been introduced.'

'This is Miss Hopkins, Vicar. And her two nieces, Lily and Alice.'

'How do you do,' the vicar said gravely to each of them in turn, in a voice so posh that Violet fought an urge to curtsey. 'I am Reverend Clewson.' He stood aside. 'Well, you'd better come in. My wife has arranged for tea in the sitting room.'

He watched carefully as all four of them trooped past him into the vicarage, Violet avoiding his gaze as she followed Hazel into the large, tastefully decorated sitting room. She had never liked church and all its trappings. Not since a bad day at Sunday School, when one of the old blokes helping out had put his hand up her skirt. She'd been too scared to say anything. And anyway, nobody would have believed her. But ever since then, she'd steered clear of anything to do with God, apart from her nightly prayers.

They were all introduced to the vicar's wife, Mrs Clewson, who was the wrong side of fifty and looked smart in a knee-length floral dress. Her face was powdered, with lipstick too brightly red for her age, but she had a kind smile.

'How do you do?' Mrs Clewson said, standing to shake everyone's hand, even Alice's, who gripped her hand far too tight, making the poor woman wince. 'Please, sit. I hope there are seats enough for everyone.' She turned to a young woman in a pinny who had entered the room after them. 'Kitty, bring more hot water for the tea. And four more cups. And another two chairs.' She gave Eva a thin smile, obviously a bit put out. 'Well, when you said others were coming, I didn't realise you meant so many.'

'I'm so sorry, Mrs Clewson, what an idiot I am. I'd completely forgotten the girls were coming too.' Eva smiled at them all from under the wide brim of her dark blue hat. 'But I'm so glad you could make it. We've been having a terrific chinwag here. Nearly sorted the whole business between us.'

'Though we will need to finalise the details with my husband first,' Mrs Clewson added hurriedly, glancing at her husband, who was standing in front of the unlit fireplace, his hands clasped behind his back. 'The church hall is his province, after all.'

'Of course,' Eva said, and transferred her broad smile to the vicar, who said nothing but raised his eyebrows.

'This is very kind of you,' Hazel said awkwardly.

'Not at all, Mrs Baxter.' But the vicar's wife sat down without looking at Hazel, and for the first time Violet heard a frosty note in her voice. 'You're all very welcome here. In times of war, we need to pull together.'

The words sounded pleasant enough. All the same, Violet saw Hazel flinch, and felt quite annoyed on her friend's behalf; it wasn't Hazel's fault her old man couldn't keep his hands off the bottle. But that was posh folk for you, she thought grimly, always pointing the finger of blame at somebody else, never themselves.

'And a community dance is an excellent idea,' Mrs Clewson added with careful emphasis, 'if organised correctly.'

Eva said nothing, but shot Hazel and Violet a wary look before taking charge of the fresh hot water that had arrived. 'Jolly good,' she said with forced cheeriness. 'Shall I be Mother?'

Mrs Clewson nodded, as though conferring a great favour, and Eva busied herself with topping up the large teapot and then pouring weak tea through a strainer, with a splash of milk, into dainty china cups for them all. Violet sat next to her, and Hazel sat on Eva's other side, leaving the girls to grab the remaining seats that the vicar had helped arrange around the table.

Eva handed her a cup that rattled in its thin saucer. 'There you go, Violet.'

'Thank you,' Violet breathed, and set it down as carefully as possible. The tea smelt fragrant and unlike the coarse, bitty stuff she was used to drinking, barely a fleck of tea to be seen on the surface of the milk.

The sitting room was very posh. There was a thick woollen rug underfoot and a grandfather clock in the corner was tick-tocking away in a loud, impressive manner. All the furniture was antique and well polished, not a mark in sight. Thank goodness the table was covered in an expensive white linen tablecloth, Violet thought, resting her hands lightly on it. If it had been bare wood she would have been terrified of scratching it accidentally. As it was, she dreaded spilling a drop of tea on the immaculate white linen.

Violet looked longingly at the jam-and-cream sponge cake in the centre of the table, from which two healthy slices had already been removed. But she did not dare touch anything until permission had been given. She could see Alice eyeing it too, and shot her a warning look.

Meanwhile, Mrs Clewson had been admiring Lily. 'Do pull your chair closer,' she told the girl. 'What a lovely face you have. How old are you, my dear?'

'I'll be eighteen this August,' Lily said, looking pleased.

'So soon? We have a daughter of nearly twenty. She's gone to work in Surrey. For the war effort, you know.' Mrs Clewson was smiling, but her anxiety was evident.

'I'm sure she'll be fine,' Violet said impulsively.

'Thank you.' Mrs Clewson sounded surprised, and her smile grew warmer. 'I . . . I expect she will, yes.' Then her attention was caught by Alice, whose hand had been creeping towards the silver cake knife. 'Would you like a slice of cake, my dear?' Alice, wide-eyed, nodded enthusiastically. 'Then you must allow me to cut it for you.' She cut a meagre sliver of cake, and Alice's smile faltered. 'Maybe a little more?'

'Yes, please.'

'Alice!' Lily hissed across the table.

But Alice got a thicker slice, much to her delight, and the rejected sliver of cake was handed to the vicar instead, who studied it in a disappointed manner and then retreated to an armchair on the other side of the room.

'Cake, Miss Hopkins? Mrs Baxter?'

They all got a slice of sponge cake on a delicate side plate that matched the teacups. Violet nibbled on hers at first, longing to stuff it greedily into her mouth, but aware of the vicar's wife watching them, perhaps in expectation of exactly such a breach of etiquette. It was hard to resist though; the jam was so sweet and the cream so fresh and thick, and soon it was gone and she was licking her fingertips with pleasure.

The others were tucking in with the same hungry intent too, nobody speaking except for Alice, who kept murmuring, 'Cake,' in a delirious voice.

Thankfully, Eva distracted the vicar and his wife while the others devoured their cake. 'So, Reverend, I do hope you'll lend your support to our little project. I know it must seem frivolous, dancing when there's a war on. But we're going to try to keep expenses down, and obviously any money raised from an entrance fee will go towards the church funds.' Her smile was dazzling. 'And I have to say, my father thoroughly approves. He thinks it'll be good for the men's morale.'

'Ah, Colonel Ryder.' The vicar nodded, smiling. 'How is he?'

As they discussed the colonel's health and the weather and several other topics of little interest to Violet, she met Alice's eye and surreptitiously indicated that her niece had a smear of jam her nose. Once that had been wiped off, sadly on Alice's sleeve, Violet turned her attention to finishing her tea, now lukewarm and not as fortifying as she'd hoped. But at least she didn't spill any on the tablecloth, much to her relief.

'So you're sure we don't need to provide any refreshments for this dance?' Mrs Clewson was asking. 'There'll be no expense on our part at all?'

'Absolutely not,' Eva promised her.

'Because the parish council can be rather strict about that kind of thing.'

'There's no question about it, Mrs Clewson.' Hazel leant forward. 'I've drawn up a list of the refreshments we're aiming to make for the dance. We'll be clubbing together with some other ladies in the village, and using our own rations and supplies. Nothing from the parish council. I can let you have a copy if you like.'

'Well,' Mrs Clewson sat back, eyeing her thoughtfully, 'I'm sure that won't be necessary.'

'Not necessary at all,' the vicar agreed.

'I suppose, in that case, there can be no reason for us to raise any objections. The dance can go ahead.'

Alice gave a strangled whoop, and Lily smiled happily over the rim of her teacup.

Violet nudged Eva, and grinned at her and Hazel.

They'd done it!

'Thank you so much,' Eva gushed. 'You won't regret it.'

'Well, let us hope not.'

The vicar brought his plate back to the table. 'One of you ladies will need to collect the keys two or three days before the event, so you can decorate the hall and prepare the refreshments in advance.'

'I can do that,' Hazel said bravely.

'Very good.' Mrs Clewson gave her a searching look, and

then glanced up at her husband, who was still loitering by the table. 'Was there anything else, dear?'

'Only that those persons attending your community dance should remember that the hall belongs to the church,' the Reverend Clewson said, back to his stern face again, 'and no bad behaviour can be tolerated on or around the premises.'

'Bad behaviour?' Alice echoed, looking at Violet in confusion.

'He means hanky-panky,' Violet whispered to her niece, and then blushed hotly when she saw the vicar's eyes on her. 'I mean, no . . . Of course there won't be none of that. They'll be dancing, that's all. Good, clean fun.'

'And it will all be over before dark falls,' Eva reminded them, smiling.

'Hmm,' the vicar said.

Eva stood up, still smiling. 'Well, thank you so much for your hospitality, Mrs Clewson, Reverend. We won't take up any more of your time.'

Mrs Clewson stood too as the others got up. She smiled at Alice. 'Did you enjoy your cake, dear?'

'Oh yes, it was scrummy.'

'I shall tell Kitty you said so. She made it this morning.'

'Though it weren't as good as my gran's sponge. Gran bakes the tastiest cakes in the world,' Alice said, oblivious to her hostess's dismay. 'She makes 'em at home to sell in her caff. Back in Dagenham.'

'In the East End,' Violet said, seeing Mrs Clewson's air of bewilderment. 'That's where we're from. My mum runs a little café there and I help out. Well, I used to. Now, Mum . . . My mother has to run it on her own.'

'How awful,' Mrs Clewson said, looking sympathetic.

Violet nodded. 'We came down 'ere to get away from the air raids, see.'

'And the street gangs,' Alice added knowledgeably.

Lily, hurriedly finishing her cuppa, almost choked on the tea she'd just gulped down. 'Alice!'

Thankfully, Mrs Clewson didn't seem to have noticed, the vicar's wife already asking Violet about the air raids in London.

'Is it very bad in London? We hear such terrible stories . . .'

Violet hesitated. 'It's pretty bad. My sister Betsy . . .' But her voice gave out, and she found herself swallowing hard, tears blurring her vision. She'd had no time to fret about Betsy's death since coming down to Cornwall, but saying her sister's name had set her off without warning. 'There was a bomb. A big 'un. It flattened the whole house. Betsy had just gone back in and . . .'

Alice came round the table and gave her a tight hug.

'I'm so sorry.' Mrs Clewson had tears in her eyes too. 'But you girls survived. That's a . . . a blessing, isn't it?'

'Amen,' the vicar said solemnly.

Eva gave her a hug too. 'Oh, you poor thing.' She put her arms around the girls too, and bent to kiss Lily's cheek, who was looking rather pale. 'Something similar happened to a dear friend of mine too. This bloody war! Pardon my French, Vicar.' Her smile wobbled but she added firmly, 'That's just the way of it, though. We've all to look out for each other now, haven't we?'

The vicar cleared his throat, and said something about making sure the church hall was tidied up at the end of the dance, but his wife paid no attention.

'It was so nice to meet you all,' Mrs Clewson said, steering them into the hall. She pressed a biscuit each into Alice and Lily's palms. 'Here, for the drive home.' Then nodded to Eva. 'Do give your father our kind regards, Miss Ryder.'

'Of course, and thank you for the tea and cake. Delicious!'

They all thanked the couple profusely as they trailed out into the afternoon sunlight. Violet gave the girls a quick hug once the door had closed behind them, worried they might have been upset by that mention of their mother's death. But Alice smiled at her bravely, already tucking into her biscuit, and Lily, who was saving hers for later, merely whispered, 'I'm all right, Aunty Vi.'

Reaching the green army truck, Eva turned to wait for them. The corporal, who had hurriedly stubbed out his cigarette when he saw her coming, was already inside at the wheel.

'Excellent work – that went better than expected,' Eva told them briskly. 'So you know the drill. I'm going to organise a band to come and play for us. No dancing without music, after all. Meanwhile, posters need to be finished and up about the place within the next few days. Spread the word among the other staff at Eastern House. And I'll get Geoff over there,' she said, nodding over her shoulder at the soldier, 'to tell all his mates in the camp. Then Hazel collects the key, we make most of the refreshments at home, and turn up on the day two hours before the hall doors open.' She hesitated, glancing anxiously at Violet. 'If that timing fits with your work schedule?'

'I'll have a chat with Mr Frobisher,' Violet told her, not without inwardly quaking. 'See if me and the girls can get off early that day.'

'Me too,' Hazel agreed.

'Good show.' Eva grinned at them all. 'Well, ladies, it looks like we're putting on a summer dance. Can't wait to get dolled up and have a proper spin around the dance floor at last. How about you?'

'Sounds lovely,' Lily said, wreathed in smiles.

Violet gave her a sharp look. 'You and your sister will be

helping with refreshments, missy. Not getting all dolled up and dancing. You're not eighteen yet, you know.'

'Oh, but—'

'I'll dance with you, sis,' Alice said stoutly.

Lily suddenly glowered. 'That don't seem fair, Aunty Vi. Not when we're helping with the posters and refreshments.' When Violet began to speak, she cut across her, blurting out, 'And we both know you'll be dancing with Joe, if he goes.'

Eva's brows shot up. 'Joe? Who's Joe?'

'Nobody,' Violet said shortly, and silenced her nieces with a look.

CHAPTER TWENTY-EIGHT

Hazel finished cutting the last of yesterday's brown loaf into wafer-thin slices, ready for an even thinner layer of butter, and laid down the bread knife with a sigh. No fried or scrambled or poached eggs for breakfast today, sadly, only bacon and buttered bread. Henny Penny had stopped laying a few days ago, after a near-fatal brush with a passing fox, and who knew when she might produce more eggs? And while Hazel might be able to make vaguely edible sponge cake with powdered egg, there was no way to fry it!

Frankly, she didn't know where the time had gone. Almost three weeks had passed since Eva had persuaded the vicar and his wife to let them use the church hall for a dance, and the big event itself was now only days away. They had decided on a Friday night before the moon was full again, so it was light enough to walk home, but not so light that they'd make a target for a bomber. And although only a few soldiers would not be on active duty that evening, the colonel had apparently agreed to allow those who wished to attend the dance to do so. Which meant more partners to go around.

It was hard to get excited when there was still so much to

do. Yet somehow Violet's nieces were not put off by the amount of hard work, squealing with excitement every time the dance was mentioned. Especially Lily, who she could not help noticing had developed a crush on Charlie.

Lily was older than Charlie, of course. But there were few young men near her age in Porthcurno, unless you counted the wet-behind-the-ears recruits, and Lily seemed to have little time for soldiers. The girl clapped her hands over her ears whenever a plane flew overhead, and barely glanced at the boys in uniform at the Porthcurno encampment, a tented barracks that seemed to have doubled in size since they started work at Eastern House.

'The government are keen to protect their assets,' George had told her only the other day, after a new convoy of troop trucks turned up at the barrier into the camp. 'They're extending the sea defences further along the coast, so more men are needed to dig holes and patrol the coastline.'

Hazel had been unnerved by this. 'Do the Germans definitely know about Porthcurno, then?'

But he had refused to say any more, turning the subject back to matters closer to home. 'How's Charlie these days?'

Hazel had bitten her lip, wishing he had not asked that question.

She started buttering the bread while keeping an eye on the bacon slices, which were curling saltily in the pan now, the fat browning nicely.

George had not come near the house since the evening of Charlie's 'fight' with him, much to Hazel's relief. She loved her boy and hated the thought that she'd turned him against her, even if he had calmed down somewhat in recent days.

But what a stupid thing to do!

It wasn't that she regretted kissing George, as those few minutes in his arms had been the most marvellous thing she'd ever experienced. That kiss had shown her, once and for all, that her marriage to Bertie was dead. Because there was no way on God's earth that she could have felt so wonderful kissing another man, if she had even a shred of love left for her husband. All his years of drunken fights and jealous rantings had turned her heart cold towards him.

But she deeply regretted letting Charlie see her kissing George. That had been a wicked thing for a mother to do, and she winced whenever she remembered it. Purely an accident. But dreadful, nonetheless. She still didn't quite know what had possessed her to kiss him. Except that it was something she'd been dreaming about for ages, and suddenly could no longer resist. And she knew in her heart that George felt the same about her.

Meanwhile, Charlie had barely spoken to her since that night.

'He'll come around,' Violet kept telling her.

But how on earth could she believe that? Charlie spent less and less time in the house, preferring to sit in the ancient shed out back, as his father had often done after an argument, among the cobwebby pots and gardening tools. The boy was like a stranger these days, looking the other way whenever she tried to have a conversation, or just stamping sulkily out of the house.

Lily came hurrying into the kitchen. 'I can't find my work shoes,' she declared, a little panicked. 'I've looked everywhere.'

'Where did you take them off?' Hazel asked.

Lily thought for a moment, then brightened. 'In the sitting room. Alice and I were playing cards with Charlie last night, to celebrate him leaving school. Maybe I kicked them off under the sofa.'

She scampered off to find them.

Violet came downstairs, tying her work headscarf over smooth rolls of fair hair. Behind her trailed Alice, her nose in a book as usual.

'Breakfast, is that?' Violet asked, peering over her shoulder at the buttered slices of bread. 'The bacon smells bloody gorgeous.'

'Is there enough for all of us?' Alice sat down at the table, still reading. 'I had to share my bacon with Lily yesterday.'

'I'm sorry about that, love,' Hazel said, feeling awkward. These were her house guests, after all, and she felt responsible for feeding them all adequately. 'I've done what I could with the ration books you gave me. But you know what it's like. Everything's scarce these days, even the home-grown veg. Besides, Mr Cuthbert only comes around with the butcher's van once a week, and the cupboard's bare until tomorrow.' She paused, nodding towards the labelled can she'd left out on the dresser. 'Except for that new American stuff. But I'm saving that for tonight's supper.'

Violet picked up the can, frowning at the label. 'Specially Pressed American Meat? What on earth is that?'

'The butcher says people are calling it "spam" for short. It's cheap, whatever it is. Thought I'd give it a whirl once the real meat had run out.'

'I get so hungry these days, I'd probably eat shoe leather if it was dipped in gravy,' Alice moaned, looking up from her book with a doleful expression.

They all laughed, though it wasn't that funny.

'Blimey, watch out, that bacon's going to burn!' Violet made a lunge for the frying pan, grabbing it off the stove top. 'Think I saved it just in time,' she said breathlessly, laughing as she turned the meaty slices over with a fork. 'I like my bacon crispy. But not black.'

Hazel became aware of Lily standing in the doorway. The

girl was very pale, wordlessly holding up an old dark green canvas bag, its thin sides bulging, for them all to see.

'What's the matter, love?' Hazel asked her, carrying the buttered bread to the table with one eye on the clock. They no longer had to leave for work so early, now they had a vehicle of their own. But it was surprisingly easy to get carried away and end up being late anyway. 'What have you got there? That looks like Charlie's old school satchel.' She frowned, perplexed and a little worried by the girl's continuing silence. 'Where did you find that?'

'Under the bloody sofa,' Lily croaked, and Hazel could see tears in her eyes.

'Language, young lady,' Violet reprimanded her sharply.

Hazel said, 'I don't understand.'

'He's been keeping it hidden from us. All this time.' Lily dropped the satchel on the table and emptied it out. 'So we wouldn't know what he was planning.'

'Careful of those slices of bread . . .' Hazel stopped and stared at the contents of her son's old satchel. 'What on earth . . . ?'

The satchel held a change of clothes, a spare pair of socks, a book, folded papers of some kind, and her husband's second-best tobacco tin, battered and dented, with BERTIE scratched across the lid. He'd given it to Charlie at the start of the war, even though the boy didn't smoke, of course. It had been intended as a joke present, one that would annoy Hazel, as he knew she didn't want her son to take up smoking; it was such a filthy habit. But Charlie had treasured the baccy tin ever since.

Lily pulled out one of the folded papers, opened it with a flourish and handed it to Hazel. 'See? Do you see what it is?' she demanded, her tone hysterical.

'Calm down, please,' her aunt said, arms folded across her chest in a disapproving manner, but Lily continued to ignore her.

'*Dear Master Charles Baxter, I am pleased to inform you that . . .*'

Baffled, Hazel had to read through the typed sheet and its blunt message several times before she fully understood what she was looking at.

Then she gasped, and put a shaking hand to her mouth.

'What is it, love? Christ, you look bloody awful.' Violet put the pan of bacon back on the now-cold stove, staring at her. 'Hazel?'

'He . . . He's enlisted!' Hazel could not seem to breathe properly, her chest was so tight. She handed the official letter to her friend; her vision was too blurred with tears to see the words anyway. 'My boy, my Charlie . . . He's only gone and joined up!'

'Bleedin' 'eck!'

Lily, who had clearly read the document when she first found the satchel, buried her face in her hands and began to weep noisily.

Alice looked shocked, putting her book down at last. 'That can't be right. Oh, do pipe down, Lily. Your nose is turning red. What does the letter say, Aunty Vi?'

'It says that Charlie's to report to the barracks outside Penzance next week. Then he'll be assigned to a training centre somewhere in England.' Violet gave Hazel a sympathetic look. 'He's done it behind your back, after everything you said to him. You poor thing!'

'Well, it's obvious he can't go,' Alice said firmly, also scrutinising the letter before folding it up again and placing it on top of Charlie's spare socks. 'He's too young, for starters. And too stupid. Who hides their running-away bag under the sofa, for goodness' sake?' Then she made a face. 'Though I suppose we've nabbed his bedroom, so he can't have had many hiding places to choose from.'

'You're right, I didn't,' Charlie said angrily from the doorway.

Hazel sat down abruptly at the table, her legs trembling so hard she was no longer sure they could support her.

Her son, who had been outside in the back garden all that time – conscientiously keeping out of everyone's way while they got ready for work, or so Hazel had thought – had come back in, and was glaring at the contents of his satchel littering the kitchen table.

'Is it true?' Lily half-ran at him, but stopped short, her face crumpling to tears. 'Are you g-g-going to war?' When he said nothing, his face averted, she shouted, 'You stupid boy! I hate you!' Then she ran upstairs and into the room that used to be his, slamming the door so hard the whole house shook.

Aghast, Hazel looked across at her son, one fat tear rolling down her cheek, swiftly followed by another. 'Oh, Charlie, whatever have you done?'

'What I told you I was going to do,' he defended himself stoutly, and began stuffing his belongings back into his old satchel. 'I've enlisted, and I'll be shipping out to join my dad and the others as soon as I've finished my basic.'

'But you're still a schoolboy!'

'No, Mum, I've finished with school. I'm a soldier now. Or as g-good as.' His voice shook on those last words, and she guessed his bravado was just for show. 'Anyway, it's done now. And you were wrong. It was just like my mate Louis told me. The army took me, no questions asked.'

'And has Louis joined up too?'

'That's right. We'll both be going out there together, to do our bit.' He fastened the satchel with clumsy fingers, defiance in his face. 'And nobody can stop us.'

Hazel did not know what to say or do that might stop her

precious boy from throwing his life away. But her heart was breaking. She had never felt more helpless in her whole life.

Violet had stood without comment all this while, listening intently to their exchange. Now that Hazel had fallen silent, she launched into a tirade, tearing a strip off the boy while he glared at her, not interrupting but not seeming guilty either. 'Talk about ungrateful,' she finished, shaking her head in disgust. 'Your mum needs you, or hadn't you noticed? Poor thing, she's worked all the hours God sends, and even gone without, to keep food on *your* bloody plate. And now you're going to turn your back on her, and for what? So you can join your good-for-nothing father and his mates out at the front . . .'

'Don't you dare speak like that about my dad!' Charlie yelled back at her suddenly, his cheeks flushed. 'He's not good-for-nothing. You don't even know him.'

'I know what he's done to your mum. She's told me.'

His furious glare turned on Hazel. 'What have you been saying about Dad? That's not right, telling fibs about a man when he's not even here to defend himself. When he's out there, risking his life every day, fighting for his country.' Charlie slung the satchel over his shoulder as though ready to march to war right there and then. 'You're not fit to be his wife! And what's more, you're not bloody fit to be my mum!'

'Charlie . . . !' Hazel wailed. That was too much for any woman to hear from her own son. She gave a great, gasping sob, and buried her face in her hands.

There was a knock at the door. Not a polite knock, but a loud, insistent thump that made Hazel sit up in a panic, her heart beating fast. She lifted the hem of her blue cotton pinny and dried her eyes with it.

'Who on earth . . . ?' Alice said, going to the front door

and peering out of the narrow side window. 'It's a young lad in uniform.'

Hazel clutched her chest in terror. Had they come for her son already?

Charlie stood in a daze too, his eyes on her face.

'See what he wants, Alice, there's a dear.' Violet stooped over Hazel, rubbing her back as she gasped for air. 'Now, deep breaths, Hazel. That's it,' she said reassuringly. 'Nice and slow. In through the nose, out through the mouth.'

Everything around her a fog, Hazel heard the front door open, a few muttered words between Alice and the visitor, then the door close again.

'Oh, what is it? Please, someone tell me.' She felt Violet push a hot mug of tea between her hands, and shook her head vehemently, thrusting it away. 'I don't want a drink. I want to know what's happening. Who was at the door?'

Alice came back into the kitchen, holding something in her hands. Some kind of buff envelope, it looked like. Her face was ashen.

'It's for you,' she whispered, reading off the name on the envelope. 'Mrs Albert Baxter. That's you, Hazel, isn't it?' She handed it to Violet first though, not to Hazel. 'It came with one of them telegram boys.'

A telegram boy. Everyone knew what that meant. Hazel felt utterly numb inside. She was shaking from head to toe though, like she had a high fever. It was warm in the small kitchen, but her teeth were chattering.

'He brought a telegram? For me?' She stared at the buff envelope as Violet held it out, and shook her head. 'Oh God, no, I can't.' She felt a familiar sickness, deep down, and covered her mouth, thinking of the baby inside. Poor little lamb. What kind of future would it have? 'Open it for me, Vi, would you?'

'Hazel—'

'If it's bad news, I don't want to hear it. I don't think I can cope. Not now, not today.' She saw Charlie's face, his eyes wide and very dark in a pale face, and a wave of love and sympathy crashed over her. After all his fury only moments before, he looked so forlorn and lost. She would have to be strong for him, at least. 'Come here, Charlie. I need someone to hold my hand.'

But he ignored her, standing mute and unmoving.

Violet tore open the telegram, and read the words aloud in a flat voice. *'We regret to inform you that your husband, Corporal Albert Baxter, has been killed in action. Letter to follow.'*

Before she had even finished, Charlie gave a terrible howl like a wounded animal and fled through the front door, running out of the house.

Hazel called after him in vain, then sank back down, weeping for the man she had once loved enough to walk up the aisle with, for her son, for her unborn child . . .

CHAPTER TWENTY-NINE

Without Hazel, the domestic staff were short-handed at Eastern House. Violet's feet were soon aching as she traipsed about the place, doing the work of two women instead of one. But it was only right, Mr Frobisher had agreed solemnly, on hearing of her loss, that Mrs Baxter should have a few days off work to deal with her sudden bereavement. Not that Hazel had wanted to stay at home. But when she'd driven them all into work that morning, a little later than usual, Hazel had gone to see George Cotterill straightaway. And had told Lily in passing, when she re-emerged from his office half an hour later, red-eyed, that she'd been instructed to go back home.

After several hours spent cleaning and chopping vegetables, Violet hurried out during her luncheon break to find Eva, grabbing a raw carrot to munch on her way. She regretted missing a proper cooked lunch, but this mission was more important. *More than ever,* she thought, *we need something to cheer us up and take us out of ourselves. And this dance might be just the thing.*

She passed Lily and Alice just outside the mess. The two girls had asked permission from George Cotterill to put up posters around the place and Lily was pinning one to a wall near the entrance door. They had already put some up in the village and on the church noticeboard too, making sure everyone in Porthcurno knew about the dance.

'Don't forget to have lunch,' Violet reminded them both.

'Yes, Aunty Vi,' Alice said, then added with a sly grin, 'Though Lily's watching her figure. So she looks good at the dance.'

'Lily?' Violet stopped to stare at her niece. 'Please tell me that's not true. You girls need to eat properly.'

But Lily only blushed and busied herself with the poster she was pinning to the wall.

'I'll talk to you later.' Violet shook her head, and headed outside.

What Lily needed were some sober words of wisdom about boys, like her mum would have given her if she'd been alive. But right now, Violet couldn't think of any wisdom worth handing on. Not when she herself couldn't get Joe Postbridge out of her mind. And she knew both girls had been left upset by Charlie's distress over his dad's death. Going easy on them had to be her priority right now.

Eva was sunbathing on the lawn, as always during lunch breaks. Though today she was flicking through a small booklet too, her face intent.

'Oh, fantastic, you got my message,' Eva said, looking up with a smile as Violet reached her. She closed the booklet and slipped it back into the pocket of her skirt with odd haste, almost as though she didn't want Violet to see what she was reading. 'I had a visit from the rather fearful Reverend Clewson this morning. Did you know, he had all but decided to cancel the dance on Friday?'

Violet stared, horrified. 'Lord, no! What the bleedin' 'eck . . . ?'

252

'I believe tales of planned debauchery had reached his ears.'

'What?'

'Ridiculous, I know.' Eva picked up the sandwich she'd been eating and grimaced at it, then put it down again. 'Reverend Clewson demanded to know exactly how many people were coming to our shindig. He seemed to be under the impression that we were inviting thousands of sinful, godless soldiers, with only one thing on their minds. I told him it would only be a few dozen clean-cut soldiers, plus some very well-brought-up ladies, upon which he relented . . . and even agreed to provide home-made cakes courtesy of his wife, as a kind of apology.' Eva grinned at her expression. 'So, it's all sorted.'

'But whoever could have told him such a load of old cobblers?' Violet was bristling with indignation.

'Who indeed?' Eva raised her eyebrows, then leant forward and whispered, 'I was given to understand that the information came from the kitchens. Apparently, you ladies have a tendency to gossip while preparing meals, and Mr Frobisher likes to listen.'

'Frobisher?'

'It seems he's one of Reverend Clewson's flock. And he likes to gossip too, by all accounts. To the vicar's wife, no less.'

'Bleeding traitor!'

'Well, quite. But I think I've scotched that rumour, so no need to worry too much.' Eva glanced up as the sun went behind a cloud, and shivered. 'Probably best to watch what you're saying when Frobisher's about, though. You have a spy in your midst.'

Violet clutched her stomach, suddenly uncomfortable. 'A what? A spy?'

'Oh, I didn't mean for the enemy. The man just likes to be officious, that's all.' Eva peered at her, frowning. 'You all right? You look peaky.'

'Right as rain,' Violet said stoutly, though in truth the conversation had left her on edge. Stupid, to be harking back to the bad times they'd suffered in Dagenham. This was another world, wasn't it? 'I s'pose you won't have heard the news yet? About Hazel's old man?'

'Not a word.'

Briefly, leaving out the more private details, like Hazel's pregnancy, Violet told Eva about the telegram, and Hazel's absence from work today.

'Poor Hazel, she's in a bad way over it,' she finished. 'Though her son's taking it hardest, if you ask me.'

'Charlie?'

'That's right.' Violet shook her head in disapproval. 'The lad scarpered, soon as he heard the news. I only hope he turns up soon. His mum'll be going out of her mind with worry.'

Eva looked thoughtful. 'Was it a happy marriage?'

Violet bit her lip, not knowing what to say and unwilling to heap blame on a dead man's reputation. *Speak no ill of the dead* was what her mum always said. Even the most curmudgeonly of their neighbours had become saints, according to Mum, as soon as Saint Peter had met them at the pearly gates.

'I thought as much' was all Eva said, sparing her the need to say anything. 'And I do hope Charlie realises how much his mother needs him, and goes back home.'

'You can say that again.' Though the way the boy had been behaving, she thought secretly, there was little chance of that. All the same, she dredged up a lopsided smile. 'So, it's all on again? The dance, that is. The girls have been putting up posters, like we agreed. Should be a damn good bash, and no mistake.'

'It's going to be splendid.'

Hurriedly, aware of their time running short, they spent the next few minutes going over the arrangements for the dance: who was bringing what, what time they'd all meet up, and who might be expected to turn up.

'And what about you?' Eva asked at the end, her grin teasing. 'I believe you have a beau lined up for the dance. Joe – was that his name?'

The posh girl was too bloody good at remembering things, Violet thought, feeling her cheeks redden. If only Lily hadn't mentioned his name in front of her . . .

'I don't know about that,' she mumbled, looking away. 'The man's got his own business to attend to. I doubt he even remembers my name.'

'Oh dear. What a slow-poke this Joe must be.'

Violet felt her temper rise and excused herself before she could say something that might cause offence. But she practically ran back to the kitchen, barely glancing at the soldiers she passed in the corridor, her head whirling with a mass of new possibilities that were both disturbing and exciting.

The dance was going to be 'splendid', all right. Something to break the daily boredom and drudgery of their work at Eastern House. But now she couldn't stop imagining how it would be if a certain Joe Postbridge walked in the door . . .

When Violet and the girls started to walk home at the end of their shift, she was surprised to see the old ambulance parked up on the verge just beyond the barrier.

'It's Aunty Hazel!' Lily cried, pointing.

'That's Mrs Baxter to you,' Violet reminded her, though she knew Hazel rather liked being called 'Aunty' by the girls. 'Careful now, watch those trucks.'

A convoy of new troops had just arrived, three dust-streaked trucks pulled up on the road while the sentry checked their documentation. They slipped between the trucks, glancing briefly inside. Men in uniform stared out at them, their faces weary and flushed with heat, but excited too. They had finally arrived at their destination, after all. God knew how far they'd come, Violet thought, sure she wouldn't want to spend hours being bumped about in the back of one of those crowded trucks. Cornwall was a long way from everywhere.

Lily had reached the old ambulance. She dragged open the passenger door and stared in, her face glowing. 'Has Charlie come back yet?'

Crossly, Violet pulled her away. 'In the back,' she told the two girls in a voice that would normally leave them quaking, but today only made them traipse slowly round to the rear of the vehicle. She climbed in beside her friend, ready with a sympathetic smile. One look at her face had told her that Charlie was not yet home. 'Good of you to drive over for us. How you bearing up, love?'

'A letter came for you late morning,' Hazel said by way of response, speaking softly so the girls in the back wouldn't hear. 'I hope it's not b-bad news.'

Violet could see that Hazel had been crying, and was ready to cry again, by the shake in her voice. She took the flimsy envelope from her friend, desperate to reassure her. But how could she, when she knew how bad the situation was in London these days? They'd all seen the newspapers and heard the whispers. Bombing had intensified in recent weeks, and loss of life had risen steeply, even though so many had already left the capital. And her mum hadn't replied to her last letter, which wasn't like her. That was what she'd been worrying about, at the back of her mind . . .

But the handwriting on the letter looked like her mum's. So she was still alive, whatever else might have happened.

'You'll want to read that on your own, I expect,' Hazel said quietly, watching her.

'Five minutes. Will you wait?'

'Of course.'

Violet got out again and shut the door, then walked hurriedly away from the vehicle, head down, not wanting to catch anyone's eye.

She tore open the envelope and read the contents swiftly, her heart beating fast. The butcher's shop next to the café had taken a direct hit, and there wasn't much left but a crater in the ground. Miraculously, the café was still standing. But the air-raid wardens had told her the building wasn't safe, and had closed the premises by official order.

That had been bad enough. But two nights later, a bomb had exploded near the shelter at the end of their road. A few people near the entrance had been killed, and her mum herself had been hurt, taken to hospital with a broken arm and a few fractured ribs.

'Oh my God!' Violet exclaimed, her hand over her mouth.

'It's nothing too serious,' her mum had written with a flourish, trying to play down the incident.

But Sheila had decided to leave the East End. She was planning to take a train down to join them in Cornwall, as soon as she could scrape together the fare. Obviously, given the awkward situation over Uncle Stanley, she couldn't stay with her sister, and wanted to know if there was space for her at Hazel's.

Nothing too serious . . .

Violet was crying, despite her best intentions. She should have been there for her mum. Not down here in Cornwall. Who was looking after Mum? She had a broken arm, for

God's sake. Broken ribs too. How could she manage to do everyday things for herself? Was she in pain? How was she coping?

'You all right, love?' one of the newly arrived soldiers asked as he and the rest of his mates jumped down from the truck into the road. 'Bad news?'

He sounded friendly enough. But she couldn't speak, her throat clogged up with tears. She muttered something, she didn't know what. Then made her way back blindly, stumbling, to where Hazel had parked the old ambulance.

''Ere, watch out,' one of the other soldiers complained in an East End accent as she blundered through their little group, by his voice she guessed not much older than Charlie. He was lighting a cigarette, hands cupped in front of his face. 'Don't touch what you can't afford!'

The men around him laughed.

She looked round crossly, tempted to give him a piece of her mind. Then stiffened, recognising him too late. That sharp face, the pale eyes, the narrow chin . . .

Patrick Dullaghan!

She lowered her head again and hurried on, praying he hadn't realised who she was. She had no wish to speak to the nasty bully who'd made her and Mum's life a misery back in Dagenham.

But it was too late.

'Well, well,' Patrick called after her, malice in his voice, 'if it isn't Vicious Violet. I'd heard you and that German spy's kids were snug down here in Cornwall, safe from the bombs. But I didn't expect to find you somewhere *top secret*.' She ignored him, not looking back. But that tactic had never worked in Dagenham and it didn't work now. 'I do 'ope the brass know about your family, that they ain't trusting you near any *sensitive* information. Because they shoot spies, don't they?'

Violet didn't respond.

Back in the East End, she might have stopped and given the little thug what for. But things had changed, and she was no longer on her own territory.

As soon as she got into the old ambulance, Hazel started the engine without comment, and they got going. It was unlikely she'd even heard that exchange, thank God. But this wouldn't be the end of it.

Violet sat staring ahead, her mum's letter crumpled in her fist, her heart thumping hard under her ribs. Patrick bloody Dullaghan. Here in Cornwall.

Talk about a bad penny!

Surely the mean little sod wasn't old enough to have joined up? Though maybe, like Charlie, he'd managed to find a recruiting sergeant willing to turn a blind eye to his age, or perhaps he'd even doctored his papers to get in. Probably running from some trouble back in London. He and his mates had always had their fingers in some dirty pie or other. 'Cold-blooded criminals,' her mum had always called them, warning her to steer clear of their gang.

However he'd done it, it seemed he was in the army now, and stationed in Porthcurno, of all places. And that meant an end to their peaceful life here. Because a nasty lad like Patrick Dullaghan took pleasure from other people's misery and misfortunes, and if they didn't have any, he'd go out of his way to cause them.

I do 'ope the brass know about your family, that they ain't trusting you near any sensitive information.

Oh yes, she knew what that threat meant.

She'd thought, by escaping to the other end of the country, that she would have left behind all those horrible suspicions about her missing brother-in-law, Ernst. But they had followed her, and now she didn't have a clue what to do.

What would Eva say when she found out? More to the point, what would her father, the colonel, do when he found out someone with links to a suspected spy had access to the underground listening post?

They shoot spies, don't they?

CHAPTER THIRTY

It was Friday morning, the day of the dance, before Eva got a proper chance to speak to her father alone. The colonel was so busy these days, as more soldiers arrived to reinforce the defences surrounding the camp, it was hard to pin him down. But she desperately needed to ask him about Rex. It wasn't exactly that she distrusted the professor; that would be absurd. But she did wonder if there was more going on with him than anyone realised. At times, she wondered rather romantically if perhaps he had some secret mission, and it was causing him to act a little oddly. But the logical side of her brain told her not to be too trusting. Up on the cliff edge, right after he kissed her, she'd had the most disturbing notion that he was thinking of tossing her to her death on the rocks below.

But why on earth would he want to?

Maybe she'd simply imagined it. The summer continued to be blisteringly hot, often unbearably so, and she knew a touch of sunstroke could do funny things to people.

Nonetheless, she decided to ask her father about him. Just in case.

Getting up fearsomely early so as not to miss him, she found him still at breakfast in the officers' quarters, along with a few others also there still finishing their scanty meals.

'Good morning, Daddy!' She sat down next to him with a ready smile. 'Now, you haven't forgotten about this dance that we've got planned, have you?'

'What's that, m'dear?' The colonel looked at her absent-mindedly over the top of the newspaper he was reading. 'Oh yes, the church hall dance. My ADC did remind me about it yesterday. Well, I'm no spoilsport. So long as the men involved are back in barracks before curfew, and don't make a nuisance of themselves, I'm sure I don't object to a spot of dancing.'

'Thank you, Daddy. I knew you'd understand.' She beamed at him approvingly, then hesitated, aware of the others looking their way. 'By the way, is there any chance of a private word later?'

Her request seemed to filter through. His eyes narrowed suspiciously on her face, and he lowered the broadsheet to give her his full attention. 'Trouble with the professor?'

It was almost as though he could read her mind!

She bit her lip, looking round at the other officers.

'Walk with me.' Her father folded the newspaper, tucked it under his arm, and nodded to the men still at breakfast before bustling her out of the door. 'Two minutes. That's all I can spare you, Eva.'

'Daddy!'

'I know you're my daughter, but duty calls.'

Eva pursed her lips, but didn't bother pointing out that duty only seemed to call when it meant her father could avoid spending time with her.

She waited until they were outside, crossing the lawn to

Eastern House and no longer in earshot of anyone, before blurting out, 'I think Rex wants to kill me!'

Colonel Ryder stopped dead and stared at her. 'I beg your pardon?'

'Well, I can't be absolutely sure,' she conceded, a little concerned by his expression. She didn't want to get an innocent man into hot water over nothing. 'But I got the oddest feeling when he was kissing me . . .'

'When he was *what*?' he thundered.

'Daddy, do pay attention. We were up on the clifftops the other evening for a picnic. And when Rex kissed me—'

'Stop right there. First of all, who in God's name is this Rex character?'

'Professor Templeton, of course.'

'Templeton?' He looked astonished. 'But I thought his first name was Reginald.'

'Well, it is. Only he prefers Rex.'

'Wants you to call him Rex, does he?'

She got the impression her father was about to explode. Which was something she should probably avoid, if possible.

'Anyway, that's not the point.' She drew a deep breath, then hurried on when his mouth opened again, hoping to forestall him, 'The point is, I made the mistake of mentioning a top-secret message—'

'*Top secret* . . . !' Now he looked like he was having a bilious attack. 'Keep your voice down, girl!'

'Don't worry, I'm not going to repeat it here. Only I *did* repeat it to Rex, because we were all alone up there, and then I got the most awful feeling he was planning to throw me off the cliff. Only he changed his mind.'

'Good grief . . .' Her father groaned and clutched his forehead, the newspaper under his arm dropping to the grass as he did so.

263

'I know, it is rather unsettling. What do you think I should do?'

'Do?' He stooped to retrieve *The Times*, and then straightened, glaring at her as he rolled it feverishly into a cylinder again. 'Stay the hell away from clifftops and picnics and fellows called Rex – that's what I think you should do.'

'Daddy!'

'My God, whatever will you say next? You can't go around accusing people of trying to murder you. It's simply not the done thing. Besides which, Professor Templeton is one of our top men. He was sent here specially from Communications HQ in London, and I won't have him maligned.' His eyes flashed at her. 'Or seduced.'

'I say, that's not very fair—'

'Mark my words, Eva, if anyone's ever been tempted to throw you off a cliff, it's me, your long-suffering father.' With that unnecessary remark, the colonel strode away, shaking his head and muttering, 'What was I thinking, bringing the damned girl down here during a war to pester me? *Trying to kill her!* Whatever next . . . ?'

Eva frowned, chewing on her lip as her father disappeared into the deep shadow surrounding Eastern House. Oh dear. That conversation hadn't gone as well as she'd hoped. In fact, he'd seemed more concerned for his blessed professor than for his own daughter. *He was sent here specially from Communications HQ in London.* How very important-sounding. That presumably gave a man the right to toss people off cliffs willy-nilly, she thought crossly.

But at least the colonel hadn't vetoed the dance at the church hall tonight.

Rex had promised he'd be there.

Time for a little amateur sleuthing, perhaps.

*

Hearing the buzz of conversation gradually rise to a cacophony of voices, Eva peered round the door of the church's kitchen, and her eyes widened in shock.

The small hall was packed. So tightly packed, in fact, she could only see a crowd of uniforms, cap badges, smart frocks, hats, and smiling faces . . .

'Soldiers, soldiers, everywhere . . .' she murmured, a slow smile creeping across her face. The word had gone out, and it looked like dozens were still trying to get in. 'Goodness me. This is going to be a humdinger of a dance!'

'Blimey!' Lily came to stand in the doorway too, her face flushed and excited. She wiped her hands on her pinny, wide-eyed, staring past Eva. 'I hope we'll have enough refreshments to go around. Look at 'em all.'

It was only seven o'clock and still bright outside, the steady glow of evening sunshine filling the hall through generous windows. It had been a lovely summer's day, and the hall was sunny and warm. A mite *too* warm, Eve thought, fanning herself with her hand as she returned to making the refreshments.

'The fruit punch won't last long in this heat,' Alice said, preparing to carry the large bowl brimming with locally donated fruit through to the hall. 'Especially once they realise there's a splash of gin in the mix . . .'

Eva grinned. 'Shh, not so loud!'

She held the door open as Alice passed through with hesitant steps, her expression tense as the girl attempted not to spill the punch before it reached its final destination on the refreshments trestle table.

Much to Eva's admiration, Hazel had bravely volunteered to help Violet take money on the door, despite her bereavement. She stopped beside Hazel, who was checking the change in her money tin, and put a hand on her shoulder.

'Hazel, how are you doing?' Eva asked gently. 'I was so sorry to hear about your husband.'

Hazel managed a smile. 'Thank you.'

'I'm glad you were able to make it tonight though. All these people . . . I don't know how we would have managed without you on the door.'

Hazel looked troubled. 'I daresay folk will talk, seeing me here. But I'd rather be busy than sitting on my own in a dark house, worrying about Charlie. Besides,' she added, biting her lip, 'I'm hoping to ask around about him later. Someone must have seen him.'

'I heard he'd run away, poor boy.'

'He'll turn up soon enough,' Hazel told her, though she didn't sound too convinced. She looked hurriedly away as more soldiers poured in through the door, saying, 'Good evening, gents. It's a shilling a head, please.'

The vicar's wife had persuaded some parishioners to part with a little food, including home-grown fruit and veg from their own gardens, to help make this dance a success. 'Anything for our brave lads,' Mrs Clewson had told them when they'd wandered, astonished, into the kitchen area of the church hall, to find fresh produce set out there, along with a few dusty bottles of home-made wine. 'Just make sure the band isn't too loud.'

The 'band' had arrived mere minutes after them, a motley crew consisting mainly of elderly gentlemen and young boys, bristling with steely tubas and French horns, since all the other players had enlisted. Not exactly what Eva had envisaged when she asked around for a band to play at the dance. But they seemed cheerful enough, and had immediately begun setting up on the low dais at the far end of the hall, waving away any suggestion of payment.

'Though a jug of beer at half-time wouldn't go amiss,' one

old boy said, winking at Lily, who had blushed fierily and almost run back into the kitchen.

Suddenly it was Eva's own turn to blush.

'Hullo again, Miss Ryder,' a cultured voice said, and she turned to find Rex in the doorway, his hat set at a dashing angle, spectacles in hand, smiling at her so charmingly she felt her tummy turn over. 'I say, you look busy. How are the preparations going?'

'Swimmingly,' she said, chin up.

'Good-o.' The brass band stuck up at that moment, a stirring tune that was more patriotic than melodic. Rex grinned, raising his eyebrows. 'I shall expect a twirl about the hall with you later, did I mention that?' He gave her stained pinny a quick glance. 'Assuming you're permitted to leave the kitchen, Cinders?'

'I'd love to dance,' Eva said smoothly, ignoring his jibe.

That was no exaggeration. She certainly would enjoy dancing again. How long had it been since she left London and its vibrant nightlife? Only a few weeks, but it felt like an eternity.

She knew she had to be careful with this man. He had behaved very fishily on the cliff, giving off a distinct air of menace when she mentioned that odd message . . . *Polly put the kettle on.* She still had no idea what that code meant, and was never likely to find out, what with all the secrecy shrouding everything in the listening room. But whether or not he'd been threatening her on the cliff, he was definitely hiding *something*.

Her father would call that far-fetched, no doubt. Her overly vivid imagination, making trouble where none existed. She was not going to risk being alone with Rex again. But that didn't mean she shouldn't be ready to follow him, if required. Just to make sure he wasn't up to anything underhand.

Oblivious to her suspicions, Rex gave her a broad smile. 'Let me know when you've been released from culinary duties, and I'll be there in a flash.'

'I will.'

He nodded in a friendly fashion at Lily, who was washing up a few utensils at the sink. The girl's eyes widened and she said nothing, but returned feverishly to her work, arms plunged into soapy water up to the elbows.

'Lily's shy,' Eva whispered.

He edged inside the kitchen and peered down at the platters of triangular sandwiches and stuffed rolls she'd been arranging, ready to carry out to the dancers.

'Those look tasty. May I?'

'If you must.'

Tentatively, he picked up one dainty triangle and sniffed it. And recoiled. 'What in God's name . . . ?'

'Sardine and watercress.' He went to put the sandwich down in horror, and she tutted. 'You've picked it now. You should eat that one.'

'My hands are clean, honestly.' When she said nothing, her eyes narrowing, he pointed – no touching this time – to the sandwich next to it. 'What about that one?'

'Salad cream and celery.'

'Good grief.' He grimaced. 'And that one?'

'Anchovy butter.'

'Suddenly, I'm not all that hungry.' He gazed about the assorted platters on the table. 'Erm, do any of these contain good old-fashioned meat? Or even something akin to meat?'

'Fish paste?'

He hesitated, then shrugged. 'Very well. Sounds better than sardines, at any rate.' Taking the sandwich she had indicated, he bit into it gingerly. 'Hmm, not bad,' he muttered after finishing his mouthful. 'Fills a hole.'

She finished arranging the sandwich triangles to her satisfaction, and then picked up the heavy platter. 'The vicar's wife found us a very useful card listing meat substitutes for party food, and we've been largely following that. Though we have mock sausage rolls too. They're still in the oven.'

'*Mock* . . . ?' He made a face. 'I'm almost afraid to ask.'

'Probably best not.'

Rex laughed. 'Look, can I help you with that?' He took the platter from her unresisting hands. When he wasn't being grave and absorbed with work, his smile was really quite dazzling, Eva thought. 'Sorry if I offended you just now. I never was terribly good at being polite.' He studied the neatly arranged sandwiches with a dubious expression. 'And salad cream and celery doesn't sound too unappetising.'

Eva scooped up a smaller platter of rolls and followed him into the busy hall. It was hard at first, threading their way through the crowd to the refreshments table, but people seemed to fall back at the sight of the professor with a platter of sandwiches. Several of the soldiers laughed, then descended into silence at his tense, bespectacled frown.

'How's it going?' she asked a harassed Alice, who was hurriedly and inexpertly ladling fruit punch into glasses for those waiting.

'These soldiers are like bleedin' camels,' Alice moaned, sloshing another ladleful into a glass, a small amount of sticky liquid pooling on the tablecloth beneath. 'I can't ladle this stuff as fast as they're drinking it!'

Eva laughed at her expression. 'Just keep breathing. I'm sure your aunt will be finished helping Hazel on the door soon enough. Then she'll be here to help you.'

'Oh Gawd!'

The band was playing a jaunty tune now. Eva looked about the packed hall, smiling. A small dance area had been cleared in front of the raised platform and a few couples were already whirling about.

Her feet began to tap. The band was playing. People were dancing. Everyone seemed flushed and happy. For a few golden moments, the restrictions and fear of the war had been forgotten.

This was precisely why she had wanted to hold a dance.

Close beside her, Rex was also surveying the room. His gaze moved over the dancing couples, then turned to light on her face. 'Well done,' he said softly.

'It does seem like a success.'

'Hard work though. All this for a dance?'

'I like dancing.'

His eyes flickered, as though registering her wistful tone. Then he unfastened Eva's pinny and dropped it behind the refreshments table, much to her surprise.

'Come on,' Rex said peremptorily, holding out a hand.

'Sorry?'

'Could I tempt you to a dance, Miss Ryder?'

Eva bit her lip. It was indeed a temptation. She had not intended to dance this early on in the evening's proceedings. There were still so many things to be done in the kitchen. Food in the oven. And she had left Lily alone there, without instructions.

'But the mock sausage rolls—'

'Hang them!'

'Oh!' She was taken aback by his stern, no-nonsense tone, but rather liked it. Better a backbone than none, she always thought. Automatically, her hand found his, and she let him lead her to the dance floor. 'I suppose one dance won't hurt.'

She was still suspicious of Rex. But the dance hall tune had wormed its way into her ear, and she wanted to dance too much to care. Besides, there wasn't much he could do to her in front of all these people. And goodness, she thought a few minutes later, breathless and smiling, this man could dance!

The professor was surprisingly light-footed, she discovered. When his muscular arm wasn't about her waist, it was spinning her round or turning her back towards him with consummate ease. And he avoided the other couples without difficulty, making the dance a delight rather than a series of embarrassing collisions, as was often the case with some partners.

And every time he smiled, meeting her eyes, she smiled at him in return. She didn't mean to. Didn't want to, in fact. There was still too much she didn't know about this man.

But whenever their hands met, or their bodies brushed in the dance, she kept thinking of the kiss they'd shared on the clifftop, its warm, dangerous excitement, and how it had fizzed inside her for hours afterwards. The way she had secretly wished it could go on forever.

Surely she couldn't be falling in love with him?

CHAPTER THIRTY-ONE

To a cheer of recognition, the band swung into 'Boogie Woogie Bugle Boy', and Hazel's feet could not help tapping to its fast, infectious beat.

'That's the last of them, Miss,' the jovial sergeant said as he squeezed through the hall door and began to close it. 'Happen you wouldn't have got many more folk inside, anyway.'

Hazel, looking up from the table where she'd been taking money, could well believe it. The shilling she'd been charging on the door would go towards church funds, as Eva had promised the Reverend Clewson. Nonetheless, her small takings tin was bulging with shiny coins, and the hall was thick with people.

'Look at 'em all dancing now.' The sergeant winked at her. 'You and the other ladies must be right proud of yourselves.'

'Yes,' Hazel said, forcing a smile for his sake.

She was proud of what they had achieved, of course. Deeply proud. Their evening of dancing had turned out to be a huge success. But how to explain why she was not glowing with happiness?

Her husband was dead, and her young son had enlisted, and might soon join his father in a foreign grave. She had not seen Charlie since he had charged out of the house, his face dark with turmoil and confusion. Poor boy, he must be devastated, having defied her by joining up and then losing his father before he could even reach the continent.

'Hang on!' a familiar voice called, and the sergeant looked round in surprise as somebody shoved the hall door open again.

It was George Cotterill, standing breathless on the threshold in a tweed jacket and muddy boots.

His eyes met hers.

Hazel sucked in her breath, her heart thumping in guilt and confusion.

The last thing she could think about right now was romance, and so she'd told him when she went up to Eastern House after receiving that awful telegram. Bertie might not have been the world's best spouse, but he had died for his country and she owed him a decent period of mourning.

To her relief, George had understood and kept his distance. But she knew his feelings towards her hadn't changed. And nor had hers towards him.

All the same, it wasn't proper.

'Room for a couple more?' George asked a little roughly, and stepped into the hall, dragging somebody behind him by the collar.

Hazel stood up jerkily, nearly knocking her takings tin flying. 'Charlie!' she gasped, staring wide-eyed at her errant son. 'I can't believe it!' George had promised to keep an eye out for the boy. But she hadn't imagined he would have time to search for him, not with all his other duties at the listening post. 'Oh, George . . . You found him for me.'

George gave a sharp nod, and pushed Charlie forwards.

'Go to your mother, boy. Remember what we agreed. You owe her an apology.'

Her son looked back at her, sullen and red-eyed, and then muttered, 'Sorry, Mum,' before hanging his head.

She hugged him tightly, and to her surprise Charlie didn't pull away. It was such a relief to feel him in her arms, she could have wept, but somehow controlled the urge. She knew how her son hated it when she cried.

'Charlie, dearest! You gave me such a turn, running away like that. I thought my heart would burst. Please don't ever do that to me again, all right?' The boy said nothing, but she could feel him shaking. She peered suspiciously at George over his head, guessing he must have read Charlie the riot act on the way to the hall. But at least he had found her son. 'Where was he?'

'On his way to Penzance with a friend.'

'What friend?' She took Charlie by the shoulders, though he was taller than her these days, and shook him slightly. He pulled away, still sullen. 'Charlie?'

'Clive Derricks. He's joined up too like Louis did,' Charlie admitted reluctantly, not meeting her eyes. 'We were walking into Penzance to find lodgings until our call-up date.'

She knew Clive, a thin, pale, freckly boy of eighteen. Old enough to enlist legally, but still wet behind the ears, like her own son. His parents must be frantic too, she thought with a sudden rush of sympathy. 'You young idiots, going to war at your age . . . Why, you're not even old enough to shave!'

'Don't fret yourself,' George told her, and now Charlie turned to glare at him with real dislike. 'I had a word with the enlisting sergeant. Told him how Charlie had doctored his identity papers to join up too young. He scratched Charlie from the list.'

Amazed, Hazel stared at her boss, speechless with gratitude. 'You're not making that up? Charlie's not enlisted anymore?'

'He's a free man,' George agreed, and ruffled the lad's head, though Charlie shot him a violent look, as though he wanted to take a pop at him. 'Now let's hope the war's over before he gets old enough to put his name down for real.'

She did not know what to say. Her heart felt twice its normal size as she took in what he'd said. Charlie was no longer going to war? It seemed too good to be true.

But one glance at her son's face told her the truth.

'This is for the best,' she told him, on the brink of tears, her voice indistinct, and she gave him another compulsive hug. 'You've just lost your dad. Last thing he'd have wanted is for you to be rushing off to foreign parts without even giving him a proper send-off.' She paused, scouring his pale face. He was watching some of the girls carrying platters of food to the refreshments table, a sudden yearning in his face. 'When did you last eat?'

'Dunno.' Charlie gave a careless shrug, as though not inter-ested in such boring stuff as food, but she was not fooled.

There were tears in his eyes. And he looked secretly relieved rather than angry. Perhaps the reality of enlisting had finally hit home after he learned of his dad's passing. Before that news, it had probably seemed more like an adventure. Now, he understood the true cost of war a little better.

Hazel looked about for her helper on the door, but Violet had disappeared. Then she recalled that, a few minutes ago, she'd muttered something like 'Be back in a jiffy,' and slipped away into the crowd.

'Go and ask Miss Ryder if you can have a sandwich or two in return for washing up,' she told the boy, giving him a little shove towards the kitchen. 'And mind you watch your manners, you hear?'

'Washing up?' Charlie looked horrified.

'Do what your mother says, boy,' George said, not unkindly, and her son gave him a sharp look, but then made a face and sloped off in search of food.

Definitely not as angry and disappointed as he would like them to think, she decided with a profound sense of relief, watching him weave in and out of the noisy crowd. She only wished it had not taken his father's death to make her son see sense.

Hazel fastened the metal lid carefully on her tin of takings. 'There,' she said, and put the tin into the drawer under the table, locked it and pocketed the key. 'I doubt there's room for anyone else, anyway.'

'I have to hand it to you, Hazel, you've worked a minor miracle here.' George was taking in the busy hall, his eyebrows raised almost to his fringe. She enjoyed the way he used her Christian name for once, though he didn't seem to have done so deliberately. 'I had no idea so many would come.' He had to raise his voice as the band swung into a loud, fast number that had even Hazel's feet tapping. People crowded onto the tiny area set aside for dancing, and the noise level rose steeply. 'Good grief, looks like everyone's dancing too! I hope the floor doesn't collapse.'

Two ladies she recognised from the local Women's Institute came out of the cloakroom beside them, heading for the dance floor too, and they moved aside automatically.

Suddenly she was standing right beside George.

'Thank you,' she said. 'For bringing Charlie back to me, I mean.'

'Honestly, there's no need.'

'I don't know what I'd have done if he'd managed to go to war.' She shook her head. 'He's just a boy!'

'I know.'

'If I'd lost him too, I'd probably have run mad.'

'I know.' George ran a hand through his hair, looking everywhere but at her. 'That's why I did it, love. I couldn't bear to see you suffering.'

Love.

Had he really just called her *love*?

Such a tiny word, and yet it changed everything.

It made her feel cared for.

Loved.

As though they were lovers.

He had called her 'love' once before, she thought wildly. One summer, when she was about fourteen, a bunch of kids from Porthcurno had travelled on the bus into Penzance, to the picture house there, and she'd gone with them. It had been a grand adventure, and she had curled her hair specially the night before, copying what her mother did. But on the way back from the pictures, it had started to rain and her hair-do had started to wilt. She'd not been wearing a coat, so George had taken off his jacket and held it over her head, saying, 'There, love.' Nobody else had heard at the time, and she had not known what to think. Except that he must be sweet on her, which was what her friends had said later, giggling, when she told them about it. But he had not asked her out.

Then she remembered the telegram. Bertie's full name and rank typed there, in stark letters. Her wordless shock. The way Charlie had fled the house, distraught.

And the child she was carrying.

Suddenly, Hazel couldn't seem to breathe. Her face was flushed, her chest heaving. 'I'm sorry, I . . .' Her head was swimming. 'It's so hot in here. I feel . . . dizzy!'

She slipped past him and out of the hall, desperate for fresh air.

George followed her. 'Hazel?' He sounded concerned. 'What is it? Are you unwell? Please wait.'

To her relief, it was cooler outside. The sun was setting over towards the west, casting a golden syrupy glow over everything. She could hear music echoing across the valley through the big open windows of the hall.

She stopped and took a deep breath, looking out over the familiar Cornish landscape. 'That's better. I just need a minute.'

'Of course.'

Hazel wrapped her arms about herself, shivering despite the warmth of the evening. She kept thinking about her wedding. It had been a perfect summer's day like this one. They had married because of Charlie. But that had been their secret, hers and Bertie's, and not something she cared to share with George, however she felt about him. *And now I'm carrying Bertie's child again*, she reminded herself.

'Hazel—'

'Please, don't.' She spun around, shaking her head at the look on his face. 'I know you have feelings for me. But I'm a widow, George. And he's only been gone five minutes.'

'I'm willing to wait.'

'I have Charlie to think of. You may be waiting a long time.' Hazel raised her chin defiantly, pushing away the temptation to tell him about the baby. 'I know what you think, but . . . Bertie wasn't a bad man.'

'Only a bad husband?'

Hazel met his eyes, and saw the understanding in them. She bit down hard on her lip, and wrenched her gaze away. She couldn't stay there another minute or she would betray how much she loved him. But she couldn't go back inside either. She was crying, a salt tear rolling down her cheek and into the corner of her mouth, and she couldn't risk Charlie seeing her like this.

Hurriedly, she walked away a few steps, turning instinctively towards the ocean, and heard George follow her again.

She stared out across the milky ocean. The Atlantic was so huge; her problems had always seemed tiny in comparison with its vastness. Some days early in her marriage, when Bertie had raised his hand to her in anger, she had run from the house in tears and stumbled cross-country to the cliffs, to stare down at the sea, losing her pain in the churning crash of the tide against rocks.

George wasn't Bertie though, and she was no longer that frightened young woman who had not known where to turn, faced with her husband's brutality.

He also didn't know that she was pregnant with Bertie's child. But once he did, she doubted he would be quite so keen to rekindle the love they had felt as teenagers. This was all hopeless and she knew it.

A car was coming their way, somewhere in the distance. She tensed, listening to the engine. Not wanting anyone to see her out here with George, she turned swiftly off the road and slipped through a gate into a wooded area.

To her surprise, George came after her into the trees, always a few steps behind her.

The car passed on the road, slowing to a halt as it approached the hall. More people wanting to dance and have a good time before night fell and lights-out began, she guessed. She wasn't there to take their entrance shilling. But perhaps Violet would have found her way back to the front desk by now.

'What do you think you're doing, George?' she asked wearily, turning to face him. 'Why are you still following me?'

'I'm making sure you don't get yourself in trouble.'

'I'm already in trouble,' she admitted, unable to conceal her despair any longer, and saw his gaze flash down to where her hand was splayed across the slight swell of her belly. Not that anything was showing yet. But she was constantly aware of that tiny life inside, Bertie's child, who would be born now without a father, without ever having known the man who had given him or her life.

George sucked in a breath, staring. 'You're pregnant?'

She gave a little moan. 'I shouldn't have said anything. Please don't turn me off from the job.' She entreated him with her eyes. 'I need the money.'

'Of course not. But I had no idea. My God . . .' His face was pale, his voice hoarse. 'What are you going to do?'

'I'm going to have his baby. What else can I do?'

'Hazel.' He took a quick step towards her, and she backed away under the low-hanging branches, shaking her head in instinctive denial.

'No,' she whispered.

He made a noise under his breath and ran a hand through his hair again, his look frustrated. 'I shouldn't, I know,' George said flatly, 'but I can't help it.'

'Shouldn't what?'

'Want to kiss you again,' he told her. He came towards her again, and this time Hazel found she couldn't walk away.

This was wrong, she kept thinking. Yet somehow nothing had ever made as much sense to her as the thought of George Cotterill kissing her. The last time had been amazing, despite the guilt she'd felt that Charlie had seen them together and nearly come to blows with George. But she couldn't pretend she had not been thinking about it ever since, and secretly wondering if he would ever repeat that tender, loving kiss.

Bertie had never kissed her like that.

She had been holding her breath, Hazel realised, and abruptly exhaled. 'I'm not sorry,' she blurted out. 'I'm not sorry he's dead.'

He stopped, his face inches from hers, and their eyes met.

Her heart was thudding wildly. The relief of that admission was overwhelming. Bertie had been her husband and she ought to mourn him. And she had tried. Neighbours had been dropping by the cottage and expressing their sympathies ever since that telegram arrived, and she had told them what they expected to hear. That she was devastated and bereft and all those other painful emotions a young war widow ought to feel.

But in truth, she was simply numb inside. Whatever love she had once felt for Bertie had seeped away years ago, leaving only habit and duty in its place.

'Do you think that makes me . . . wicked?' she asked him, terrified he might say yes.

'No, it makes you human.'

Then George took her in his arms, and kissed her.

She clung on to him with eyes closed tight, wishing things could be different, that she had never married Bertie – but no, then Charlie would never have been born, and she loved Charlie so much – or that Bertie had not died, and she could have divorced him decently and married George instead.

He could never possibly want her for his wife. Not after Bertie, and certainly not now she was carrying another man's child. But perhaps it would be enough just to love him, and take comfort from that.

Suddenly, he pulled back, and she could see him frowning.

'What is it?' she whispered, bewildered.

'I can hear something.' George released her and walked out from under the trees, staring up at the milky gold evening sky. 'A plane. You hear it too?'

When Hazel said nothing, he pointed to a dot in the far distance, high above the waves, flying towards them along the coast. And now she could hear the droning note of its engine too, and felt her skin turn clammy with fear, her heart thumping.

'There . . . And there . . . More than one plane.' His voice changed. 'Oh, Christ.'

'What is it?'

'Run,' he shouted hoarsely. 'Back to the hall, warn the others. We need everyone to get to a shelter.' George grabbed her hand when she did not move, pulling her along with him. 'For God's sake, move. They're not ours. They're Jerries!'

CHAPTER THIRTY-TWO

Violet, seated reluctantly behind the table in Hazel's absence, hoped to goodness that the vile toad Patrick Dullaghan was not here tonight. She had crept away from the entrance early on, pretending to have a chore to do elsewhere, but in fact hiding out in the ladies' cloakroom, which was about as large as Hazel's outdoor lav, so not terribly comfortable, especially now it was full of hats and summer jackets. But she had dared not come out until most people had arrived, in case he and his East End buddies turned up and spotted her.

The last thing she needed was to be labelled a spy again, here in Porthcurno, where it might be taken seriously.

She had been sitting as still and quiet as a mouse, not venturing out to dance or even grab a cuppa for herself, though she was parched.

Now the entrance door opened, and she shrank back, horrified.

Only it wasn't Patrick Dullaghan.

She put a hand to her mouth.

Joe Postbridge paused in the doorway, leaning on his stick and accompanied by a small group of uniformed, laughing friends. Behind him, she could see the sun setting on a perfect summer evening.

She froze behind the table at the sight of him, and did not know where to look, not even able to occupy herself with the takings, for she couldn't see the metal tin anywhere and the drawer under the table was locked. No doubt Hazel had decided nobody else would arrive this late, so had removed the money tin. Either that, or she'd wanted to discourage late arrivals, given how full to bursting the hall was, all the windows open but the air still hot and stuffy.

'Room for a few more?' one of the soldiers asked as they all piled in, some of them already pretending to dance with each other on the threshold as the band music swelled.

'I . . . I'm not sure,' Violet said, suddenly shy for once, carefully avoiding Joe Postbridge's gaze. 'By rights, I ought to turn you away, coming so late.'

'But we came specially for the dance. And look,' the soldier said, nodding towards Joe's stick. 'We've walking wounded here.'

'Frank, for God's sake!' Joe said, a flicker of irritation in his voice.

'See for yerself. There ain't room to swing a cat.' Violet met Joe's eyes, then looked hurriedly away. The Cornishman's dark gaze had narrowed on her face. 'But I suppose it won't do no harm. Go on then, in you go. Though it's a shilling a head, mind.'

'Even for us brave soldiers?' The one he'd called Frank pinched his buff uniform and shook it, giving her a broad wink.

'Especially for you,' she said, unable to resist, and they all laughed at her disapproving tone.

'Don't worry, boys.' Joe rummaged in his pocket and dumped a handful of coins on the table, some of them rolling merrily away. 'That do you, Miss?'

Violet gathered the coins together without bothering to

count them, her eyes on his face. He looked even more handsome than when she'd seen him on the beach at Penzance, if that was possible. Why nobody had nabbed him yet was beyond her. He might have a false leg, but he had the face of an angel. She knew a dozen women in the East End who'd kill for a juicy piece of flesh like Joe Postbridge. Not that she was like that. She had manners.

'Thank you,' she said, aware of heat in her cheeks as he gazed steadily back at her. Trying to distract attention from her growing embarrassment, she pointed through the crowd. 'You get a sarnie apiece for your shilling, plus a slice of cake and a cuppa. Down the far end.'

'You go ahead, lads,' Joe told the others, tapping his metal leg with his stick as they moved eagerly away. 'I'm all puffed out after that long walk. I'll catch you up.'

Joe leant his stick against the wall opposite her table, and reclined there too with his arms crossed, watching her pile up the coins.

Violet dared not look up at him, but bent her head, pretending to count but failing miserably. She kept losing count, too aware of his nearness to concentrate on her task.

'I met you on the beach,' he said. 'Down at Penzance.'

'That's right. I was with my nieces, Lily and Alice.'

'I remember them. Nice girls.'

'They're here somewhere,' she said. 'Been slaving away in the kitchen most of the afternoon, poor things.'

She smiled, recalling how eager Lily had been to help out, after her constant pleas had finally softened Violet's resolve to forbid her and Alice from dancing.

Not that Alice was very keen on the idea of dancing. Too young still, perhaps. But she enjoyed spotting the different uniforms and noting down all the various regiments that had been drafted out here to defend Penzance and Porthcurno.

Lily, however, was almost beside herself at the thought of dancing with a real partner, instead of her sister. Apart from family weddings, she'd never really had the chance before. And she might end up dancing with a soldier, which probably made it all the more romantic in her imagination.

'You helped organise this do, then?'

'Me and a few mates, yes,' she admitted, giving up all hope of counting their shillings after starting again for the fourth time. She scooped them up and popped them into her pocket instead, since there was no sign of the takings tin. 'We thought it would be a nice idea, what with rationing and all. Give people round here a chance for a right good knees-up.'

'Not to mention sandwiches and cake,' he said, grinning.

'Them too.' She laughed, then could not help her glance flicking down to his false leg, hidden beneath his trousers. He was a dab hand with that walking stick, she thought wonderingly. If she hadn't known, she would never have guessed that he'd lost his leg. 'Do you ever . . . ? I mean, I suppose you don't, but . . .' Hot-cheeked, she floundered in sudden confusion, mumbling, 'Sorry, forget I said anything.'

His eyebrows arched. 'I don't think you *did* say anything.'

Violet jumped up at his tone, not knowing where she was going, but only aware of a pressing need to escape. Her blasted tongue . . . !

But Joe moved with surprising speed, catching hold of her before she could run away. 'Hang on a tick. You haven't offended me, if that's what you're getting all flustered about. Yes, I do dance, though no, it isn't easy and sometimes I can't get the steps right. But I do my best not to make a complete fool of myself.' He held her gaze. 'That was what you wanted to ask, wasn't it?'

She nodded silently.

The band came to the end of the dance tune, and for a

moment there was a pause as people stopped talking to applaud.

'So, how about it?' Joe slipped an arm about her waist, taking her breath away with the warmth of his hip against hers. 'You want to risk it, next tune they play?'

His smile was so sweet, it could charm the birds from the trees, she thought, gaping at him in astonishment.

She opened her mouth to say, 'Yes,' but suddenly realised he was no longer listening. He had stiffened, his head turned with a frown.

There was shouting outside, she realised. Loud, urgent shouts. And beyond them, she could hear a deep, familiar, spine-chilling drone.

'Air raid! Get to shelter!'

Joe released her and tore open the door just as George Cotterill came running up the road, breathless and yelling, 'Get out, everyone! Enemy bombers are nearly here.'

The whole hall descended into chaos.

'Where's the nearest shelter?' Joe asked her crisply.

Violet was too shocked to think straight. 'D-dunno,' she managed to stutter, before adding with sudden inspiration, 'How about the vicar? He's here, he'll know.'

But George had entered the hall now, followed by a panicked-looking Hazel. 'There's a shelter under the church,' he shouted, standing aside as people flooded out of the building, soldiers flocking together and making way for the civilians. He pointed behind the hall to where the old church stood, half hidden by trees. 'Through the churchyard and to the right. There are steps down into the crypt. It's sign-posted.'

The Reverend Clewson appeared out of the crowd, sweating and red-faced. He ran ahead of the others, gesturing to everyone to follow him, while his wife bravely stayed behind to make sure the hall was emptied.

'Everyone out,' she was saying in a posh accent, clapping her hands to get people's attention. 'Two exits. One at the front, one at the rear of the hall.'

Nobody was really paying much attention to her.

'I can't see Lily and Alice.' Violet clambered onto a chair to see more clearly as the guests hurried past them. 'Oh, where the hell have they gone?' She saw Eva among those leaving, but couldn't reach her. 'Miss Ryder, have you see the girls?'

'Sorry, no,' Eva yelled back. 'They were handing out refreshments last time I saw them. Haven't you seen them go past?'

'I don't think so.' Though in this crush, it was possible she might have missed them, if they'd got out before she thought to stand on a chair.

'Maybe they went out the back door,' Eva called reassuringly before she too was swept out of the hall.

'I'm sure that'll be it,' Joe said, rescuing his stick as the room gradually emptied. He took Violet's arm, helping her down from the chair. 'Come on, Miss, you need to leave too.'

'Just one more minute,' she pleaded. 'I need to be sure the girls are out. I promised my sister I'd look after them, and I can't let her down now.'

But though they checked the kitchen and the cloakrooms, there was no sign of Lily or Alice anywhere.

'Time to go,' Joe said firmly.

The brass band were among the last to leave, by which time the drone of the approaching bombers was so loud, Violet felt quite nauseous. All she could think about were the times she had heard that same noise above the streets and houses in the East End, swiftly followed by sudden, terrible death as buildings exploded, the night sky bright with that horrible, unnatural orange glow as the city burnt all around them.

Violet clapped her hands over her ears, stumbling as she followed the others out of the church hall. 'I can't bleedin' stand the sound of them Jerry planes,' she moaned, tripping in her haste. 'I'm sorry, I'm sorry . . .'

'Miss?' Joe helped her back to her feet. 'Violet?'

'I can't help it. It's just like it was at home, when the bombing raids went over.'

He said nothing, but she could see from his expression that he understood.

Violet tried to stay calm as they made for the churchyard, though her heart was thumping. Back in London, she had grown accustomed to the nightly terror of the Blitz. Like everyone else, she'd learned to shrug off the fear of death, and even make jokes about Hitler and the bloody Jerries. The boys had sung rude songs in the street about him, and sometimes she'd joined in with a grin and a little jig. But it had been weeks since she'd had to cower in some flimsy tin-roofed shelter in the dark, listening to explosions nearby and praying to live to see dawn, and somehow she'd lost that armour plating she'd grown over her nerves.

The sun had not yet set, but it was dim and cool in the shaded churchyard, the sturdy trunks of yews looming over the lichened graves of yesteryear.

'I'm sure we'll find them,' Joe said, walking as fast as he could, his stick clacking against the stones of the path.

'Sorry?'

'The girls. They'll be down in the crypt with everyone else – mark my words.'

Violet gulped, suffering a terrible pang of guilt. She'd been so worried about a bomb dropping on her head, for a moment there she'd clean forgotten about Lily and Alice.

'Of course.'

Mrs Clewson came running after them, her heels clacking.

'That's everyone, I think,' she said, a tremor in her posh voice. Joe stood politely aside to let her descend the steps, and then gestured for Violet to follow her.

'Ladies first,' he said gravely.

Inside the crypt, the narrow, low-roofed space was packed with warm bodies, some crouched with hands over their ears, others standing to listen to the planes as they flew overhead, the air shaking with their passage. A very young woman was weeping in the corner, rubbing her eyes with a white hanky, while an elderly gent tried to comfort her.

Violet gazed about, seeing the same terror she was feeling on other faces.

'You'll be all right,' she told the woman next to her, as kindly as she could, though she had no idea if they'd even live through this. But what she remembered from air raids in London was that a little white lie could be helpful at times, to keep people's spirits up and stop them from panicking.

The woman nodded stiffly and said nothing, her face very pale.

'They're not used to seeing bombers here in Porthcurno,' Joe said in her ear, as the Reverend Clewson went up to close the trapdoor. 'Though we sat through a good few raids at Penzance, me and Mum, down in the shelters. That was one reason I insisted she came with me when I moved into the farm. To get away from the bombs.' He shook his head. 'Seems like Jerry's bombing everywhere now.'

Probably looking for Eastern House, Violet thought worriedly, but said nothing.

Once the trapdoor was shut, there was almost no light in the crypt. The noise of the planes was considerably dimmed though, which helped her nerves. But Violet was also aware of her old enemy from the shelters, the fear of small spaces, rising inside her like a tide. She bit her lip, trying hard to push her fears aside. But she could feel her heart beating hard, her breathing fast and shallow . . .

A hand found hers and squeezed. Not hard, just enough to be reassuring. She looked into Joe's eyes and managed a nervous smile.

'Sorry,' he whispered, and dropped her hand. 'I don't know why I did that.'

'No, it's all right.' She sought his hand again. 'I like it.'

He smiled too then, and his fingers laced with hers like he was never planning to let go. It sounded soppy when she thought too hard about it, but it gave her new strength, just having someone hold her hand.

'Lily?' she called out across the heads of those nearest to her, trying to sound cheery. 'Alice? It's Aunty Vi. Are you down here, girls?'

A slim arm rose above the dark sea of shoulders, right at the far end of the crypt, and waved a hand in her direction. 'I'm over here, Aunty Vi!' Alice's voice bounced off the low roof, bright as a skylark in this dark, sweaty, underground hole. 'Lily's with me too. And Miss Ryder. We're both fine, don't fret yourself!'

'Oh, thank Gawd,' she said under her breath, sagging with sudden relief, and then forced herself to call back jauntily, 'I can't get to you, love. But you two mind your manners. No stepping on anyone's feet, you hear?'

Heads turned, and there was an uneasy ripple of laughter through the crypt, either at her East End accent or her gallows humour, she wasn't sure which.

But she didn't mind, smiling along with them. That was how they'd always kept their spirits up in the shelters in Dagenham, after all. If you laughed at something terrible and made it ridiculous, suddenly it didn't seem so bad.

'Who knows a song?' she said loudly. 'Might as well pass the time with a bit of music.'

There was an awkward silence.

Then one of the band members took the saxophone tucked under his arm and played a few notes before looking at her, grinning. She recognised the popular tune at once as Glenn Miller's 'In The Mood' and began to hum the tune. Several other people took up the humming, including Joe, who was still holding her hand. They were halfway through when a deep rumble shook the walls and the stone-flagged floor of the crypt. The humming wavered, then stopped.

'Jesus, that was a bloody bomb!' a soldier called out in the stunned silence that followed the explosion.

'Nowhere near us though,' his mate added quickly as one of the women shrieked in fear. He turned to her. 'No need to get your knickers in a twist, love. That was a tidy way off. We're all right down here.'

'It wasn't that far away,' the Reverend Clewson said, his head cocked to one side as though listening for more explosions.

George Cotterill, who had been standing to one side with Hazel, squeezed his way through to the foot of the crypt steps. He looked tense, a smudge of dirt on his forehead. 'Not Eastern House, surely?'

Violet was horrified, thinking of everyone she knew at Eastern House. The buildings were heavily camouflaged, but that kind of disguise probably worked best at night. The Germans would have seen it straight away in daylight, especially flying cross-country rather than coming in from the sea.

Had that bomb landed on the listening post?

The vicar looked pale and shocked. 'Perhaps. They flew straight over us, didn't they? I'm sorry, George. Let's hope they heard the raid coming and got to a shelter in time.'

Violet thought of the fortified tunnels, but said nothing. That was top secret.

'Those bastards . . .' George spluttered, almost incoherent.

'Language, please! There are ladies present.'

'Sorry, Vicar, but . . .' George shook his head angrily. 'It's not even dark yet. Nobody will have been expecting them. Enemy planes flying over in the daytime, bold as brass?' He looked disgusted.

'If the Jerries think there ain't no anti-aircraft guns, they do sometimes chance coming in the daytime,' Violet told him eagerly, wanting to help. 'We had one or two afternoon fly-bys in the East End.'

'And us,' Joe said, nodding at her side. 'We've had a few bombing raids down in Penzance while it was still light. They've brought in anti-aircraft guns now, but it doesn't seem to stop the Germans trying their luck.'

George sighed. 'I suppose we've got used to feeling safe here in Porthcurno, that's all. But there are plenty who've had it worse than us. Like those poor souls in London.'

'Oh, that's for sure,' one of the soldiers agreed, stepping out of the darkness at the back of the crypt, an unlit cigarette dangling from his lip. 'Ain't it, Vi?' His smile was unpleasant. 'But maybe someone went and tipped the Jerries off. Told them where to look for Eastern House. Now, who'd play a nasty trick like that on their own countrymen, eh?'

Violet stared at Patrick Dullaghan, unable to say a word.

CHAPTER THIRTY-THREE

Eva felt sure that her father must have been safe in the underground tunnels at Eastern House during that bombing raid. But that didn't mean everyone was safe. What about the soldiers gathered in the camp below or bravely manning the little pillboxes along the coast? And what of the civilians in Porthcurno, some of whom would have been sitting down to supper as that bomb struck . . .

It was too horrible to contemplate what might be happening out there.

She had lost Rex in the confusion early on, but dutifully followed everyone else to the church crypt anyway. Some of the locals had seemed quite scared and bewildered by the intrusion of the war into their quiet lives, but she'd reassured them as best she could, telling tales of bombing raids she'd survived. They had not seemed very comforted by this, to her surprise. So she'd made her excuses and squeezed in tight next to Violet's plucky young nieces, who at least were unfazed by the sound of enemy bombers overhead. They too must have been through many such air raids.

Being at the back, she and the girls were among the last

to leave the dank little crypt once the Reverend Clewson had declared the raid over – though how he could be sure, she had no idea. Unless he'd received a personal message from the Almighty, she thought, and then scolded herself for being such a cynic. The poor man was just doing his best in a frightening situation, jollying everyone along as they headed home in the twilight, the dance well and truly over.

People were pointing to a thick, ominous plume of smoke rising in one spot along the coast, roughly in the direction of Eastern House. Some of the soldiers had clambered onto a wall to see better, and were speculating how bad the damage would be. Others had already started to double-time it back to base, quite rightly assuming they'd be needed on duty tonight after all.

'Do you think Eastern House was hit?' Lily asked her, wide-eyed.

'I'm not sure, to be honest.' Eva struggled against her fear, studying the sinister pillar of smoke rising into the evening air as nonchalantly as she could. There was no point alarming the girls with her worries. 'I certainly hope not.'

She also hoped her father had been able to evacuate the buildings in time, if that really was Eastern House on fire. Most of the staff, trainees and officers would have been safe enough in the underground tunnels, unless the cliffside had taken a direct hit. She could only pray it had not, as that would have been catastrophic for everyone in the tunnels. And she felt sure the soldiers in the tented area had designated areas for sheltering in the event of a raid. Assuming they'd received adequate warning, of course.

She tried not to fret herself into a panic. As her father would have said, there was nothing anyone could do about it at this remove. But she had to admit to a flutter of genuine fear in her chest. What would she do if she lost her father?

Despite the fact that he'd been a career soldier all her life, the thought of him dying had never really occurred to her before. Not with any seriousness. Daddy always seemed so capable and indestructible. But nobody was indestructible. She had learned that lesson the hard way with her mother, who had died of tuberculosis nearly five years ago, yet somehow she'd pushed the memory aside. Now it came flooding back, making her breath catch in her throat and her eyes blur with sudden, unexpected tears.

'You all right, Miss?' Alice asked bluntly, tugging on her sleeve. 'You look right peaky. You going to chuck up?'

Through her shimmering vision, Eva grinned down at the girl and shook her head. 'No, thank God. Though if I do, I'll make sure I throw up on you. What a brat you are!'

Alice laughed, seeming deeply pleased by this insult.

Expecting to catch sight of Rex at any moment, she popped her head inside the church hall as the others milled about outside, but found the place dark and empty, except for Hazel and her son, who were hurriedly collecting the remnants of the food.

'Waste not, want not,' Hazel said, looking at her guiltily. 'Since the dance seems to be over, I thought we could take this lot home. Have a feast for a few days.'

'Jolly good idea,' Eva said with a smile, aware that Hazel was kindly housing Violet and her two nieces, not to mention her son Charlie, all of whom probably ate enough for a small army. 'Have you seen Rex? I mean, Professor Templeton? I haven't seen him since the planes came over.'

'Sorry, I haven't seen anyone. George – I mean, Mr Cotterill – went straight back to Eastern House with the men. Maybe the professor went with them. There's only my Charlie here.'

The lad flicked her an uninterested glance, then carried

on stacking sandwiches into a cake tin, his expression distracted. He'd just lost his father, poor boy.

Though at least Charlie had come back after running away, Eva thought, recalling what Lily had told her in whispers during the air raid. George Cotterill had brought him back, apparently, so all was well that ended well. Though the details were muddled. She had only been half-listening to Lily, her mind on Rex and her frightening suspicions. Though it would probably turn out to be a silly mistake on her part. It usually was where affairs of the heart were concerned. Her mother used to say she was always dashing in where angels feared to put a toe, let alone tread, and ending up in hot water.

Still, she wasn't the only one in trouble at the moment. There was something 'going on' between Hazel and George Cotterill, as her dad had put it yesterday, his tone rather disapproving. That was the gossip buzzing around Eastern House, anyway. Not that Eva cared one jot about that. So what if Hazel had been carrying on with someone behind her husband's back? The husband had been a thoroughly bad sort, from what she'd heard. Besides, in case nobody had noticed, there was a war on. The usual rules no longer applied.

She froze as she heard what sounded like a truck coming fast up the hill, crashing through the low gears, then squealing to a halt outside the hall.

Hazel's head turned. 'What on earth . . . ?'

They all hurried outside to find Lily and Alice staring at the newly arrived vehicle, which turned out to be an army truck. It was nearly dark outside now, the sun having set at last in the far west.

A corporal jumped out of the truck, calling out, 'Joe Postbridge of Swelle Farm?' He turned to look at them, squinting through the darkness, the headlights partly covered to comply with blackout rules. 'Hello? Is a Joe Postbridge in there?'

'Never heard of him,' Eva said crisply. 'Sorry.'

'I know Joe.' Behind her, Hazel stood in the doorway to the hall, wiping her hands on her apron. 'He was here earlier, at the dance. And in the shelter too. But I don't know where he went after that.' She frowned. 'Why, what's the matter?'

'I was sent to fetch him up to his farm.' The soldier stopped, turning his head.

'Hello? Someone called my name?'

Eva looked round at the sound of an unfamiliar voice.

Violet had appeared from the field opposite, conspicuously picking grass from her hair. A man climbed over the stile behind her and jumped awkwardly to the ground. He collected a walking stick from beside the stile, and then limped heavily across to them.

'I'm Joe,' he said shortly, looking the soldier up and down. 'What's all the to-do?'

His bearing was upright, despite what was obviously a bad leg. A war injury, Eva guessed. That was the face of a man who'd seen action. Tough and determined. She'd met plenty of men like him before, having spent much of her childhood on or around army bases with her father.

'Bad news, I'm afraid,' the corporal said uneasily. 'Your farm took a hit in that raid. Mr Cotterill sent me to fetch you home.'

The man looked almost grey in the poor light. He swivelled, staring back in the direction of the smoke they'd seen earlier. 'M-my mother . . .' he stammered. 'How bad is it? Was she there when the bomb fell?'

'Sorry.' The corporal climbed back into the truck. 'I don't know nothing about it, beyond I'm to fetch you away to Swelle Farm, soon as may be.'

Eva felt awful for Joe Postbridge, discovering that his property had been bombed. She only prayed his mother had not been hurt in the blast. But at the same time, she felt a wave of relief that Eastern House had not been hit. After all, they had only heard one explosion from down in the crypt, so it was possible nowhere else had been damaged by the bombers.

Joe glanced round at Violet, strain in his face.

'I'll come with you,' she breathed, before he'd even spoken.

'I'd like that,' he said.

'Would you mind the girls for a bit, love?' Violet asked Hazel. 'I'll be back at yours soon as I can, I promise.'

'Of course I'll mind them.' Hazel pulled Alice near and affectionately ruffled her hair. 'You go. They'll be all right with us.' She nodded to Joe, her expression sympathetic. 'I hope your mother's safe.'

Eva watched as the two jumped into the truck and the corporal turned it smartly in the narrow road, then roared off again, back towards the smoke rising.

'You should have gone with them,' Lily said, right behind her.

Eva turned to her with a rueful look. 'You're right. I'm stranded now, no question about it.' She peered up and down the road, but everyone else had left, most of them on foot. What an idiot she was. But she'd been so relieved to know the bomb had missed Eastern House that she'd felt quite dazed, unable to think straight. 'Oh well, Shanks's pony it is,' she said, and then glanced down at her dancing heels. 'If I take these off, it shouldn't be too bad. How far is it cross-country to Eastern House? Two miles? Three?'

'Don't be silly,' Hazel said bluntly. 'I'll give you a lift. If you help me get the last of the food into my van, I'll take you to Eastern House myself.'

'But it's so far out of your way!'

'Maybe. But without you, there never would have been a dance tonight,' Hazel pointed out. 'And it was good fun until the Germans decided to crash the party. So, no more arguments. You're coming with us.'

'That's very kind of you,' Eva said, accepting with a smile. And she was genuinely glad, because she hadn't really fancied walking barefoot for miles through rough fields of long grass and nettles, especially in the pitch-black. Besides, she needed to get back to Eastern House as soon as possible, to reassure herself that only one bomb had fallen on Porthcurno tonight and her father really was safe.

'Better wait till you see the van, Miss.' Alice was looking a little fragile. No doubt the news of Joe's farm being bombed had shaken her. She pointed to the field opposite the church hall that some people had been using as a space for leaving their vehicles. There, Eva could just make out the sturdy, high-backed shape of what looked like an ambulance, glimmering in the dark. 'It's not what you might call comfy.'

'If it means not having to walk, it'll be perfectly comfy for me,' Eva assured her, and then turned cheerfully to Hazel. 'Right, leftover food, snippety-snap.' She took Alice's hand and marched back into the gloomy hall with her, determined to rally their spirits. 'Did you know that if you whistle while you work, the job gets done in half the time? How are you girls at whistling?'

Hazel dropped her at the guard post below Eastern House, and drove away in the dark, lights off and relying simply on local knowledge to stay on the road.

Eva showed her ID papers to the guard at the gate, though really it was just a formality. They all knew her by now at the listening post. 'Is everyone all right?' she asked the corporal on duty. 'I heard the bombers going over earlier.'

'No need to fret, Miss Ryder.' The corporal grinned at her. 'Jerry missed us, didn't he? Bombed some farm up the way instead. I guess he took a wrong turning.'

She'd been dreading bad news ever since hearing that explosion. Now she took a deep breath, desperately thankful to hear that nobody there had been hurt. Especially her father.

'Is the colonel up at the house?'

'No, Miss, he's gone out to visit the farm that got hit, to see what can be done for the poor souls.' The corporal shouldered his rifle and let her in through the fortified barrier. 'He was looking for you earlier though.'

'Oh, bloody hell.'

He grinned appreciatively. 'Colonel said to tell you to head straight for the tunnels.' He winked at her. 'That's where the civvies are sheltering tonight. In case Jerry comes back.'

Eva thanked him, and trudged wearily up the slope to Eastern House in the warm stillness of the summer evening. So, a long, stuffy night underground, was it?

No doubt the others would be in the tunnels already.

Including Rex.

Pausing outside the looming edifice of Eastern House, its walls draped in camouflage, Eva felt a shudder run through her.

In the distance, it seemed still and peaceful, though she knew that somewhere along the coast, a farm was burning.

Swelle Farm.

Strange how life could turn in a second, she thought, nothing ever the same again. Life one minute, death the next. That was how it had felt in London, when the bomb exploded nearby, blowing her into oblivion. It could have been forever, but for that American. She remembered the handsome pilot who'd sacrificed his life in saving hers, and wondered what her future might have looked like if she'd got a chance to know Max better. There'd been such chemistry between them that night . . .

But it was pointless living in the past, dwelling on what might have been. Poor Max had died. She was still alive. For how much longer, though?

She listened to the drag and roar of the tide over the beach at Porthcurno, and recalled how Rex had looked at her so strangely on the cliff edge. Had she imagined the grim look in his eyes? Or had he really been intending to cast her down to her death?

In that split second, Eva made a decision.

Turning away from the tunnels, she trod lightly across the front of Eastern House in the shadowy gloom of blackout, heading for the low building where she knew Rex had his quarters, along with some of the other 'civvies', as the guard had dubbed the non-military personnel who worked at the listening post.

The house was dark and quiet. Nobody home. And the front door was unlocked, of course. Why wouldn't it be?

She knew exactly which room belonged to Rex, as he'd leant out of the window one sunny afternoon to wave at her.

'Rex?' she whispered, opening the door to darkness.

The room was empty, its occupant sheltering from German bombers in the tunnels. Where she ought to be.

Closing his door behind her, she stood a moment in the silence, gathering her nerve. The blackout curtain was in place, covering the window, so she put the light on.

Her heart was thudding wildly at her own audacity.

If she was caught in here . . .

She pushed that fear aside and began to search regardless, hunting first through the loose papers on his narrow desk, then opening his drawers, peeking hurriedly in his wardrobe, even kneeling to rummage under his bed. Finally, about to give up, she lifted his mattress clear off the metal bedframe, noting how bumpy it felt . . . and a piece of folded paper fluttered to the floor.

Eva bent to retrieve it, blinking as she realised what it was.

The strange, childish phrase she had intercepted from the machine in the tunnels that he usually manned alone. *Polly put the kettle on.* A secret coded message. He had not seemed surprised to see it, and had said he would deal with it.

Yet here it was, pushed out of sight under his mattress.

She lifted the mattress again and ran a hand along its bare underside. Yes, there it was again. An odd little bump. Like a concealed pouch. It was sealed though, she realised on closer examination, with a row of neat, almost invisible stitches. Almost as though something had been sewn inside the mattress itself.

'Oh, Rex . . .' She bit her lip. 'What have you been up to?'

There was a penknife on his bedside table.

Breathing fast, Eva picked it up and began to cut the secret pocket open.

CHAPTER THIRTY-FOUR

'Looks like the old barn got the worst of it,' Joe said, straining to see through the gathering dark. He had wound down the window, and leant out now, staring ahead. 'That's where we kept the spare gas canisters. They must have exploded. The house looks untouched though.'

'That's a blessing,' Violet said, holding on for dear life as the truck bounced violently up and down over the farm track ruts.

'Yes,' he said slowly, but he still looked tense.

'Edna will be right as rain,' Violet said, trying to reassure him. 'Your mum won't have been out in the barn at this time of the evening.'

'But the shelter's dug in right beside the barn. If she heard the plane coming over, she might have run out there for safety.'

Violet wanted to say something cheery, to keep his spirits up. But she had too much experience of neighbours in the East End who'd thought themselves safe in their cellar or Anderson shelter, only to be found dead in the rubble the next day – or never found at all. Nothing and nobody could survive a direct hit from a Jerry bomb.

But she could hardly tell him that, could she?

As soon as the truck drew up outside the smouldering ruins of the barn, Joe jumped straight out. He ran to where the colonel and a small group of soldiers were trying to explore the wreckage. 'Where's my mother?' he called out. 'Was she here when the bomb fell?'

He sounded half out of his mind, Violet thought, following him with a sick feeling in the pit of her stomach. The soldiers were all looking down at their boots in an unhappy manner she recalled from bombings in Dagenham. Nobody ever wanted to be the one who had to break the bad news to a grieving relative.

'Somebody talk to me, for God's sake!' Joe insisted.

'It's bad news, I'm afraid, Joe,' Colonel Ryder said grimly, and put a hand on Joe's shoulder. 'Best prepare yourself. The shelter was destroyed along with the north end of the barn. Not much left. My men are digging there . . . We couldn't find anyone in the house.' His voice tailed off, his expression compassionate as Joe let out a groan. 'I'm sorry, son.'

Joe turned away, shrugging off his hand. 'Why here?' he demanded hoarsely, rubbing at his eyes. 'Why my farm? What use was it to the Jerries, bombing this old place?'

Nobody answered.

'It's because of Eastern House, isn't it?' Joe answered his own question, bluntly voicing the thought that was running through Violet's head. He turned on his heel, pointing up into the black sky. 'The Germans flew up the coast with some garbled intelligence, probably looking for "a large white house near Porthcurno", and bombed Swelle Farm by mistake.'

'You're upset,' the colonel began awkwardly, but was interrupted.

'I only brought my mother up to the farm to keep her safe. She was happier down in Penzance, wanted to stay there, despite the bombing. I told her that I couldn't cope without a woman about the place. It was the only way to get her to come with me. She . . . she called me selfish. And she was right. If I'd left her in Penzance like she wanted . . .' Joe ran a hand across his forehead. 'This is all my fault.' Then he straightened, shaking his head as he turned back to the colonel. 'No, it was *your* fault.'

'Now, son . . .'

'I'm not your son. And you're not my superior officer. I'm not in the forces anymore. I've done my time and paid my price.' Joe banged his metal leg furiously. 'Or so I thought. You set up camp in a quiet Cornish village, knowing it made us a target for the enemy. Yet you've done sod all to protect the locals. And now this . . . my mother is the one who's paid for what you're doing at the listening post.' He drew in a sharp breath, his voice uneven. 'Get off my land! You and your bloody men. She's my mother, I'll dig her body out myself.'

As Joe finished, another shadowy figure loomed up out of the dark night, lit up by the faint light of the moon, rising slowly behind Violet. A young soldier whose pinched, familiar face made her shudder, her stomach queasy with apprehension.

''Ere, you watch what you're saying to the colonel!' Patrick Dullaghan said, squaring up to Joe and punctuating each word with an insolent jab of his index finger. 'You ain't got no right to speak to 'im like that, all right?'

Joe stared at the young soldier, speechless.

'We'll get your mum out of that bleedin' mess, no fear. But there ain't no amount of yapping will bring 'er back to life.' Patrick Dullaghan pushed him backwards. 'So just you shut yer gob, sit down out the way, and let us work.' Abruptly, his gaze swivelled toward Violet, and she shrank back, appalled by the cruel glint in his eyes. 'Though if you want to blame someone for that Jerry bomb, you might want to start wiv your lady friend there.'

Violet sucked in her breath in horror.

He was going to accuse her of being a spy.

This was precisely what she'd feared the moment she'd clapped eyes on that nasty piece of work. It was all lies. But would they realise that? He was so good at twisting words, making a lie sound like truth. If they asked him what he meant . . .

Shaking her head in instinctive denial, Violet put a hand to her mouth. 'No,' she tried to say, but no sound would come out.

At this, the colonel rapped out, 'Private, that's quite enough! What in God's name . . . ? Who gave you permission to speak?'

'Sorry, Colonel.' Patrick took a few steps back and saluted, his back very straight. 'Don't know what come over me, Colonel.'

'That's not good enough. Explain yourself.'

Patrick flashed her a vengeful look. Though what he might have to feel vengeful about, Violet could not imagine. He'd always had it in for her – that was all. Perhaps because her mum ran a café, and his family had nothing, like so many others in the East End. She was sorry for him, but that didn't excuse his reputation for petty pilfering and telling whoppers. Nor for him wanting to dob her in with the colonel, who was listening intently.

'She's not to be trusted, sir. Her whole family neither. They had dealings with the enemy, that's what we used to say back in Dagenham.'

'What?' the colonel thundered.

'That's where I know her from, sir,' Patrick said hurriedly. 'The East End. Nobody with any sense spoke to Violet back there. Well, what do you expect, with a bleedin' Jerry for a brother-in-law?'

The colonel turned to her, his face unreadable in the darkness. 'Does this private know you, Violet?' He paused. 'I apologise, I don't know your surname.'

'Y-yes, sir,' she stammered, her knees fairly knocking at the steel in his voice. 'He knows me and I know him, more's the pity. That's Patrick Dullaghan, and I bet them in Dagenham are glad to be shot of the nasty little sod, if you'll pardon my French.' She saw what looked like the suspicion of a smile on the colonel's face, and added with more bravado than actual courage, 'And I'm Violet Hopkins.'

'Is any of this farrago of nonsense true, Miss Hopkins?'

'I d-don't rightly know what a f-farrago is,' she said, struggling to get the words out, her chest was heaving so much with hurt and indignation. 'But what he said . . . It's not true, Colonel Ryder.'

'What about this brother-in-law of yours?'

'He's half-German, sir. But Ernst joined up soon as war broke out. He wanted to fight for King and country – that's what he kept saying. They shipped him out to the front straightaway. As he talks the lingo, I expect the army thought he could be useful.'

'Yes, I rather imagine they did.'

'Only he . . . Well, he's gone missing in action.' Violet wrung her hands together. 'I know it looks bad, sir. But Ernst is a good bloke, sound as a pound. He's not a Jerry spy, I swear!'

'Hmm.' The colonel considered her, then called one of the other soldiers over. 'Drive Miss Hopkins home, sergeant.'

The sergeant saluted, and gestured to her to follow him. 'This way, Miss.'

But Violet was looking at Joe.

Joe had been staring at her since Patrick Dullaghan's first

horrible accusation; she had felt his tormented gaze on her face the whole time. And she badly wanted to explain herself, to protest her innocence. Only he didn't give her the chance. Without saying a word, Joe turned to stumble away towards the ruins of the old barn.

Poor Joe, she thought wretchedly, watching him go. To have lost his mother in such an awful way, and all through a misunderstanding, the white farmhouse mistaken for Eastern House, the Germans' real target . . . He must be in pieces. And she wanted to comfort him, to hold his hand again, like she'd done during the drive over here. But she could see her sympathy was not wanted, that Joe needed to be alone right now.

Besides, the sergeant was waiting and Patrick Dullaghan was sneering at her, like he knew he'd won.

What could she do?

Nothing, she thought bitterly. Nothing at all.

A tear rolled down her cheek.

The colonel cleared his throat. 'Come and see me tomorrow,' he told her, though his tone was a little distant now, as though he half believed the accusations against her. 'I'll need to investigate this properly. Make a full report to headquarters.'

Violet allowed herself to be led away by the sergeant to a waiting vehicle. But all the time her gaze was following Joe as he dropped to his knees beside the bombed-out rubble that had been his barn, now covering the shelter where poor Edna's body lay. Her own pathetic troubles were nothing in comparison. His life would never be the same again.

CHAPTER THIRTY-FIVE

Charlie and the girls had already taken themselves off to bed by the time Hazel heard a car in the distance. She jumped up, her heart beating fast, hoping that was Violet back from the farm at last. She'd been sitting in the kitchen for several hours, reading a magazine in a distracted way, trying not to think about kissing George at the dance, but cast it aside as the car drew to a halt outside the cottage.

Outside, the engine died. A car door opened and shut, but she couldn't hear Violet's familiar clacking heels approaching the house.

'Is that Aunty Vi come home?' a voice said from the top of the stairs, and she turned, schooling herself to look unconcerned.

'I expect so. You should be in bed, Alice. You must be exhausted after tonight. All that work we did to get the hall ready in time. Not to mention the dancing.' She tried to smile. 'Don't think I didn't see the two of you having a twirl!'

'My feet hurt, for sure. But I can't get to sleep.' Alice gave her an unhappy look. 'I keep thinking about Joe's mum. I hope she's all right.'

Alice and Lily had met Joe Postbridge and his mum on the beach at Penzance, they had told her on the drive home, and liked both of them instinctively. They were sad that the farm might have been bombed. But there had been weary resignation in Lily's voice when she expressed a hope that the bomb had missed 'Joe's nice mum'. That was how they had lost their own mother, of course.

'I know, it's awful. But with any luck—'

Someone knocked at the cottage door.

Alice came down a few more steps, wide-eyed. 'That can't be Aunty Vi. She wouldn't knock.'

'No.' Hurriedly, Hazel opened the door, which was unlocked, and felt winded when she saw who was standing there. 'G-George!'

'Sorry to disturb you so late.' He stumbled over the words, his gaze fixed on hers. There was a strange light in his eyes. 'But I had to speak to you. If you don't mind, that is.' Removing his hat, George ran a hand through his dishevelled hair, and then tugged at his crumpled jacket, as though trying to pull himself together. 'I can come back tomorrow evening, if it's more convenient.'

'What's happened, Mr Cotterill? We ain't heard nothing and it's been driving us mad.' Alice scrambled down the stairs, apparently oblivious to the fact that she was barefoot and wearing a too-short nightie, which was hardly appropriate in front of visitors. 'Where's Aunty Vi? Is it true Joe's farm got bombed? Was his mum hurt?'

George looked dazed, perhaps unsure which question to answer first. 'Swelle Farm was hit in the raid, yes. But I haven't seen the damage first-hand, so I'm afraid I don't know anything beyond that.'

'Poor Joe,' Alice whispered.

'You'd better come in,' Hazel told George firmly, then

turned to her young guest. 'Alice, perhaps you should try and get some sleep. I'd like to speak to Mr Cotterill alone.' Her smile was placatory. 'As soon as your aunt's home, I'll send her up to you, I promise.'

Alice cast her a frustrated look, but did not argue, sighing and heading back upstairs without another word. She was a good girl at heart, if a little eccentric at times.

George turned towards the sitting room, but she caught him in time, signalling him to be quiet. 'In the kitchen is best. I don't want to disturb Charlie.'

'Charlie?' He looked confused.

'He sleeps in the sitting room now. Gave up his room to Violet and the girls.'

'Of course.' George put his hat on the table, then drew up a chair. 'He's not a bad lad, your Charlie. Running away like that wasn't the cleverest thing to do, besides scaring you half to death. But under the circumstances . . .'

'I don't know what I'd have done if you hadn't found him. Thank you for—'

'You already thanked me, Hazel.'

She loved the sound of her name on his lips. But she couldn't think like that. It was madness. And far too soon to be proper.

'Shall I . . . make a brew?' Uneasily, she turned to put the kettle on the stove.

But he stopped her with a swift, 'No, I didn't come for tea. I came to talk to you.'

She sat down at the table next to him, suddenly tongue-tied. It didn't help that she had been pushing away memories of her and Bertie all evening. Her late husband. How strange it seemed to think of him as being dead. Though, awful as it was, she couldn't pretend to be genuinely mourning. She was sad for him. But not distraught, as people might expect her to be, especially once it became known that she was carrying his child.

It had been a long time since she'd felt any love for Bertie. But the shock of his death was so recent and raw, she wasn't sure she could manage these feelings for George on top of that emotion.

He took her hand. 'Hazel,' he said, speaking her name so lovingly that she did not know where to look, 'I know it's probably too soon. What with Bertie, and all . . .' George seemed as awkward as her, his usual professional air replaced by something more like desperation. 'But I want you to know that I'm here for you. Whatever you need, you only have to say the word.'

'That's very kind.'

'I'm not saying that out of kindness.' He drew her hand towards him, then raised it to his lips, amazing her by kissing the back gently. 'But out of love.'

Her lips parted in astonishment. 'S-Sorry?'

'I'm in love with you, Hazel.'

She stared at him, pulling her hand back.

'Is that so hard to believe?' George asked gently. 'We've been friends since school days, and I think you know that if you hadn't married Bertie . . . Well, no point crying over spilt milk. You did marry him, and what I'd hoped for never happened.' He smiled at her bewilderment. 'What, did you think I was only after one thing?'

'I don't know. I wasn't sure . . .'

'Oh, Hazel.'

She looked down, unable to find the right words for the feelings sweeping over her. Sadness? Joy? Tears pricked at her eyes. Yet she was happy. She shouldn't be. It was wrong to be happy at such a bleak time. But she couldn't help the love in her heart.

'Do you remember when we ran off to the woods together after school one day? We can't have been more than nine or ten years old.' He smiled when she nodded. 'We'd been learning about the Wild West in school, so I made a wigwam for you with twigs and fallen branches.'

'I made mud pies for us,' she said with a shaky laugh, remembering how they had pretended to keep house together, even sheltering inside when it started to rain. 'My mother gave me such a scold when I got home, I was covered in dirt.'

'Did she?' He shook his head. 'I only recall how beautiful you looked, kneeling in the opening to that wigwam.' George ran a hand through his hair. 'I know it's too soon,' he added. 'Far too soon.'

'Yes,' she managed to croak, overcome with emotion.

'And if things were different, I wouldn't have said anything. I'd have given you a year to get over your loss. God knows I've waited long enough, another year wouldn't have made much difference. And there's a war on. Not the best time to be tying the knot.' Seeming troubled, his gaze dropped to her belly. 'But ever since I heard your news, I've realised we can't wait. If you want that baby to grow up with a father, that is.'

Hazel could hardly believe what he was saying. 'You want to . . . ?'

'I'm asking you to marry me, yes.' He paused, frowning when she didn't say anything. 'I'm not love's young dream, I'm the first to admit it. But I've got a steady job, and you're going to need someone to take care of you and the baby.'

George knew she was carrying Bertie's child.

And it hadn't put him off.

In fact, he wanted to marry her. And as fast as possible, by the sound of it. So her new baby could grow up with George Cotterill as his or her father, instead of as the child of a lonely widow.

'Oh!'

He dropped her hand and stared at her, clearly taken aback. 'Hazel, what is it? You're crying. Have I upset you?'

Hazel rubbed her eyes with the back of her hand. 'No, I just thought . . . At the dance tonight, when you kissed me, and then . . . and then left . . .'

'That I was only flirting?'

'How could I have known you wanted to *marry me*?'

'I wanted to say something then, but you seemed so fragile. And then the bombers came over.'

'I know, I know. I'm sorry I misunderstood.' She waved a hand at him, struggling not to blub too loudly, in case Charlie heard and came in to see what was going on. 'I'm not upset, silly. I'm happy!'

'Thank God.'

'And you don't mind that the baby . . . that it isn't yours?'

'Of course. I won't lie to the child, though. I couldn't do that. I hope you understand. Boy or girl, they'll be told about their real father and what happened to him. That's only right and fair.' He cleared his throat, speaking with an effort. 'Whatever else Bertie Baxter may have been, he died a hero, fighting for his country.'

'Agreed.'

'And you probably want to wait a while to marry so folk don't gossip. A few months to grieve.' He paused. 'But before Christmas, if you approve?'

Hazel nodded, her eyes misty. 'I can't believe this is happening.'

'I haven't done this properly, have I? I've always prided myself on being methodical, doing things carefully so they get done right. And the most important thing in my life, the moment I've been dreaming about for years, I manage to completely fluff . . .' George dropped to one knee and took her hand again, looking up with a shy smile. Something in his face transported her back to when they were stupid kids together, falling in love and not really sure what they wanted, so making a complete shambles of it . . . 'Hazel, will you do me the honour of accepting my hand in marriage?'

So many mistakes in her life. So much regret.

But this would not be a mistake.

This was something she would never regret.

Hazel did not even need to make that promise to herself; she knew it instinctively, gazing down into his eyes. He was offering her a fresh start. This was true love, not a mockery of the real thing.

And she was going to grasp this love with both hands and never let go.

'Yes, George,' she breathed, 'I will.'

For five blessed moments, they were alone together in the kitchen, just kissing and holding each other close. Then she heard the creak of a door opening, and turned to find Charlie in the doorway, wearing blue long johns and staring bleary-eyed at them both.

'Oh, d-did we wake you?' she stammered, moving away from George, who had also taken a quick step back, looking embarrassed. 'Sorry, dearest.'

'What's going on?' he asked suspiciously, staring from her to George, and no doubt noting their heightened colour. 'Were you kissing my mum again?'

Before she could say anything, George cleared his throat and nodded. 'That's right, I was,' he said firmly. 'I know it probably feels too soon after your dad's passing, and I'm sorry for that. But I love your mum, and I want to marry her and look after her properly for the rest of my life.'

There was a long silence, while Hazel dared not move,

terrified that Charlie and George would argue, and maybe even come to blows. She was so used to Bertie's hair-trigger temper, she half believed her son had inherited the same prickly temperament. And perhaps she ought to tell Charlie she was expecting again, and that she and George didn't have time for a long courtship. But really, it was too soon in the pregnancy to be sharing her news, even with her son, and she wasn't sure it would make any difference to him anyway.

To her amazement, Charlie merely ran a hand through his dishevelled hair, studied George for a moment, then gave a sharp nod.

'You'll treat her right, Mr Cotterill? No funny business?'

'You have my word of honour,' George told him, solemn and straight-backed, and went to shake Charlie's hand. 'You're the man of the house now. Do I have your consent to come courting your mother?'

'Only so long as you don't hit her.'

Hazel clapped her hands to her cheeks, horribly embarrassed by her son's frankness. 'Charlie, please!'

'I swear on my life that I'll never raise a hand to your mother, either before or after we're wed.' George shot her a wry smile over his shoulder. 'My own mother taught me better than that.'

'Well, then,' Charlie said, yawning, 'I'm going back to bed.' And with that sleepy statement, he disappeared, closing the door behind him.

Hazel thought she might cry. But from pure joy, not sadness.

My son is growing up, she thought.

And growing up to be *nothing* like his violent dad.

As George was leaving, they heard an engine roaring up the hill towards the little row of terraced cottages. An army vehicle, no doubt bringing Violet back.

They stood waiting together at the end of the garden path until her friend had stumbled out of the truck, and it had driven slowly away in the darkness.

Violet was weeping, and it was clear that things had gone horribly wrong since they'd seen her drive off to Swelle Farm. Hazel was horrified by her appearance and shaking hands. How much damage had the bombing done?

'What is it, Vi?' With George's help, Hazel supported her into the house and shut the door. The woman looked awful, her face blotchy, eyes red-rimmed. 'What on earth's happened?'

'Joe's mother is dead,' Violet told them both in an agonised whisper, clawing at her face as she sobbed. 'And the c-c-colonel thinks I'm a spy.'

CHAPTER THIRTY-SIX

Everyone else had gone outside for their morning tea break. Eva alone still sat at her desk, her back to the underground room, peering down at the silent machine in front of her.

Come on, she kept thinking. All the other machines were whirring round noisily. But not hers.

Do something, damn it.

The chair she was sitting on was straight-backed with an uncomfortable seat. Ordinarily, she would have been waiting in the comfier chairs in the training room down the corridor and only come out when she heard the machine start up as a message arrived. But she dreaded not being in her seat at the right moment and messing up the timing.

Finally, to her relief, there was the ticking and clacking of an incoming message.

Right on cue.

She ran her finger along the ticker tape as it spewed off the roll, and smiled to herself before tearing the section cleanly.

'Better give that to me,' a voice said smoothly from behind her.

She jumped, looking round into Rex's face.

'How long have you been standing there?'

'Long enough to know you've been sitting there for ages, waiting for a message as though you knew one was coming.'

She felt her colour rise, but said nothing.

'Come on.' He snapped his fingers, his expression calm and expectant. 'Can't have top-secret messages falling into the wrong hands, can we?'

'Funnily enough, that's just what I was thinking.' Eva whisked the piece of ticker tape behind her back as he reached for it. 'Sorry, Rex, no can do. I have a feeling it wouldn't be a terribly good idea to let you take it either.'

'What on earth are you talking about?' He paused. 'Is this about last night? I know you were planning to dance the night away. You can't pin that on me though. Hardly my fault the damn Jerries flew over.'

'Isn't it?' she asked lightly.

'Sorry?'

'Well, it's odd how the bombers knew about Eastern House.'

He blinked. Then gave a short laugh under his breath. 'You're such an innocent, Eva. It's charming, really.'

She stared, puzzled.

'It's hard to keep anything a secret when the place is crawling with soldiers,' he explained gently, 'half of them writing letters home to Mum and Dad.'

'You think someone here talked?'

'Loose lips sink ships.'

'Or get bombs dropped on civilians, in this case. Someone was killed in last night's raid, you know.' She studied him closely. 'The Germans missed this place and bombed a farm-house further along the coast by mistake. I expect the two buildings look quite similar from the air.'

'Yes, I heard that. It's too bad.'

'Will they come back and try again, do you think?'

'Depends on whether the Jerries know they hit the wrong target. I don't imagine they realise that yet.' He reached around her for the piece of ticker tape, and she backed away again. His frown intensified. 'Here, what are you playing at? This isn't funny, Eva. Are you going to give me that message or do you want me to tell the colonel?'

'Maybe I should save you a job and find my father myself.' She took a deep breath, her heart beating fast. 'You see, I don't think you can be trusted with this message.'

Especially, she thought, if it was true what he'd said about the enemy not knowing yet that they had hit the wrong target. To keep Eastern House safe from further bombing raids, it was vital that Rex Templeton should be prevented from passing on more intelligence to the Germans.

His eyelids flickered but his expression didn't change. 'Very funny, ha ha.' He clicked his fingers again. 'Now come on, be a good girl and hand it over. I think you're the one who can't be trusted.'

'I imagine Daddy would be quite curious to hear about your other life.'

'My other life?'

'As a spy.'

'What in God's name . . . ?' His jaw hardened. 'How dare you?' There was a tense silence, then he took a step towards her. 'All right now, enough of this nonsense. Give me that message or face the consequences.'

Eva was a little alarmed by the menacing look in his eyes, but kept her hand firmly behind her back. 'No,' she said, raising her chin as she added, 'and I really don't think you ought to be threatening me.'

'Is that so?' Rex made a snatch for her arm, but she danced out of reach. Flushed, he swore loudly, moving after her. 'You spoilt brat! Wait until I get hold of you . . .'

'Admit you're a spy!' she hissed, ducking round behind a large row of glass-panelled cabinets that divided the room, housing machines that constantly whirred and ticked.

'You're insane.'

She ran to the far end of the machine cabinets and looked round, only to find him advancing upon her, having guessed what she would do.

Fleeing back the other way, she yelled, 'There's no point denying it. I've been in your room, Rex. I've seen what you keep hidden there, sewn into your mattress.'

His heavy footsteps stopped.

She too shrank to stillness with her back against a glass-panelled door, listening to the sound of his laboured breathing on the other side of the cabinets.

'I don't know what you mean . . .' he began cautiously.

'Liar!'

Rex trod swiftly round the end of the cabinets, his eyes narrowing as he saw her. 'Very well,' he drawled, his manner changing now his secret was out in the open. 'So you've got me. I've been moonlighting for the other side.' He came slowly towards her, an unpleasant smile on his face as she walked backwards, her eyes wide with apprehension. 'The problem is, little Miss Know-It-All, I've got you too. There's nobody else here. What's to stop me from taking that message away from you, and strangling you before you can tell your precious daddy about me?'

Eva swallowed, convinced that he meant it. 'Well,' she said huskily, 'there is one thing that could stop you.'

'And what's that?'

'I'm not as stupid as you think. I already told Daddy about you.'

Rex stopped dead, staring at her in disbelief.

'Right, I've heard quite enough.' To her relief, her father

came out from his hiding place in the adjacent messages room, flanked by two other officers. He was holding a pistol, and his voice boomed the full length of the room, making Rex jump and look round. 'Step away from my daughter at once, you traitor.' He shook his head, sounding magnificently angry. 'Spying for the enemy, eh?'

Rex froze, staring at him in silence.

'Cat got your tongue, Professor Templeton?' her father continued. 'I'm afraid that will never do. Especially after those incriminating papers we found in your quarters. I think it's time you and I had a chat, man to man. Before I have to send you back to London under arrest. Yes, your presence has been requested. Seems there are a few people in Whitehall who'd like a word with you too.'

But Rex had other ideas. He grabbed Eva before she realised what he was planning, twisting her in front of his body like a human shield.

'Better not shoot, Colonel,' he said coldly, 'or you'll be killing your own daughter. Put that gun down.'

Her father looked horrified, but did not lower his pistol. 'Don't be a fool, Templeton. The place is crawling with soldiers. You can't get away.'

'Oh, can't I?' Eva felt Rex wrestle with something in his jacket pocket, then found herself staring into the dark, business-like muzzle of a pocket pistol. He pressed it against her temple with a cracked laugh. 'Time for us to go. Not a move or I shoot the girl.'

Eva felt her skin go cold at those words. Would he really kill her?

Rex pushed her forward a few steps, and then a few more, all the time heading for the tunnel that led outside. They passed her father and the other officers, who watched their progress in silent consternation.

One of the officers made a move, but her father held him back. 'Steady, there.'

'That's right, better not try anything stupid.' Rex sounded oddly calm despite his desperate situation. 'Let me go, Colonel, and your daughter gets to live. Try to stop me, and her brains will be all over the floor.'

Eva blenched, sure now that he wasn't bluffing.

It had seemed like such a good plan when she spoke to her father after the air raid had finished. To entrap Rex into revealing himself. They'd hoped he would give away precisely who he was working for, and why, perhaps in order to boast to her about it. But although Rex had admitted to being a spy, perhaps because her proof had been too conclusive to bother denying, he had not given away anything else of use to the British government.

And why would he?

Rex had never been genuinely attracted to her, after all. She had been a means to an end. Walking out with her had been one more way to gain the trust of the brass higher up, getting close to the colonel's daughter while covertly passing on decryption keys and classified messages to the enemy.

She could not let this evil man get away. He would probably shoot her anyway. Unless she could disarm him before he was out of the tunnels.

As they reached the doorway, she spotted the fire bucket a few feet ahead, full of sand. Pretending to stumble, she slumped against him with a groan.

'Stand straight!'

'Sorry,' she moaned, 'I feel so faint . . .'

'For God's sake!'

As she drooped in his arms, Rex tried to grab her up again, but she had hold of the heavy metal fire bucket. Using all her strength, she swung it round into his knees, taking him by surprise.

He swore in pain, staggering back, and raised his arm to shoot. But a sharp, deafening crack dropped him to his knees, and his gun skittered away across the floor. At first, Eva didn't understand what had happened, backing away in bewilderment. Then she saw her father's arm still pointing in their direction, pistol in hand, and smelt smoke on the air.

The two officers ran forward to secure their prisoner, who was groaning now as he rolled about on the floor.

'Got him in the buttocks, by the look of it,' her father said crisply, holstering his pistol, and then apologised to her. 'Sorry, not what I'd have liked you to witness. But couldn't let him escape. Or risk him shooting you, eh?'

'Quite,' Eva agreed drily.

Her father reached her and gave her a quick, rough hug. 'Bit shaky, my dear? Perfectly natural. You've had a nasty shock.'

'I'll survive.'

'Of course you will. You're my daughter, aren't you?' He beamed down at her indulgently, then turned to Rex, his look suddenly fierce. 'No need to make all that noise. We'll get a doctor to you soon enough. Not that you deserve it, threatening to shoot my daughter, and bringing those bombs down on us last night. An innocent woman was killed in that raid. You'll pay for that.'

Eva looked down at Rex too, feeling sick now that it was all over. 'Why did you do it? Why betray your country?'

Rex grimaced, clearly in pain. 'We didn't all have your advantages in life,' he spat out. 'Don't judge what you can't understand.'

Her father made a noise under his breath, and drew her

away. 'Come on, m'dear,' he said gruffly, 'let's get you away from that worthless man.'

Her father supported her out of the tunnel, into the bright sunshine, where she stood dazed, watching seagulls wheeling above them in a brilliantly blue Cornish sky. He hurried away to send for a medical team to attend the professor, and then guided her to a bench on the lawn below, in the shade of a large beech tree.

'Right, where's that message?' her father asked. 'The one our friend was so eager to intercept.'

'Oh, yes.' Eva took a deep breath and handed over the ticker tape. She watched curiously while he read it. 'What's it about, anyway?'

'Nothing more important than a shopping list,' he said with a wink, and pushed it into his pocket. 'But the trick worked a treat. Now, if you're feeling better, I've got something for you.'

Eva was surprised. 'Something for me?'

He drew out a crumpled letter from inside his jacket pocket. 'It arrived a while ago, but I didn't feel right letting you read it before now. No hard feelings, I hope.'

She turned the envelope over and saw her name on it, yet it had already been opened.

Outrage filled her. 'You read a private letter? Addressed to me?'

'A father's prerogative,' he said gruffly. 'Listen, you were quite shaken up after that near miss in London. I was just trying to protect you.'

'Daddy!'

'You've got the letter now, haven't you? No point making a big song and dance.' He cleared his throat, then gave a nod. 'Right, I've got business to attend to. People waiting to see me. If there's anything else you need—'

'I'll be fine,' she said firmly.

'Well, well.' He looked quickly about as though to check nobody was listening, then bent towards her, saying, 'You were brave in there, Eva. Quick thinking too. That fellow nearly got away, and that would have been a bad deal all round. Now he'll face justice.' He bent and dropped a kiss on her forehead. 'Must say, I was very proud of you.'

She blushed, smiling as he walked away, hands in his pockets, whistling in the sunshine. Then turned her attention to the letter.

It was a single sheet, signed *Flight Lieutenant Max Carmichael*.

He was alive!

Her heart beating fast, Eva smoothed out the crumpled sheet and read through it quickly, then more slowly a second time.

Dear Miss Ryder,

It seems like a century since the night we met in the club in London, and I hope you don't think it an impertinence for me to be writing to you now. But ever since I came to, I've been thinking about you and wondering how you are. I've been told you survived the blast, but nobody seems to know what happened to you after you were taken to hospital.

As for me, I'm a bit of a mess. Swathed in bandages like an Egyptian mummy! But at least I didn't bite the dust. Not everyone was so lucky that night.

One of the men in my ward knows your father, Colonel Ryder, and kindly suggested where I should send this letter. I hope it reaches you. I'm to be discharged to a convalescent home as soon as I'm fit enough. As luck would have it, there's one in Cornwall

*that might be able to take me. It's in a town called St
Ives, but I don't know how far that is from you, and
they have no free beds at present.*

*Anyway, if you could find the time to reply, I would
be relieved to know you weren't badly hurt.*

Still very much your admirer,

Flt Lt Max Carmichael

So, this time, her worst fears had not been realised. The
pilot had survived the bombing. It sounded like he was in a
bad way, though.

Swathed in bandages . . .

Eva bit her lip at the frightening mental image that phrase
inspired. How severe were his injuries? It was impossible to
tell from his letter. Yet he seemed in good spirits, despite
everything that had happened to him. What a strong, resilient
soul he was, she thought, closing her eyes as she remembered
that awful moment when Max had pushed her to safety, just
before the bomb hit . . .

A tear crept from under one eyelid, trickling down her
cheek in the sunshine. Oh goodness, what was she like? It
wasn't as though she were *in love* with the man. She had only
known him a few hours, in fact, before disaster struck. But
she had wasted so much time on Rex Templeton this summer,
and he had not been worth a single minute of it. Max was
worth a hundred Rex Templetons. A thousand, even.

All the same, it was only a letter. And a short one at that.

Should she be thinking about turning her life upside down
over a man again, so soon after being deceived by an enemy
spy? On the strength of a single sheet of paper?

She folded the letter, replaced it in the envelope, and
pressed it to her chest. Despite today's appalling events with
Rex, this news felt like the hand of Fate on her shoulder. And

maybe her father had been right to withhold the letter, seeing her so absorbed by her work at the listening post, and her preparations for the dance. She might not have been able to cope with this exciting news any sooner.

Now though, she felt ready to look beyond Porthcurno again.

She had been shaken up by the bombing in London, it was true, and happy to hide down here in rural Cornwall. That night had definitely affected her behaviour, making her more cautious than usual and almost afraid to look beyond surface appearances. If she had been her normal self, she would have spotted far earlier that Rex was hiding something. But last night's dreadful air raid had reminded her that she had survived one brush with the enemy already, and that life had to go on – otherwise what was the point of it all?

It had been lovely this summer, discovering the southern Cornish coast and falling in love with its sandy coves and sleepy countryside. And she had enjoyed spending more time with her father too, even if he could be a bit overbearing at times, always thinking he knew what was best for her. But she had no intention of hiding down here forever, acting the role of dutiful daughter. Not when she had unfinished business elsewhere.

Still very much your admirer, Flt Lt Max Carmichael.

Oh, was he, indeed?

Eva grinned as she hurried back to her room, already mentally rehearsing how she would persuade her stubborn father to let her leave Porthcurno.

A convalescent home in St Ives . . .

Maybe it was time to brush up on her nursing skills.

CHAPTER THIRTY-SEVEN

Violet could not meet anyone's eye.

Lily and Alice were seated either side of her, their slight bodies still and tensed, as though waiting for the next blow to hit their troubled family. Lily had been weeping, and Alice had her nose in a book, no doubt trying to escape the reality of their situation. They must be starving, she thought, having eaten the scantest of breakfasts this morning, and no lunch whatsoever, knowing they had to be at the colonel's office for midday.

Only midday had come and gone long ago.

Hazel was pacing the narrow corridor outside the colonel's office, pausing now and then to glance out through the window. When Violet had arrived back at the cottage last night, George Cotterill had been there with Hazel, and both of them had listened in horror to Violet's explanation of why she had been brought back by a soldier.

But although George had reassured her that the colonel wouldn't put any store by Patrick Dullaghan's claims, she had seen the wary look in his eyes and suspected he was in fact questioning whether the stories about her brother-in-law might be true.

Did Joe harbour the same suspicions, she wondered? Did he blame her for his mum's death, perhaps?

She remembered Joe's drawn face as he left her, stumbling away towards the ruins of his bombed-out barn, and despair gripped her. At the dance, she had thought, maybe . . . But no, even that tiny hope had been extinguished now. She would never see Joe again, unless it was to point an angry finger of accusation in her direction.

Violet bent her head, staring down at her hands, clasped tight in her lap. She didn't have a clue what would happen now. But she was sure it wouldn't be anything good.

Perhaps they would send her away from Porthcurno. Her and the girls. Just to be on the safe side. Except they had nowhere else to go. They might end up having to return to London, where bombs still fell every night . . .

Patrick's jeering voice echoed in her head, however hard she struggled to shut it out. *They shoot spies, don't they?* This was so unfair. She wasn't a German spy! And neither was Ernst. But how to convince the colonel of that?

'Don't fret, Aunty Vi,' Lily reassured her. Such a good girl, she was. Poor pet though, she must be as terrified as Violet herself. To lose first her mother, and now possibly her aunt . . . 'Those rumours about Daddy . . . They're not true. It's all a terrible mistake, you'll see.'

Violet squeezed Lily's hand, muttering, 'Thank you, pet.'

Alice looked up from her book with a loud harumph. 'Don't be an idiot, Lil. Them Dullaghans don't give up easy. I mean, look at them, making trouble for us even down here.' She tapped the open page of her book emphatically. 'Run away, Aunty Vi – that's what you should do. Scarper before the colonel can clap you up in irons.'

'Clap your aunt in irons? What nonsense. The colonel won't do any such thing. Where on earth did you get such an idea?' Hazel peered at the tatty paperback on Alice's lap. 'What is that book you're reading?'

'*Treasure Island*,' Alice said, her chin raised defensively, and she snapped the paperback shut. 'Nuffin' wrong in that. I've read it three times already.'

'Three times too many if you ask me,' Hazel murmured, shaking her head with a faint smile. 'Though you're an unusual girl, Alice. I'll give you that.'

Violet jumped up, unable to sit still a moment longer. 'For goodness' sake, where's the colonel? It's nearly two hours since we came up here and no sign of him yet. All this waiting about . . . I tell you, me nerves won't stand it.'

'Yes, it's not right to keep you waiting this long.' Hazel stopped, looking out of the window again, apparently mesmerised by something going on below. 'Hello, how odd. I wonder if that's what the hold-up is about.'

Curious, Alice went to stare out of the window too. 'Well, I never,' she said, sounding surprised. 'It's that toffee-nosed bloke Eva's so sweet on. Professor what's-his-name.'

'Templeton,' Lily said promptly, joining them at the window. 'Gosh, it looks like the professor's under guard. I wonder what he's done wrong.' She giggled. 'Forgot to dot his "i"s and cross his "t"s, maybe!'

Too distracted to care about a man she hardly knew, Violet sat down again and wrung her hands. 'Hazel, I don't think I can bear this waiting.'

'Chin up,' Hazel told her cheerfully, bending to give her a quick hug. 'I'm here to defend you, aren't I? And you heard George last night. He doesn't think the colonel will pay any attention to that nasty Dullaghan boy.'

'He doesn't know that for sure, though.' Violet felt her chest constrict with fear. 'And what will happen to the girls if I'm arrested? Who will look after the poor little pets if . . . if I'm . . . ?'

She couldn't finish that sentence, tears rolling down her cheeks.

'It won't come to that.' Hazel hesitated, then put her arm about Violet's shoulders, lowering her voice so the girls wouldn't overhear. 'But you know I'll look after them until your mum arrives, so don't worry about that. You did say she was on her way down from London, didn't you?'

'As soon as she can get the train fare together.' Violet rubbed at her damp eyes, and sucked in a great shuddering breath, trying to calm herself down. She had to stay strong for the girls' sake, at least. It wouldn't do them any good to see their aunt crying, would it? 'Mum don't know nothing about this though,' she whispered back. 'What a shock for her, rolling up in Porthcurno to find me banged up for spying, and her granddaughters all alone.'

'That's not going to happen.' But Hazel was chewing her lip, clearly uncertain about the whole business.

They fell silent as they finally heard footsteps coming up the stairs. Tough, military footsteps. The girls spun round from the window at once, nervously tidying their hair and skirts. Violet stood, and hoped nobody would see how scared she was. Even Hazel straightened, but kept her arm about Violet's shoulders.

'Now, see here, Colonel,' Hazel began crossly, but was interrupted.

'Excellent,' the colonel's loud voice boomed out, 'all present and correct. Just what I like to see.' Colonel Ryder threw open the door to his office, ushering them inside. 'That's it, in you all go. Sorry to have kept you waiting so long, ladies, but I had some urgent business to attend to first.'

Behind him came George Cotterill.

'Yes, please join us, Mr Cotterill,' the colonel insisted, closing the door and heading for his desk. 'You need to hear this too.'

George did not look happy, which made Violet even more nervous. She noticed how his unsmiling gaze searched Hazel's face before he took up a position behind the colonel's desk, hands clasped behind his back, his expression very stern indeed. Maybe that horrible boy Patrick Dullaghan had somehow managed to convince them that she was a spy, or that her brother-in-law was, making her look suspect too.

She refused to believe that Ernst could ever be a German spy. So they'd better not try to tell her that he was, she decided stoutly.

'Sit down, sit down,' the colonel told them, squeezing himself into his chair and picking up his unlit pipe.

There were three chairs ranged in front of his desk. The girls sat, and Hazel took a seat near the window, facing them.

Violet, however, refused to sit down, standing bolt upright before her chair instead, a damp hanky crushed between her hands. 'I'm not guilty,' she blurted out before he had a chance to accuse her of anything. 'I swear that's the truth, Colonel. I'm sorry about the bombing, truly I am. But it was nothing to do with me. That Dullaghan lad . . . He's a wrong 'un. I told you last night, you can't trust a bleedin' word he says. I'm innocent. I would never . . . I mean, it's just not true . . . Oh, you've got to believe me!'

She was crying again, she realised, and staunched the flow with her crumpled hanky before blowing her nose violently.

'No need to cry, there's a good woman,' Colonel Ryder said, not unkindly, fiddling with his pipe as though it was more interesting than she was. 'Truth of the matter is, we know it wasn't you behind last night's bombing raid. And George here has vouched for you personally.'

Violet stared at George. 'He has?'

'That's right. So you can sit down and stop blubbing.'

Stunned, Violet sank onto her chair. 'Oh . . .'

'We've got somebody else in the bag for last night. So you're off the hook. And frankly, you know, I never believed that boy. Lads his age, they're always looking to make mischief.' He blew into his pipe bowl in a uninterested way, and then tapped it in the ashtray. 'Private Dullaghan . . . Knew you back in the East End, did he?'

'Th-that's right.'

'George told me there was some kind of bad blood between the two of you.'

She nodded, speechless with gratitude for George's intervention.

'Then last night, Dullaghan saw an opportunity to get his own back, with all that spy nonsense. Am I right?'

'Yes, sir. That's it, exactly.'

'Well, no need to trouble ourselves over it. Clearly not a word of truth in the whole thing. So you can go about your business as usual, eh?' He waved a hand to dismiss them. As they all stood up to troop out of the room, he pointed at Violet, and cleared his throat. 'Though I'd like another word with you in private, Miss . . . erm . . .'

'Hopkins, sir,' she supplied.

'That's the one. You stay behind a minute for a quick chat.'

Violet sat down again, her face pale as she watched Hazel and the girls leave the room, followed by George. She had told him she was innocent. Somebody else had been arrested. So whatever was this about?

The door closed behind them, and she was alone with the colonel.

'Now, don't fret,' he said kindly, and lit his pipe. 'You don't mind if I smoke, do you?' She shook her head, watching him in trepidation. The thick fragrant smoke filled the air. 'Thing is, what I'm about to say to you is top secret. You signed the Official Secrets Act when you came to work here, didn't you?'

'Yes, sir.'

'Well, you'll know not to say a word to anyone outside this room. Not even those two girls of yours.'

'They're my nieces. Lily and Alice.'

'Quite so.' The colonel puffed on his pipe for a moment, regarding her through the smoke with clever eyes. 'I really am sorry to have kept you waiting so long. But I had to chase the story up, you see, and that took a bit of time. That nonsense about your brother-in-law. Can't have that kind of wild accusation doing the rounds. Talk of a German spy and his accomplice down here in Porthcurno, where we're all meant to be top secret and watertight? Bad for morale.' He laid his pipe down in the ashtray, its bowl still smouldering. 'So I made some phone calls last night. Did a little digging. And this morning I heard back about your brother-in-law, and had my secretary take down some notes. Would you like me to tell you what they say?'

Violet nodded, her heart thudding fit to burst.

He unlocked one of his desk drawers, pulling out a thick manila folder, which he dropped onto his blotter pad. Reading upside down, she could see words stamped across the folder in red ink.

TOP SECRET

Colonel Ryder opened the folder and shuffled through various papers inside, then drew out a handwritten sheet and studied it thoughtfully. 'Ernst Fisher,' he read aloud, the words filling her with dread. 'English father, German mother. Joined up early in the war, currently missing in action. Last known location classified.'

'He wasn't a spy, Colonel. Not our Ernest.' She could feel the tears starting again. But this time, there were tears of anger. 'He was as English and patriotic as they come. He'd never have betrayed his country. It's just spiteful rumours, on account of his name, and him being able to speak German proper. That's all it ever was. Nasty, spiteful gossip.'

'I believe you,' he said calmly.

'And now my sister's dead, and I don't want his two girls growing up thinking their dad . . .' She suddenly realised what the colonel had said, and stopped dead, staring at him. 'Oh . . . You don't believe he was guilty either, then?'

With a faint smile, Colonel Ryder slid the paper back inside the folder and closed it. 'Not one jot, Miss Hopkins. You see, I believe your brother-in-law has been most helpful to this country.'

Violet could not believe what she was hearing. *Most helpful to this country.* Was he suggesting that Ernst had been spying for England when he was declared lost in action?

'What do you mean?'

'Can't say any more, I'm afraid.' He tapped the side of his nose. 'And nor should you. Not even to your family.'

'I see.' Violet frowned. 'I think.'

'Not one word, there's a good woman. Or my head could be on the chopping block . . . and so could yours! Is that clear?'

Violet quaked inwardly. 'Yes, sir.'

Colonel Ryder opened his desk drawer, dropped the manila folder back into it, and then turned the key again.

'Now,' he continued briskly, 'I've heard on the grapevine that you're bunked up with those two girls in Mrs Baxter's place, and your mother's been hurt in London and will be joining you shortly. Is that right?'

'I've got no complaints,' she said hurriedly, worried that Hazel might be in trouble for putting her up.

'Mrs Baxter is an excellent woman. But there's no need for you all to be squeezed together like sardines in a can.' He smiled. 'Not when we have some perfectly good accommodation available for you right here in Porthcurno.'

Violet stared. '*What*?' She remembered her manners too late, adding, 'I mean, what did you say, sir?'

'It just so happens that one of my officers and his young family have been sent back to London this week, and their quarters have fallen vacant. It's only a tiny place up the hill in Porthcurno. Little better than a fisherman's cottage, frankly, and probably quite damp. But you and your family are welcome to make a home of it.' He cleared his throat, looking at her significantly. 'Least we can do, with the girls' father still missing in action. And all that.'

Her eyes widened. So he was serious. Ernst had been a spy, but for England, for their side. And now he was missing, presumed dead.

Or was he?

Perhaps the government knew perfectly well where Ernst was, but he was working for them undercover, maybe part of the resistance on the ground in Germany. To admit that he was still alive could cost lives, including his own. But the colonel seemed intent on making sure Ernst's children were being taken care of, at least.

'Thank you,' she managed to say, though her voice came out as a squeak. 'But what about Patrick Dullaghan?'

'Never you mind about that foolish young lad. Private Dullaghan is soon to be shipped off. First thing tomorrow, in fact. Seems they need some extra manpower over in Wiltshire. So I've made sure he'll be among the detail being sent over there.' He gave her a wink. 'The boy's been told to keep his mouth shut about your brother-in-law from now on, and the fear of God put into him if he doesn't.'

She held both hands to her hot cheeks, shaking with relief. 'Oh, sir . . . Colonel . . . I dunno what to say.'

'No need to say anything at all, Miss Hopkins.' He got up and opened the door for her. Outside, she could see Hazel and George waiting for her, their faces worried, and the girls too, huddled together in apprehension. 'Now, off you go. And once you've finished your duties for today, come back and I'll get one of the orderlies to take you over to your new quarters.'

The girls ran towards Violet as his office door closed. 'What happened, Aunty Vi? What did the colonel say to you? Will we have to leave Porthcurno?'

She was half-laughing, half-crying, but shook her head at their questions. Over their heads, she met Hazel's surprised look with a tremulous smile.

'No, nothing like that. Blimey, the colonel's such a nice man. He was just saying to me . . . Oh, girls, girls . .' She clutched them both close to her chest, her heart swollen with emotion. 'How would you like us to live together in a nice little cottage of our own? And Mum too, when she fetches up from London?'

Both girls started to talk at once, demanding to know what she meant, but she could only weep happily into her hanky.

'Give us a minute, girls. My head's in such a tangle, I can't think straight.'

Waking up this morning, she could have killed herself if it hadn't been for the girls, she'd been in such flat despair. She'd been so sure the end of the world had come. That she was about to be condemned as a spy. Or sent away from Porthcurno and her new friends, at the very least, which would have been devastating.

Now, everything had changed, and instead the world was just beginning.

But what about Joe Postbridge?

Because of nasty Patrick Dullaghan, Joe probably still suspected she was a spy for the enemy. Worse, that she had told the Germans where to drop their filthy bombs. And she couldn't even tell Joe the truth. She had signed the Official Secrets Act, and she didn't think the colonel had been entirely joking when he said she might get her head cut off for blabbing about Ernst, even to her own flesh and blood. Let alone a near-stranger, however she might feel about him in her heart.

But maybe Joe would hear that someone else had been arrested for betraying their location to the enemy, and realise she was innocent.

Even then, she thought sadly, it would probably take time for him to trust her again. And he had his grief to work through too, his mourning for his mother. Because that wouldn't be easy. She knew how it felt to lose a loved one to a bombing raid. The shock and horror, the raw suddenness of it all. And then you had to get up the next day, and the day after that, and somehow carry on with the business of being alive.

George put a gentle hand on her shoulder. 'I take it the colonel told you about the cottage for you and the girls?'

She nodded. 'Did you tell him about our situation?' When he shrugged, looking modest, she gave him a quick peck on the cheek. 'Thank you, Mr Cotterill. For that, and for speaking up for me. You're a gent. I won't forget it.' She smiled mistily at Hazel. 'I'm proper grateful to you for putting us up, don't get me wrong. You and Charlie have been the best ever. But it's time we moved on. Got a place of our own. I hope you're not offended.'

'Of course not,' Hazel said warmly, and gave her a hug. 'George told me all about it while you were in there. I think it's smashing news.' She blushed a little, whispering in her ear, 'It's good timing anyway. There's going to be a happy event later this year, so I'll need the extra space. And I don't just mean for the new baby.'

Violet's jaw dropped. 'You and Mr Cotterill?'

'That's why George was at the cottage last night. He came round to propose.'

'Oh my Gawd!' Violet heaved a great sigh, considering this. 'What did Charlie have to say about that?'

'He wished us both happy.' Hazel nodded at Violet's surprised stare. 'I know, you could have knocked me down with a feather. All the same, we're going to wait a while before tying the knot. Charlie and his dad didn't always see eye to eye; it's true. They had their arguments, and Bertie raised a hand to him more than once. But when all's said and done, Bertie was still his father, and Charlie needs time to mourn him properly.' Hazel shot a quick glance at George Cotterill as though unable to keep her eyes off the man. 'I think he'll come around to the idea of George as a stepdad eventually, though.'

'Well, I never.' Violet dried her eyes, so happy for her friend that she could hardly speak. 'Congratulations. That's bloomin' marvellous, I'm telling you. The best news I've heard in a good long while.'

Arm in arm with Hazel, Violet followed George and the girls downstairs to work, not minding for once that a steaming mop and bucket would be waiting for her in the kitchen. She felt like she was living in a dream, and what a gorgeous dream it was too!

She wished she could let Lily and Alice in on the amazing news she'd heard, but the colonel had been so stern about keeping her lips sealed, she didn't dare. But the girls' dad might not be dead, after all, and though it was all top secret at the moment, Ernst could yet turn out to be a national hero. And her old mum would be beside herself to arrive in Porthcurno and find them all tucked up cosily in some seaside cottage.

Today had started off so horribly, like a nightmare. But suddenly the sun was shining and the sea was calm, and it looked like a perfect Cornish day.

'Now all we need is to get this war done and dusted,' Violet said airily, 'and we can live happily ever after. Ain't that so, Hazel?'

George laughed. 'We're working on it, trust me.'

If you enjoyed *Wartime with the Cornish Girls*, don't miss the next book in the series, *Christmas with the Cornish Girls* – coming soon.

Acknowledgements

What a wonderful thing it is to have a novel published!

My grateful thanks first to my marvellous agent, Alison Bonomi from LBA, who has been there for me through difficult times this past year, my number one supporter and friend.

Thank you also to my editor, Tilda McDonald, whose clear-sighted suggestions have made this a much better book, plus Phoebe, Ellie, Sabah and all the incredible publishing team at Avon Books.

I'm also extremely grateful to the helpful staff at the Telegraph Museum Porthcurno, Cornwall, who answered my long series of questions with great patience and friendly enthusiasm. The brilliant museum exhibitions helped me envisage how life at Porthcurno might have been during the Second World War. Any inaccuracies are my own fault, with the caveat that I had to use creative licence occasionally in this story. *Mea culpa.*

Finally, a huge thank you to Steve for being such a considerate husband, and to my kids Kate, Becki, Dylan, Morris and Indigo, for putting up with an absent-minded writer for a mum, and for making me endless cups of tea!